This book is a late wedding present for
Janet and Neville Partridge, with my love.

Diamonds and Daisies

Bernadette Strachan

LARGE PRINT
Oxford

Copyright © Strawnygawn Words and Music, 2006

First published in Great Britain 2007
by
Hodder & Stoughton
a division of
Hodder Headline

Published in Large Print 2007 by ISIS Publishing Ltd.,
7 Centremead, Osney Mead, Oxford OX2 0ES
by arrangement with
Hodder & Stoughton
a division of
Hodder Headline

British Library Cataloguing in Publication Data
Strachan, Bernadette
    Diamonds and daisies. – Large print ed.
    1. Women novelists – Fiction
    2. Single women – Fiction
    3. Aristocracy (Social class) – Fiction
    4. Love stories
    5. Large type books
    I. Title
    823.9'2 [F]

        ISBN 978–0–7531–7836–2 (hb)
        ISBN 978–0–7531–7837–9 (pb)

Printed and bound in Great Britain by
T. J. International Ltd., Padstow, Cornwall

Acknowledgements

I'm so grateful to everybody who bought the last two books, and it's nice to see you back for number three. I must also thank: my agent, Annette Green, who manages to be patient, indulgent and dynamic all at once; Monika Moysova for amusing my daughter with fishfingers and CBeebies while I write; Jen and Keith Strachan for letting their granddaughter clamber all over them at short notice; Sergio Giannasso for doing my hair and lending me his name; Penny Warnes, Julia Tyrell, Kate Haldane and Janet Partridge for being stalwart and supportive; Domenic Sforza for ensuring that my Italian character sounds credible; Tamsin Ruhrmund for the comment about studio flats which has stuck in my memory for years; Michael Anderson for oh-so-vital legal/fencing detail; Aunty Maisie, Aunty Doris, Aunty Eva and my mum, Lily, for providing inspiration for the Aunts (the real ones are *much* nicer); the friendly, clever, inspirational Hodder people, particularly Isobel Akenhead, Emma Knight, and most especially, my precious editor, Sara Kinsella; and finally Matthew — all my books are for you, really . . .

CHAPTER
ONE

"Don't," whispered Helena, husky with desire. "We mustn't."

"We only have tonight, my queen." Carlos's breath was hot on her trembling neck. "To gaze upon your dazzling face, I have travelled a thousand lonely nights across burning desert."

Jojo banged on the bedroom door. "BAKED POTATO'S READY!" she bawled, sounding as if her mouth was full. It generally was.

Pressing "save" on her laptop, Sunny called, "OK!" and stretched her limbs like a weary tabby. She'd written a lot today. The cunning little word-count feature informed her she'd bashed out almost four thousand words of exotic romance, and all on one fried-egg sandwich. She was more than ready for her dinner, even though it was her cousin Jojo's turn to cook.

Jojo, small, perfectly spherical and upholstered in a robe from her endless selection of lurid leisurewear, was doling out spuds when Sunny reached the kitchen. Whenever the merciless rota put Jojo in charge of the kitchen, baked potatoes were on the menu.

Sunny's other flatmate and cousin, Ellen, had come in from work. With many an "Eek!" and a "Shit, that's hot!", she was encouraging her allotted potato out of its foil overcoat.

"You're early," commented Sunny, as she sat at the table, a manoeuvre that had to be approached carefully. Alongside all the traditional kitchen paraphernalia, this room also supported a sofa, an armchair and a television. To afford even this draughty flat on the third floor of a crumbling mansion block, Sunny and the two sisters had been forced to convince the sitting room that it was a third bedroom. The high ceilings and graceful covings had attracted them; the dry rot and prehistoric carpets had only registered after the deposit had gone through.

Such a furniture arrangement was not ideal: when the girls relaxed on the sofa, their eyes were level with the table, and when they sat up to the table, they had to hold their breath in order to squeeze into the chairs. It was fun, if you were in the mood.

Sunny wasn't in the mood. It had been a long day. She slathered a landslide of comforting butter on to her potato.

"Easy now," warned Jojo. "Watch those calories."

Sunny goggled at her. Jojo didn't seem to know she was fat, just like some dogs don't know they're dogs. Jojo didn't notice the goggling: she was blessed with rhino-calibre skin.

"Is there any sweetcorn?" asked Ellen, wiping her chin daintily. She did everything daintily. She was the archetype of a Celtic princess, all tumbling auburn locks and green eyes.

"Jojo ate it. Obviously." Sunny was no princess. Her warm brown hair was abundant and wavy, and it matched her warm brown eyes, but pretty though all her features were, they never seemed to add up to beauty.

Jojo, oblivious to that "obviously", suggested grated cheese. "It's lovely. Goes all melty," she enthused, unaware of the splodge of Cheddar on her freckled nose. "And it's only a week past its eat-by date."

Silence reigned. They were comfortable being quiet together. Every summer of her childhood, Sunny had been exported from London to spend the holidays in Dublin with her mother's clan. The two Irish girls felt more like sisters than cousins.

"How's the latest book coming along?" asked Ellen. Intelligent and enquiring, Ellen was interested in her cousin's work. Unlike some people Sunny could mention, sitting not too far from her, and garnished with cheese.

"Fine. Carlos and Helena are just coming up to their first dot-dot-dot."

"Ooh, the sexy bit. The bit we don't let our Mas read," smiled Ellen.

Jojo scoffed — not easy to do with your mouth full of nuclear-heat carbs. "Carlos and Helena! Why don't people in books ever have normal names? Like . . ." She scratched her head with her fork as she waited for inspiration. "Trevor. Or Pam."

"Would you want to read about a Trevor and a Pam dot-dot-dotting?" asked Sunny.

"I don't want to read about *anybody* shagging," said Jojo, with a distinct lack of that poetry the Irish are famed for. She shuddered. Jojo's romance gland had atrophied. She'd reached her mid-twenties without hankering after a man, and she was prone to sneer at Sunny's romantic predicaments, fictional and otherwise.

"Well, plenty of women do." Sunny was stout in defence of her work. The overblown, torrid novellas she bashed out were sold by mail order to thousands and thousands of readers who couldn't get enough of lustful behaviour by women with great hair in foreign climes. "It's a bit of colour in a bland world," she maintained. Sometimes Sunny felt like a social worker, a social worker in pink who made sure that needy housewives received their romance benefits. "It's not art, but it's not easy either."

"Don't know how you do it." Ellen sounded admiring, as she dissected her potato neatly. It politely fell apart, giving up its almost-cooked middle with a sigh. "I wouldn't know where to start."

Praise from Ellen, who was hard to please, was always welcome, but it made Sunny smile ruefully. If anybody was to be admired, it was her diligent, industrious cousin, who put in long hours at a specialist family law firm, defying her bosses with her insistence on representing the lowest-income clients.

"You always did have a brilliant imagination." Ellen deftly carved out the edible bits of her dinner, leaving a small, hard, Easter Island potato statue in the centre of her plate.

4

"Head In the Clouds" their mutual O'Brien grandmother had called Sunny during those Irish summers that now seemed a thousand years away. Typing up market research in Soho advertising agencies, the adult Sunny had used her famous imagination to conjure up the glamorous lifestyle she would enjoy if, when, if she ever became a bona fide, honest to God published author. Champagne had figured heavily in these daydreams, along with a minimalist riverside penthouse, a sports car and various ardent beaux.

True, 13 Chudleigh Court teetered on the top floor and was opposite the Thames, but it was distressingly maximumalist, stuffed with the landlord's car-boot tat. The sports car had morphed into a travel card, and the beaux were represented at the moment by Calum, who was prone to telephone-number-related dyslexia.

"Quick!" yelped Jojo suddenly. "Switch on the telly. QUICKLY!" she bellowed as Sunny reached awkwardly backwards above her head to reach the tiny set balanced precariously on the mantelpiece.

As the theme tune of the latest reality show whistled through Sunny's hair, Jojo's face assumed the look that Sunny struggled to describe for her heroines when they were in the throes of ecstasy with brave and handsome firemen.

"Oooh, *Celebrity Bus Conductor*! I love this!" squeaked Jojo.

Ellen unfolded herself from the table like a paperclip. "I'm off for a soak." She looked tired.

Crouching, in case she impaired Jojo's vision of the attention-hungry freaks on the screen, Sunny followed her. Out in the hallway, she hissed, "How come Jojo always chooses what we watch, even though she has worse taste than Jordan's dressmaker?"

For an answer, Ellen asked, "Why don't you go back in and ask to watch another channel?"

Sunny raised her eyebrows expressively.

"*That*'s why," said Ellen.

Sunny noticed that Patrick was in the same jeans he'd worn when she'd chucked him.

Four years ago.

In the intervening years, they'd met in the Volunteer every Thursday at eight for a drink and a chat. They never discussed their past relationship.

"They do *have* clothes shops in Hammersmith?" Sunny asked conversationally, as she carefully deposited his brimming pint on the table.

"Stop about the jeans," warned Patrick, without looking up from his paper. His right hand snaked to his Guinness by instinct.

"But they're —"

"Stop about the jeans," Patrick repeated. He folded the paper into a small square and concentrated hard on it.

"I know, I know," said Sunny, archly. "You have to wear them for work. But surely even a landscape gardener deserves some glamour?"

Finally, he looked at her. It was a look she knew: he was pondering how to respond. He settled for, "Fancy some pork scratchings?"

6

Sunny Parkinson, twenty-eight, single, addicted to Maltesers, with hair that would never co-operate, was in love with love. Always had been. But love had never returned the compliment.

She dreamed of finding The One, the man who would ignite her passion, make her espadrilles walk on air and appreciate her lopsided smile.

Unfortunately, love was not only not in love with Sunny, it had huffily ignored her since her first kiss. Kevin O'Gorman, famed for the ever-present sty in his left eye, had grabbed her and snogged her for a dare in front of a whooping gang of their fellow first years. Sunny didn't feel that the standard of her men had improved noticeably in the intervening seventeen years.

True, Patrick didn't have a sty, and, as far as she knew, their two-year-long relationship hadn't been the result of a dare from a giggling mob of landscape gardeners. In fact, Patrick was very presentable when he could be prised out of his mediaeval denim. But, as the most significant man in her past, he was conspicuously unromantic.

There had been no heat, no passion in their break-up. Patrick hadn't threatened to throw himself on his shears when she'd ended it. He hadn't even had the common decency to spiral into a destructive vortex of despair and self-abuse. In fact, he'd bought a camper van and started talking about going to Cornwall for long weekends.

It wasn't that Sunny expected overblown gestures like the ones she wrote about. She wasn't unrealistic. She was simply after a little more sensitivity, a little more respect. It would be nice to have fewer bruises to show for her love affairs.

"How are the ladies?" Patrick always asked after her cousins.

"Jojo is psychotic, borderline autistic and morbidly obese. So no change there. Ellen is still congenitally elegant, overworked and worryingly single."

"Why 'worryingly'?" Patrick lit a flame under a topic they often warmed up.

"It's not right. It's not normal. She never shows any interest in blokes."

"Neither does Jojo," pointed out Patrick.

"No, but she's *Jojo*. She's always been odd. Embroidered fluorescent polyester is her fabric of choice: you can't use her as a yardstick for acceptable behaviour." Sunny flicked a crisp down at Ozzie, the curly little mongrel she'd encouraged Patrick to buy as a Sunny substitute after their split. She and Ozzie, as Patrick liked to point out, were eerily similar: both favoured greasy snacks and lying down. He admitted that Sunny had better breath.

"Perhaps Ellen has her reasons."

"Don't go all wise on me. What reasons?" pestered Sunny, who was apt to diagnose a nice shiny new boy as the cure for all ills. "She's so lovely, and I hate to see her on her own."

"She's got you." Patrick paused. "And Jojo, God help her."

"We all need somebody special." Sunny was on solid ground here: romance was her business. "Like I've got Calum."

"Ah." Patrick unsuccessfully tried to conceal what looked suspiciously like a mocking smile. "I wondered when the C word would crop up." He looked at his watch. "Well done, Agent Parkinson. You went a whole forty minutes this time."

"You're just jealous," accused Sunny.

"Yes. I am violently jealous," deadpanned Patrick, taking up his paper again. "It's killing me."

Sunny sighed. If only that was true. Some display of emotion might defuse the burden of sadness that could still overwhelm her when she remembered the tiny tragedy that she and Patrick had weathered. It had ruined everything between them and left her with a hole that ached to be filled. She glanced at Patrick, immersed again in the crossword. She wondered if he knew how the memory still burned. This was an ancient rut for her thoughts to trickle down, and she always reached the same conclusion: how could he possibly know that she still smarted, when they never, ever discussed it?

Sunny aimed another crisp at Ozzie. It landed four inches from his nose, but he seemed disinclined to get up and snaffle it. "You really are the world's laziest dog," she chided, prodding him with her toe.

"He's depressed," muttered Patrick, chewing the end of a stubby pencil. "He needs a girlfriend."

"Ha, ha."

"That special doggy someone."

"We get the joke."

"He is a worryingly single mongrel."

Determined not to encourage Patrick, who had a very male tendency to stretch jokes as thin as Jojo's knicker elastic, Sunny whipped out her notebook.

It wasn't unusual for Sunny and Patrick to sit in companionable silence like this. He was unable to leave a crossword half finished, and she was driven to scribble down inspiration as it struck. It struck now, in this uninspiring environment.

The Volunteer was not an obvious place to find a romantic novelist. Sunny would have preferred a chic gastropub, all Farrow & Ball colours and newspapers on rods that stuck out from the wall. However, Patrick would only countenance "proper" pubs. The Volunteer certainly fitted the bill: it had the requisite sticky carpet, terrifying toilets, shambling customers and bar staff whose teeth were straight from Victorian London. She'd given in, anxious to preserve their weekly meetings and fashion a friendship from the ashes of their romance. Even at the time, she'd known she was clinging on to reassure herself that not *everything* she and Patrick once shared had been swept away.

By now, Sunny was so immune to the anti-charm of her surroundings she could jot down a dot-dot-dot chapter mindless of the ghostly scent of beer spills through the centuries.

Helena pulled away from his hungry mouth. "We shouldn't . . ." She struggled like a sparrow with a broken wing.

"I want you," muttered Carlos gruffly.

Helena slid her hand down his taut body until her slender white fingers found his . . .

10

His what? Sunny always had trouble with this bit. Her publishers, Entwined Hearts Limited, were very specific. They wanted rude but not too rude. Saucy but not explicit.

Perhaps Helena's fingers could find his manhood? She winced: that was so lame. His proud member? Nah, the reader would visualise an MP between the lovers. She settled for "his ardent desire". It would have to do.

Sunny's own slender white fingers relaxed. Her mind had wandered (it didn't take much: it was easily led) to Calum, and his ardent desire. She couldn't fault her boyfriend in that department: the sex was plentiful and exciting, they dot-dot-dotted with abandon whenever they met. But . . . She scrawled the ugly little word in capitals in the middle of a line.

BUT

. . . they didn't meet very often. Sunny frowned. She knew Calum fancied her. She even knew he liked her. But Calum wasn't at all, in the slightest, not a jot, never would be, in love with her.

She pressed down with her felt-tip and underlined the "BUT". (If she'd had access to her desk drawer, she'd have highlighted it in fluorescent pink: Sunny had a mild stationery fetish.) She didn't much like the woman Calum turned her into; a woman happy to do all the running, desperate to keep their ragged affair from running out of steam. Sometimes Sunny suspected that if she dared to test him by not calling,

Calum would let a week go by, and then a fortnight, then a month, until he would stumble on somebody else content to settle for cracking sex and a slap-up Pizza Express American Hot once in a while.

Sunny shook her head and scored out the "BUT." What did a stupid little But know? She and Calum had fun together. She made him laugh and agreed to keep her high heels on in bed: he wouldn't throw it all away just like that. Besides, he'd agreed to escort her to her best friend's dinner party next week without batting an eyelid. Surely he would have made some excuse if he was only in it for the sex? No, thought Sunny, glad to have derailed her train of thought, Calum really wasn't such a bad boyfriend after all.

Sunny took a sip of her wine-box white, and persevered with describing good old Carlos's ardent desire, painfully aware that she wouldn't dare describe Calum as her boyfriend if he was within earshot.

From the other side of the table, Patrick peered over the top of his paper and murmured, "There's no X in 'ecstasy'."

CHAPTER
TWO

Soft-hearted Sunny reckoned the muffin looked lonesome, so she tucked a double-choc brownie beside it to keep it company. Inching her tray along the self-service counter, she nodded across the café at Sarah to confirm that she had understood the frantic semaphoring telling her that they had a table.

Glowingly blonde, Sunny's best friend in the entire world was at odds with the tatty surroundings. Pert diamonds glittered at her ears, and her almond-coloured trouser suit was sharp enough to cut the sandwich that Sunny had also bought.

Her Top Shop bling jangling, Sunny set the tray down. "No decaff," she announced, apologetically.

"No problem." Sarah took a deep slurp of coffee. "I need the caffeine." This was heresy: Sarah's body was a temple, as opposed to Sunny's, which was more of a 7/11.

"How are the Beasts?" Sunny spaced her goodies out so they wouldn't look quite so greedy opposite Sarah's sunflower 'n' nut bar.

"They're *horrific*." Sarah was emphatic. "They're rude, they smell, they destroy everything in their path. They really shouldn't be allowed by law."

"Such an inspiring advert for motherhood." The Beasts were Sarah's twin two-year-olds, and although any eavesdropper might assume that she loathed them, Sunny knew different: Sarah had adored them both from the moment they'd made their messy exits from her undercarriage. But Sarah was a natural ranter, and she loved to go on, and on, and *on* about the Beasts in a half-ironic, half-serious way that was designed to amuse, even though her spiel sometimes tempted strangers to call Social Services.

"*You* have them for half a day," yelped Sarah. "See if you wax lyrical then. Sam and Charlie might look adorable, but they're the toddler arm of al-Qaeda." She bit into her pallid snack as if she had a personal grudge against it. "Having kids isn't just about the kids, it's all the shit that comes with them. I had a conversation with the new nanny this morning that made me long for death. I mean, what *is* the fucking Portuguese for 'kettle-descaler'?"

Sunny admitted she didn't know and lapsed into silence as Sarah raved on. It was advisable to let her work off her head of steam before attempting normal conversation. As Sarah warmed to her theme of how the nanny was plotting to kill her, Sunny remembered the olden days, when Sarah would start every Monday morning in the offices of Waldhorn Truss Levy Advertising with a similar tirade. Back then the subject had been men, and their habits/shortcomings/peccadilloes. None of them were good enough. Until she'd started going out with Alfie, the Goldenballs of the company.

14

Alfie had been good enough. In fact, Alfie had been good enough to cry over when it looked as if things were going awry. Sarah had never cried over a bloke before, but when Alfie had asked her to marry him, she'd cried all over again.

"And as for Alfie," Sarah was despairing, "he's never around to help. Even today, Saturday, he's in the office. He works late every other night. It's more like having a flatmate than a husband."

"Working late equals diamonds," Sunny pointed out.

Sarah feigned shock. "And here's me thinking you're the romantic one!"

"I'm quoting *you*," Sunny reminded her. "It's what you said back when you first got married. And now look at you. Earrings, rings, bracelets — you're P Diddy on a slow night."

Suppressing a giggle, Sarah said, "I know I moan, and I know a lot of women would kill to be in my position, swanning about at home with an au pair and a Range Rover and a Barclaycard, but I'm worried. About *Her*."

"Her" was also known as "Porqy Peeces Woman". Waldhorn Truss Levy had landed the contract to relaunch one of Britain's neglected foodstuffs: Porqy Peeces luncheon meat ("Not Spam. *Definitely* not Spam," as Alfie insisted) was making a comeback, and Alfie was masterminding its hugely expensive ad campaign. The owner — Her — of Porqy Peeces Limited was called Liz, and was rather demanding.

The complaints from Sarah had trickled in at first ("She calls the house in the evening — do you think

15

that's OK?") but had recently escalated into a tidal wave ("SHE'S AFTER MY HUSBAND!").

Sunny attempted to pour oil on her friend's troubled marital waters. "Let's act calm until we meet her at your dinner party." Personally, Sunny felt that Sarah and Alfie's marriage was cast iron. They'd weathered health scares, in-law problems and Sarah's obsession with cleaning the fridge: Liz wouldn't pose any sort of threat.

Sarah's face lit up. "I'll meet Calum at last!" she practically sang. "I can't wait." Living vicariously through Sunny's love life was a habit she had fallen into since slapping on the manacles of matrimony. Sunny didn't encourage it.

"I hope he's not a disappointment."

"You said he was gorgeous. You said you'd chew your way through garden furniture to get at him. Don't backtrack on me now."

"Oh, he's gorgeous all right." Sunny conjured up Calum's sardonic face. He was certainly handsome, in a rough-hewn way, with his large nose and his fleshy, kissable mouth. "He's just so . . ."

"Are we going to be treated to some of your lusty prose? He's just so *wild*. He's just so *exotic*." Sarah spun all the value she could out of the shiny adjectives. "He's just so *wanton*."

"I was going to say he's elusive."

"But in a good way? Elusive, aloof, *enigmatic*."

"Yes, yes, in a good way." Sunny sidestepped analysing her relationship (for want of a better word) in the middle of a bustling café. He wasn't just elusive . . .

16

Sunny shivered. Calum was cold. "The latest book's coming along nicely," she offered, to change the subject.

"Fab." Sarah gobbled up her friend's books as soon as they appeared. She was proud, she often said, of having a real, live author in the fold. She never allowed Sunny to modestly pooh-pooh her achievements, self-righteously insisting that books that only sold by mail order were still books. "Another happy ending?"

"Of course."

"They don't happen in real life, you know." Sarah banged a sullen tune on her coffee cup with a spoon. "I should know."

The mansion block squatted opposite the river, broad marble steps leading to its elegant black doors. Stately Edwardian red brick, it was built in a classic quadrangle, enclosing traditional gardens dotted with roses. Chudleigh Court emanated an air of ladylike disapproval for the traffic that buzzed irritably past it all day. Like many of its residents, it had seen better days.

Ben from the basement was approaching the steps as well. "Hi, there," he said, with a jut of his chin. Ben was very shy.

"Hi," echoed Sunny. She wasn't shy, but Ben's shyness was catching. "Nice day," she heard her voice saying woodenly as they pushed open a door each.

"We've had a hell of a summer." Ben looked amazed at his own daring repartee as he escaped to the back of the wide tiled hall and fled down the stairs.

Risking the volatile embrace of the cast-iron lift, Sunny clanged the gates shut and pressed a button. As she rose, slower than Mao Tse-tung's funeral cortège, up the three flights to number thirteen, she fretted, mildly, about Sarah's frame of mind.

Sarah's cynicism was familiar, but the scale of today's bitterness had been unexpected. Sarah wasn't right about happy-ever-afters, was she? They were Sunny's business. Admittedly, her own life hadn't delivered one yet, but Sunny was hopeful.

The lift juddered on, complaining.

Like a politician with an out-of-date manifesto, Sunny believed in love. Watching Sarah and Alfie fall for each other, she'd ached for the same thing to happen to her. It hadn't been soppy or soft focus: they'd fought like that cat and dog we hear so much about. Sarah was driven and ambitious, with a wild streak that would alarm Colin Farrell. She'd broken many a heart, and sprained many a penis, but with Alfie it had been love. What else could make Sarah, who'd planned to be the most powerful woman in advertising, hand in her notice the day she got engaged?

All that nonsense in the café had to be taken with a pinch of salt, thought Sunny. It was Sarah's thwarted ambition talking. She'd agreed with Alfie that one of them should be at home while the kids were young, but she perversely kicked against it with her power-dressing trouser suits and her refusal to darken the door of Tumble Tots.

No, Sunny wouldn't let Sarah's gloom influence her. I believe in love, she reassured herself. There was romance in life, even in Sunny's prosaic existence, as long as you looked out for it.

Somebody was waiting for the lift as it reached her floor. "Hi, hi, hi!" sang the funkily dressed girl with an infectious grin.

It didn't infect Sunny. She was immune to the Thin Girls. "Hi," she said, lacklustre.

The three Thin Girls lived in the flat next door and were, as you'd expect, thin. But they weren't just thin; they were really very thin indeed. Kate Moss thin. Their fashionable clothes looked great on them, they had expert streaks in their long hair, they wore cheeky little boots and were always happy.

Sunny hated them.

"Looking forward to tonight?" beamed the middlingly thin Thin Girl, as she thoughtfully held the iron door open, at some risk to her fingertips.

"Er, yeah." Sunny had no idea what this clear-complexioned, bright-eyed beauty might be alluding to. Even her teeth, Sunny noticed, were thin.

"Me too!" chirruped the Thin Girl, taking Sunny's place in the lift and leaving a trace of subtle perfume.

"Good, good." Sunny, baffled, put her key in the front door of number thirteen. She breathed in the delicious scent the Thin Girl had bequeathed her. See, she smiled to herself, there is beauty and romance everywhere.

Jojo was yelling, "You *did* fart, Ellen, you fecking liar!" as Sunny stepped through the door. Jojo was careering down the hall in an egg-stained dressing gown, a Sooty glove puppet on her left hand. "It's to

19

cover me eczema," she enlightened Sunny, as she dashed past.

Perhaps, Sunny corrected herself, not quite *everywhere*.

Throwing down her bag, Sunny nabbed Ellen and lowered her on to a kitchen chair. In a voice that would take no argument, Sunny told her victim, "I'm going to manipulate you." Sunny had recently bought a *Teach Yourself Massage* book and DVD.

"Manipulate away," breathed Ellen. "My shoulders are like tangled knitting."

Inexpertly, Sunny kneaded at her cousin, sneaking looks at the book open on the table. "Does that hurt?" she asked, anxiously.

Surprisingly, Ellen was groaning with what sounded like orgasmic bliss. "Oooh," she growled, contorting with pleasure. "You'll make some lucky man a wonderful wife."

Jojo, now full length on the sofa and reading *OK!* as if she were a scholar studying the Dead Sea Scrolls, tutted and commented, "The lucky man won't be Calum, that's for sure." She laughed gently to herself and turned the page to the wedding of somebody who had been in one episode of *Spooks*.

Sometimes Jojo reminded her cousin and her sister of their aunty Annie. This was not a good thing: Aunty Annie was the most vindictive woman ever to wear a cardie. She was renowned for her sarcasm in Dublin, a city renowned for its sarcasm. They didn't like Aunty Annie much, and at times they didn't like Jojo, but they tried not to let it show.

"Shut up, you beach ball," said Sunny.

20

They didn't always try very hard.

Jojo assumed a smug look. "Sticks and stones —" she started.

"Can be arranged," finished Sunny darkly. She was trying a fancy move on Ellen, a kind of hard tapping. Significantly, the orgasmic groans had tapered off, to be replaced by timid ouches. "I bumped into a Thin Girl."

One day they'd tried to determine if they really did hate the Thin Girls. "I wouldn't call it hate," Sunny had said hesitantly, not wanting to be the kind of sad cow who hated people because they were attractive.

"Maybe we're jealous?" Ellen suggested.

"Jealous? Of those Twiglets?" snorted Jojo, the seams of her polyester kaftan straining. "I think we just dislike them."

"But why?" probed Sunny.

They had sat and thought of the Thin Girls and the way they chattered on their mobile phones, the way their tinkly laughter could be heard through the walls as they threw dinner parties for their thin friends, the way they clattered about in expensive heels on the stairs, the way they baked cakes for the neighbours' birthdays, the way they always smiled and said hello in the hallway.

"Yup, we hate them," Ellen had sighed.

Back in the here and now, Sunny was recounting her conversation with the Thin Girl. "Asked me if I was looking forward to tonight. Said she was, too."

"Skinny eejit," Jojo summed up succinctly. "Nothing's happening tonight. Well, not here. Nothing ever happens here."

This was indisputable. When one flatmate is sociopathic, one is celibate to the point of supergluing her knickers on, and the third has an absentee boyfriend who doesn't believe in spoiling girls by actually ringing them, nothing much is bound to happen.

Sunny tightened her grip on Ellen's shoulders. Ignoring the "OW!", she gasped, "Something *is* happening tonight! We're hosting the monthly Residents' Association meeting!"

A refrain of "Tonight?" and "Here?" and "No!" and "Are you sure?" and "Feck, feck, feck" was only halted by Sunny holding up one hand and saying, "They'll be here in twenty minutes. Get cracking."

The three of them jumped up, looked wildly at each other and realised they had no idea what to get cracking on. They had never hosted a Residents' Association meeting before, and had only volunteered for this one because Jojo had thought she was putting up her hand for more cake.

They were dull affairs run by the formidable Mrs Wilde, whose shape suggested she was trying to smuggle circus tents under her lurid clothes. She would cajole, threaten and bamboozle a dozen or so people to each meeting, so she could chair tedious discussions about parking spaces, where to hang washing and swearing in communal spaces.

"There's usually food at these things." Ellen looked nervous. She didn't like being caught on the hop: Ellen's life was neatly organised and subdivided, like her Filofax.

"It's shopping day tomorrow," winced Jojo. This translated as "There isn't a scrap of food in the house."

"Leave the nibbles to me," said Sunny recklessly. "Jojo, you clean the toilet. Shut up," she ordered, before the inevitable whinge could shape itself on Jojo's lips. "Just get on with it. Ellen, you tidy around."

"Sir!" Ellen clicked her heels and saluted, before dashing off to civilise the hall, which was an obstacle course of junk.

Sunny opened the large larder that took up one alcove of the kitchen/sitting room. The contents weren't very inspiring. Feeding a dozen people on a tin of own-brand beans and a mislaid hairbrush wasn't covered by Nigella or Jamie. Her eyes lit on a box on the bottom shelf.

"Porqy Peeces, my darling little chums," she whispered reverently. When Sarah had forced the box on her, saying, "Alfie's brought home tons of the stuff. Take it. It'll come in useful," Sunny had scoffed. Now it was saving the day. She grabbed a tin and set to work.

When Ellen and Jojo rejoined her in the kitchen, the table was groaning with goodies. "Anyone for a Porqy Peeces boat?" asked Sunny, with a Bree from *Desperate Housewives* smile, holding aloft a platter of boat-shaped slabs of luncheon meat with cocktail-stick masts and jaunty sails of stale bread.

"Is it past its sell-by date?" asked Ellen, dubiously.

"Not at all!" Sunny's smile was still in place, but looking a tad forced. "It's yummy. It's delicious. It's luncheon meat." She whimpered, and the smile dropped. "Work with me here, will you?"

The doorbell sounded and Jojo trundled off in the slightly cleaner dressing gown she'd put on for receiving guests.

Sunny fiddled with a Porqy Peeces giraffe and lined up some Porqy Peeces cars. Behind her, Sunny heard Ellen exclaim, with muted panic, "Marmite!"

Through the kitchen/sitting-room window sauntered their cat. She was indeed the colour of Marmite, and, like that foodstuff, you either loved or hated her. All three flatmates loved her, despite her habit of vomiting in the CD tray, but Mrs Wilde would hate her: animals were strictly forbidden at Chudleigh Court.

Down the long hall they heard Jojo say, "Come in, Mrs W."

"Do something!" hissed Sunny, as Marmite leaped daintily on to the table and capsized a Porqy Peeces armada.

"Like what?" Ellen hissed back. She often complained that the others always expected her to know what to do, as if she was their mother, and this seemed to be one of those occasions.

"*Something!*" Sunny repeated desperately, scuttling off down the hall to slow the progress of the association's chairwoman. "What a beautiful dress!" she gushed inaccurately, as many yards of manmade fabric hurtled towards her.

"Twenty-nine ninety-nine. Drip-dry," barked Mrs Wilde, without breaking step. "What's all this?" she boomed as she reached the kitchen. "This won't do at all."

Peering warily around their guest's bulk, Sunny was relieved to see not a single Marmite hair. She awarded Ellen a covert thumbs-up.

"Tea!" Mrs Wilde demanded. "Where is the tea? Tea is the rocket fuel for my meetings."

As Sunny helped Mrs Wilde dig out all their tannin-streaked mugs, she frowned questioningly at Ellen. Her cousin was wincing silently on the other side of the table, hunched over in a strange position that reminded Sunny of an evening of modern dance she had once endured in order to impress an arty boyfriend.

The doorbell rang again and Ellen slumped to the sofa, lips pursed, her expression reminiscent of Tudor portraits of martyrs.

In moments the kitchen was full of neighbours. The woman who lived below them and never complained even when they held Abba festivals and sang "Waterloo" at midnight put herself in charge of the kettle. Ernest, a dapper old gentleman from the basement, complimented all the ladies, even Jojo, which was over and above the call of duty. Mrs Wilde's other half, Leonard, pressed himself against the brooms in the corner. Covering only a fifth of his wife's acreage, Leonard was beautifully house-trained: he rarely spoke, and when he did, it was nothing more controversial than "Yes, dear". The Thin Girls all arrived together, glowing and chic in the skinniest of jeans, wearing tops that they seemed to have fashioned out of scarves. They were exquisitely polite to everybody and brought homemade organic muffins: Sunny wanted to tip scalding tea over them.

Mrs Wilde was still unhappy with the arrangements. "This room is insufficient," she bawled, as residents squashed up together on the sofa and insinuated themselves into the chairs around the table. "And here is our dear Mrs Gibbs! She simply must have a comfortable seat."

Mrs Gibbs was dear to nobody, and her slow entrance, marked by much wheezing and puffing, parted the company like Moses's trick with the Red Sea. Moses possibly didn't achieve his miracle by smelling of biscuits, but that was why everybody leaned away from Mrs Gibbs. Squat, layered with cardigans that myth-mongers whispered she never removed, Mrs Gibbs was the oldest tenant of Chudleigh Court by about a century. Racist, homophobic and living in the certain belief that every man was after her handbag, she didn't improve meetings.

Sunny had wanted to like her, she really had. When they'd moved into number thirteen and heard that an octogenarian lived on the ground floor, she'd daydreamed about running errands for the grand old lady, listening to her fascinating stories of the Blitz, being a comfort to her in the evening of her days. But that was before Mrs Gibbs had tipped a bucket of water over a West Indian friend of Ellen's, claiming the girl was trying to start a riot as she sat listening to Classic FM in a Ford Focus.

"Blimey. This place is a proper rat 'ole," commented Mrs Gibbs, in the strange slur her pre-NHS dentures dictated. "Get up, son, and let me sit down." She poked Ben with her walking stick, which seemed to be wrapped with old bandages for some reason. "Come on. Me insides went bad in 1953, and I'm on doctor's orders to rest me legs."

"Settle down, everybody. BEN!" hollered Mrs Wilde. "Do find a seat and stop fidgeting, dear. Put down that Spam football. We're starting."

"It's not Sp — Oh, never mind." Sunny looked around for somewhere to place Ben. He rarely emerged from the basement and the cousins theorised that his pallor was a result of this mole-like existence. Ben looked in need of a good meal or seven, but he was shy and sweet and could be relied upon to know about arcane boy stuff, like fuse boxes. He was unaware that they called him "Boiled Egg" behind his back. "Try and squeeze in beside Ellen on the end of the sofa," she said.

Looking murderously at her cousin, Ellen shifted to one side so that Ben could perch beside her once he'd managed to negotiate his way through the forest of people and furniture that overwhelmed the small room. Ellen grimaced and writhed, then was very, very still. Sunny sent her a "What's the matter?" raise of the eyebrows, but Ellen ignored it. She was, Sunny noticed, sweating: a very un-Ellen activity.

One Thin Girl poured Ben a cup of tea, and the least Thin Girl whispered sweetly, "Try a little boat. They're so delicious. Sunny made them herself. Isn't she clever?"

Sunny itched to put an axe through her head.

Mrs Wilde scanned the room momentously, like a wartime prime minister about to impart news of the invasion. "Are we all here? There is much to discuss tonight." A Mexican wave of dismay travelled around the room. "I could talk at length about the myriad contraventions of the bye-laws: sunbathing on the lawn, eating soup in the lift, coughing after midnight, etc., but I must start with . . ." Mrs Wilde paused, then lifted her permed head high to snort, with a whiff of Boadicea, "KNICKERS."

"Knickers?" said Jojo, who was alone in not being shit-scared of Mrs Wilde. "Don't tell me the fecking bye-laws prohibit knickers?"

As Leonard's eyes widened at such daring, his wife surveyed Jojo witheringly. "Believe me, miss, I am not interested in your undergarments."

And neither is anybody else, thought Sunny, communicating this with a furtive grin to Ellen. But Ellen was still grimacing as if in silent pain, with her hands clamped, somewhat unsettlingly, to her own breasts.

Sunny had no time to puzzle, as Mrs Wilde swept on. "There is a pervert in our midst!" she said dramatically, causing a Thin Girl to choke on a Porqy Peeces swan. "A fiend of cunning depravity who derives a squalid thrill from snatching knickers!"

A kerfuffle by the door signalled a latecomer. Guy from the neighbouring block was a professional actor and had contrived to be the last arrival. As usual. He bowed low. "My apologies, one and all," he enunciated gloriously, bestowing his even, white smile on the company. "The stage is a demanding mistress." Guy's

28

main claim to fame was a series of three adverts for a probiotic yoghurt drink that was only shown in East Anglia. Handsome, and aware of it, he was expert at hogging the spotlight. "I heard what you were saying, Mrs Wilde, and I cannot keep it in any longer." He flung out his arms, narrowly missing Ben's startled face. His noble head fell back. "It is I!" he breathed. "*I* am the swine for whom you search. I am the Chudleigh Cad!"

The Thin Girls applauded, mewing with delight. Mrs Gibbs belched and shouted, "Getoutafit, yer Mary-Ann." Sunny had seen it all before.

"I apologise, Mrs W." Guy bowed again. "We thespians can be such children. You have a mission, and I'm in your way. I'll sit here, quiet as a mouse. Do go on." Guy lithely folded himself into a sitting position that looked like sadistic yoga to Sunny, but which he evidently found comfy. He assumed a listening face, offering the room his best profile.

There had been complaints, according to Mrs Wilde, from various "lady residents" that their underwear had vanished. Usually, announced Mrs Wilde with I-told-you-so glee, as it was drying by an open window. This was strictly prohibited in the exhaustive Chudleigh Court bye-laws. (They also proscribed thinking about Communism, and hopping.) "Recently," she thundered on, "there has been a worrying escalation in the swine's activity. The latest item to be snatched — I believe it's called a *thong* — disappeared from a closet in a ground-floor bedroom." A small gasp escaped her audience and Mrs Wilde smiled, pleased at the reaction. "We must act swiftly and decisively before his lusts drive him to even worse atrocities."

Not considering a pilfered thong to qualify as an atrocity, Sunny felt it was time to introduce a hint of sanity. Perhaps the panties had got lost in the wash. Putting up her hand, she started, "I'd just like to —"

"Excellent! Our first vigilante." Mrs Wilde was beaming. "You can man the stake-out."

"Eh?" Sunny, panic-stricken, glanced over at Ellen, who could usually be relied upon to help in a calamity, but Ellen was still hotly contorted, leaning heavily against Ben, who seemed to be enjoying it in his mild, boiled-egg way.

Mrs Wilde thundered on. "I am happy to donate a pair of my own underwear. I suggest we hang them on the washing line by the pond, in order to lure the creature into our clutches. Well, into Ms Parkinson's clutches." She smiled benignly in Sunny's direction.

"But I . . ." Sunny flailed. She was distracted by the fact that one of Ellen's breasts was moving under her V-neck. This information was difficult to compute.

"Marvellous. Let's move on." Mrs Wilde looked sternly around the room. "Pets," she breathed, in a quavering voice. "There is a mammal at large. Does anybody know the whereabouts of the little tortoiseshell cat I've seen wandering about as if it owned the place?"

Sunny winced. Of course. The little tortoiseshell cat was up the jumper of Ellen. By the looks of things, the cat was as unhappy about it as Ellen was. Sunny could just imagine those razor-sharp claws digging in as Marmite struggled to get free.

30

The rest of the meeting seemed to take for ever. Sunny watched Ellen anxiously, barely registering the heady rumour of a new wheelie bin. However, even the tedium of a Chudleigh Court Residents' Association meeting wasn't enough to tempt people to the Porqy Peeces buffet. As the door closed on Guy, always the last to leave, Jojo scraped the leftovers into the bin.

"OHMYGOD!" Ellen whipped up her jumper and released a hot and bothered Marmite into the wild. The cat shot under the table and stayed there for some time, as Ellen examined her enviably flat but now very red midriff.

"What the Jayzus . . .?" Jojo could be very slow on the uptake.

Sunny went to find something soothing. She had vague ideas of calamine lotion, but their bathroom was understocked in that department. Cheapo bubble bath they could do, but medication was thin on the ground. She returned with some Clarins bust-firming gel, her hand carefully over the label.

"Ouch," empathised Sunny, as Ellen rubbed it on her tummy.

"I wondered why your knockers were jiving." Jojo was piling mugs in the sink for somebody else to wash. "I thought it must be some new kind of bra."

Ignoring the very long conversational dead end this remark opened up, Sunny wailed, "I'm a vigilante and I can't even spell it. One of you'll come with me?" Sunny looked expectantly at her flatmates. "Won't you?"

Although they expressed themselves differently — "Sorry, but no" and "In your hole" — the sisters were equally adamant.

CHAPTER
THREE

Her neighbours' knickers had always been low on Sunny's list of priorities. Her new status as the Chudleigh Court vigilante didn't change this. She dodged Mrs Wilde's insistence that she name a day for the stake-out by pleading pressure of work.

It wasn't just an excuse. Sunny had struggled to finish her latest epic on time. Sitting in her publisher's office early on Monday, waiting for Camilla to finish a call, Sunny tugged nervously at the floral vintage sundress she'd chosen to make the most of the lingering warmth of the late summer.

Much of Sunny's wardrobe was vintage. ("It's fucking *second-hand*," Patrick had insisted when they were together. "Vintage schmintage. Some old woman probably died in it. It was chucked in the bin and now you're buying it for ten times as much as it cost when it was made. *Before we were born*." And so on. Men, Sunny decided, didn't understand.) She liked *vintage* clothes because they were unusual and required some creativity to put together. But she was acutely aware that if the wind was in the wrong direction she could look like a batty aunt, fresh from years in the attic (another Patrick quote).

Jojo had agreed with Sunny that the dress, cinched with a wide belt and topped with a pastel cardigan, looked very Audrey Hepburn. Now, Sunny wasn't so sure: Audrey Hepburn didn't have Sunny's childbearing hips. She looked around the head office of Entwined Hearts for distraction.

Her surroundings were disappointingly unromantic. On her first visit, a few years earlier, Sunny had naïvely expected velvet chaises longues and the scent of roses in the air. Today, all she could smell was photocopy toner: Camilla was a hard-headed businesswoman who would sell parsnips, or toothpaste, as easily as she peddled love stories. It was only after Sunny had signed on the dotted line that she had appreciated why Camilla insisted on dealing with authors direct, without the fuss of an agent: she got them cheaper that way.

And, boy, was Entwined Hearts cheap. They churned out Sunny's lovingly written fantasies on greyish paper with lurid covers featuring manly chests and heaving bosoms, created by the "Graphics Department", a man named Reg whose drink problem was evident at twelve paces.

As Sunny waited patiently, quietly regretting her outfit, Camilla sat with her back to her, murmuring into the phone in tones mangled by centuries of the highest-quality inbreeding. Camilla always claimed to be speaking to the Coast when Sunny visited. Knowing that Entwined Hearts had no New York office, and didn't even sell to the States, Sunny was highly dubious about these calls. She deduced that Camilla was probably browbeating another author, or maybe dealing with her husband, a man so dementedly posh that he couldn't do up his own cufflinks without hurting himself.

"Byesie bye!" barked Camilla into the phone, slamming it down and swinging round to face Sunny with one easy move. "Look at this!" She whipped out a diagram on laminated plastic. "This is a graph of your sales." Camilla pointed to the zigzag that was happily climbing the page until, Sunny couldn't help noticing, it suddenly plunged, lemming-like, back to the bottom. "Doesn't look good, does it?"

"Well, no." Sunny guessed she was looking at any old graph that Camilla had swiped from the Internet at random. It might be the incidence of rainfall on Ben Nevis, or how many mice like jam.

"We pay you a pretty penny to write for us," continued Camilla, as Sunny's eyebrows shot up under her fringe. Pretty the pennies might be, but there weren't many of them. "In return, we expect certain standards."

Feeling her stomach contract, Sunny braced herself for criticism.

"Your work is not romantic enough."

Accusations of inaccuracy, plagiarism, even persistent use of made-up words might have been fair, but Sunny couldn't believe her ears. She blinked hard. "You're serious?"

"Oh, yes, perfectly serious. You underestimate our readers' appetite for escapism. For God's sake, Sunny, your last heroine worked in a hardware shop!"

"Only until she discovered she was really an Andalusian gypsy abandoned at birth in a Croydon bus shelter," protested Sunny.

34

"Croydon." Camilla held the word between two fingertips like a snotty hanky.

"It can be a very sensual town," claimed Sunny, who had once taken a salsa class there. She was baffled. Sunny considered herself to be the Queen of Romance. She looked for it in the most mundane situations. "My new heroine is called Helena. She has lots of sex on various beaches with a matador with long hair," she gabbled, as if on trial for her life.

Camilla arched one over-plucked eyebrow. "Might I ask what this Helena does for a living?"

"She's a . . ." Sunny caved in. "All right, she's a lollipop lady." As Camilla threw her hands in the air, Sunny spluttered, "But at the beginning of the book, she sees her husband killed crossing the road to buy her a cushion in the shape of a cat." Her voice rose to a wail. "She's only a lollipop lady to blot out the pain!" Sunny was reasonably certain that she was the first person ever to utter that sentence.

"Listen to me," said Camilla dourly. "When you're writing the next one, crank up the romance. By that I mean crank up the unlikely bits, crank up the sexy bits, crank up the escapist elements. *That*'s what sells. If he's going to be a lord, make him an archduke. If she's going to have ample breasts, make them double Es. If they're wealthy, they should be richer than Elton John's florist. If they're poor, they should be eating gravel. And I don't want orgasms, young lady, I want EARTHQUAKES!" Camilla brought a fist down hard on her blotter. A pencil sharpener jumped off the desk. "Got it?"

"Yes, Camilla." Sunny was meek. She didn't want to provoke her publisher into shouting about orgasms again. "More romance. Got it."

"Excellent. Good." Camilla patted her impressive hairdo. "On to lighter matters. Your pen-name."

Still reeling from the unexpected attack on her style, Sunny straightened her spine. "Here we go again," she thought. This time she would win the argument. According to the Entwined Hearts catalogue, Sandra Parkinson hadn't written a book in over a year: Sunny's output was so prolific that Camilla had insisted on pseudonyms. She had also insisted on supplying them. So far, Sunny had been Eugenia Farquahar, Donatella Doubleday, Mimi Swash and Dame Candida Whyso-Blu. Evidently, Camilla's talents lay elsewhere — beating servants to death, perhaps — but it wasn't really the quality of the names that troubled Sunny. She wanted to hold an Entwined Hearts novelette in her hands and, once again, see the name her parents had given her on the cover.

This time she would stand up to Camilla.

By the time Sunny was back out in the sunshine, she was Muffy Purejoy.

This never happened: the flat was empty. Suspiciously, Sunny peered into wardrobes and under beds: Jojo was *always* in. It was one of the laws of the universe that you could rely on. E always equalled mc^2, rivers always ran downhill, and Jojo was always in. Apart from brief forays to the supermarket, the launderette or Tacky

Dressing Gowns "R" Us, Jojo was in number thirteen Chudleigh Court.

"Jojo!" called Sunny down the echoing hall.

Her cousin hadn't always been such a homebody. Jojo had worked as a bank clerk until a few months ago. Admittedly, her job was only two streets away, but she'd gone there every day, until the afternoon she'd fallen off her office chair and damaged her knee slightly. (She later admitted that she'd been reaching for her colleague's last Rolo while he was in the loo.) Before you could say "malingering fat Irish girl", Jojo had sued the bank, courtesy of a shonky legal firm she'd spotted in a Channel Five ad break. Now she lived comfortably on the settlement, which kept her in Toffee Crisps and lurid loungewear. She didn't like nightclubs ("Too noisy"), and she didn't like the cinema ("Sure, it'll be on the telly in no time"), and she didn't like parties ("A roomful of gobshites talking bollocks") and seemed perfectly happy just to hang around the flat all day watching television and talking to the cat as if it were human. Sunny no longer watched Jojo's behaviour for signs of agoraphobia. She'd accepted that her cousin wasn't depressed or phobic, merely staggeringly antisocial.

A Jojo-less flat meant that Sunny could knuckle down to some writing and sketch out a new, hyper-soppy plot without the insistent blare of the television to distract her. She was switching on her laptop when a better idea struck.

"Hi." Calum sounded so sexy on the phone, like he was licking your ear. "What's up?"

"Oh, not much." Sunny twiddled a lock of hair. "Just checking you're still OK for tonight. My friend's dinner party, remember?"

"What time do you want me?"

Sunny could hear the white noise of the busy trading office behind Calum. "It's interesting that you should put it like that," she said softly, bowing her head as if she might be overheard. "I want you now."

"Easy, tiger," laughed Calum. "Don't get me all hot and bothered. I've got work to do."

"The flat's empty." Sunny paused. She could hear Calum's breathing at the other end. "I thought you might like to fool around." She paused again. "We wouldn't have to keep quiet like we normally do." The deal wasn't quite struck. "I'm wearing those pink panties you like."

"Don't you dare move." The line went dead.

It took him half an hour to get to Putney, by which time she'd actually put on the little chiffon nothings she'd claimed to be wearing. (The very large white tummy-tamers she'd really had on might do it for Daniel Cleaver, but she knew Calum was an Ann Summers kind of guy.)

As Sunny heard his motorbike crunch on to the gravel of Chudleigh Court's communal gardens, she tousled her hair and stepped into her highest heels, a pair of sixties gold stilettos. In bars, Calum was trendy, with waxed hair and layered Tees, but in the bedroom, he was staunchly traditional: it was big hair and high heels all the way. Sunny was happy to oblige. She inspected the girl in the mirror. The girl looked good, she decided. Sunny swatted away the uncomfortable thought that the girl also looked a little lost and vulnerable. The girl in the mirror knew that the only way to get Calum to her side was with the promise of no-strings sex.

Sunny shut the wardrobe door and that girl who knew too much was gone. A moment after the doorbell sounded, Calum was in the hall tearing off his leathers, with his lips locked on Sunny's.

Forty minutes later, flat on their backs and sweating on the duvet, which had found its way to the floor, they grinned dopily at each other.

"Bloody hell," said Calum.

"Exactly," said Sunny.

It had been sensational. And acrobatic. A lack of Jojo meant that they could be as noisy as they dared, and they'd taken full advantage. Gasping, shrieking, yelling urgent instructions about exactly what to do to each other, they'd dusted all the surfaces in the room with their bodies.

"You are one sexy girl, sweetheart." Calum kissed the top of Sunny's head gently.

Sunny's toes curled with pleasure. That kiss on the head, so throwaway and so *loving*, gave her more genuine happiness than all the eye-popping activity that had preceded it.

"Am I?" She snuggled into his hard, damp body, hoping to milk this moment. Perhaps they could inch forward slightly, talk about how they felt.

"Which makes this even more difficult." Calum sat up, dropping Sunny mid-snuggle.

She scrambled to a sitting position, too, panic knitting in her chest. "What do you mean?"

A look of distilled discomfort on his handsome face, Calum said, "This isn't really going anywhere, is it?"

Leaping to her feet, Sunny squealed, "You went somewhere pretty intimate ten minutes ago, mate! What do you mean, not going anywhere? What was what we just did all about, then?" Suddenly aware of her nakedness, she delved into the nearest drawer and came up with her most recent Christmas present from Jojo. It was a Teletubbies towel, and although it didn't add much to her dignity, it was large enough to cover her sticky-out sections.

By now Calum was standing, too. In fact, he was jumping into his Calvin Kleins with a speed that Sunny could only interpret as hurtful. She wanted to say pleadingly, "You kissed me on the top of my head," but instead she spat, "Is that all you've got to say?" Even she didn't like the tone of her voice, shrewish and belligerent.

Swallowing a sigh, Calum put down his trousers and sat on her bed. "C'm'ere," he said kindly.

"No, thanks. I'll stand." Sunny turned mulish. She *really* couldn't handle kindliness from Calum. Passion, even anger, was fine, but she had no use for a condescending Calum in her fragile state.

Slowly, Calum said, "It's great seeing you. We always have fun. You're a great girl." He was talking to Sunny but staring at his trousers, as if he yearned to be reunited with them. "But . . ."

Sunny actually felt sorry for him. Calum wasn't equipped for this. He was all about fun and spunk; right now, there was none of either. Taking pity on him, she whispered, "I know. Like you said, it's not going anywhere." She suspected he'd already spent twice as long breaking up with her as he'd planned: there was no way he could devise an alternative get-out phrase at this kind of notice.

"Not really, no." Kindly Uncle Calum shook his head. A hand inched towards his shirt.

"Oh, get dressed, Calum, and go," mumbled Sunny, suddenly desperate to be on her own so she could embark on an Olympic cry. She tugged at the Teletubbies towel in an attempt to cover more skin in front of this man she'd just had sex with.

"Don't be like that." Calum was in his trousers. "We knew it had to end sometime." The shirt was on.

"Yeah, but not straight after making love and immediately before my best friend's dinner party," Sunny reminded him, a soupçon of irritation possibly creeping into her delivery.

"Shit, yeah." Calum paused in knotting his tie. "Sorry about that." He pushed the tie up under his collar with a lightning action.

"You're desperate to get away, aren't you?" It was meant to be light, but it came out cynical. Sunny felt as if she'd suddenly aged a decade or five. If she opened the wardrobe door now, Mother Teresa would be staring back out of the mirror.

"No, no, we can talk more if you like." Calum did his best, but he still looked as if he'd rather sauté his own testicles than "talk more".

"Don't worry," spat Sunny. "You're off the hook. You got your free shag. You can go now."

Calum appraised her and seemed about to say something, but instead just pursed his lips.

Sunny shadowed him down the hall, like a mongrel waiting for a morsel. He zipped up his leathers in surly silence. He opened the door. Sunny realised with a sickening jolt that Calum could walk out on her without saying goodbye.

"Calum!" Her whisper was cracked. "Goodbye."

Calum softened. "Goodbye, girl." He smiled through the closing gap as he pulled the front door shut. "G'night, Tinky Winky. G'night, Po."

Sunny managed a watery smile. Then she was alone, in a sad silence that was only broken by a voice coming from way behind her, in the kitchen. Jojo shouted, "Oi, Audrey Hepburn! I can see your arse!"

CHAPTER
FOUR

"I told you not to wear your jeans," said Sunny crossly as Patrick clambered into the taxi.

"You told me not to wear my usual jeans." Patrick was, as ever, calm. "These, my little fruit fly, are not my usual jeans."

"No," frowned Sunny, taking in the spatters of paint and the missing belt tabs. "They're worse."

"Who's doing who a favour here?" asked Patrick lightly as the taxi chugged towards Chiswick.

"I'm not asking you to donate an organ. It's a lovely meal in the lovely house of two people you're very fond of." Sunny had left her gratitude and her manners at home, along with one of her earrings. Heartache was having its usual effect.

"Her's here!" whispered Sarah, anxiously, as she answered the door.

Unbuttoning her velvet jacket, Sunny said, "In this country we say, 'Hello' or maybe, 'Good evening. Gosh, don't you look nice.' "

Prada sequins reflected crystal patterns up on to Sarah's strong, handsome face. "You're not Calum," she accused Patrick.

He grinned fondly and wrapped his long arms round her. "You really haven't got the hang of this greeting-people lark, have you?" He then held her by her shoulders at arm's length and said slowly, "Now, repeat after me: 'Hello, Patrick, it's great to see you.' "

"Oh, it is!" Sarah's features relaxed. "It's always great to see you." She turned to Sunny as she took Patrick's hand and led him across the wide white hall. "I'd forgotten how nice his hair is."

"Never mind his hair, what's Her like?" asked Sunny in an undertone.

"Stunningly beautiful," said Sarah decisively. "No, she's frighteningly ugly. Oh, how would I know?" She kicked open the door to the drawing room like a disgruntled toddler.

As they entered the vast white space (Alfie and Sarah worshipped at the Church of Modernism), Sunny noticed Patrick surreptitiously eyeballing his own hair in one of the massive mirrors. She suppressed a smile. He *did* have nice hair. The same deep brown as her own, it curled lazily along his neck, but it had argued with his comb some years ago, and now they rarely met. In the olden days, when Sunny had been in the habit of running her hands through it, she'd sometimes encountered leaves.

The fact that Sunny and Patrick had met at one of Sarah's infamous toga parties had given Sarah special rights over their relationship: she was their self-appointed fairy godmother. Even though that particular toga party had been six years ago, Sarah still felt propietorial about Patrick. She treated him like an indulgent big sister, taking liberties with him that were beyond other women. For his part, Patrick seemed to find Sarah's bulldozer ways endearing. His real older sister was a dull woman who bred cockatiels on the Isle of Wight, and he infinitely preferred the spirited, sexy, outspoken and clumsily affectionate version he'd acquired in Chiswick. "Even if she did lumber me with you," he was fond of saying to Sunny.

The toga party had been part of Sarah's cunning plan to rescue Sunny from the aftershocks of another failed affair. Sunny was fresh from a wounding encounter with an art director at Waldhorn Truss Levy and had vowed, loudly, that she would never get jiggy with it again. However, there was something about the tall bloke in the corner, the only person in the room not wearing a toga, that had caused a rethink. That and the seven vodka jellies. And, possibly, Sarah hissing, "He is, he's looking at you!" all night.

Sarah had been there for the giggly bits at the beginning; she hadn't shirked the messy bits at the end. The weekly rendezvous had been her idea: "If you stay friends, you'll salvage something," she'd reasoned, touched by Sunny's pain.

Alfie wasn't quite so proprietorial, but he loved them both. Wearing a linen suit as bright as the modern art that pricked the white walls, he came over to bear-hug Sunny and offer a manly handshake to Patrick.

"This is a surprise!" He grinned at them. He was small and round and pink-cheeked: in other words, not at all Sarah's type. She had always bought in bulk, going for the broad-shouldered, stooping-to-get-through-the-door types. The cynical view at the agency had been that Alfie looked a lot taller standing on his wallet, but Sunny knew that Sarah had planned to make her own fortune and didn't find wealth an aphrodisiac.

Alfie was frighteningly smart, but he wore it lightly. He made Sarah laugh, and he challenged her, and he was worth listening to. Besides, although not the conventional romantic hero, Alfie dressed well and cleverly kept his depleted hair closely cropped. He looked a bit like a baby. A big, fashionable baby.

"Are you two . . . ?" Alfie pointed from Sunny to Patrick, a question in his eyes. "You know? Again?"

"God, no!" Sunny caught his drift. "Patrick's just a stand-in."

"I see." Alfie winked at Patrick. "They sure know how to make a guy feel good, don't they?"

Sarah thrust her face between them. Despite the expert *maquillage*, it looked sallow. "Are you planning to get them a drink, Castro?" she nagged. Sarah only used her husband's surname when she was miffed (which was a shame, as it was such a splendid and unlikely one).

Sunny saw Alfie's face cloud briefly at his wife's tone before he said, "Champagne OK? I'll be right back."

Introductions were made. Infuriatingly, Her was out in the conservatory with her back to them, but Sunny met Karen and Phil. He was tall, black and monosyllabic, wearing a shiny blue suit that cost more than Sunny's parents' first home. He stared into the air above their heads, leaving his tiny girlfriend to fill in the gaps with machine-gun Glaswegian chatter. Tiny and approximately chopstick-shaped, all the calories in her frame had leaked out into her hair, fizzing in a wild triangle around a face that, although pretty, looked as if it had been sucking lemons since the millennium.

"Oh, I *love* your earrings. *Earring*," Karen corrected herself mid-gush. "Of course, Himself neglected to tell me about this invitation until this afternoon so I had to throw myself together."

Sunny murmured that she looked great.

"Thanks. If some people didn't hog the bathroom —" she cast a glance of pure citrus up at Phil's impassive face "— with their scuffing lotions, and their re-texturising moisturisers, and all their other *gay* crap, some of us might have been able to get in and wash our hair. But no." She appealed to Sunny and Patrick with the air of somebody who expected sympathy. "Oh-ho no. Muggins here has to make way for his nibs."

Sunny produced a noise between a laugh and a tut that she hoped hit the spot.

On Karen went, tirelessly traducing the silent Phil, although never referring to him by his name. "And then, of course, Little Lord Fauntleroy wants a cab, even though it's only a ten-minute walk. So we get stuck in traffic, and we're late. I'm doing my nut, but Joe Cool here isn't bothered. But it's rude, isn't it, to be late?"

"We were late," smiled Patrick.

"Oh. Well." Karen flailed. She rallied with, "Lord Snooty always blames it on me when we're late."

It was a relief to be led away to meet Her. Out in the glowing glass cube that was the Castros' groovy take on a conservatory, they shook hands with Liz, a comfortably built woman in a navy dress that even Sunny's mother would have deemed old-fashioned.

"Nice to meet you." Her smiled. Sunny detected a slight lisp. "Isn't this house stunning?" She seemed overawed.

"It is," agreed Sunny. She was used to her friends' level of opulence and had long ago conquered any awe: leaving a menstrual bloodstain the shape of India on a white leather couch had been a breakthrough. "You work with Alfie?"

"Actually, Alfie's saving my company's life," asserted Liz. She played with her necklace, nervously. "My grandfather created Porqy Peeces." Behind her back, Sarah raised her eyes to the ceiling, having evidently heard all this before. "We've gone right out of fashion, but Alfie's come up with a spectacular advertising campaign that will make us — dare I say it? — *trendy* again." Liz pulled a face at her own daring.

"I love Porqy Peeces," claimed Patrick unexpectedly.

"You do?" Liz was delighted. When she smiled she looked kind of goofy, but it didn't stop her doing it often.

"Yeah! You can do anything with it. You can fry it, or you can make a sandwich, or you can just lie in bed sharing it with Oz."

"That's his dog," explained Sunny.

48

"When I was a student we practically lived on Porqy Peeces and fried eggs." Patrick's gaze went dreamy, the way some men look when they think of page three.

Alfie had been earwigging. "Lots of people feel like that about it, but they're secretive, as if there's something shameful about luncheon meat." He was animated, as he always was when he spoke about his work. "The public is very knowledgeable about food and what's in it these days. My own darling wife —" he gestured at Sarah, who was listening to Karen describe Phil as gay for the tenth time "— can recite the additives in chicken nuggets like a nun saying the Lord's Prayer. When I took home a few tins of Porqy Peeces for her to try, she threw her hands up in horror, suspecting there were all sorts of evil little additives in there. Now she even gives it to the kids."

"Shame." Patrick looked crestfallen. "I rather liked the frisson of guilt."

"Sorry. From now on it's a virtuous product. Isn't that right, Liz?"

Her nodded, and took a gulp of champagne.

"I might not buy it now," sulked Patrick, with a cheeky twinkle.

"Oh, I bet you'll change your mind when you see Alfie's wonderful commercials," Liz said, admiringly.

"Now, now," said Alfie, unable to see his wife behind him miming being violently sick into a Philippe Starck plant-holder. "Without far-sighted clients like Liz, no decent advertising gets made."

They were joined by Karen and her silent man. She announced, "I want an extension like this, but do you think You Know Who will even discuss it? Of course not. Can't afford it, he says, before he even knows the price."

You Know Who doggedly behaved as if Karen was a very small wasp that might stop buzzing if he ignored it. They were an uncomfortable couple to be around, so Sunny was relieved when Sarah volunteered her to help in the kitchen.

In a blank chrome room so minimalist that Sunny had once been reduced to tears trying to find the kettle, Sarah hissed, "Whadyathink? Am I going mad, or is something going on? Would you fancy her if you were Alfie? Is she fat, or is she just shapely? Can a man overlook that kind of bum if a woman has personality? I suspect she's got a lovely personality, the cow. Is that lisp irritating, or is it cute?"

"If I could only see a frying pan in this tundra, I'd whack you over the head with it," laughed Sunny, incredulously. "Get a grip, you silly old bag. She's just a . . . a . . ." Sunny floundered. "She's just a woman, a really ordinary, obviously nice woman. She's not a femme fatale, and Alfie's treating her like a client. Honest."

Sarah was biting her nails, a habit she'd abandoned in the Brownies. "There's more to it. I know it. I *feel* it." She turned lunatic eyes to Sunny. "You should understand that. Your books are full of people who just *know* things. Remember *Love Against the Odds*? Samantha just *knew* that Sebastian needed her and she was right — he'd been kidnapped by crazed pygmies."

Even Sunny could see that it wasn't sensible to use her novels as a blueprint for life. "Samantha's not real. I made her up. And I was premenstrual when I did it." Sunny was treading carefully. There had to be more to Sarah's behaviour than met the eye: this mania couldn't be triggered by jealousy of somebody as mousy as Liz. "Look, have another sip of shampoo, get the starters on the table, and we'll talk about Her to our hearts' content tomorrow."

"Yeah. You're right. I'm going bonkers, aren't I? I can be bloody unbearable when I get an idea and run with it." Sarah shrugged with rueful self-knowledge and tucked a stray strand of blonde hair behind an ear. "Sorry, Sun."

"Do not sorry me. Now, where's the starters?"

Sarah gestured to an array of small white plates. Trying not to sound alarmed, Sunny asked, "What exactly is this pink stuff?"

"It's Porqy bloody Peeces pâté," snapped Sarah. "The things I do for that man."

"Hmmm." Sunny pulled a face. Hoping that Sarah wouldn't shoot the messenger (it wasn't out of the question for there to be a chic little chrome gun somewhere in this spotless room), she said, apologetically, "I heard Karen say she's a vegetarian."

"Brilliant," growled Sarah.

"I'll rustle something up," declared Sunny, foolhardily. She was a bad rustler-up at the best of times. After a fingertip search, she located the fridge and peeked inside. "Christ, it's a tofu warehouse. Is all your food white? Where's the normal, unhealthy stuff?"

Lobbing a frozen bag of green goo at her friend, Sarah said, "I don't do unhealthy stuff. That's watercress soup. Unless she has a conscience about harming tiny green plants, that'll do her."

"OK, I give up," wailed Sunny after a minute or two. "Where's the hob gone?"

Sarah pressed a button and an electric ring appeared in the middle of the worktop.

"Why can't you have a nice country kitchen?" complained Sunny. "With herbs hanging up to dry, and Beast artwork stuck to the fridge?"

"Do you know how many bacteria thrive on just one frilly blind?"

This rampant desire for hygiene had increased with the Beasts' birth. It was one of Sarah's best-kept secrets that she adored her noisy, smelly children and worried constantly about them. Only Sunny and Alfie knew about this, and understood that something in her proud, complex nature compelled her to disguise her love with a patina of offhand boredom. The couture armour had never fooled Sunny: she'd recognised Sarah's vulnerability the moment they'd met in the ladies' at Waldhorn Truss Levy. Sometimes Sunny wanted to shake Sarah and crack the brittle façade she offered the world, but tonight she just wished Sarah wouldn't be so hard on Alfie.

"Oi." Sarah pointed a ladle at Sunny. "Where's the gorgeous Calum? What happened? He didn't let you down at the last minute, did he?"

"Just slightly." Nudging a watercress iceberg around the pan, Sunny recounted the story of Calum's exit.

"The monumental sod." Sarah prodded a joint of lamb with bloodthirsty empathy. Before now, she'd been known to track down, and tip drinks over, blokes that had done her friend wrong.

"Yup. One minute we're throwing each other about like Soviet gymnasts, the next he's on his bike." Sunny sniffed. "Literally." She swallowed. She didn't want to splash tears into the homemade soup: Sarah was puritanical about salt levels.

"Poor you," sighed Sarah. "You should have cancelled. I would have understood."

"I knew I'd feel better if I went out. I'll have a good cry in bed tonight, though."

"He didn't touch your heart, did he?" asked Sarah gently, her façade shifting to reveal one of the chinks that Sunny cherished.

Sunny reassured her: "I always kept something back. I knew he was never going to fall for me." She could only be this honest around Sarah. "Strange, but I wish he *had* touched me." She shook her head. "No, I don't mean that exactly. I mean . . ."

"You wish *somebody* would touch your heart?" suggested Sarah, slicing thin, crisp toast into slender triangles.

"Exactly."

"That's when the real trouble starts," muttered Sarah. Before Sunny could respond, she carried on brightly, "At least Calum actually chucked you, even if the timing was cruel. It was the non-callers I couldn't bear."

"Yeah. You see them five or six times and then they just tumble off the side of Love Mountain, never to be heard of again."

"I mean," theorised Sarah, transferring the toast to a plate, "do you call *him*?"

"And if you do, what do you say?" Sunny hadn't noticed that the thawed soup was bubbling like Vesuvius.

"Are you breezy? Are you concerned? Do you ask if he's been ill? Do you pretend you've been given two tickets for something?"

"And when you've finally worked yourself up to call, but you get his answerphone, how do you stop yourself from screaming into it, 'PICK UP THE PHONE, I SLEPT WITH YOU, YOU BASTARD'?"

The soup boiled over on to the virgin worktop, flooding down to the glossy white floor. Sarah said, "I think that's ready."

"What about you, Patrick?" asked Sarah. "What's the most interesting thing that's happened to you this week?"

This was an old conversational gambit that the Castros dusted off for dinner parties. Each guest had to think of one interesting thing that had happened to them over the past seven days, and then they'd all vote for their favourite story. The winner brought home a bottle of pink champagne, which flowed like tap water in this house.

Sunny loathed the game. It was so false. She only ever joined in facetiously. One evening, she'd been amazed to win with her tale of how she'd mistaken a small tramp for Bruce Willis in her local Spar.

Pulling a face, Patrick said languidly that nothing ever happened to him, interesting or otherwise. "I garden, I go home. That's about it. Oh." He held up a forefinger. "Once a week, I have a few Guinnesses with madam there."

"And believe me," Sunny was sombre, "it's not interesting." She didn't mean that. She and Patrick could talk in detail and at length about any subject on earth. He was good at careering off at a tangent, dragging Sunny, her hair streaming, with him.

Patrick was being honest when he claimed that nothing ever happened to him. His life was predictable. When they had been together, Sunny had tried to goad him into being more exciting. He'd insisted, with his trademark infuriating calm, "I get my excitement watching the plants I tend grow." She would inevitably snarl, "Oh, shuddup, Alan Titch-fucking-marsh," and secrete ski brochures in his seed catalogues.

"Hang on." Realising something, Patrick smiled and said, "Actually, something vaguely interesting did happen to me yesterday. I was offered my own TV programme."

All cutlery clatter ceased.

"Oh, get off!" scoffed Sunny.

"Give, give!" urged Sarah, her face animated at last.

"You're serious?" marvelled Sunny.

There was a pause. Sometimes Sunny could kill Patrick: only he would choose to take a long, deliberate slurp of his Guinness after such an announcement.

(And only Patrick would have switched to Guinness when there was Moët et Chandon on offer.)

"Well." Looking as if he regretted ever starting this, Patrick unfolded his "interesting happening". He'd been contracted to landscape a large plot behind a sumptuous house. The client had a fat budget but zero inspiration. The only brief he'd given Patrick was "My wife's a country girl, and she misses wild flowers."

"So," Patrick told them, his eyes faraway, "I gave them a gently undulating wilderness at the end of the garden, dotted with bluebells and sprinkled with daisies. Nearer the house I laid a soft lawn and curved a pebbly path through it. They looked like they entertain a lot, so I built them a pergola with a brick barbecue and laid a terrace using these fantastic old stone flags with a really nubbly edge in a soft greyish, charcoalish colour . . ." Patrick had slowed right down as he recalled the garden. "And I trailed a honeysuckle around the garden doors to scent the dusk when they brushed against it."

Gently, Karen murmured, "I can almost feel the sun on my face."

"I love daisies," said Sunny, dreamily.

The others nodded, all lulled by the quiet intensity in Patrick's description. Snapping out of his reverie, Patrick said cheerfully, "The bloke really liked it. On my last day, he had some business associate round for a drink, and he asked me to describe what I'd done. So I did, and this other guy tells me he runs a television production company and asks would I be interested in talking to them about being involved with a new programme."

Eyes narrowed, Alfie interrupted to ask, "Which company? There are loads of little ones out there, jostling for position. They have ideas every ten minutes, but hardly any of them make it to the screen."

Patrick thought for a moment. "Er, Curiosity Films. Something like that."

"Curiosity?" Alfie looked taken aback. "They're massive." He was so obviously impressed that everybody else was, too. Even the impassive Phil leaned forward to hear the rest of the story.

"It seems that they want to create a — is this the right word, Alfie? — *mainstream* gardening show." On a nod from Alfie, Patrick carried on. "They want a presenter who knows his stuff, but is unknown. They want to . . ." Patrick hesitated, as if he suddenly had a bad taste in his mouth. "They want to make somebody a star." Having gone slightly pink, he took another sip of his Guinness. "Don't know what made them think I'd be right for it."

Karen did. "It's because you're easy on the eye," she said, precipitating Phil's first reaction of the evening, a peeved snort.

"Oh, it's nothing like that. It's a *gardening* programme," Patrick reminded her, looking uncomfortable.

"Don't be so naïve," chided Sarah, standing up to clear the plates. "Sex sells. I know what I'm talking about. Before I spent my days Beast-wrangling, I used to make ads, remember. We always used attractive actors because that's what people want to see when they turn on their televisions. With no hunk at the helm, it would be just another bloody show about geraniums, and who'd watch it?"

"I'm not a hunk," insisted Patrick, as if she'd accused him of stealing her purse.

"No, he's not." Sunny backed Patrick up, earning herself a funny look from him. "I mean, you're good-looking in an intelligent sort of way, isn't he, Alfie?"

"Oh, yes." Alfie was trying not to laugh.

Karen said emphatically, "He's a fucking hunk in my opinion," which even won a grunt from Phil.

From the doorway, Sarah said, "You win the competition hands down. Unless one of us has shagged an Oscar-winner, you have done the most interesting thing."

"I can't take it in," said Sunny incredulously. "You're going to be famous." My silly old Patrick, she was thinking, a telly star. Her scalp tingled with the excitement of it.

Patrick looked puzzled. "Obviously I turned him down."

From the kitchen came Sarah's voice. "Somebody stab him."

"Why?" howled Sunny. "Patrick, people *dream* of having their own television programme. You could be a celebrity. And rich."

"I've never dreamed about it." Patrick was employing his let's-change-the-subject voice, one that got trotted out a lot around Sunny.

Sarah's voice drifted through again. "Tell him he's not getting any dessert."

Relentless, Sunny banged on. "You've got to call them and say you've changed your mind."

"Do I?" That tone was dangerous. Sunny didn't pick up on it, but Alfie evidently did.

"Here's dessert!" he shouted, as Sarah reappeared, holding aloft a large dish. "What is it, darling?"

"Porqy Peeces ice cream," simpered Sarah. She broke the heavy silence by saying, "As if. It's tropical fruit salad."

The evening was winding down. Karen had whinged herself to a standstill and was dozing, head back and exhausted mouth open, on a colossal sofa. Phil was staring into his espresso, ignoring Sarah's polite conversation.

She didn't notice his rudeness, because she was eavesdropping on Her and Alfie's chat about the Minehead railway line for signs of sexual innuendo.

On another huge sofa, like a neighbouring desert island in the ocean of the drawing room, Sunny tried to convince Patrick that he should reconsider. She was at her most animated; he was like a statue of himself.

"You needn't think I'm being starry-eyed, because I'm not," she said, fabricating an assumption for him before dealing briskly with it. "It'll be hard work, a steep learning curve, and who knows, you might be useless at it. Then you'd get terrible viewing figures and that would be that. Psssht." She made an inexplicable gesture with her fingers to signify something or other.

"But," she said loudly, tracing the word on his grubby jeans to emphasise her point, "you might enjoy it and be an instant success, make a fortune and suddenly start popping up in Sainsbury's ads."

"Do you think there's any more Guinness?"

"Remember how I went on and on at you about getting a dog?"

After a pause, Patrick said, "Oh, you want an answer. Yes, O bully, I remember."

"You were yapping on about how they were a burden and you were allergic and you'd been bitten once in Torbay?"

"Totnes, actually."

"But I dragged you to Battersea Dogs' Home, and you met Oz and fell in love? I was right then, wasn't I? Imagine your life without Oz."

"I think I saw more Guinness earlier."

"The point I'm making is that I had to nag you into that, but it turned out for the best."

"Even a glass of champagne would do. I'm not proud."

"I'm going to do it again. I'm going to wear you down. I'm not going to let you pass up this opportunity. It could change your life."

"Exactly. Sunny, not everybody wants their life changed." Patrick got up and left the room.

Harrumphing, Sunny wasn't alone for long. Sarah abandoned Phil to his intense inner life and joined her amongst the Heal's cushions. She got her trajectory slightly wrong and almost suffocated Sunny with Prada.

"How are you doing?" she asked in a kind undertone as they budged up clumsily.

"All right." Sunny smiled weakly. "It'll hit me when I get on my own, I suppose, but for now I'm fine." She felt like a doctor discussing a patient: there was a coolness about her reaction to Calum's callous departure that surprised her. "I'm not turning into a hardened old slapper, am I?" she asked anxiously.

"You?" smiled Sarah. "Hardly. You're Snow White. You'll never be cynical." She paused. "Unless something happens to make you that way."

"Will you *stop* watching them like that?" whispered Sunny. "You're being so obvious. The poor woman will think you've got a personality disorder."

"Poor woman my expensively-exfoliated arse," hissed Sarah. "She's after him. She's using her womanly wiles and will stop at nothing."

As they spoke, Liz was laughing goofily, exposing a sliver of kiwi fruit between her front teeth.

"See what you mean." Sunny felt the situation called for high levels of irony. "She's a right *femme fatale* in those support tights." Hesitating, because she rather liked her head where it was, neatly on her shoulders, Sunny ventured a "What's really the matter?"

"Can't you see?" Sarah struggled to keep her voice down. "Alfie hasn't looked at me all night. Or all week." Her face, so perfectly made up, twisted like a discarded tissue. "My jokes don't make him laugh. He works late and then sits up while I go to bed." She clutched Sunny's arm, a passionate gesture out of place in this

61

austerely beautiful room. "Are we having a real crisis, do you think? Has he gone off me?"

Sunny couldn't possibly know, but she could tell that Sarah needed an answer. "You two need to talk," she said, sagely.

"What about?" Sarah was back in control of her features again. "About *Her*?"

"Her is so not the problem." Sunny didn't like to be too certain about anything (she suspected God of having a twisted sense of humour), but she felt on safe ground. "Alfie is not lusting after Liz."

"Maybe not." Sarah smoothed out Sunny's sleeve where she'd creased it. "But he likes her better than me."

Patrick joined them, cutting the emotional conversation short with his male presence. "What's the latest on the Beasts?"

"We're in what parenting magazines refer to as Me Time, Patrick. You know I don't talk about them during the hours of darkness." Sarah relented, and admitted with a grin, "Actually, Charlie did do something very sweet today." It was a long anecdote, culminating in Charlie asking if he could marry the hoover.

Liz drifted over to them for the punchline, her hand nervously at her tonged hair. "They sound like lovely children," she said, with banal politeness. "I hear so much about them from your husband."

"Well, he must make it all up." Sarah flared her nostrils in a way recognised as dangerous in both racehorses and West London housewives. "He never sees them."

62

"Oh . . ." Liz didn't seem equipped for this kind of sophisticated rudeness, and looked down at her feet in their Clarks sandals.

Anxious to help Liz out, and steer the conversation into sunnier waters, Sunny said, "Alfie makes up for it when he takes you all away, though, doesn't he?"

"He brought a pile of Porqy Peeces paperwork on our trip to Disneyland Paris last month." Sarah was almost knocked out of her Manolos by the massive nudge this comment elicited from Sunny. "But," she carried on, perhaps ashamed of her own lack of grace, "I understand. It's a demanding job." She paused, and looked over at her husband, who was managing to winkle almost complete sentences out of Phil. "He's a good man," she added, almost to herself.

"Yes," nodded Liz, grateful to be back on pleasant turf. "He's my hero." If she noticed the sideways look this comment earned her from her hostess, she didn't show it.

"Ready for the off?" said Patrick, yawning and stretching unabashedly. He had no problem with taking his leave of parties; Sunny always felt vaguely guilty and scattered extravagant goodnights and kisses and hugs randomly and repeatedly, until everybody, frankly, wished she'd bugger off.

As they scanned the Chiswick horizon, Cherokee-like, for taxis, Patrick said, "You were in a hurry to get out. I usually have to use grease and levers to extricate you from Sarah's."

"It's been a long time since you and I went anywhere together apart from the pub," Sunny realised.

"Aha," said Patrick. "That old Parkinson subject switch. Obvious, clumsy and oh so revealing. Tell me why you wanted to leave: I know you haven't argued with Sarah; that's not possible."

"I never argue with anybody," said Sunny tetchily.

"Technically, you're arguing with me now," Patrick pointed out. After a gap, which Sunny didn't rush to fill, he said, "You don't need to tell me if you don't want to."

This induced a massive tut from Sunny. (She had learned tutting from her mother, a noted tutter, and was good at it.) Why couldn't Patrick ever demand, or insist? He never showed any passion, just like back when . . . She didn't want to revisit their break-up just now; that was pointless. And he would be astonished at the hard nugget of disappointment she still carried. Patrick was Patrick: he was a good friend if a bad boyfriend, but maybe he was just the person to share what was troubling her.

"This sounds so pathetic." She started off with a disclaimer, in case he thought she was a romantic fool. "But I find it so hard to cope with Sarah and Alfie having difficulties in their marriage. They're a kind of totem pole for me; they *have* to be happy. If their relationship dissolves, then what hope is there for the rest of us?"

"Have I missed something? I didn't notice any difficulties."

"No, well you wouldn't, would you? You own a willy."

They passed a streetlamp, and Sunny had to laugh at the consternation on Patrick's face. She clarified: "Blokes just don't notice the subtle stuff," she opined, like a venerable Oxford don giving an undergraduate the benefit of her years of study. "Alfie was withdrawn tonight. He barely looked at Sarah, and he talked *about* her rather than to her. Did you see any of that?"

"I was too busy enjoying my dinner," muttered Patrick.

"Exactly. Sarah's really concerned. She thinks he might be going off her." She waited a moment before revealing, "She suspects him of having an affair with Liz."

This didn't produce the bark of amusement that Sunny had expected. "Nah," said Patrick, dismissively. "Liz seems like a very nice woman, but nah."

"Sarah's convinced something's going on."

"You know how us poor, dim, village-idiot blokes don't notice the subtle stuff?" began Patrick.

"Ye-es." Sunny sensed a trap.

"Sometimes you laydeez don't notice the fucking obvious."

"Like what?"

"Sarah needs a job. She's going potty in that show house. She's far too bright and smart and dynamic to spend all day torturing au pairs. She's bored, and her underused mind is joining up the dots to make a picture that isn't there." He folded his arms, maddeningly certain of himself, and looked down at her, waiting for her agreement. "Well?"

"You might have a point . . ." Sunny knew instinctively that Patrick had hit Sarah's nail on the head. She leaned into his creaky leather jacket. "Clever clogs," she said, sullenly. He smelled of Guinness and peat.

"At last." Patrick stuck out his arm and a gleaming black cab purred to a halt at the kerb. "In you get."

"What are you doing?"

Sunny yanked the window down as Patrick slammed the door behind her and said, "Putney, please, mate," to the driver. It was the second time that day a man had put a door between them.

"Get in, silly."

"I'll walk. It's a lovely night. Sweet dreams."

Sunny slumped in the back seat. Out of habit, she dug out her mobile. There was a text message. That evil fairy who controls the part of the brain that relates to exes whispered that it might be from Calum.

The message was from Ellen. "MRS W SEZ STAKEOUT TONITE OR ELSE!" she read. Sunny growled, low and guttural, alarming the meaty driver who asked if she was all right.

"No," wailed Sunny. "I'm not." She sat up straight. "Turn round!" she ordered. "I need that man!"

The taxi turned with a screech and hurtled back along the dark street. Patrick's tall, distinctive shape was just crossing the road.

The taxi slowed. "Oi!" The driver stuck his head out of the window. "Your luck's in, mate!"

CHAPTER
FIVE

The tent was designed for two. "Two what?" wondered
Patrick grouchily in the blackness, contorting his long
limbs in an effort to get comfortable. "Two hamsters?"

"There's loads of room!" fibbed Sunny gaily, trying
to ease a numbed arm out from under Patrick without
disturbing him.

"It's like being in somebody's pocket." Daringly
attempting to sit up, Patrick leaned on Sunny's hair.
"Don't scream like that," he advised evenly. "You'll
alert the enemy." That tight note in his voice told Sunny
he was trying not to laugh.

The zip of the tent whizzed down and Mrs Wilde's
face appeared above them. Her balaclava ensured that
only her teeth and eyes were visible, hovering in the
darkness. Leonard was just visible behind her.
"Comfy?" she whispered.

"It's positively Ritz-like," muttered Patrick.

"Some supplies." Mrs Wilde's teeth danced in and
out of vision as she spoke. "I made paste sandwiches,
and there's a flask of tea." She handed them in. "And
here's a torch. And a whistle. Blow hard if you catch the
blighter. And you might need this." The disembodied

eyes looked slyly from side to side as she handed over a small, stubby item.

Patrick's voice was unusually stern. "I hope that gun's a toy."

Sunny's heart leaped. She'd always wanted to hold a gun. Well, to wave one around while wearing a catsuit and high heels, to be precise.

"Of course it is," reprimanded Mrs Wilde. "But Johnny Boy Psychopath's not to know that, is he?" She handed over the gun, along with a pad and a pen. "Make extensive notes. I want to know details of who creeps about in the small hours. Goodnight and good luck." The floating face disappeared, the zip flew up, and a small squeal was heard from Leonard as his wife stood on him.

When the Wildes' squelchy footsteps had grown faint, Sunny burst out, "Leonard in a balaclava! He looked so funny."

"Everybody looks funny in a balaclava," Patrick reminded her. "Mind you, there's something about Leonard in one that's extra special."

"And why did they have to walk like that?" The hundred yards from the block to the tent had taken five minutes because Mrs Wilde had insisted on zigzagging and clinging to walls, to "confuse the enemy".

"Where are we? All the zigzagging disoriented me," said Patrick.

"We're only by the pond, near the communal washing line," Sunny told him. "And apparently we're completely invisible because of all the leaves Leonard stapled to the tent."

"Hmmm," mused Patrick. "*Completely invisible* as opposed to *bloody unmissable due to being covered with stapled-on leaves*."

With some difficulty, Sunny wiggled over to the zip. "I want to see the decoy knickers." She stuck her head out. "Oh, dear God!" she squealed. "They're ginormous. The thief could be in them for all we know."

Sticking-plaster pink, the pants glowed on the washing line. Possibly visible from a satellite, they certainly wouldn't be missed by any passing snatcher.

By dint of careful manoeuvring, Patrick managed to look out, too. "Jesus," he spluttered in real fear, and hurriedly pulled up the zip. As they rearranged themselves like two hairpins, he said, "I have to admit they're not the most irresistible lingerie I've ever seen."

"Maybe knicker-maniacs go for quantity over quality. If that's the case, he'll be the envy of every pervert for miles."

Patrick scowled as his knee came into contact with some soft bit of Sunny. "They'd be roomier than this sodding tent."

"It might be better if we, you know, kind of . . ." Sunny was blushing in the dark. "Cuddled up?" She felt Patrick tense. "Don't worry, I'm not planning to revisit ancient history. I'm speaking from a sensible, Brownie-style perspective."

Relaxing, Patrick agreed with her. Snuggling together, they soon found a spooning position that worked. "Aaaah, that's better." Sunny could hear his smile. "Just like old times."

Teasingly, she warned, "Don't go getting any ideas. Picking on a poor heartbroken girl."

"You're not heartbroken, Parkinson." Patrick hesitated. "Are you?"

"Nah." That was true. It also wasn't the whole story. "Battered, maybe."

"You were always moaning about him." Patrick spoke carefully, as if practising Esperanto. "You said he was a . . . What was it? A commitment phobe?"

Mouth turned sourly down, Sunny said, "He wasn't love's young dream, that's for sure."

"So you're glad he's gone?"

"Nooo." Sunny knew she was talking to the wrong person: Patrick had never been able to discuss their own relationship, let alone other people's. Dissecting and analysing was a job for Sarah, not her very male, very circumspect ex-boyfriend. Despite this, the throbbing of the recent wound made her plough on. "I wanted it to come right, somehow. I didn't want him to give up on me so soon."

"So it's ego?"

"No." She was exasperated. "I mean, is it really too much to ask of the universe to send me a decent man who likes me a lot, is nice to me, *might* fall in love with me and, along the way, brings some romance to my life? I'm not asking for an end to world hunger or a flat stomach, just a nice-looking bloke who won't twitch like he's in the electric chair if I refer to him as my boyfriend."

"And that wasn't Calum, *ergo* good riddance."

Patrick would never get it, so it was easier to curtail the discussion. "Sure. Good riddance." His blunt logic collided with her wounded rationalisation. "Can we change the subject, please?" She needed to purge her brain of Calum, especially as she couldn't help imagining what would be going on if he was sharing this tiny tent with her. It would be sweaty, and it would be frantic, and it would be great. "Let's talk about this telly offer."

"Ssh." Patrick put his hand over Sunny's mouth.

This was direct, even for him. Sunny was insulted until she heard the noises outside and cottoned on that he was listening to them.

They heard the unmistakeable scrunch of footsteps on the gravel that skirted the pond and the washing line. Sustaining mild bruising, they managed to pull the zip down a tiny bit. Through their V-shaped peephole, a fuzzy figure could be seen out in the night. Sunny felt a jolt of adrenaline: it was Guy.

He was still, staring up at the line with a rapt expression on his face. He looked as if he was in church.

Surely, thought Sunny wildly, Guy couldn't be the man they were looking for? That was absurd. He was famous. Well, semi-famous in the Norwich area. Could a man who advertised healthy drinks spend his evenings fingering contraband underwear?

"Where's the gun?" she said in the tiniest whisper.

"I don't believe you sometimes," was the only answer she got.

Guy was reaching out towards the knickers. This was incredible. Inside the tent, both Patrick and Sunny held their breath.

A voice came from beyond the washing line. A female voice. It was short-tempered. "For Christ's sake, Guy, you'll do anything to get out of discussing my ovaries, won't you?"

"But these are amazing!" There was real wonder in the actor's fine tones. "It's like a modern-art installation. I mean, they're so fucking *pink*!"

"Yes, yes." Chloe, Guy's on/off girlfriend (or "inamorata" as he preferred to introduce her), stepped nearer. "The world is an amazing place and you are a sensitive soul: we get the message. Now, are we going to get pregnant or not?"

"Darling, who knows?" Guy flung his arms wide and leaned back theatrically, showcasing his suppleness. "We are all in the lap of the gods!"

"We're actually in Putney," said Chloe sharply. "And I'm in my forties. We've got to talk about this."

"Chitter-chatter, chitter-chatter," sang Guy amiably. "Talk away, my love."

"Sometimes, Guy . . ." started Chloe.

Sunny felt a pang of empathy as the woman choked off the end of her sentence and stomped off uncertainly on heels that were too high for gravel.

"Goodnight, sweet maid," whispered Guy after her. Then he bowed to the panties and was swallowed up by the darkness.

"Blimey." Patrick summed up the little tableau.

"So he really is like that all the time," said Sunny. "We often wondered."

They'd only just got comfortable again when more footfalls sounded. This time they synchronised their movements and unzipped the tent without injury. Very near to the tent, a dark, slender outline was evidently talking on a mobile (unless she had an imaginary friend). "Yah, yah, gorgeous," said a musical voice that Sunny recognised as belonging to the second thinnest Thin Girl. "What a fabulous idea. I've never been to Switzerland. And your aunt really doesn't mind lending us the castle?" The voice moved away.

Safely zipped up, Sunny snarled, "Castle. Get her. What's wrong with a . . . a . . ."

"Tent?" suggested Patrick. "She's very slim, isn't she?"

"Skinny," Sunny corrected him. "Bag of bones. *Too* thin. Not healthy, really. Eating disorder, probably."

"Looks good in a mini."

Grateful for the darkness, Sunny poked her tongue out.

"I can see you, you know."

After a few moments spent recreating their previous comfortable position, he asked, "What are you writing at the moment?"

"I'm waiting for inspiration to strike," she told him. "I'm under orders to beef it up. More romance. More spectacle."

"I don't understand why you don't write something simpler. Leave out all the frills and flounces and daydreams. Just write about a young woman in love."

In a small voice, Sunny said, "I don't know how that feels."

Even in the khaki gloom, Sunny saw Patrick's features droop. "What?" she snapped. "What have I said now?"

A crunch on the path outside distracted them both. They peeked out to see Ben come to a halt by the washing line.

"It's Boiled Egg," whispered Sunny, rapt, as Ben edged nearer, stepping off the gravel and moving on to the damp grass. Her hand tightened on the whistle in her pocket.

"He's shaking," Patrick murmured. "Perhaps Mrs Wilde's knickers are just too much, even for a deviant. All that nylon's sending him into a fit."

"He's laughing," Sunny corrected him. "And hiccupping. He's drunk."

Clutching a kebab to his chest, Ben stumbled off in the direction of his flat. "Aww," smiled Sunny, relinquishing the whistle. "Off to have his little takeaway on his own, bless him."

"Why all the sympathy? He's in the holy state known as bachelorhood. Don't waste your pity, Barbara Cartland."

Haughtily, Sunny asserted, "I'm sure he'd rather have a nice girlfriend waiting for him than a cold flat and a doner."

"Nice girlfriends can be underappreciative when you come home burping," Patrick said as they reverted to spoonage. "They point out your shortcomings in a loud voice. They invite you to sleep on the sofa. They call you bad names when they step on a spring roll."

"Not me," said Sunny confidently, as she snuggled down.

"A bachelor can sprawl on the sofa in his underpants, dribble chilli sauce all down himself and fall asleep in front of the footie without any distractions. Ben doesn't need your 'awwww's, believe me."

"Love improves everybody's life." Sunny was sleepy now. She had the enviable capacity to drop off anywhere.

"How would you know?" muttered Patrick.

"Romance, then."

"Hey. Don't go to sleep." Patrick prodded his partner. "I'm only the assistant, you're the vigilante."

Sunny rubbed her eyes. "Let's talk about your television career, then."

"We've covered that. I'll talk to my client about it."

"That's all I ask," said Sunny virtuously, vowing inwardly to hound Patrick into the dirt until he accepted the job.

CHAPTER
SIX

Unfamiliar with this early hour, Sunny sprawled on the sofa, bleary-eyed and reeling from the discovery of a caterpillar in her bra.

By way of contrast, Ellen was sharply drawn in her conservatively cut navy suit. Administering reviving coffee, Ellen commented that Sunny wasn't much of an advert for life under canvas. "Where's Patrick?"

"In my bed." Sunny shivered appreciatively as the coffee hit various spots, like a ball in a pinball machine. "And you can put those eyebrows back down where they belong. He's just napping before he sets off for work."

"Shame." Despite having a love life quieter than the Pope's, Ellen nursed a hope that one day Sunny and Patrick would reform. Like Duran Duran. She turned at the sound of shuffling in the hall. "I'm off to put me face on." She nipped out at her customary speed.

Disney slippers trundled in. "You woke me up," Jojo accused the wounded figure on the couch. "I needed a lie-in: I was up late watching a horror film," said Jojo severely, as if talking of vital research.

"Sorry." Sunny was too busy aching to bite back. In a weak voice, she asked the inevitable question of Jojo.

"Nope, nobody called." The tone was irritable. "And don't ask me if I'm sure: I'm not a gobshite. Nobody called. Not even," she added with emphasis as she poured boiling water on to a Pot Noodle carton of strange dust, "*Calum*. OK?"

"Got it," said Sunny sadly. She was quite glad that she had spent the night folded up like a Swiss Army knife: the pain took her mind off things.

Green eyes twinkling, Ellen was shouting her goodbyes from the hall door. "Cheerio, gang!" she sang, in her best Dick van Dyke. "Sunny, don't work too hard. Jojo, don't lie on the sofa watching TV too hard." Her hand on the latch, she added, "Jo, did you pass on Calum's message?"

The stare was long, it was hard, and it was evil, but it skidded straight over Jojo's head. "So you *are* a gobshite," said Sunny eventually.

"Only a half gobshite," corrected Jojo, with an air of erudition. "There wasn't actually a message. He just said to tell you he'd called."

"So," Sunny warmed to her theme, "perhaps any normal functioning human being might *tell me he called*?" She was on her feet now, hands on hips. Evidently, bile has a restorative effect.

"It doesn't mean he wants you back." Jojo was infuriating when she was like this. And she was always like this. "And you know now, so what's the problem?"

After a pause, Sunny answered, "Nothing. There is no problem." If the delivery was a little robotic, Jojo didn't notice, and she carried her steaming snack back to her room.

One brief mime of throttling a shorter person later, Sunny initiated the mandatory fretting that Calum's phone call demanded. Should she call him back? she wondered rhetorically. Sunny knew, of course, that ten out of ten cats would ignore it, forget it and carry on as normal. But what if, a whining little voice asked, it was urgent?

Try as she might, Sunny couldn't conjure up an urgent reason for Calum to call: "Come quick, you've left a pair of laddered tights at my place!" perhaps. The only urgent reason to call her would be to beg her to take him back. Ardent lovers tended not to say, "Just tell her I called." It certainly wasn't the kind of phone message Romeo would have left Juliet.

It was, therefore, sensible to put it to the back of her mind. Particularly as her mobile was out of steam. Unfortunately, the back of Sunny's mind was a cluttered place where sunlight rarely penetrated, and within moments she was at the other end of the hall lifting the phone receiver with the care of a spy.

In many ways 13 Chudleigh Court was the flat that time forgot. Along with a pot-bellied boiler, an overhead oven grill and a loo that flushed with a chain, it had a retro phone. Fire-engine red, with a circular dial and a clunky receiver, it also had a very short lead, so all calls had to be made in the open, where flapping Irish ears could hear every word.

By now, Jojo would be in a Pot Noodle reverie, and Patrick was asleep, if the sounds, like a horse being masturbated, coming from Sunny's room were anything to go by. Sunny gently inserted a chipped fingernail into the dial.

Behind her, the doorbell erupted and Sunny threw down the phone as if it was electrified. Foaming with guilt and irritation, she swung open the door to reveal the Wildes.

"A debriefing!" demanded Mrs Wilde, stepping over the threshold, shadowed by her bootlace of a husband.

Scanning the hall anxiously for Marmite, Sunny said apologetically, "Not much to report, I'm afraid. Ben came home with a takeaway."

"Or did he?" asked Mrs Wilde portentously, with a knowing look at Leonard. Her husband returned the look, then reverted to his customary nervous demeanour.

"Er, yes, he did," insisted Sunny.

"Could it have been a red herring?" Mrs Wilde leered.

"It looked like a kebab."

"I'll make a note of that." Mrs Wilde gestured to Leonard, who produced a small notebook from the folds of his cardigan and scribbled in it.

Sunny remembered something else: "Guy walked past. He was with his girlfriend. Ernest walked around, smoking his pipe. Oh, and Mrs Gibbs came out to . . ." The old woman had turned Sunny and Patrick's stomachs by enriching the fish pond with the contents of a battered chamber pot. "To water the flowers," she fibbed.

"So, no real progress was made?" Disapproval wobbled Mrs Wilde's jowls.

"Not really." Sunny did her best to look saddened.

"Then, how, madam, do you explain *this*?"

With a sweeping gesture, Mrs Wilde handed the floor to her husband, who cleared his throat and read gravely from his notebook. "Upon checking the decoy at 5a.m., I noted that my wife's intimate apparel had been purloined."

"Eh?" Sunny's hand flew to her mouth. She and Patrick had been so keen to escape their canvas cage at dawn they hadn't even looked up at the line to make sure the monstrous knickers were still there.

Savouring the moment, Mrs Wilde asked, "So you fell asleep?"

"Only for a minute or two." Sunny had dribbled all over Patrick's head.

Daringly, Leonard interjected. "When I checked the site at 3.14a.m., the lingerie was intact."

"So a person or persons unknown," Mrs Wilde boomed, "got their evil paws on my nether garments while you snored. I'm very disappointed in you." Mrs Wilde prided herself on being candid. "You were even less effective than I feared." And insulting. "I suspect your heart wasn't in it." And correct.

"I'm just as keen as you to catch this . . . this demon," Sunny assured her, frowning to cover the giggles that were threatening.

"Hmmm." Mrs Wilde looked unconvinced. Leonard looked, well, he looked the way he always looked. Mrs Wilde examined Sunny for a moment too long. "I can't stay here all day," she suddenly exclaimed, as if Sunny had been begging her to do just that. "Keep them peeled."

"Always." Sunny was very glad to finally close the front door behind her uninvited guests and return her attentions to the coquettish red telephone. She picked up the receiver, took a deep breath and then shouted, "Oh, what? WHAT?" at Patrick, who had emerged, bed-headed, from her room. Why did everybody around her have such perfect bad timing?

"Bloody hell. Good morning." Patrick turned and walked to the kitchen, stiff-legged like a cowboy. He muttered, "If I were you, I'd ask for my money back from that charm school."

Down clattered the phone. The call to Calum would have to wait. "Frosties or Coco Pops?" she asked Patrick, in the manner of one accusing him of war crimes.

I'll make him a count, mused Sunny to herself, as she tinkered with the notes for her next novelette. She went further, remembering Camilla's advice/threats. An *Italian* count. There was something about Italians that was innately romantic. The only Italian she'd ever actually known was Guido, who lived next door to her grandparents and kept pigeons. He was a binman, and there is nothing whimsical about pigeon shit, but she clung to her notion.

Abba boomed out at full blast from the next room. Jojo was a fan. No, that is far too mild a word: Jojo felt the same way about Abba as Aunty Jane the nun felt about God.

Sunny was not a fan. Abba were fine when she was the far side of a bottle of Chardonnay, but sober and trying to write, their simplistic Nordic way of looking at things was extremely annoying. Sunny just knew that Jojo would be winding a tatty boa around her neck as Agnetha (or was it Freda?) philosophised that breaking up is never easy.

The Swedish racket ruled out phoning Calum. In one way, Sunny was grateful: what on earth was she going to say, anyway?

Despite the background music, she'd managed to come up with the title of the new book by her usual method of gluing two OTT words together: *Fatal Crescendo*. She'd also conjured up her count. Sergio was tall, with tousled black locks (no, not hair; this guy definitely had *locks*), he was intense, passionate and in-the-market-for-a-yacht rich.

His blonde (natch) counterpart was Lucinda. Willowy and ethereal, she looked great in the silky slip dresses that her creator insisted on trying on in Jigsaw, even though Sunny had to receive counselling afterwards. Despite a trust fund that kept her in cashmere, Lucinda worked tirelessly in a children's hospital.

Vehemently backspacing, Sunny pictured Camilla's face: a day job plus sickly tots did not equal high romance. On a whim, Sunny installed Lucinda in a chichi pastel terrace in Notting Hill. One tap of the keys and Notting Hill became a sunbleached villa on the Côte d'Azur. Sunny had never been to the south of France. Making empty vows to do some research, she

scribbled down a few key words to create ambience —
"sun/palms/waiters with nice behinds" and was grateful
for the distraction of a call from Sarah: this gooey
material was not flowing.

Just back from a gruelling hour with her personal
trainer, Sarah was fizzing with endorphins. Sunny was
rarely bothered by the little devils, thanks to her
sedentary career and an inclination to reunite her bum
with the sofa at every opportunity. She let Sarah canter
on in her customary way.

"I mean," Sarah was gabbling, "what was that Karen
on? She never stopped insulting her poor boyfriend all
night. Was the lamb all right? Not overdone? I like that
beaded cardie, by the way. It brings out your eyes. And
so does Patrick, for that matter. He was on good form.
And what about that television offer? I couldn't believe
it. Alfie got pissed after you all left and spilled red wine
on the Beasts' rabbit. He thought it was very funny, but
he didn't have to wash and comb the bastard. Now."
She paused for breath, before tackling the big one.
"What about Her? Am I going mad or not?"

"The problem isn't Her." It was succinct and it was
true, but it introduced a tin-opener to a can of worms
that Sunny would have rather left on the shelf.

"What do you mean?" Panic hovered at the fringes of
Sarah's voice. (She was definitely *not* a panicker: she
had infuriated the fire warden at Waldhorn Truss Levy
the day the top floor burst into flames by insisting on
retouching her make-up. "Well," she'd explained,
"*firemen*, darling!") "Can you smell trouble? Am I
right? He's gone off me?"

Sunny had always presumed that getting married, and accumulating children, a mortgage and a Range Rover, changed women so that they no longer applied *Jackie* magazine theories to their relationships. Apparently not. "It's not as simple as that!" she insisted. "I just couldn't help noticing —"

"What? What did you notice?" Sarah quivered, like a cartoon cat who'd spotted a mouse. "Tell me!"

"Calm down, you're making me nervous." Sunny wanted the old Sarah back: the witty one who dealt with crises by opening another bottle of champagne. This fidgety neurotic could detonate at any moment. "I couldn't help noticing that you and Alfie seemed a bit estranged. Not very . . . happy."

"So you think he's not happy with me!" wailed Sarah, taking the ball and running very, very far with it.

"No, no, that's not it." Sunny sighed. "Perhaps Patrick was right. You do need a job."

"A job?" Sarah pounced on the word, turning it around in her mouth like a boiled sweet. "A job."

An idea swirled out of the mist towards Sunny, the way her plots did. "Forget the gym, your brain needs a workout." Sunny warmed to her own suggestion. "You've got a head for business that only gets used for creating dinner-party menus and removing red wine from rabbits. Get involved with Alfie's work. You know advertising inside out. Be his unpaid PA. Organise this Porqy Peeces project. Annoy him with ideas that he'll roll his eyes at and then use. Feel you've been a part of it when he wins yet another award." There was silence from the other end. Sunny chose to believe that this

84

was positive. "Get acquainted with the Porqy Peeces campaign the way you used to at Waldhorn Truss Levy. Know it inside out. Poke about in the budget. Help with the casting of the ads. Look at all the designs for the packaging." Still no response. Her confidence slightly eroded, Sunny finished with a side effect of her plan that appealed to the romantic in her: "You and Alfie will be much closer if you do this."

Finally, a little gasp sounded. "You're a genius!" The line went dead.

"Tea! Tea! Tea!" Ellen recited, in pace with her brisk steps down the hall. Like many of her fellow countrywomen, Ellen believed that tea was the answer to all life's ills.

"You look like you've been freshly dug up," said Jojo, from her nest on the sofa.

"Period," said Ellen curtly, filling the kettle and switching it on. "You must have heard of them: Earth women have them."

Laughing appreciatively, just as if the remark hadn't been aimed at her, Jojo said, "You're in a rush."

"She always is," Sunny pointed out, coming in to perch on the end of the sofa. A whole day thinking about lurve can be exhausting, and she was glad of the distraction of Ellen's homecoming.

"I'm going out," said Ellen, nose buried in the tea caddy.

Sunny's ears cocked. Going out? Ellen? This was news: even Jojo's Munchmallow halted en route to her lips.

"Oh?" Sunny smiled. "Anywhere nice?" Her romance gland kicked in. "Anyone nice?"

Ellen didn't answer. She wasn't ignoring her cousin; she simply hadn't heard her. Her brain was trying to compute a simple fact. "There's. No. Tea." Her voice was robotic. Her stare, flinty, was directed at Jojo, who was grasping a large mug of the very stuff.

"Well, no. But there's green tea in the cupboard," offered Jojo hopefully.

"Don't even . . ." Ellen seemed lost for words. "I'm having a bath. When I come out, I'll want a cup of proper tea, with milk and sugar." She left the room with stiff dignity.

"It's only a cup of fecking tea," said Jojo disdainfully.

"Oh, come on," said Sunny, unwilling to let Jojo get away with an outrage of this dimension. "She fantasises about that cuppa all the way home."

"One of us had better go out and get some more." Jojo was so expert at this kind of thing that Sunny almost said, "I'll go."

Instead she said, looking away because she was brave but not stupid, "Perhaps the person who took the last tea bag should go."

Incredibly, Jojo stood up. Marmite, taken by surprise, rolled off her lap and landed in a very awkward, most un-catlike way on a pile of wrappers on the rug. "All right, all right, don't go on," said Jojo.

"You mean you'll go? Just like that?" Sunny was amazed.

"Yeah." Jojo was acting as if she went to the shops for somebody else every day of her life. "I need some Ginger Nuts, anyway."

That explained it. Watching with interest as Jojo wrestled on some jeans, Sunny whispered, "Where do you think Ellen's going? Could it be a date?"

"It might be a work thing."

This prosaic possibility deflated Sunny. "I'll ask," she decided.

"She won't let on if it's a date." Jojo tittered. "It'd be a gas if it was a fella. Imagine. Ellen and a fella. Wonders'll never cease."

That didn't hit the right note for Sunny. Ellen and a man was nothing to titter at; it was something to celebrate. "Get some hummous while you're out," she said to change the subject.

"I might," said Jojo, which meant she wouldn't.

With Ellen locked in a steamy bathroom, and Jojo at large on Putney High Street, Sunny had an opportunity to call Calum.

Without thinking too hard (common sense is such a spoil-sport), she dialled Calum's mobile. Half hoping it would go to answerphone, she coughed and cleared her throat just as he picked up.

"Hi." There was no recognition in his voice: he had already wiped her number.

"It's your ex," said Sunny, rather too breezily.

"What? Who is this?" The backdrop of a noisy bar was making it difficult for Calum to hear her. "Phoebe?" A sound system jolted into life and Robbie Williams noisily bared his soul.

"It's Sunny." This was already off-the-scale humiliating. And who the fucking hell was fucking Phoebe? thought Sunny, using up all her swear words for that week.

"Hang on, I'll go outside." Calum did just that. His voice was gentler. "Hello, sweetheart. How are you?"

"Oh, you know. Learning to live again." Sunny clutched the phone, hoping she'd injected enough irony into that quip. "How are you?" *And how's fucking Phoebe?* she silently added, eating into next week's curse quota.

"I'm great," he said glibly, aiming a sharp little shard straight for Sunny's heart. "Just out with the boys. Having a pint." He seemed to be groping for conversation. "Having a laugh. You know." He paused. "Was there something . . .?" Calum tailed off.

Was there something? Sunny blazed with embarrassment, feeling like a cold-calling estate agent. "Well, yes, there was. You rang me. I wondered if *you* wanted something."

"I rang you?" Calum sounded baffled and Sunny's heart lurched unpleasantly, like a lumpen gymnast.

"Last night," she prompted uneasily.

"Oh, shit. Yes." Calum was straying even further from her misty-eyed template. He was about to make things a lot worse, and Sunny sensed it coming. "You know how it is. You're drunk. You've got the number of a cracking girl. You might get lucky." He sounded sheepish. "It was worth a try. Sorry, babe."

Sunny hated being called "babe". She hated even more being Calum's short-notice shag of choice.

"That's OK," she said, with, if anything, even more breeze than before. He had subtly devalued all the time they'd spent together. Like a fool, she'd invited this ugly postscript to their relationship. "As you say, it's worth a try."

"I don't suppose . . .? I mean, tonight . . .?" Calum caught the vibes whizzing his way. "No. No. Stupid idea."

"See you."

"*Ciao.*"

How, wondered Sunny, had she ever slept with somebody who said "*ciao*"?

Bathed and tea-ed, Ellen looked and smelled great. "I'll be back about eleven," she said absentmindedly, loading her bag with purse and mobile and keys.

"I like that top." Sunny was quietly envious of the way clothes always looked new on Ellen. "Must be somewhere special."

"Not really." A tiny spark of green fire, like an emerald being cut, flashed from Ellen's eyes. She pulled on a fitted jacket. "Bowling, if you must know."

"Bowling!" Sunny didn't mean to sound quite so amazed. She winched down her surprise to say, "Ah. Bowling," again, in a much quieter voice. Just as if people went bowling all the time.

"Yes." Ellen was patient. "Bowling."

"With . . .?"

She wasn't that patient. "See you later, Chief Inspector Parkinson." And she was gone.

★ ★ ★

Sunny relished being a suburban Zeus, orchestrating the lives of her fictional characters from her cosy room. Tonight, though, she was constantly doubting herself and tweaking every comma. Is this romantic enough? she kept asking. Consequently, she had more cups of coffee than usual, more little chats with Jojo than usual and spent rather longer than usual leaning back with her chair balanced on two legs. Sunny had just manoeuvred the first meeting between Sergio and Lucinda when there was a thump on her door.

"Oi!" bawled Jojo. "Have you forgotten the launderette?"

For once the interruption was welcome. "Are you sure it's my turn?" shouted Sunny suspiciously. The housework rota had been more complex to draw up than a Middle East peace accord, but that didn't stop Jojo trying to wriggle out of her obligations.

"I did it last week, and Ellen did it the week before."

This was true: Sunny remembered how she and Ellen had tricked Jojo out of the flat by throwing a packet of Frazzles into the lift. She rose and stretched. Having a legitimate, unignorable excuse to switch off her laptop was great, but did it have to be the launderette? For a second, the contrast between the life she was living and the one she was writing about sharpened unbearably. She'd left Lucinda on the bank of a crystal Provençal river, where the glamorous yet sweet-natured heiress was rinsing the muddy hem of her (designer) skirt, unaware that the richest, sexiest bloke in all fictiondom was watching her. Their eyes had just met, with the usual pyrotechnics, when Jojo disturbed the scene.

Laden with lurid checked laundry bags, Sunny trudged round to the Washeteria. A Formica womb migrainously lit by a fluorescent tube more appropriate for a stadium rock concert, the Washeteria hummed with the drone of the machines. The smell of fabric conditioner was pleasant, the chewing gum fossilised on the yellow bench less so. Shoulders slumped, Sunny filled two giant machines with knickers and bras and jeans and jumpers and socks and tights and cardigans and one Bagpuss pencil case, which was probably there by mistake. Her shoulders always slumped in the Washeteria, despite its manic candy colours.

Settling down on the bench, Sunny scanned the walls for any new handwritten signs. There was one by the slot of the dry-cleaning machine she hadn't seen before: "DON'T 20P'S!!!!" it barked warningly. Sunny's favourite sign was the one Sellotaped to the wall over the hook for lost property. Above a bedraggled sock, it asked, "AM I YOURS?"

If things didn't improve, Sunny might pop herself on that hook. Post-Calum, she wasn't anybody's. Again. Which was, she reminded herself sharply, fine. No, it was more than fine. It was liberating. She could get on with her work. And her life. All right, so it was a life that consisted of relentless typing, sleeping in tents under exaggerated underwear and being used as a knocking shop by her ex, but it was her life.

For the next hour, it was a life that centred on watching the whites go round and watching the coloureds go round. And worrying that the one little coloured she could see among the whites would turn everything pink.

Truly, thought Sunny, I am steeped in glamour. Lucinda would never set foot in a launderette; she'd finger the machines wonderingly, like a Martian. Lucinda's creator was all too familiar with her surroundings.

Bundling clothes into a dryer, she caught sight, out of the corner of her eye, of a tall male figure slowing as it passed. She sensed him dawdling, but when she looked round, the street outside was empty.

There were forty minutes to go. Lulled into a kind of daze by the dryer's tumbling, Sunny leaned her head on a washing machine and gazed out of the plate-glass frontage. She was in a little reverie, eyes glazed, mind scampering far away, when she realised that she was being watched.

That tall figure was back, but standing stock still and gazing in from the sooty street outside. Lifting her head, Sunny pulled back from her daze and met the eyes of the man who was watching her.

Pyrotechnics. The eyes she met were so beautiful, of such an edible brown and so clearly *intent* on her that they set off a brief but exhilarating series of sodium flashes inside her head.

Straightening up, she kept staring but didn't think to smile.

The man smiled. It was dazzling. It took a moment for Sunny to accept that he was real and not a flowering of her muscular imagination. And then she smiled, too.

92

She was aware that her teeth couldn't match his for whiteness and her lips couldn't match his for plumpness, but confronted with such beauty, it was the only possible reaction.

Later, when she looked back on this strange tableau, she realised that she'd expected him to move on, to swim off into the dark, leave the glow of the launderette's fluorescent strip. But instead, emboldened by her smile, he stepped into the Washeteria.

CHAPTER
SEVEN

Number thirteen wasn't the sort of establishment to sport a drinks cabinet, but there *was* a prehistoric bottle of crème de menthe and an alcopop at the back of the kitchen dresser. Jojo mixed these together and ladled them into Sunny's mouth, like Florence Nightingale tending to a cholera victim. "Better?" she asked.

"How could it possibly be better?" gargled Sunny, noxious minty fumes filling her head. "Christ, what is that?"

"It's a stiff drink. For shock."

Sunny was slumped at the kitchen table, a giant plastic laundry bag either side of her. She hadn't been able to speak since she'd got back to the flat, and evidently her glazed look had frightened her cousin.

"What happened?" probed Jojo, concerned and perhaps a touch too excited. "Were you mugged? Did somebody flash you? It wasn't the Chudleigh Cad, was it?" Her face shone with hope.

"No. No." Sunny, recovering from Jojo's cure, said wonderingly, "A man asked me out to dinner."

"Well, yeah, that is shocking, I suppose." Jojo returned to the sofa, disappointed. Marmite leaped up to her slithery nylon lap.

"But this wasn't just any man ..." Sunny was breathless just remembering him. "He was ... a god."

"Yeah, yeah." Jojo didn't seem convinced.

"No, I mean it. I've never met anybody like him. He's stunning."

"And he asked you out to dinner even though your cardie's inside out?"

"What!" Sunny jumped and glared down at the unmistakeably lumpy seams on her M&S angora. "Oh, shit."

Jojo moved on, to ask suspiciously, "You didn't mix up the whites and the coloureds, did you?"

"No," lied Sunny. She said slowly, "His name's Fabio. Isn't that a lovely name?"

"Foreign, then?" Jojo turned up the volume on Ricky Gervais.

"Italian."

"Like your new hero."

Sunny gave a funny little half-laugh of realisation. "Oh, yeah." She stretched like a cat. "Maybe he's a count, too."

"Yeah. You get a lot of them in launderettes. If you're just going to sit there, you may as well make the hot chocolate."

"OK." Shock was making Sunny very amenable. "Hello, you, you lovely cousin you," she sang happily when Ellen appeared.

"Drugs? Drink?" queried Ellen, shrugging off her jacket.

"Love," clarified Jojo sourly.

"Love? Since I went out? How?" Ellen poked Sunny the way tourists poke David Beckham in Madame Tussaud's. "What's the matter with her? What's been going on?"

"She met a handsome Italian in the Washeteria, and he asked her out to dinner. She's been like this ever since." Jojo loved to nip in and tell other people's stories before they could.

Sunny corrected her. "Actually, I met the most handsome Italian in the whole history of handsome Italians." Her dreamy gaze hardened slightly. "Hey, you're back early from your date, Ellen."

"Who said it was a date?" That stern look presumably came in handy in the courtroom.

"Nobody." Sunny crumbled. "Nobody at all. Not me, that's for sure." She couldn't resist pushing a little. "Fun, though, was it?"

"It was bowling. It was exactly as much fun as bowling is."

"Was there a crowd of you?"

With an exasperated shrug, Ellen said, "You obviously won't rest until you know, but there's nothing much *to* know. I was with Dave, who used to work in our firm until he was poached recently, and we were just catching up on work stuff. And bowling." Ellen carried her chocolate off to her room.

That qualified as fascinating, but it took approximately one gazillionth of a second for Sunny's mind to return to Fabio.

★   ★   ★

Chiswick, always pretty, looked like Shangri-La through Sunny's pink sunglasses, on Saturday.

"Blimey. Have you been hosed down with Botox?" asked Sarah, as Sunny joined her in the garden, shielding her eyes from the unseasonably late sun.

"No." Sunny had decided to save her thrilling new development until after lunch, when Sarah had finished her inevitable epic moan. She'd waited a whole three days, unwilling to share it over the phone. Oh, what the hell. "I'm going out to dinner tonight with the sexiest man ever to walk the face of Putney!" she almost screamed.

Sarah lapped up the story. "In a launderette!" She was full of admiration for Sunny's powers of allure. "This calls for champagne." Almost everything did in this house, but Sunny was glad to get her hands on something that tasted as bubbly as she felt.

Squeaks erupted from the conservatory doors. A Beast was at large.

"Shunny!" shrieked Sam Castro, launching himself like a blond missile across the lawn.

Sarah snatched up the champagne glasses. "He's filthy!" she warned.

"I don't care." Sunny was knocked off her lounger by Sam, who didn't know his own toddler strength. "Hello, gorgeous!"

"Nanny gone!" yelled Sam, smearing something gluey and suspect on Sunny's jeans.

This had been one of his first phrases. Nannys left the Castros with the same reliable frequency that soap stars check in to rehab.

"No notice, no nothing." Sarah rolled her eyes. "And before you accuse me, I was as nice as pie to her."

Cuddling Sam hard, Sunny whispered to him, "It's a pity you can't make full sentences yet, Beast. I'd ask you if Mummy called the nanny any bad words." Sunny studied Sam's curvy arms and his goofy jowls. She loved the way he smelled, and it made her want to dance when he clung to her. Sam was indisputably a good thing, with his buttery curls and his fat feet; perhaps, though, she'd feel differently if he was her responsibility day in, day out. A hiccuping scream from an upper window reminded her that there was another one where Sam came from.

Charlie, in the new nanny's arms, was shouting gibberish down at them. Sam was answering in faultless Toddlerese. "Sooogwey!" he said urgently. "Soogwey flah!"

"Suki, come and take him!" Sarah yelled. In an aside to Sunny, she theorised, "She's probably been sleeping off last night's binge-drinking. She's Australian, and she seems to know every other Australian in London."

It wasn't that Sunny didn't *like* Sarah in her role as Rich Mum — that would be sacrilege — but Sunny didn't like her as much as she liked her sensitive, interested, generous girlfriend. Looking around at this landscaped garden, studded with seats and benches and loungers, she found it hard to empathise with Sarah's dissatisfaction. Was a glorious house, a loving husband, two healthy kids and all the money she could eat really so hard to cope with?

Then Sunny remembered that the loving husband bit was in question and endeavoured to cut her friend a bit of slack.

Lunch was an organic affair of fruit, artfully laid out on a platter.

"Everything you see is certified by the Soil Association," said Sarah, piling Sunny's plate with slices of apple, kiwi, orange and banana. "No pesticides, no genetic modification, no freezing."

"But it's still bloody fruit," said Sunny, crestfallen. She could just murder a Cornish pasty. "Is dessert as puritan as this?"

"Chocolate pudding," promised Sarah. "The chocolate's organic, the eggs are free-range, the cream is from a named farm in the West Country."

Sunny, who had stopped listening after "chocolate", nodded approval. When the spoons had been licked (Sunny having revolted Sarah by leaning over to lick hers), they went back into the house to see Sarah's new office.

There was a gleam in Sarah's eye as she showed off the brand-new desk and laptop that had been installed in one of the sundry spare rooms. She waved a diamond-sprinkled hand at a row of files standing along the skirting board. "That's all Porqy Peeces stuff. I'm submerging myself in it, like you said. I've been emailing the factory, finding out all about the production process. I'm having lunch with the art director in Soho tomorrow. I've created a dozen different pie charts. I've highlighted possible faults in the current budget, probably saving Waldhorn Truss

Levy about ten grand." She looked the way women look in films when they've just had a bouncing baby after years of fertility treatment. "It's almost like being back at work."

"And Alfie?"

"He's glad to have me on the team again." Sarah put her head to one side. "I think I might be saving my marriage by doing this, you know. We've talked more over the past couple of days than we have for weeks. Obviously, it's about work, but it's early days."

"I'm glad." Sunny smiled. "Now, please, please can we obsess about Fabio some more?" She grasped Sarah's thin arm. "Like what the hell am I going to wear?"

Hair tamed, face carefully painted, nails varnished, brain back-flipping, Sunny slipped into the slithery, silvery, expensive piece of nonsense she'd fliched from Sarah's walk-in wardrobe. On the hanger it looked like a chain-mail hanky; on her body it became a stylish, stunning, sexy and demure dress. Sarah had been right. It did work miracles. Sunny didn't even mourn the extra inch she usually longed for on her boobs' behalf.

When the minicab driver rang the doorbell, she was hopping about on one leg, pulling on borrowed mules. "Hang on!" she shouted, limping down the hall. The drivers from their local firm were infamously moody and had been known to bugger off if left hanging about on the doorstep for longer than a minute. "Be with you in two ticks," she said breathlessly as she opened the door to Patrick. "You're not Cheep Cheep Cabs," she told him.

"I am not," he agreed. Patrick looked her up and down. "Blimey. Going somewhere special?"

"Yus." One of the reasons she was glad she wasn't Patrick's main squeeze any more was the fact that he considered "blimey" to be the highest praise. "Come in. In. *In!*" She flapped her hands as if he were a flock of slow-on-the-uptake sheep. She hurried lopsidedly back to her bedroom. "Follow me!" she ordered, wondering why he was there: they'd seen each other two nights ago at the Volunteer. "And can you see an earring anywhere? A dangly, diamondy one?"

"Er, no. Yes!" Patrick triumphantly retrieved a gaudy clip-on from the rug. "Are you going on a . . . like a . . . date thing?" he asked as if this was the most extraordinary notion in the world, as if he was asking the Queen if she was off to bingo. "You never mentioned it at the pub."

"It's not a date thing. It's a date. And I don't tell you *everything*." Sunny shuddered with excited nerves as she slipped on the earring and gave her hair yet another fluff with a shaking hand. "With the most handsome man I've ever seen."

"Great." Patrick said it again. "Great."

"It is. It fucking is." It suddenly seemed to register with Sunny that she had a visitor. "Tea? Water? Er, luncheon meat?" she asked speedily, and without much finesse.

"No, no, you're in a hurry. I just came round to tell you —"

"Seriously," Sunny interrupted him. "Are the earrings too much?"

"In what way?"

Sunny growled. She needed a girl, but the nearest approximation was Jojo, and she was in the bath. "Never mind. But are they?"

"Yes. No. They're too much. No, they're not. They're perfect." Patrick looked desperate.

"They'll have to do," scowled Sunny. The bell went again, and she jumped a foot in the air, landing out of one of the mules. "Get that," she told Patrick, who obeyed meekly, like a faithful servant of long standing.

Despite his protests that he didn't want one, Sunny gave Patrick a lift. In a back seat smelling of Magic Tree and hair oil, she took deep breaths and checked her little bag (another Sarah piece) for mints. "I wish I'd worn trousers," she muttered.

"Eh?" shouted the bad-tempered driver, who was a native of a country yet to feature on any map. "You what?" he snapped.

"Nothing. Sorry." Sunny always felt cowed by the belligerent Cheep Cheep drivers. She turned to Patrick. "What were you going to tell me?" she asked.

He beamed, slowly and face-splittingly. "I accepted the offer."

"The offer?" Fabio had infested Sunny's brain like a computer virus. History had begun for her three days ago in the Washeteria.

"The TV programme." Patrick's grin disappeared like the sun on a bank holiday. "You bugged the hell out of me about it," he reminded her.

102

"Oh, my God! Of course!" Sunny squealed. She wrapped her arms around Patrick. "Oh, I'm so pleased! That's brilliant!"

Slightly mollified, Patrick's smile returned, smaller and rueful. "I'm terrified now, of course," he said.

"No, no, no, you'll be fine." Sunny was airy. She was disengaged again. Were the shoes right? she wondered.

"I'll jump out here," said Patrick.

Hearing the name Fabio di Sica improved the haughty manner of the woman guarding the front desk of the tiny Chelsea restaurant. "Ah. Good evening." Her eyes widened and she smiled ingratiatingly, taking Sunny's jacket and introducing it to the first padded hanger it had ever met. "Follow me."

Past tables of palpably rich people, Sunny tailed her new best friend. Trembling and tingling, Sunny barely noticed the starched white tablecloths and the crystal glassware and the candles. She was fighting an urge to upend a tureen over her head and run out into the street. Calum had never provoked such collywobbles.

In a booth at the back of the room sat a man, his face in the shadows created by the peachy lighting. Sunny narrowed her eyes. His outline was blurry, as if he were flickering into life on a screen. As he leaned forward into the gentle pool of light, he sharpened up. She took in his faultless grooming, the clean lines of his clothes. He was like a star of a Fellini film in his perfection.

An absurd thought struck her that the man wasn't quite real. As if he was too good to be true, and he and this hushed room could disappear in a puff of candle smoke. She trembled harder, chilled by this fancy.

"Sunny." He looked up and said her name.

"Fabio." She said his.

Something else had to happen, but neither of them seemed able to move on. Looking amused, the receptionist left them to it.

Fabio stood up, unfurling six feet three inches of Italianate gorgeousness to good effect. "It's wonderful to see you," he said, and he seemed to mean it.

"Thanks." Sunny managed to sit down without knocking anything over, or farting. It was a good start, she thought.

Slowly, Fabio sat, too. His dark eyes glowed almost amber in the candlelight. Sunny felt warmed by them. "This place is lovely," she said.

"It's my favourite restaurant," he told her, in a voice designed to mutter sweet nothings. "The veal is particularly good."

Their stilted, slightly nervous conversation had a surreal edge to it, as if they both actually wanted to shout, "God, I want you!" and rip each other's tops off. At least, that's how it seemed to Sunny. Her heart was beating so fast she felt sure it must be disturbing the silver dress.

There were a thousand questions she wanted to ask him. She wanted to know how he had acquired his accent, which was smooth, sleek and educated, frilled around the edges with charming Italian cadences. She wanted to know where they sold the sort of well-cut, touchable jackets he was wearing. She wanted to know how it felt to own a nose so faultlessly drawn. But most of all she wanted to know what on earth he saw in a London-Irish girl who always carried that handy extra half-stone and wore her cardigans inside out. She simply said, "Oh, good. I love veal." Which wasn't true.

The menu was long and confusing for somebody who had a Pizza Hut loyalty card. Perhaps Fabio sensed this, because he suggested that he order for them both. "We'll dine like Italians," he promised.

By the time the tiramisu arrived, Sunny was marvelling that anybody in Italy could walk. Presumably, they didn't operate heavy machinery after sitting down to course after delicious course of briney mussels, tangy rocket, pasta jewelled with cherry tomatoes, dense bread, pearly broth . . . Even Sunny, with her healthy greed, might have wilted if it hadn't all been so irresistible.

"I like to watch you eat," purred Fabio, leaning over to steal a bite of Sunny's dessert.

Longing to blurt, "Oh, shuddup," Sunny raised her glass instead. It wasn't the first overblown thing Fabio had said, and she was beginning to suspect he meant them. It was still difficult not to bat them away with embarrassed sarcasm. "To you!" she sang happily.

Very seriously, as if he was making a statement to the police, Fabio said, "To us, Sunny. To us."

He reached across the table and took hold of her hand. It was the first time they'd actually touched, and Sunny felt a current race up her arm. She paused her breathing as he lifted her hand and pressed his warm lips to it. His eyes never left hers, so surely he could see her naked excitement?

Remembering to breathe, she smiled. It was a smile that surprised her: it was real and full of delight, not coquettish, or flirtatious, or faux sexy like the smiles she usually doled out on dates. It was a smile of pure happiness.

Fabio laughed. "We're having far too good a time," he said in his rolling, rich baritone. "Shall we spend the rest of our lives trying to live up to it?"

From Calum, that would have sounded like he was trying to fast-track her into bed. But Fabio had said it, and it sounded fresh and new-minted, as if he was simply saying what he thought.

"I am scaring you? I am going too fast?" He seemed anxious.

"You are going too fast," Sunny told him. "But I'm not a bit scared."

"Do you want to know why I asked you to dinner?" Her response seemed to have relaxed him. He put his elbows on the table and leaned towards her.

She really, really did want to know.

"It was that cardigan. A girl with such a beautiful face who was unperturbed that her cardigan was inside out, she just had to be worth knowing." He waved a hand disparagingly. "I hate vanity, you see. Beauty, of course, I adore," he added silkily, somehow managing to convey that he was thinking about her and her alone. "But girls who primp and preen, they are boring," he concluded. "And you, Sunny Parkinson, could never bore me."

Sunny liked the girl he described. Even if the bit about being beautiful made her want to gulp and go, "Gworrrrn!" *à la* Mrs Gibbs. Nobody, not even Patrick (especially Patrick), had ever told her so casually that she was beautiful

Maybe I am, she thought dreamily, reluctant to let go of his hand. I certainly feel it tonight.

The table was strewn with the delicious rubble of their meal. They'd sipped at dessert wine and had a chat with the owner. It was indisputably time to go. With a discreet movement worthy of Fagin, Fabio palmed his credit card to the waiter.

Sunny's jacket reappeared, she was showered with goodnights and then she was on the pavement beside Fabio. He had taken her hand, and her own felt small in his.

Night in West One has a different quality to night in Putney. The air pulsed. Sunny felt shaky to be alone and in the darkness with this tall stranger. But he didn't feel strange, she realised, as she looked up at his hawkish profile. He felt familiar, like a warm country she'd just arrived in but had anticipated for years.

Fabio was bending towards her, his dark hair flopping. She could smell the sweet dessert wine on his breath as he whispered, in a voice as soft as moss, "A gentleman should wait, but I'm more of a man than a gentleman. I'm going to kiss you, Sunny."

For some reason she struggled when he told her that. Perhaps the warning confused her: she was accustomed to being rugby-tackled outside pubs. However, when his lips reached hers, she became totally docile.

His lips were gentle, but not weak. Like the easy way he moved, his kiss was confident. Sunny responded ardently, and he reached his arms around her. They clung to each other, like drowning people, for a long moment.

Fabio pulled away. He raised his eyebrows. Not the sort of man you would expect to be stuck for words, he seemed uncertain what to say.

"Blimey," said Sunny. Patrick's word had been substandard earlier, but now it was all she could think of, except *marry me*.

"Yeah. Blimey." It sounded so sweet in his hybrid accent. "Well," he said, stepping back and feeling his mouth with the tips of his long fingers. "Well." He smiled, like a schoolboy caught stealing apples. "Well."

"Is that it from now on? You're only going to say 'well'?" teased Sunny, rather enjoying her new role as a *femme fatale* who could strike hunks of man silent.

"Oh, no. I've got a lot more to say to you." Suddenly, he flung out an arm and whistled. "TAXI!" He shot off to the end of the street to nab the cab he'd seen. "Wait here, we'll turn round," he shouted over his shoulder.

As the cab manoeuvred its way back to her, the door of the restaurant opened and a waiter leaned out. "The gentleman's credit card, *signorina*," he said politely.

"Oh. Thanks." Sunny took the card. Evidently, she made hunks of man forget to pick up their American Express as well. It was, she couldn't help noticing, black. She had read that only the super-rich have those. She glanced at his name, in bold relief along the middle, and her smug composure wobbled. "Hang on . . ." she murmured, suspiciously. The first name was different and — she frowned — the surname was different as well.

Sunny hesitated, but climbed into the taxi. Fabio, or whoever he was, had one arm stretched invitingly along the back of the seat.

"You forgot your card." She tossed it into his lap as the driver accelerated.

"Thank you." He tucked the small plastic rectangle into a soft wallet. "You are unhappy, Sunny." He cupped her chin in his hand. "Why are you sitting so far away?"

"What's your real name?" Sunny asked him bluntly. "The name on your card isn't the one you use for picking up girls." She swallowed, gulping away the maddening tears that were threatening. "Just because I can't put on a cardigan properly doesn't mean I'm an idiot."

"What?" He looked shocked, then impish. "Ah, I understand. I *did* tell you my real name, *cara*, just not my whole name." He dug out the card. "See?" He traced the raised letters. "Conte Agostino Cristiano Carelli." He frowned playfully at her. "You look so stern, Sunny, like a judge. Fabio is my family's pet name for me. I only answer to Fabio. As for di Sica . . ." he shrugged ". . . my complete surname is so long it just wouldn't fit on the card. And you know what 'conte' means, don't you?"

"It's your first name," she muttered stubbornly, vaguely aware that she'd made a first-date fool of herself.

"It means 'count'," he said. "It's my title, not my name." His face got nearer. "Can we be happy again now?"

I've kissed a count! thought Sunny. Then, *Correction. I'm kissing a count.*

CHAPTER
EIGHT

Despite having a nun in the family, Sunny didn't live her life according to the ways of the Bible. She regularly coveted her neighbours' ox (or their designer shoes), she sometimes forgot to honour her mother and her father (except when she needed a little something to tide her over), and she didn't rest on the Sabbath day. In fact, Sundays were, paradoxically, Sunny's most prolific time. The fact that most other people, with "normal" jobs, were resting spurred her on. She felt wild and free and bohemian, typing like a tornado while the rest of the world slept off their hangovers or washed their cars.

This post-Fabio Sunday was different. She had been invited (or summoned, to be precise) to lunch at Sarah's place.

"Well?" Sarah practically threw her into a garden chair, standing over her with hands on hips. "Is Fabio as fabulous as you thought?"

"Nah," said Sunny, with mock sadness, before bouncing on the chair like a kangaroo. "He's more fabulous!"

"Yes!" Sarah punched the air and grabbed a champagne bottle. "Get this down you and tell me all about it." She sank into a hammock and looked over expectantly. "Did you . . .?"

"We did not," said Sunny piously. "He was the perfect gentleman."

"Aw." Disappointed, Sarah folded her arms. "Tell me you at least got a snog out of him."

"Nope."

"Give me back that champagne!" ordered Sarah, sitting up in the hammock with great difficulty. "You don't deserve it."

"But we did kiss," simpered Sunny. "It was definitely *not* a snog. It was like being kissed by Cary Grant." Snapshot memories of the evening had flickered in her mind all morning. In the taxi Fabio had been passionate, but he had been respectful, even distant, when they got to her door. Sombrely, he had kissed her hand, then treated her to a burning glance that had scorched her mascara before leaving her. The thought of the kissing made her toes spasm, and once or twice she had even squealed out loud. Where, she wondered, was the worry? The anxiety? Sunny and Calum had exhausted the *Kama Sutra* on their first night together. Then, after two weeks of non-communication, she'd caved in and called him, after long nights banging her head against the wall and shouting, "Hide the phone!" at her flatmates. Even with Patrick, she hadn't felt secure about his feelings for her until . . . She realised with a start that she'd never felt totally secure about them.

This was different. Sunny knew that she was having an effect on Fabio. And she knew that he would call when he said he would. She could tell instinctively that this man was not a game-player.

"Tell me all about him." Sarah snuggled down, ready for the traditional post-date analysis. "*Everything*," she warned.

An unusual reserve descended on Sunny. She didn't want to tell Sarah *everything*. Much as she loved her friend, the burgeoning relationship with Fabio was too precious to cackle over in this sunny corner. "Where's your old man?" She bought some time with conversational sleight of hand. "I'd like to give him some good news about my life for a change."

"He should be back any minute." Sarah gulped down some champagne. "In theory. He's already late."

"He's . . . working?" Sunny was surprised. Sundays were sacred to Alfie, who claimed that nothing was important enough to keep him away from his wife, his kids and a large dead roast animal.

"He's escorting Her around some food exhibition. Checking out the competition." Sarah pursed her lips, and she looked older. "I should be with them, really, now that I'm involved, but it's the nanny's day off."

Strangely disappointed that Sarah wasn't spitting with fury about Alfie being with Her (a tantrum would have been easier to handle than this unconvincing acceptance), Sunny asked, "And are you still enjoying being involved?"

"God, yes!" Sarah lit up. "Of course I can only make suggestions. But it does help that I sleep with the boss." She pulled a face. "Or used to."

Two small Red Indians shot out of a makeshift teepee constructed of Conran chairs and 300-thread linen sheets: the Beasts had heard their dad's key in the front door, using that special sonic radar shared by mongrels and toddlers.

In the hallway, Sarah and Sunny came upon Alfie on his knees, small blond boys swarming over him like heavy-metal groupies. Faces smeared with mud, Charlie and Sam were telling their dad they were glad to see him, by shrieking, "GWOOOOO!" in his face.

It was impossible not to laugh at poor Alfie, who was giggling despairingly himself. Sunny looked across at Sarah and was surprised to find her expression blank.

"Where have you been?" asked Sarah, flatly.

"You know — ouch! — where I've been," Alfie told her from beneath their sons. "I had to take — not my groin, Charlie, not Daddy's — OW! — Liz home."

During lunch Alfie looked tired. Sarah looked wound up. Charlie put mint sauce up his nose.

Sunny concentrated on her organic pork belly.

"This summer just doesn't want to leave," said Ellen, dreamily, chasing a moustache of ice cream off her top lip with her tongue.

"Mmmmm." The riverside early evening was a gentle, washed-out pink. Slumped on a bench alongside her cousin, Sunny felt gently washed out herself, after all that dead animal and marital tension. She couldn't summon more than a murmur of agreement.

A sly look came her way from Ellen. "I hear he kissed your hand. Very *Gone With the Wind*." When she got no response, she tried, "According to my spy, he's gorgeous. And you know Jojo's not easily impressed."

That was true. Despite her own aesthetic shortcomings, Jojo considered Brad Pitt to be "quite nice" and grudgingly conceded that Johnny Depp would do in an emergency.

Even with her eyes closed against the fading sun, Sunny could tell that Ellen was staring at her expectantly. Still unwilling to tip the details of her date on the bench and trawl through them with forensic care, Sunny felt she should throw Ellen a bone. "The best thing about Fabio is that he's a romantic. A genuine romantic."

"You found one at last," smiled Ellen.

"Anyway, never mind about me. What about you and Daaaaaaaaaaave?" Sunny opened her eyes and drew the word out like a twelve-year-old teasing another twelve-year-old.

"That's different. It's platonic." Ellen's body language switched instantly from languid to spiky. She folded herself up like a deckchair.

Deciding not to chance a "Platonic, my bum", Sunny said, "It's your birthday soon."

"And?" Ellen sounded suspicious.

"We should have a party!" said Sunny toothily.

"No, we should not."

"Oh, go on. How about a fancy-dress one?" Sunny had always, always wanted to throw a fancy-dress party. Their surreality appealed to her. "It'll be a laugh." And it might show you that it's not illegal to have fun, she added silently.

"Will it make any difference if I say no?" Ellen sounded resigned.

"Of course," said Sunny, attempting sincerity. "It's your birthday."

"Oh, go on, then." There was a half-smile threatening on Ellen's lips, the memory of which would help Sunny deal with the fallout from her impetuous decision in the weeks to come. "We'd better get back. Mrs Wilde forged our signatures on the rota to scrub the rubbish chute."

Thank God for Fabio, thought Sunny, as the rest of her life was as prosaic as ever.

It was Monday, the fatally glum day that inspires schoolyard shoot-outs, but the words were tumbling on to the screen of Sunny's laptop. She was writing *Fatal Crescendo* the way firemen put out fires. Sergio and Lucinda were exchanging burning looks, undressing each other with their eyes, trembling with desire, etc., etc. as Jojo threw chicken pieces down the hall for Marmite to chase: it was her weekly exercise session.

Just as Lucinda was warding off the advances of a scheming ex-lover, Jojo pounded on the door. "Patrick's here!" she yelled at her customary volume.

"But it's not Thursday," complained Sunny, as she emerged from her room, tying her hair up hurriedly into a scrappy bun.

"I do exist on other days of the week," chided Patrick. He looked different.

"You've had your hair done," Jojo said, leading the way to the kitchen.

"Cut," Patrick corrected her. "Women get their hair done. Men get their hair cut."

"Looks done to me," insisted Jojo, who had never cottoned on to the fact that men have egos. "It's all bouffant."

Patrick shot a horrified hand up to his head and went a similar shade of puce to Jojo's shortie dressing gown.

Rescuing him, Sunny scoffed. "It's not 'bouffant'," she said decisively. "It's fuller, that's all. It's a lovely cut. Very trendy." And bloody bouffant, she thought. "What made you do it?" She knew all about his paranoid distrust of hairdressers, stemming from an accidental perm in his teens. Many times she had tried to coax him through the doors of Sizzorz or A Cut Above, but he had always resisted strenuously, like Damien at the doors of the cathedral in *The Omen*.

"Well, my producer kind of made me do it," Patrick said, his gaze averted.

"'My producer'?" echoed Sunny disbelievingly. "Listen to you; you sound like a television pro already. You'll be talking about my public next."

"You were the one who pushed me into it," Patrick reminded her.

"And I'm glad I did." She prodded him playfully. "I'm only teasing."

Patrick rubbed his arm. Sunny's playful prods had put men in sickbay before now.

"When do you start filming?"

"A week or two. There's some contractual things to tie up with the commission and a load of pre-prod to get through." Patrick eyed Sunny, presumably to see if she was going to leap on this bit of industry-speak as well. When she didn't, he said, "I'm scouting out a location now. We need a big garden that needs a lot doing to it and whose owners won't mind a television crew camped out on their property for weeks."

"You sound excited." Sunny was intrigued by this new Patrick, galvanised and keen. She was accustomed to the old model, which had untidy hair and had to be prised out of the pub.

"I am. A bit." Patrick looked sheepish. "It's more fun than I thought it would be."

Jojo couldn't hold it in any longer. "Will you move your bum, Patrick? I can't see the screen."

"Sorry." Patrick knew better than to come between Jojo and an imported American game show. "At least you're more interested today than you were the other night," he said, in a softly accusing way to Sunny.

"I was . . . very distracted," she agreed, with a moony smile. "If you'd seen the guy, you would have understood."

"So it was a good night?"

"The best," said Sunny dreamily.

"He kissed her hand," Jojo chipped in.

"Sounds like a nonce," posited Patrick.

"He's a gentleman." Sunny was too serene to rise to the bait. "A titled one. And a romantic."

"Seeing him again?"

"Of course. This one's going to be around for a long time."

"Uuuuurgh!" Jojo turned up her nose. "Can we talk about something else? I'm sick of loverboy Fabbypants already."

Patrick had a theory. "He'll be using this romance stuff to get his leg over, of course."

Repeating the phrase, Sunny assumed the air of a disgusted OAP. "'His leg over.'" She shook her head slowly. "I bet he's never even heard that expression."

"Well, whatever the titled equivalent of it is," persevered Patrick. "He'll want to get his aristocratic end away. Dip his noble wick. Get his royal oats."

"I understand." Sunny held up a hand. She heard Ellen's key in the door and shouted down the hall, "Ellen, come in here and rescue me from these vulgar sods, will you?"

"Hello, vulgar sod." Ellen kissed Patrick on his cheek. "Ooh, new hair." She stood back, surveying him and trying not to smile. "It's a bit . . ."

Sunny hissed, "Don't say 'bouffant'."

Ellen plumped for "high", which was almost as bad, judging by Patrick's expression. "What are you doing here, Paddy?" she asked him.

"On my way round to Vine House."

"How's that going?" Ellen asked, unburdening herself of various briefcases and bags.

"Really well. We've dug out the paths, and I'm ready for planting."

"Vine House? Is this something to do with the television programme?" Sunny felt vaguely riled, for some reason, that Ellen knew what Patrick was talking about.

"You never really listen, do you?" said Patrick, with a long-suffering air. "Vine House is an old people's home just up the road. I'm tarting up their garden."

"For free," added Ellen approvingly.

"Oh, the glamour of it all," said Sunny, tartly. She thought it was admirable, but couldn't say so. A three-year-old seemed to have crept into her brain and was calling the shots: this was a recurring problem. "Fabio does a lot for charity," she added. "His family are famous philanthropists."

"He told you that, did he?" Patrick sounded sceptical.

"It's true. He wouldn't lie." Sunny was starting to feel irked. Why didn't anybody understand that Fabio was different?

"I'll love you and leave you." Ellen kissed Patrick again. "I'm off out."

On the sofa, Jojo paused in her diligent ingestion of Fig Rolls to ask meaningfully, "Is it *Dave* again?"

"Might be." Ellen's pale cheeks turned pink. A nice pastel shade, not the Ribena that Sunny always produced.

"Dave?" asked Patrick, with a raised eyebrow.

"Just a quick pizza."

Ready to leap in with a "Yeah, right", Sunny paused, because Patrick's expression was telling her to. It was something about the way he was looking at her, part stern, part knowing. "Have a nice time," she said instead.

"Yeah, enjoy yourself," Patrick ordered. "You work too hard. You deserve a nice night out every now and then."

"Oh, it's nothing fancy. Just a —"

Jojo growled, "A pizza. We know. Will you feck off, it's the prize question and I'm missing it over youse lot."

The pizza didn't take long. Ellen was home and in bed by eleven, leaving Sunny and Jojo plenty of time to talk about her in the kitchen before they retired themselves.

"We have to get a look at this Dave," said Jojo, with an unusual air of determination.

"You have to be careful with Ellen." Sunny was more circumspect. "She's very private."

"But we're related. We have a right to know who she's bowling and eating pizza with."

"That's true," mused Sunny, even though it patently wasn't. She was crazy with curiosity about the colleague who was taking her cousin out on such fifties-style dates. "I can't remember the last time she was interested in a man."

"Not all of us measure our lives by men," said Jojo, acidly.

"No, some of us measure them by KFC family buckets," said Sunny, goaded into snappiness by the uncomfortable truth that Jojo had laid bare.

"A KFC family bucket never lets you down," philosophised Jojo imperturbably. "When are you seeing the eye-tie loverboy again?"

"He has a name. And I'm not sure."

"Oh." Jojo sensed trouble. "Not sure, eh? Has he rung?"

"Nope. And you can't get me going, Jojo," she warned. "He said he'd be away for a few days at his house in Cannes, and that he'd call when he got back in the country."

"That's as good an excuse as any, I suppose." Jojo evidently didn't believe in any house in Cannes. "We'll see."

"Yes, we'll see."

"I read the first few chapters of *Fatal Crescendo*," said Jojo unexpectedly.

"I'm honoured." Sunny knew that Jojo rarely read anything more taxing than the TV listings page. She hesitated before asking, "What did you think?" Her cousin could make the most vicious critic sound like a benign novice.

"All right, actually." Jojo paused. "Quite good, really." She checked herself. "For arsey romance rubbish, you know."

That was five stars coming from Jojo. "Glad you like it," smiled Sunny, feeling a rush of warmth towards her difficult, prickly relative.

"I noticed what you did with Lucinda and Sergio's first meeting," sniggered Jojo.

"How do you mean?" Sunny stopped twiddling her Top Shop diamond ring and looked puzzled.

"You know, writing it like you and Fabio."

"Don't have a clue what you mean."

"Yes, you do." Jojo was impatient. "You and Fabio met in a launderette, so you made Lucinda and Sergio meet while she was washing her skirt in a stream. It's a romantic version of what actually happened."

"Except I wrote the chapter before I went to the launderette." Sunny smiled. "Sorry to disappoint you, but it had nothing to do with Fabio and me."

"Hmm. Spooky."

"Why spooky?" Sometimes Jojo's trains of thought were too rackety to ride.

"What you wrote came true." Jojo added, "Kind of," possibly aware that she was stretching a point.

"You're losing it, Jojo. You've watched too many *X Files*."

"Maybe you're a witch. Like Nana O'Brien."

"Nana O'Brien wasn't a witch," scoffed Sunny. "Granddad used to like saying that when he was drunk."

"She could tell whenever the woman next door was pregnant."

"The woman next door was always pregnant."

"And she predicted that Granddad would hurt his leg."

"Yes, just before she pushed him down the cellar steps."

"Well, we'll see," said Jojo, for a second time.

"Goodnight," said Sunny firmly.

A minute or two later, Sunny was back in the kitchen. "Have you been in my room tonight?" she asked Jojo, suspiciously.

"Why would I go in your room?" It was a habit of Jojo's never to answer a question directly.

"My top drawer is open my knicker drawer."

Jojo's little mouth formed a perfect O.

"There's a pair missing," said Sunny miserably.

"We've been targeted!" said Jojo excitedly, rushing in to look at the drawer in question. She clutched her shortie robe about her more tightly. "When did he get in? Oh, Jayzus, what a thought. Patrick's the only visitor we've had today, so the Cad's been in this flat without us knowing."

Disquieted, Sunny pushed the drawer shut. "He could be anyone. He could have . . ." She didn't want to end that thought.

"Murdered us. Cut us into bits. Fed us to Marmite," spluttered Jojo, who watched too many American TV movies.

"Let's check all the windows and doors before we go to bed." The knicker-snatcher felt real all of a sudden. "Hope he enjoys my M&S high legs," she murmured, putting the chain on the front door for the first time since they'd moved in.

CHAPTER
NINE

Fabio rang when he said he would, bang in the middle of the week. Cocking a snook at the cynical Jojo, Sunny agreed to meet him in an hour, ignoring the pinprick of guilt she felt about leaving her laptop.

Jojo leaned on the doorjamb, watching while Sunny tried on and discarded every second-hand sundress she owned. "Has he invited you to watch while he gives alms to beggars?"

"We're having a picnic, actually. In Richmond Park."

"Oooh." Jojo's greedy eyes sparkled. "Where are you buying the food? Can I have a bite?"

"He's bringing it."

"Is he gay?"

"Oh, shut up, Jojo. He's in touch with his feminine side. He's a fully rounded man who's not afraid to be sensual or creative."

"Gay."

"He's not gay!" It was so wrong to rise to Jojo's prodding, but Sunny couldn't help herself. "He's a proper romantic who's not afraid to show his feelings and treat his girlfriend like a real woman."

"Oh, so you're his girlfriend now, are you?"

"Yes, I bloody am," shouted Sunny. Throwing a crumpled dress at Jojo, she continued, at the same volume, "How do you get me like this every time?"

Jojo was smug. "I'm good at it."

Parks bored Sunny. They were all right in theory — all that greenery and fresh air and wholesome fun — but whenever she found herself in one, she became very speedily bored.

She wasn't bored now. Fabio asked gently, "Did you enjoy the massage?"

"I don't think 'enjoy' is the right word." Sunny had drifted into a realm of sublime pleasure, only previously reached by eating Magnums while watching Clooney-era *ER*. "Could you do this all day, every day, until one of us dies, please?"

"No," said Fabio with a laugh. "We must eat." There could be a slight peremptoriness to his remarks that made Sunny smile. So much of what he did had this effect.

"Where did you get this stuff?" If Sunny's voice sounded odd, she put it down to the drool. Earthenware bowls were emerging from a proper, serious picnic hamper. There was pasta salad, mushrooms in breadcrumbs, crisp crunchy coleslaw and bread sticks.

"I made it this morning," said Fabio, easily.

"You didn't," laughed Sunny.

With a grave face, Fabio stopped unfurling a linen napkin for her. "You doubt me?" There was that second-language seriousness again.

"No, no, I . . . I just can't believe that a man could cook like this." Sunny corrected herself. "That a man would *bother* to cook like this. I'd have been impressed if you'd just remembered to go into Marks and Spencers for a pack of sausage rolls."

"What would that say about my feelings for you?" Fabio didn't echo her smile. "I did this for you." He pointed at her and followed that up with a slow kiss to her lips. "I learned how to cook by watching Maria. She's been with my family since my mother was a child. She is a genius."

Maria . . . The more Sunny learned about Fabio's life, the more she felt intimidated by it. Their first date had just been dinner with a glamorous stranger, a diversion from the everyday, but now that they seemed destined to become closer, the dripfeed of detail about the cook, the chauffeur, the five (yes, five) homes around the world made her feel insecure. "Fabio," she said, grabbing his strong, lean hand and interrupting the dressing of the salad, "what on earth do you see in me? We're from different worlds."

"Shush!" Fabio kissed her fingertips. "We're from the same world: our world. And what do I see in you? I see the face I've been searching for all my life. You believe me, yes? It's important." He seemed uncharacteristically nervous.

"I think I do." And she thought she did. This was all moving at a hundred miles an hour, and although it made her dizzy, she was growing used to the pace.

"Tell me more about you," Fabio insisted, as he grated Parmesan over her griddled aubergine. "Tell me five things about your family."

"Oooh, Gawd." Sunny's mind raced. "Let's see. My mother's aim in life is to cover anything that can't fight back with doilies. My dad owns a hardware shop and won't enter into any discussion that doesn't involve drill bits. I have one brother, who had to give up accountancy because it was too exciting. Er . . . one of my aunts, Jojo and Ellen's mum, made a citizen's arrest once, on a dwarf, in Dublin. He was getting away with a three-pack of tights." She paused, wishing desperately she hadn't mentioned the citizen's arrest. "How many is that?"

"*Quattro.*"

Sunny's downstairs shivered. She loved it when Fabio lapsed into Italian. "Let me see, one more." Her family just weren't interesting enough. She'd always considered them to be quite lively, but next to Fabio's jet-setting relations, with their charitable trusts and their châteaux and their yachts, her lot were dreary. "Hmm . . ." Inspiration struck. "My grandmother was a witch!" she declared.

Impressed, Fabio asked, "What powers did she have?"

"Well . . ." This wasn't so easy to answer. Nana O'Brien's "powers", as Sunny kept reminding Jojo, hadn't been exactly jaw-dropping. "She put a curse on the woman next door, because the woman next door put it around that Nana couldn't knit. And . . ." she paused for dramatic effect ". . . the woman next door died."

"No!" gasped Fabio, who was a great audience. Credulous *and* good-looking.

"Yes," said Sunny, adding, for the sake of honesty, "a mere twenty-two years later."

"So perhaps not such a dangerous witch?" Fabio's generous mouth smiled, his lips full and irresistible. "You have more power than your grandmama. You have bewitched me."

Sunny rolled her eyes and threw in an "Oh, for Gawd's sake" for good measure. When she'd finished the rolling, she saw that Fabio's smile had disappeared. "Oh, you're serious!" she giggled. "I assumed it was a line." It was just the sort of thing that Patrick used to say, before putting his fingers down his throat.

"Yes, I am serious." There was a slight air of huffiness to the way Fabio was cutting up the Cambozola. "I don't use lines. I have more respect."

"I'm not used to . . . romance, Fabio. You'll have to forgive me. I've got to learn how to react when you say lovely things to me."

"Yes, *cara*. For a start, don't pull a face like a frog," advised Fabio.

"I'll try not to," answered Sunny, in a humbled voice.

When they were finishing off their profiteroles, Sunny's mobile phone buzzed. "Sarah. God, where are you?" From the background noise it sounded as if her friend was fleeing a civil war.

"I'm in the Range Rover, on Chiswick High Street. And my children are having a screaming competition."

Sarah seemed to be stretched pretty thin. "Bloody Suki bloody walked out, bloody girl. Over nothing. A teensy row."

"Nothing?"

"I asked — *asked* — if she just might have slightly stolen my cashmere V-neck, and she stomped out, as if I'd insulted her, or something. Please say we can come and see you? If I don't talk to a grown-up, I'll lose it and may harm myself with the Play-Doh."

Biting her lip, Sunny glanced down at Fabio, who had settled his leonine head in her lap. His eyes were locked on hers. "Well, I'm sort of tied up." She heard the gasp of despair at the other end. "Oh, come and join us. It'll be fun."

And it was.

As demented two-year-olds go, Charlie and Sam were a hoot. They found everything, from grass to handbags, hilarious, and their unsophisticated delight was infectious. When she looked through their eyes, Sunny could see why wiggling her varnished toenails was much funnier than anything Billy Connolly could dream up; she appreciated that Fabio pretending to trip over the picnic rug was worthy of a BAFTA.

As they crawled over her, she was impressed by their unerring ability to kick, press and pinch her soft bits for maximum pain. Innocently, Sam yanked down her T-shirt in his quest to find the last garlic mushroom, exposing her mint-green lace bra.

"Ah." Sarah raised an eloquent eyebrow. "Event underwear!" She leered at Fabio's receding back as he

130

went off in search of ice cream. "Can't say I blame you. I'd lock him in a cell with just a mattress and a cannister of spray cream if he was mine."

Trying not to blush, Sunny awarded the mushroom to Sam. "It's not that kind of relationship."

"You mean you still haven't . . .?" Sarah was as shocked as a Quaker at Spearmint Rhino. "Are you insane?"

"No, I'm waiting."

"For what?" demanded Sarah. "World peace?"

"The right moment."

"Listen, girl, the right moment to have sex is the moment you get your mitts on a piece of machinery like *that*." Sarah jerked a thumb at Fabio. "You jumped into bed with Calum quickly enough. The way I heard it, he'd barely got to the question mark of 'Can I come in for coffee?' before you had his combats off."

"And look how that ended," argued Sunny. "In a funny way, I think I slept with Calum precisely because I *didn't* care about him. How could I fall for a man who lists boob-job-spotting as a hobby? I was lonely, I needed male attention. Sex was the best way to hang on to him." She smiled sadly and hugged her knees. "Didn't work for long, did it?"

"Well, it's none of my business." Sarah was patently lying: she considered everything about Sunny to be her business. "But I'd be all over him like a cheap suit."

The September afternoon passed in a warm haze of ice cream, giggling and a protracted game of Kick the Silly Grown-ups. Tired out, Sunny flopped, encircled by Fabio's fudge-coloured arms, as they leaned against the solid base of an enormous oak. "Be kind to me," she purred. "I'm suffering from post-traumatic stress disorder. Having your knickers snatched takes it out of a girl."

"If I find this man . . ." Fabio's eyes narrowed, thrillingly.

"Yes?" prompted Sunny, eagerly.

"It is not for the ears of a lady."

This disappointed the lady.

There were leaves in Sarah's hair and unguessable smudges on her white trousers. Her careful make-up had long since sweated off, and there were Red Indian stripes of mud along her cheeks, as she rolled about with her sons.

"How your friend loves her babies," murmured Fabio approvingly. All afternoon he had lived up to the family-worshipping Italian stereotype, hugging and kissing the boys extravagantly, despite their indignant "Yuk!"s.

Trudging back to the car park, a snoring twin apiece, Sunny asked Sarah, "How come you're enjoying the Beasts so much today?"

Sharply, Sarah asked, "I don't normally enjoy them?"

"Last week you were Googling for a toddler boarding school."

"That was a joke," claimed Sarah unconvincingly. "But you're right: I am having a good time. Maybe it's because I have a meeting tomorrow with the Porqy Peeces board. If all I had to look forward to was days and weeks and months of Beast-related activity, I'd be all wound up. I'm achieving some kind of balance at

132

last. If I have a work project, I appreciate the time I spend with the kids. And vice versa." She gave Sunny a hug, made awkward by their twinny burdens. "All thanks to you, Claire Rayner."

A rain cloud over their heads chose that moment to fulfil its potential. The downpour was worthy of a disaster movie. Sarah broke into a sprint. "Holy shit!" she shrieked. Motherhood had not tempered her language.

Running ahead with the hamper, Fabio shouted at them to shelter with the children. "I'll come back with an umbrella," he shouted.

Under the protective canopy of an ancient tree, Sarah quivered. "That accent!" She pouted lasciviously. "I'd do whatever he told me."

"Know what you mean," said Sunny, trying to iron out the tremble in her own voice. "I argued with Patrick about every tiny thing, but there's something about Fabio . . ."

"There certainly is. And it's not just his arse in those shorts." Sarah had the air of an antiques expert valuing a commode.

"This reminds me of the time Patrick and I got stuck in a storm." Sunny shifted Sam in her arms. "We sheltered under a tree and had this huge debate about who should go and get the car. He said that suffragettes had died for the sake of equality, so why couldn't I get my hair wet."

"And your clever retort?"

"I think I called him 'blow-off breath'."

"Touché."

"Well, he'd been eating prawn-cocktail crisps. We argued, and argued, until the rain stopped, and we were late for the film, and we ended up eating Mexican, and I hate Mexican. All those fiddly fajitas and refried doodahs."

"Knowing you, I bet you wouldn't speak to him."

"No. Not until the refried beans arrived, and some went up his nose, and he had to honk them out on to a napkin. I reckoned he'd been punished enough."

"Poor old Patrick," said Sarah warmly.

"Poor old Patrick nothing. He'll be famous any second now."

"I mean . . ." Sarah took an unlikely interest in a small blade of grass in her hand. "I mean, he's never really got over you." She hesitated, before saying, "Over *it*."

"Eh?" Sunny squinted in confusion. "Are we talking about the same Patrick? Tall, big feet, mud under his nails? He was over me by the next episode of *The Bill*."

"Hasn't had a girlfriend since," said Sarah meaningfully.

"He says I put him off for life."

Sarah smoothed a Beast's hair. "You can be ever so thick," she said fondly.

Something unsaid hovered between them in the damp afternoon. The two women looked in opposing directions, seemingly lost in thought. Even the Beasts were quietened by this change in atmosphere.

Eventually, Sunny said, "You know why I had to leave him." She paused. "You of all people, Sarah."

Nodding gravely, Sarah agreed. She seemed stuck for words, rare for such an opinionated individual. "Yeah, sweetie, I do know."

"He could have fought for me," Sunny said simply, expressing an old, tired thought that she was weary of.

"I know that that's the way you see it." Sarah was being atypically gentle.

"Isn't that the way it was?" A note of irritation sharpened Sunny's question.

"Perhaps." Sarah shrugged. "It was hell, and nobody behaves all that well in hell."

"Except you." Sunny half smiled. "What on earth would I have done without —"

"Oh, shush!" laughed Sarah. "Here comes Fabio. Let's slap some smiles back on for him. No more soppiness." But she leaned over to award Sunny a quick kiss on the cheek all the same.

Relieved to see her man striding, Heathcliff-like, across the scrubby grass, Sunny noticed that he'd torn off his sopping shirt. Slung over his shoulder, its damp linen sleeve reached down to stroke his washboard midriff; she envied it, keenly. "Now, *that* is how a real man behaves in a rainstorm," she murmured, approvingly.

CHAPTER
TEN

"You're wearing new jeans." Sunny's voice was accusing as she looked Patrick up and down. She had sauntered across the lawn to ask him what he was doing at Chudleigh Court surrounded by a motley band of her neighbours, but she'd forgotten her question in shock.

"Yup. It was about time," he said.

"New, groovy jeans." Sunny actually sounded angry now, as if she'd caught him stealing.

"Are they?" Patrick looked down, bemused. "They're very comfortable."

Sunny should have been pleased. The rising irritation was totally illogical: she'd been trying to get him into some new jeans for years. "What brought this on?" she said sharply, itching to add, "After you've ignored me all this time?"

"Serena."

"And who's Serena when she's at home?" Her tone of voice was openly bitter now.

"Er, she's me." The woman standing just behind Patrick swam into Sunny's view.

Sunny hadn't noticed the tall redhead because her world had shrunk to Patrick's legs. Now she took in the boyish, rangy figure and the profuse Titian curls and the simple summer dress. Realising she was staring, she took the advice of various children's TV programmes and turned her frown upside down. This didn't, as promised, produce a smile: it produced a rather alarming gurn.

"I'm his producer," Serena elaborated. "I can get pretty bossy about stuff like jeans." She laughed, evidently deciding to politely ignore the strange look on Sunny's face. Serena turned to Patrick, took him familiarly by the arm and smiled. "She's exactly what I expected." Turning back to Sunny, she said, "I've heard a lot about you."

Exactly what she expected? To somebody with Sunny's shaky self-image, this was torturous stuff. Patrick's face held no clues. He was beaming like a fool. "We've got some news," he began.

Mrs Wilde stomped into their midst. "Chudleigh Court is going to be on the television!" she told Sunny. "These good people are giving us a beautiful new garden."

Behind her, Ernest stepped out from the small knot of residents. "Some of us like the old gardens," he said, indignantly. "I'm very partial to a rose. How do we know this fellow won't land us with gravel, and sculptures, and neon lights?"

Confidently, Sunny said, "Oh, he won't, Ernest. He loathes all that stuff." She felt a touch on her arm, as if she'd been knocked by a spanner wrapped in velvet.

It was Serena, who said, just as imperiously as Mrs Wilde if not as loudly, "Any questions about the gardens can be directed to *me*." She smiled, too sweetly to be wholesome. "OK?"

"OK."

Serena, Sunny decided, was not her type.

It was like a bad dream, the sort that sometimes plagued Sunny after late-night cheese consumption. Under harsh fluorescent lighting strode Jojo, hands on hips. "I feel very comfortable," she was saying happily. She was dressed as Hitler.

Sunny was wide awake: this was no dream, it was Saturday morning and they were in a fancy-dress hire shop. Regret that she had ever suggested the damn party swelled through her again. It had been difficult enough putting together a guest list when the birthday girl was as solitary a creature as Ellen without Jojo acting up. Patiently, she reminded her rotund cousin, "The idea is to come as your hero."

"Exactly. This'll shake things up a bit."

"If by 'shake things up a bit' you mean 'offend and upset perfectly nice people', I suppose you're right."

"Ah, sure, who'd be offended?" Jojo twirled happily in her Nazi togs.

"Me, for a start." Struggling to remain calm, Sunny hissed, "We're not discussing this. You can't come as Hitler."

"All right," conceded Jojo, so easily that Sunny suspected the hideous outfit was purely to annoy. "Shame. It flattered me figure."

"Now *that* would be beyond even the evil genius of Adolf," whispered Sunny to Ellen as their flatmate goose-stepped back to the changing cubicle. Sunny registered what Ellen was wearing and took a step back in admiration. "That's the one," she said decisively. "You look wonderful."

The Scarlett O'Hara crinoline made a feminine swoosh as Ellen moved. Her corseted waist was as narrow as Jojo's conscience.

"I can't . . ." Ellen gasped and pointed to her mouth.

"You can't what?" asked Sunny.

"Breathe," guessed the shop assistant, who had earlier alienated Sunny by suggesting she try their new Darth Vader. She expertly loosened the lacing at the back of the elaborate dress.

"Thank you," gasped Ellen, and leaned on the counter for support. Biting her lip, she surveyed the velvet gown. "It's a bit showy."

"You're the sexiest woman in the history of the Deep South. Of course it's showy." Sometimes Sunny wished she could inject some fizz into her cousin. "And trust me, Dave'll melt."

"Dave's fine at his current temperature, thank you very much," said Ellen tartly, checking her back view in a mirror.

Not an ounce of fizz, thought Sunny sadly. "We'll take it," she told the assistant.

Sashaying out of the changing room, Jojo invited them all to "get a load of this". She was a mini Elizabeth I, a cut-price monarch. "Now, this is really *me*," she asserted, as if the progression from velour tracksuits to bejewelled coronation gowns was a natural one. "Mind you," she said, appraising Ellen's get-up. "Would that look good on me?"

"No!" said Sunny and Ellen together.

The assistant added, "We don't have one in your size," redeeming herself with Sunny, who she turned to next. "And what about you, madam?"

"My boyfriend is organising my costume." Try as she might to sound casual, Sunny was smashing the smug-o-meter. "We'll match. A famous romantic couple is all he'll tell me."

Unable to resist swishing about in her crinoline, Ellen pondered, "Romeo and Juliet?"

"Richard and Judy?" suggested Jojo.

Ellen had another theory. "Adam and Eve!"

"Jack and Vera Duckworth," said her sister.

Frowning prettily at Jojo, Ellen came up with, "Napoleon and Josephine."

"It's got to be," said Jojo sagely, "Myra Hindley and Ian Brady."

Their foray into history concluded, the cousins stood like a gaggle of geese on the bustling W. 1. Street. Pointedly, Ellen told the others, "You don't have to wait with me, you know."

"We want to," said Sunny, lugging Jojo's Elizabethan gown on to her shoulder. "You might get mugged."

"It's only lunchtime. This is a busy street." Ellen knew why they were hanging about.

Jojo didn't even bother to cover up her motive. "I'm going nowhere until this Dave turns up to meet you,"

140

she said, resolutely. "I have to see what kind of fella likes bowling."

Rigidly, Ellen hissed, "Here he comes."

Dodging the traffic, and already looking uncomfortable, Dave was smallish and niceish. He was wearing a suit, despite the warmth of the day. Sunny thought he had a cute face.

"Sunny, Jojo, this is Dave." There was a very specific look on Ellen's face, and it communicated a very specific order: don't say anything funny or I'll kill you somehow with my handbag.

"Hello, Dave!" Sunny took his hand and wrung it as if she was trying to juice it. "Hello, hello, hello!" She didn't dare a "We've heard so much about you" or even a "We meet at last", as neither of these would be approved of by Ellen, who seemed to have been taking a masterclass in being uptight. "Going out for lunch, then?" she asked pointlessly.

"Yes. Lunch. That's right." Dave was pale, and he had kind eyes. His tie was knotted perfectly, but one side of his shirt collar was turned up.

Taut as a hospital sheet, Ellen said, "We should get going."

"Yeah," drawled Jojo. "Off youse pop. Don't do anything we wouldn't do." As the two marched off, to the tune of some invisible military band, Jojo summed Dave up with her usual élan: "Jayzus, she's got herself a right dork there."

All right, thought Sunny, so 10a.m. isn't early for most people on a Monday, but most people haven't been up half the night engineering two star-crossed lovers around the south of France. She'd finally dropped into bed after stranding Lucinda and Sergio on a small, not too scary island, where Sergio had managed, with much tossing of his locks and flashing of his pecs, to catch and cook a fish for them both. A nice lie-in was just what any sensible doctor would order, so the mayhem outside her window was particularly unwelcome. It sounds as if blokes in tractors are driving over the flowerbeds, thought Sunny grouchily, yanking back the curtains to see blokes in tractors driving over the flowerbeds.

Her first impulse was to call the police, but then she remembered that filming on Patrick's gardening programme was due to start today. The sedate Chudleigh Court gardens were already unrecognisable. The hillocky lawn had sprouted a number of large tents, not the Boy Scout variety that she and Patrick had shared, but marquee-style affairs. One seemed to be set up as the production office: desks, filing cabinets and computers were being carried in by meaty men. Girls with clipboards and headsets milled purposefully about, overseeing the placement of ladders and cameras and huge lights. More meaty men were pulling up the turf. A van, which might have sprung straight from Jojo's imagination, was serving fried breakfasts. The whole place throbbed with activity, as if a Wild West frontier town had sprung up in the night.

It was too exciting to resist. Sunny threw on her jeans and a T-shirt that had been washbag bound, and tore down the stairs. She found Patrick sitting at a small plastic table. All around him, crew munched their way through Desperate Dan piles of sausages and eggs.

"Didn't fancy it." Patrick looked drawn. His plate was untouched.

Sunny asked sympathetically, "Nervous?"

"It's all your fault," he accused.

"Remember that when you're picking up your awards."

"I don't think they have one for Best Imbecile in a Gardening Programme." Patrick ran his hands over his eyes. "And before you ask, yes, you can have my breakfast."

As Sunny chomped contentedly on a squelchy slice of fried bread, the smell of lard was overpowered by a waft of perfume.

Serena was wearing jeans so tight that for a moment Sunny thought she'd painted her legs blue. "You're needed in make-up in five," Serena told Patrick.

Sunny lifted an eyebrow at Serena's manner. Very headmistressy, she thought, wondering how the bolshy Patrick would take it.

"I'll be there."

Like a lamb, apparently. Perhaps, pondered Sunny, he had a secret thing for headmistresses. Size-eight ones, whose hair actually tumbled.

It tumbled in Sunny's direction, as Serena said, with a dazzling smile that belied her words, "Meals are for production personnel only." She put her head daintily to one side. "And would you mind vamoosing, Sunny? We've a lot to get through."

"I live here." Sunny was chewing hard.

"I know. But I need you to stay indoors while the cameras are turning." Serena was indeed serene. She calmly went on, "If you have any problems, take it up with Mrs Wilde. She agreed to these conditions on your behalf."

Stubborness was Sunny's middle name. (Well, Philomena was her middle name, but it could have been Stubborness.) "I like to sunbathe out here," she insisted. "Naked."

"We don't want an eighteen certificate," said Serena with the merest lift of her lips to signify a joke.

Unsure whether Serena meant for nudity or horror, Sunny swallowed the contraband fried bread and vamoosed.

Monday ended more glamorously than it had begun. The Sunny who was meandering through the West End neon nighttime hand in hand with Fabio didn't look like the sort of girl who favoured fried bread. Her pearly shoulders were bare; the spot where Fabio had kissed them glowed like a hot coal.

"Happy?" he asked.

"*Contentissimo*," replied Sunny, who had acquired an English-Italian dictionary.

Delighted, Fabio hugged her, enthusiastically at first, before his hands started to gently explore her back and pull them closer together. "If you are learning some words of my language, perhaps you care for me a little?"

With what voice she had available when Fabio came this close, Sunny breathed, "Perhaps I do."

144

I do, she told herself in the moment before they kissed and all the lights of the West End exploded in her head. I really do.

Linked, they carried on with their aimless walk, until Fabio stopped and said suddenly, "Let's have some fish and chips!"

"You? A bag of chips?"

"Like I said, we do not come from different worlds." Fabio flung his arms out and exclaimed, "I LOVE FISH AND CHIPS!"

Later, popping the last chip into her mouth, Sunny had to admit that the Savoy did a great battered cod. And the waiter was quite right: the chilled Chenin Blanc complemented it nicely.

It would take Jojo to point out, later on, that Fabio had echoed his fictional couterpart by presenting Sunny with a fish. "Goodnight, witch," she said.

CHAPTER
ELEVEN

It was the usual pub. It was the usual table. Ozzie was lying in his usual spot, right up against the quiz machine. Everything was the same, except for Patrick's jeans and a jaunty height to the back of his thick brown hair, but Sunny felt different. She couldn't be bothered to tease Patrick about the trousers: could she be coming down with a cold? she wondered.

"Earth to Parkinson." Patrick waved his empty glass, a shifting foam map drifting down its sides. "Your round, your ladyship."

"Oh. Sorry. I was miles away." Sunny rose.

"In Cannes, probably. Or were you on a yacht?" Patrick's hazel eyes were amused.

"Actually, I was under a tree in the rain." *And drawing unfavourable comparisons with you,* thought Sunny, as she approached the bar.

For the landlord of the Volunteer, it was quite a cheerful opener. "Of course, the wife's shingles is back," he told Sunny, as he sloooowly poured a Guinness. "And that new barmaid is obsessive-compulsive." The landlord leaned over the bar to say confidentially, "She's rearranging my nuts as I speak."

"What," asked Sunny as she got back to their table, "are — or is — shingles? I've never really known."

"No idea," laughed Patrick. "And I hope to live and die without ever finding out. Horrible word, isn't it?" He shuddered. "Shingles."

Sunny said it menacingly, "Sh-iiiiing-les." Then she tried wacky: "Shingles! Wahey!"

Plumping for drama, Patrick lowered his voice. "Shingles."

Breathlessly, Sunny gave him the sexy version. "*Shingles*," she moaned.

Giggling unmanfully, Patrick decreed, "I don't know why but it's a funny word." He looked hard at Sunny, then leaned down to say to Ozzie, "Uh oh. We're losing her again, Ozzie. We must be spectacularly dull tonight."

"No, no. Well, Ozzie isn't." Sunny tickled the snoring mongrel's snout with her toe. "I'm just, you know, thinking."

"He's really getting to you." It sounded as if this thought had just struck Patrick. "It's not serious, is it, Sun?"

Twiddling her glass of rancid Chardonnay, Sunny said, "It is, actually."

"Blimey." Patrick looked surprised. "But he's so . . ."

"Handsome. Intelligent. Sexy." The list could have gone on and on, but Patrick butted in.

"*Unlikely* was the word I was thinking of. He's from another world."

Nimbly forgetting that she'd used exactly the same phrase, Sunny tutted. "And you a socialist. We're all

147

equal. You can't discriminate against him just because he's got a title and squillions of pounds."

"From your description the guy is simply too handsome, too romantic and too damn perfect to be true." Patrick treated Sunny to a searching look over the rim of his pint. "Or have you made him up?"

"God, shut up! I mean, shut up!" spluttered Sunny. She could tell that her overreaction had surprised Patrick: he was unaware of Jojo's occult theories. "How's filming going?"

"Ah. The Parkinson subject switcheroo again," said Patrick, indulgently. "It's going fine. It's a steep learning curve. Weird, but fun. Did I tell you it's going to be called *The Gardener's Guide*?"

"Bit dull," complained Sunny.

"It does what it says on the tin," said Patrick, stolidly. "If I thought this programme would be just some flashy, trashy bundle of fast edits to a funky soundtrack, I wouldn't do it. I want to show the average bloke — and blokesse — how much fun and satisfaction they can get out of even the tiniest scrap of garden."

Peering at him through an imaginary magnifying glass, Sunny croaked in a very unconvincing old man's voice, "I'd heard rumours that there were a few like you left in the wild. You're a sincere enthusiast, aren't you, my lad?"

"Mock all you like." Patrick drained his pint. "It's not going to have some tacky, punning title. Luckily, Serena shares my vision."

A crisp halfway to her mouth, Sunny froze.

"What now?" laughed Patrick.

148

"Now I *know* you've changed. You're turning into a . . . well, tosser is the technical term." Sunny carefully held the crisp between her thumb and forefinger, leaned towards Patrick and enunciated carefully, "'Serena shares my vision.'" She rolled her eyes. "The old Patrick would *never* have had a vision. She threw the crisp in the air, caught it in her mouth and crunched it, saying, "Vision", scornfully through the crumbs.

Arms folded, Patrick smiled sheepishly. "I see what you mean. I apologise for offending you by having a vision."

"Will there be daisies in the new garden?" Sunny smiled as she recalled the corner of the lawn that always sprouted a host of the happy little sods. "I love daisies."

"It's a real, proper garden. Of course there'll be daisies." Patrick looked almost shocked that she should doubt him.

"Oh! Oh! Oh!" Sunny dusted Patrick with soggy crisp as she remembered a vital piece of news. "I am the latest victim of the Chudleigh Cad," she said solemnly. When there was no reaction she said, deflated, "I made the mistake of thinking you might be interested. I'm very traumatised, you know."

"Yeah. You look it." Patrick watched as Sunny crammed five crisps into her mouth at once.

"I am," insisted Sunny, trying to chew and look sad at the same time. "I don't like to think of my poor little knickers being pawed by some freak."

"You're starting to sound like Mrs Wilde. Maybe your freak is some lonely man who needs help, not persecution."

"You are nought per cent fun, Patrick Smith," moaned Sunny. "I thought you'd laugh." She fell silent. She knew Patrick quite liked silences, but she considered them to be evil, so she ended it by saying, "I was nearly knocked over by one of the production staff today. Well," she mused, "I *think* he was one of your lot: he looked tellyish."

"How is that achieved?" Patrick was intrigued.

"He was on a moped and his hair came to a point on top. And he had a Thai word tattooed on his arm. Probably translates as 'trendy wanker'."

"Or 'shingles'."

They both laughed, and Sunny put another five crisps in her mouth.

The fresh-faced girl sitting straight-backed on Sarah's mile-long sofa had answered all Sunny's questions fully and clearly. Sunny had limited experience of interviewing nannies (and was uncertain how Sarah had hypnotised her into helping out), but this candidate seemed ideal. Gentle, decent, with a spotless CV, the girl had shown a real interest in Charlie and Sam.

While the nanny enthused, with shining eyes, about her love of flowerpressing, Sarah passed Sunny a scrawled note. "OBVIOUS SLAG."

Next to dent the cushions was a German teenager who spoke three languages and managed to teach Charlie to identify colours while Sarah took a cold call from a double-glazing firm. "SHOPLIFTER PROBABLY," scribbled Sarah.

After Sarah had summed up the last girl of the day, a beautiful Pole with a diploma in childcare who had once worked for Tony Blair, with "EYES TOO CLOSE TOGETHER (PLUS SLAG)", Sunny suggested she was being a tad fussy. "They all seemed really nice."

"You're such a softie," said Sarah, with an air of hard-won wisdom. "Give any of these angels two weeks and you'll see belligerent harpies who won't grill a fishfinger without demanding danger money."

Wandering out to the conservatory, Sunny, bored with listening to nanny-related whinges, asked, "How's Porqy Peeces going?" She loved the conservatory. It was tranquil and understated, in direct contrast to the shabby-chic bombsite of her own small room at Chudleigh Court. "All set to take the world of luncheon meat by storm?"

"Quinoa shake?" Sarah offered Sunny a glass of pale sludge.

Sunny declined. "I would rather eat my own feet."

Settling herself on the arm of a Perspex cube chair, Sarah said, "Fabio OK?"

"Ohhhhh dear." Sunny didn't like this at all. "You're avoiding the subject *and* you didn't subject me to an hour-long lecture for refusing healthy, lesbian, social-worker food." Sunny narrowed her eyes. "What's wrong?"

"I've discovered something." Sarah looked troubled. "Porqy Peeces isn't quite the wholesome little snack it claims to be."

To somebody who would happily exist on kebabs from a roadside van in Armenia, this wasn't such big news. "Is that the end of the world?" queried Sunny.

"There's an ingredient in it that's under investigation in the States for various side effects. It's called Bilnius Red F, and Porqy Peeces don't own up to it on the packaging. It just says 'colourings'." Sarah drained her shake. "Part of me wishes I wasn't quite so bloody thorough with my research."

"You've told Alfie?" Sunny was rattled by Sarah's grave demeanour. The conversation was starting to feel portentous.

"He thinks it's something we can deal with internally."

Ah. Sunny could guess what was coming. "But you don't?"

"No," said Sarah, passionately. "I believe people should know exactly what they're eating. What they're giving their kids to eat." She sighed and it echoed in the elegant room, which now seemed cold, despite the sun.

"Give Alfie a chance to sort this out," suggested Sunny. They had strayed on to marshy ground. Sunny had no way of knowing how dangerous Bilnius Red F was, or wasn't, but she knew that Sarah's motives were compromised by overwhelming jealousy of Her. "You're not going to do anything stupid, are you?"

"I'm going to do the right thing."

"Even if it's the wrong thing for your marriage?"

"*Sure* you won't have a quinoa shake?"

★　★　★

The bus had crawled home from Sarah's place. Sunny was greeted by an obstacle course of wine and beer crates in the hallway of number thirteen, ready for tomorrow night's party.

A hopeful Jojo said from the sofa, "Making a pot of tea?"

"Nope. Too much work to do."

"Work," sneered Jojo. "Scribbling down makey-up stories. I don't call that work."

"Hmmm. Perhaps I should lie about all day, playing with the cat and eating twice my own weight in chocolate. Oh, no," she realised, "that job's taken."

"Shuddup. *Quincy's* on."

As the paunchy pathologist solved another baffling case involving enormous lapels and pastel slacks, Sunny bashed out her next chapter. It was the one she'd been dreading, so she just took a deep breath and tackled it head on.

It was the dot-dot-dot chapter.

Since meeting Fabio, sex had been on Sunny's mind. Partly because it was unavoidable when sitting close to the prototype that God uses to make movie stars. Partly because she couldn't wait to make the beast with two backs with him. And partly because she feared it.

Tonight she was going to Fabio's flat, or apartment as he called it, in a swanky Chelsea Wharf development, for the first time. He was cooking dinner for them both. She was staying over. It was shaping up to be the night of their very first dot-dot-dot.

Would Fabio still be crazy about her tomorrow? It wasn't just the dollops of cellulite and the marks her socks left on her ankles; he might be disappointed that she wasn't more experienced. Sunny didn't have Sarah's vast experience of one-night stands to draw on: she had always been too idealistic to be promiscuous. Even the postboy at Waldhorn Truss Levy had known that Sarah was good in bed, but Sunny couldn't make the same boast.

What a loaded phrase that was. Sunny knew she'd had good sex, even great sex. Once, she hadn't even noticed her bottom was on her curling tongs until her orgasm ebbed. But maybe, she thought paranoiacally, it had been good sex because of her partners. Maybe she was — gulp — so-so in bed.

Turning away from this self-flagellation, Sunny pounded the keyboard. Lucinda had no such doubts. She and Sergio were prowling about his bedroom in a *palazzo* (obviously, it had to be a *palazzo*) like two caged panthers.

Perhaps, Sunny thought idly, she should ask her exes how they rated her. A reference might give her confidence: a document stating that I, the undersigned, consider Sandra Philomena Parkinson to be Good In Bed.

Sunny stopped typing for a moment to visualise Patrick's face if she asked him to rate her sexual performance: that really would turn his hair bouffant.

It had been slow to ignite, the flame between them. After the drunken kisses at the toga party, they'd seen each other in a patchy way for a few months, before the rainy Sunday morning when he'd called for her and found her still under the covers. "Too wet to go out," she'd decreed, and pulled him down on to her lumpy single bed.

The sun had come out later that afternoon, but the blind didn't go up until Monday morning, by which time they were happily exhausted and Sunny had a large curling-tong-shaped burn on her bottom.

There had been no self-doubt then, but Fabio's perfection inspired it now. It wasn't that Patrick was unattractive — there had been a time when his calm face had been like catnip to her — it was more that Patrick was attractive in an ordinary way, whereas Fabio was a headturner. She didn't need to be Poirot to surmise that every square inch of Fabio would look like oiled mahogany.

With an expressive groan that expertly combined lust, terror and regret at regarding gyms as if they were leper colonies, Sunny reapplied herself to Lucinda and Sergio.

Going further than she'd dared before, Sunny choreographed the lusty couple around the *palazzo*. Lucinda howled with pleasure on a marble washstand, and Sergio playfully bit her nipple as they tumbled on the Aubusson rug.

Slightly breathless, Sunny finished them off on the bed (a Louis Quinze, naturally). As Lucinda "scaled the peaks of feminine pleasure", Sergio whispered in her ear, "I love you, my darling. I love you for ever."

And that, Sunny thought, as she slapped the laptop shut, calls for a nice cup of tea.

★   ★   ★

The antiques were "family pieces", Fabio told Sunny, as he gave her a tour of his apartment. Nodding serenely, Sunny thought of the family pieces in her parents' home: Nana O'Brien's painting-by-numbers of a dancing gypsy and Great-granddad's false teeth.

"Nice place," she murmured, with nervous understatement. It was a scaled-down stately home. "Family portrait?" She pointed at an old oil of a portly man.

"Yes. Painted after he became pope."

Sunny drained her martini. "I have an aunty who's a nun, you know."

"See how alike we are?" grinned Fabio, peeling off his shirt. "Cooking always makes me so hot," he drawled, by way of explanation.

It took four martinis for Sunny to loosen up. "Oh, Gawd, not oysters! I hate the briney buggers!" Maybe she loosened up a tad too much. "These had better be organic or my friend Sarah will kill me," she commented, as she relented and let a briney bugger slither down her throat. "Are you trying to seduce me, Mr Carelli di Sica, etc., etc.?" she asked him, coyly.

"Yes."

"Yikes."

After dinner, Fabio uncoiled himself and lay full length on an immense fur rug. "Join me." He was half commanding, half beseeching.

Feeling slightly ridiculous — *a fur rug, for God's sake* — Sunny got to her knees and crawled over to him. She felt twitchy and super-alive when she looked into his eyes. Her senses were powered up. The rug was

156

super-soft, the smell of claret on Fabio's breath was yeasty, and the impact of his lips was intense.

They had never kissed like this before. This kiss meant business. Sunny was agitated, wired. The feel of Fabio, his solidity, his maleness, overexcited her, making her feel that however fast they went, it couldn't be fast enough. She was like a hunger-striker at a smorgasbord.

"Slow, slow," counselled Fabio. "We have the rest of our lives."

That night was a revelation. Fabio took charge and Sunny was remade in his hands. The old Sunny, conscious of her wobbly bits, fell away and a new powerful, sensually confident girl emerged.

It was a long night, and as morning arrived over the window sill, Fabio crushed her in his arms and whispered, "There is something I want to say, cara."

Sunny's damp body, exhausted though it was, found the energy to jangle like a burglar alarm. All her nerve endings knew what was coming, and they weren't sure if they could cope with the sensory overload. "Don't!" Sunny put her fingers to Fabio's pout. "Not yet. It's too soon."

They fell asleep.

CHAPTER
TWELVE

There were Monster Munch crumbs in Elizabeth I's ruff.

"Leave some nibbles for the guests!" Sunny was cranky with anxiety: she knew the God of Parties frowned on her. "And your wig's sideways."

Patting her impressive ginger hairpiece, Jojo corrected her, smugly, that it wasn't.

Sunny gave it a tug. "It is now."

The swish of crinoline announced the birthday girl.

"You look so beautiful!" mewed Sunny, with a mixture of pride and envy. Severely underdressed in her pyjamas, she was impatient for Fabio to get there.

Ellen was the image of a southern belle, with her cinchedin waist and the pale blush on her cheeks. Any moment now she might lynch a slave. "Is it OK?" she asked, gingerly.

"It's stunning. Honest. Now, help me rig up the fairy lights, Scarlett."

Sunny's bedroom had been transformed into the "dancing room". The fairy lights shed their reliable, £4.99 magic over the denuded room. One of the homemade compilations they'd argued over all week ("No more Kylie!", "Please can we have just one

Morrissey?") played as Sunny sketched out her hopes for the party. "Everybody congregates in here." She mimed holding a glass, daintily. "Chat chat chat. Nibble nibble nibble. Flirt flirt flirt. Then . . ." she led the others out into the hall ". . . as it fills up they start spilling out here. Chat chat chat. Maybe get off with get off with get off with. And when they're brave enough, it's back to the dancing room for dancey dancey dancey."

"Then," suggested Jojo, "off to the loo for pukey pukey pukey."

Severely, Ellen corrected her. "Nobody will puke at my party."

"Your Highness, if I might be so bold, shut your face," said Sunny in respectful tones to their half-pint monarch. "I have only invited very nice, well-behaved people." Sunny had struggled to come up with a guest list at all. Ellen's three years in London had reaped her no more than a handful of friends. She didn't use Sunny's machine-gun approach to making chums: Ellen was guarded. "It's going to be a sophisticated affair."

"If you say so." Jojo yanked up her jewel-encrusted robe to tug at her knickers. "Thank Christ for that. The gusset was up in me throat."

Unable to frame a comment, Sunny prescribed large vodka and tonics for them all. Uncharacteristically, Ellen downed hers in one.

"Nervous?" How Jojo loved to scent trouble in the wind.

"No." Delivered with the snap of an alligator, Ellen's answer confirmed it.

Jojos rush in where angels fear to tread. "Is this Dave-related? Scared he's going to dump you?"

Icily, Ellen said, "Dave can't dump me because I'm not going out with him."

"Whatever." Jojo had learned much from the *Trisha* audience.

"I'm *not*," insisted Ellen. "That's the problem." Her shoulders sagged. "He wants more."

"And you?" Sunny took the precaution of clamping her hand over Jojo's mouth.

"I'm not sure." Ellen looked more than unsure; she looked deeply miserable. Paradoxically, this rendered her prettier than ever. "It's not straightforward. I'm not like you."

The tangled topic was curtailed by the doorbell. "Fabio! You'll meet him at last!" sang Sunny, scampering to the front door.

Already in costume, Fabio's entrance prompted a silence to fall like heavy snow over all three hostesses. "Can you work out who I am supposed to be?" he asked, unleashing one of his heartbreaker smiles.

Their voices mere growls, the girls answered in unison: "You're Mr Darcy."

Obviously concerned by their zombie-like reaction, Fabio asked anxiously, "My breeches are too tight?"

"No!" Sunny was decisive but husky.

"I am all right, yes?" Fabio's sooty brows lowered.

Taking in the polished riding boots, the taut breeches on his muscular thighs, the jacket tailored to showcase

160

his broad chest and the sideburns trimmed to echo his Elvis cheekbones, Sunny said weakly, "You are all right."

Sounding as if her mouth was dry, Ellen stopped staring at Fabio's legs to say, "Very historically accurate."

For only the third time since she'd learned how, Jojo didn't speak.

In character, Fabio bowed gracefully, and complimented Jojo and Ellen on their costumes. "Sunny, *cara*, introduce me properly to your —"

"Shut up." Sunny grabbed her boyfriend by one velvet lapel, jabbing a finger at each of her cousins as she muttered, "That's Jojo. She's Ellen." Manhandling him away, she commanded, "You're coming with me," and shoved him into the bathroom, kicking the door shut behind her. Then she reached up to grab the back of his head and pulled his face down to hers.

"I don't think," whispered Fabio a moment or two later, "that I have ever been kissed like that before."

"Off." When Fabio failed to understand, Sunny set about finding the buttons on his tight fawn trousers herself. "Hurry."

He got her drift. Luckily, Ellen had the presence of mind to scuttle off in her crinoline and turn up the dance CD. The gasps, the groans and the clatter and splat as a shelf of shampoos hit the tiles were masked by loud drum and bass.

Pink-faced and breathless, Sunny, satisfied, stopped riding Fabio as if he was a particularly naughty runaway stallion and leaned down to kiss him tenderly.

"Oh, your poor head!" Sprawled on the bath mat, Fabio's glossy curls were sandwiched between the washbasin pedestal and a chrome bin.

"Please do not feel sorry for me." Fabio blinked, disbelievingly, before awkwardly clambering to his feet.

"Surely you know the effect Mr Darcy has on us girls?" Sunny splashed her face with water, marvelling at the restorative effect sex has on the skin: Fabio was better value, and more fun, than a Clarins facial. "It's all Colin Firth's fault."

"I chose this character because he is romantic." Fabio retied his cravat. "I did not expect this . . ." he gestured with his hands ". . . *explosion*."

"Mr Darcy *is* romantic, but he's a sex god first and foremost," Sunny explained eruditely. "Even Jojo came over funny, and I thought her bits had healed over years ago."

"Beets?" Fabio looked lost.

"Never mind." Sunny kissed him on his handsome nose. "It's time for me to slip into something less comfortable."

"Something less . . .?"

"Never mind," repeated Sunny, laughing. "Help me into the costume you've brought for me."

The Elizabeth Bennett dress, and her visceral reaction to Fabio as Darcy, shed new light on the Regency period for Sunny. The high waist hoiked up her breasts like apples on a market stall.

"Charming," pronounced Fabio, who had evidently never heard the English expression "Phwoaaar!".

The doorbell rang again, signalling the arrival of actual, honest-to-goodness guests. "Show time!" laughed Sunny, throwing her bosom a last disbelieving glance in the mirror.

"One moment." Fabio pulled her against him. "I need to tell you . . ."

"Yes?" Sunny looked him in the eye.

"Sunny, you must let me say it. It is not too soon."

Dumb with expectation and happiness, Sunny nodded. She was ready.

"Sunny, I love you, my darling. I love you for ever."

She wanted to jerk away and stuff a flannel in his mouth. Why those very words?

Luckily, Fabio seemed to take her consternation for adorable feminine confusion. "You don't have to say a thing, cara." He kissed her on the end of her nose. "I am patient. It will happen."

The Incredible Hulk was pouring drinks. Queen Victoria was snogging an Oompa Loompa. Sunny's party karma had been foiled: this was a good do, even if some guests' interpretation of the term "hero" was puzzling.

The only threat to the party's success was Mrs Wilde. Not just because she had teased her bulk into a size twenty-four Wonder Woman outfit, but because of the latest move in her quest to find the Chudleigh Cad.

"Flashcards!" Hauling Sunny into the loo to show her some ordinary playing cards with supposedly provocative pictures glued lopsidedly on to them, Mrs

Wilde explained, "I'll flash these at various suspects and note their reaction."

"Most scientific." Sunny was understandably eager to get out of the loo.

"The net is closing." Mrs Wilde was complacent in her glossy black wig.

They met Guy, dressed as Nelson, in the crush in the hallway. He barely had time to salute them before Mrs Wilde shoved a picture of Britney Spears's body with Vanessa Feltz's head, at him, fruitily proclaiming, "Aha now!"

"Dear God!" Guy stumbled back, with a suitably aghast look on his face but recovered speedily. His suave self again, he asked, "What the hell was that about?" as Wonder Woman stomped off.

"Don't ask." Sunny spotted his girlfriend, in what looked like an ordinary black dress, chatting to a Munchkin. "What's Chloe come as?"

"She's come as Disgruntled Bitch. Seems I forgot to tell her it was fancy dress."

"Guy, you're a bastard sometimes."

This was sincerely meant, but Guy took it as a compliment. "Yeah. I know. I like your outfit," he told her breasts.

All evening, Sunny had felt like the dull chum her boobs had brought along to make up the numbers. "Ta," she said, turning her head at the sound of a frightened squeal.

Scrawny Ben made a very unconvincing John Wayne. He looked even less like his hero now that he was blundering through the crowd yelping, "Keep Queen

Victoria away from me! She's an animal!" Appealing to Sunny, he said breathlessly, "When the Oompa Loompa spurned her, she grabbed me. She knocked my Stetson off!"

"Oh dear." Sunny struggled to look grave. Boiled Egg might benefit from a hit-and-run snogging, she thought. It might bring him out of himself, stop him nicking knickers. With a start she realised that Ben was her prime suspect.

A spaniel joined them. Ernest was almost unrecognisable under all that fun fur. "We residents are still worried," he told Sunny abruptly. "Can we really trust your friend not to ruin our gardens?"

"Don't worry." Sunny was emphatic. "Patrick's not the type to erect neon cubes or steel orbs. You'll like the end result." Her head flew backwards as one of her ringlets was tugged. "Ow!" she yelped, swinging round. "Oh, it's you, Beckham."

"This football strip makes me feel all macho and tough." Sarah pulled another ringlet to illustrate just how tough she was.

"Hmm." Sunny looked Sarah up and down. The strip had been customised so that the top (now low cut) fitted like a second skin and the baggy England shorts had been transformed into hotpants. The painted-on stubble sat uneasily with Sarah's Jessica Rabbit bod. "Have you done anything stupid yet?" she asked, in an undertone.

"No. Well . . ." Sarah shrugged ". . . depends what you mean by stupid."

"You said you'd give Alfie and Her a chance!" hissed Sunny, glancing over at Alfie, who had come as his nan. She was his hero, apparently.

"See!" Sarah pounced. "Even *you* lump them together! Alfie and Her! Her and Alfie!" she chanted, in a manic whisper.

"If this is really about . . ." Sunny had no option but to use the word ". . . *jealousy*, then think very carefully about what you're doing."

"I *have* given them a chance." Sarah looked stung. "Porqy Peeces just aren't taking the problem seriously. Thanks for your support, by the way." There were tears in Sarah's eyes.

"I am supporting you, you twit." Sunny kissed her on the cheek. "This isn't the time or place."

"You're right." Sarah shook the tears away and scanned the other guests. "What an amazing figure Catwoman's got."

"If you like ironing boards."

"Oooh, *Catty*woman. What have you got against her?"

"Nothing." Sunny tossed her ringlets, innocently. "Serena's perfectly all right. A bit bossy maybe. And snooty. And rude. And a tad too old for her costume."

Behind them, an amused voice asked, "Who's too old for their costume?"

Recognising Patrick's tones, Sunny turned and gabbled, "Me!" Thinking on her feet was not a strong point. "I'm way too old to be Elizabeth Bennett!"

"Naw," said Patrick.

"Sir, you are too kind," simpered Sunny, who was amusing herself (if nobody else) by lapsing into Austen-speak every now and then. "If I may be so bold, dear Count Dracula, pray tell me, where are your fearsome fangs?"

Running his tongue over his non-threatening, even teeth, Patrick said, "I've a horrible feeling they're impaled on a Scotch egg somewhere."

Moving as a pack, the Thin Girls rolled up and enveloped Sunny in a fragrant group hug. "What a wonderful party!", "Thank you for inviting us!", "Oh, your boobs look fantastic. I wish mine could do that!" they twittered, like a flock of glam starlings.

They were dressed as nuns, defying Jojo's premonition that they would come as sticks. They were naughty nuns, of course, in miniskirts and suspenders. The middle Thin Girl, giddy from the punch that Jojo kept replenishing with dregs, was enthusing on the standard of costume. "Everybody's made such an effort. Just look at Superman over there."

They all looked over at Leonard, whose baggy Superman outfit seemed to have been borrowed from a taller friend. Blue tights wrinkling around the top of his red boots, it was unlikely that Leonard could leap tall buildings in a single bound. Just now he was struggling to control a sandwich and a plastic glass of Tizer.

"My favourite," chirruped the least thin Thin Girl, "is . . ." her voice dropped and became smoky ". . . Mr Darcy."

Down the hallway, Fabio was leaning one arm against a wall and talking politely to Cleopatra.

The Thin Girls and Sunny fell respectfully silent as they studied him.

"And he's really, truly your boyfriend?" asked one of them.

"He really, truly is." Sunny held out her arm. "Would you pinch me, please?"

Of course, none of the Thin Girls could do anything so horrid, and they dispersed, telling Sunny to look out for the "really lifelike gorilla" and the other nun, "much more accurate than us".

The gorilla had been sick in the loo and was looking considerably less lifelike now that an ashen solicitor's head was poking out from his hairy shoulders. One of the party's many Elvises almost collided with him as he manoeuvred down the hall with two glasses of punch.

"Dave!" Sunny pushed her way through the throng to catch up. "Enjoying yourself?"

Nodding vigorously, Dave shouted, "It's brilliant!" over the din.

Enough people had said this for Sunny to start believing it. "Great shades," she mouthed approvingly. Dave had plumped for the Vegas Elvis, so he was in a jewel-studded white jumpsuit and aviators. "Going to give us a song later?"

Behind the seventies sunglasses, Dave pulled a horrified face. He was so gloriously easy to tease that Sunny couldn't help liking him. She usually veered away from people as "ordinary" as Dave: she favoured more pepper in her recipes. Dave's ordinariness was there for all to see: he drove a hatchback; he played air guitar to Phil Collins; he had a pension plan in place and probably had done since primary school. All of this made him perfect for cautious, sensible, look-before-you-leap Ellen, who checked the BBC weather report before putting out the milk bottles.

Perhaps the most important factor, the final tick in the box, was Dave's obvious devotion to Ellen. The look on his face when he'd first seen her in her Scarlett O'Hara finery had clinched it for Sunny: Ellen could continue to pump out her smokescreen, but there was something going on between them. Dave was mad about her.

And if Ellen was as sensible as they all believed, then she should be mad about him, too, in Sunny's opinion. "Where are you headed with those drinks?" Sunny realised that she hadn't seen Ellen for an hour, since the gorilla stopped break-dancing.

"We're hiding out in Ellen's room," grinned Dave.

"Aha." Sunny punched Dave on the arm, a curiously blokeish gesture from a nineteenth century lady. "Don't let me hold you up," she leered.

Off scuttled Dave, weaving in and out of the tipsy guests. Sunny darted into the dancing room to avoid a drunken Jesus who was being carried out by Mr Happy and that busy Oompa Loompa. Lawyers were turning out to be far more raucous than Sunny had imagined.

Spotting her boyfriend ("Great word that," she thought), Sunny forged a path to him. "Why, if it isn't Mr Darcy," she giggled. "Greetings, sir."

Fabio bowed, and Sunny wondered how Jane Austen heroines got through the day without ripping the hero's kecks off hourly.

"Forsooth," said Patrick, who Sunny hadn't spotted. "And gadzooks, I suppose."

Sunny looked from one to the other. "What were you two doing?" she asked, like a suspicious constable with two hoodies in a shopping centre.

Patrick folded his arms and smiled lazily at her. "What do you think we were doing? Weaving baskets? Splitting the atom?"

"We were talking," Fabio told her straightforwardly, with no teasing.

It was a firm rule of Sunny's to keep past and present men in her life apart. "Talking about what?" she said, trying to sound nonchalant but coming across like the Regency arm of the SS.

"Gardens." It was an innocent word and an innocent topic, but there was something about the way Patrick said it.

"Yes, we've had a fascinating discussion," said Fabio eagerly. Unlike Patrick, he hadn't majored in irony. "Your friend is an expert. I have picked up many tips, which I will pass to my head gardener in Roma."

Sunny guessed how Patrick longed to react to that "head gardener in Roma". Suddenly infuriated, she wanted to protect Fabio, guileless and innocent beside Patrick's dark smirk. This man loved her, she reminded herself, even if he had told her so in a manner that had made her ringlets stand on end.

"I'll fetch us all another glass of the interesting punch." Fabio took Sunny's chin in his hand. "You stay here, cara, and keep Patrick company."

170

There was a long silence, accentuated by the bleat of a boy band.

Sunny caved in first. "Go on. Say it."

"Say what?"

"That Fabio's a plonker. Or a twat. Or whatever you're dying to call him."

"Why, Miss Elizabeth, what a potty mouth you have acquired in London town."

"I can see you're aching to have a pop at him. Just because he's rich."

"That's his business," said Patrick equably. "But he might think about buying himself a sense of humour."

Shocked, Sunny squeaked, "Fabio's got a brilliant sense of humour!"

"Come on, Sun, he's not exactly a laugh a minute. This man is not going to giggle at shingles. He's intense. Nice with it." Patrick paused. "If you like that sort of thing."

"And I do!" said Sunny, spiritedly.

"Fine. Listen," Patrick looked apologetic. "This is none of my business. You do what you want, Sunny. It's your life."

Sunny blinked hard, and suppressed the sigh threatening to rise up from her satin pumps. Same old Patrick, she thought rancorously. Still holding back, still not fighting for me, still not caring enough to interfere. "I will," she promised him.

Returning with glasses of murky punch for them all, Fabio was recovering from being flashcarded. Looking nonplussed, he said, "A big lady showed me a dog wearing a bra. Why?" he ended, forlornly.

"Mrs Wilde works in mysterious ways." Sunny led her intense but nice man away, poking her tongue out at Patrick as they went. She noted that there was a light under Ellen's bedroom door.

So Dave and Ellen were still snug in there. She wondered if Dave had been brave enough to risk a cuddle. Putting her arm through Fabio's, she felt relieved that her own relationship was so straightforward. She had to be adult about those ridiculous fears that he was somehow just a figment of her own needy imaginings. Patrick was wrong: Fabio was right for her.

Smiling down at her, Fabio whispered, "I like it when you hang on to me."

And that, Sunny determined, was exactly what she was going to do from now on.

In the crowded kitchen, Jojo had one arm protectively curled round a large bowl of Doritos. With the other she was drunkenly fending off an even drunker, practically feral, Marilyn Monroe. "Feck off!" snarled Jojo, who had lost her wig long ago. "I can have you beheaded, you know."

"Aw, the lovely Jojo is tired," said Fabio indulgently.

"Where's the shaggin' guacamole!" shrieked the lovely Jojo.

Sunny distracted the Marilyn by tossing a cheese straw into a corner and guided Jojo to a chair. "Stay there while I make coffee," she commanded, clearly and distinctly.

It wasn't easy in the scrum of historical characters, but Sunny whipped up a large mug of black Nescafé.

The gorilla was back, and gunning for a fight. "Oi! Superman!" he slurred angrily at Leonard, who was

172

rinsing a dishcloth. "Did you nick my drink?" Before Leonard could answer, the gorilla picked him up and carried him out, knocking into Queen Victoria on her way in. Her make-up was smudged, and she was keening for her Oompa Loompa.

Sunny ignored all this drama and concentrated on Jojo, who placidly accepted the coffee. Over their heads, Fabio said wonderingly, "That nun is wonderfully authentic."

Something in a deep, dark, rarely used, distant niche of Sunny's psyche pinged like an oven timer. She looked directly into Jojo's fuddled eyes: they had miraculously cleared. The same pinprick of foreboding seemed to have disturbed her cousin.

Together they looked over to the doorway. Just in front of an unsettling tableau of Superman beating off a gorilla with a stale baguette stood Aunty Jane the Nun.

"There you are, girls." The soft Dublin accent cut right through Leonard's screams and the twelve-inch remix of "Relax". "Are you not well, Jojo?"

"Phlaaaaargh," answered Jojo, her momentary sobriety evaporating.

"Aunty Jane!" Sunny said it again, in a tone that implied disbelief. "Aunty Jane?"

"Yes, it's me, Sandra." Irreproachably neat in her navy coat and ironed wimple, Aunty Jane the Nun had a small navy overnight bag in her small navy-gloved hands. "I've come to see you all. Where's my lovely Ellen?"

At that moment, her lovely Ellen shot out of her room, barefoot and hysterical. In a coarse, guttural shriek quite unlike her usual serene voice, she was yelling, "Get out! You freak! You monster! Get out!"

Whiter than his diamanté-studded jumpsuit, Dave emerged, hugging the wall. "What did —"

His question was curtailed by Ellen. "What do you think I am? Do you think I'm a prostitute!" she screamed. She wrapped her arms tightly around herself and shrank from Dave as if he was toxic.

"Please, Ellen." Close to tears, Dave put his arms out towards her, and Ellen shrieked even louder than before.

Party-goers melted back, isolating Dave and Ellen. The music had abruptly stopped.

A sick panic rose in Sunny's throat as she barged her way towards the scene. By the time she broke through the cordon of shocked onlookers, Patrick had one arm round Ellen and was holding Dave firmly at arm's length.

"Just go, mate." Patrick was sombre.

"But I can't leave her like this." Dave was in tears, his face crumpled with anxiety.

Crying into Patrick's tatty cape, Ellen's accusation was clearly heard by everybody. "He attacked me," she sobbed. "He attacked me."

Dave couldn't miss the change in atmosphere. He fled, shoving people out of his way.

"Let him go," Patrick advised softly when Sunny began to squeak about the police. "We know where he lives. Ellen's our priority."

Aunty Jane's embrace shocked Ellen out of her tears for a second or two. "Looks like I arrived just in time," she said.

CHAPTER
THIRTEEN

Number thirteen looked freshly looted. People having a good time leave a bad mess. From her sentry post at Ellen's bedside, Sunny could hear Sister Jane padding about, tidying, rearranging, issuing the odd soft command to her sulky assistant, Jojo.

Inside the bedroom, all was dark and cloistered, the curtains drawn against the nosy morning light. Sunny was grateful for the quiet. Last night's music still thumped in her brain. Even so, it didn't quite drown out her memory of the screeching that had ended the party.

A dark hillock under the duvet, Ellen was asleep. Her sobs had faded with the last of the guests, to be replaced by a resolute silence that was, somehow, worse. She'd said nothing, explained nothing, before falling into a deep sleep, her white frown buried in the pillow.

Taking turns, Sister Jane and Sunny had sat by Ellen through the night. Sister Jane's sudden appearance, like some Vatican panto genie, had been inexplicable, but Sunny was glad that her aunt was there. Calm and watchful, Sister Jane was just the person to soothe Ellen.

God knows what she must think of us, cringed Sunny. Why had fate delivered their holiest relative in the midst of a wild party? Vomiting, snogging and, just to round things off nicely, a hysterical allegation of assault. Sunny had told her, "It's not like this every night."

"Glad to hear it," had been the nun's reply.

Sister Jane had been a distant figure in their childhood. There had been occasional trips to visit her at her convent on the outskirts of Dublin, preceded by much maternal finger-wagging about the dire consequences if they didn't behave. Their aunt had always welcomed them, treating them as miniature adults. Sunny could remember being asked about school and pets as if Sister Jane had been genuinely interested; her own mother had never pretended to find the vicissitudes of Squeako the gerbil fascinating. Sister Jane had been present at Christmas, handed around the family like a human Pass-the-Parcel, but she always had "something to get back to". So her arrival on their doorstep (Sunny didn't even know she had their address) was a mystery.

Feeling redundant, Sunny pointlessly fussed with the duvet. She longed to be of some real use to poor Ellen. For the umpteenth time she wondered if she should have ignored Patrick's atypical intervention and called the police. Ellen's screams had doubled at the idea, so Sunny had relented, but the morning after brought doubts.

A tap on the door summoned her to breakfast in their unrecognisable kitchen. The table was laid with a cloth that Sunny had never seen before. The crockery almost matched. There was a napkin at each plate. Even Jojo looked as if she'd brushed her hair.

As Sunny sat down, her aunt set a cooked breakfast, sizzling and perfect, in front of her. "You didn't find this food in our fridge." Sunny was sure about that.

"I certainly did not," scoffed her aunt. "I sent Jojo out for sausages and bacon and eggs and black pudding."

"You sent . . ." The words tailed off as Sunny stared at the usually un-send-outable Jojo, who ignored her and concentrated studiously on the toast she was buttering. Maybe their aunt was a modern Mary Poppins with powers far beyond your average nun.

"How's our patient?" Sister Jane's bright eyes and upturned nose had always reminded Sunny of a woodland animal. There were a few lines now in the soft, papery, Irish skin around those eyes, but the analogy held: she was just a slightly scuffed woodland animal.

"Still asleep."

"We might get a few more details when she wakes up," said Sister Jane comfortably. She had the patience of a different era, before people relied on mobiles and microwaves.

Sunny wondered if her aunt had always had an aura of calm imperturbability, or if it had been brought on by a life of nunning. Calm aura or not, Sunny had never discussed sexual assault with a holy woman, and she didn't want to start now.

Through a mouthful of fried egg, Jojo said, "She's making it up."

177

"Really?" asked Sister Jane evenly. "And why would Ellen do a thing like that?"

"For the attention." Jojo was quietly confident, despite the egg yolk travelling at speed down her chin towards her leopardskin tricel robe.

Exasperated, Sunny huffed, "Sorry to blow your theory, but we all know that Ellen *hates* attention. And she doesn't lie." Angry on Ellen's behalf, Sunny glared at Jojo.

Trundling on, Jojo said, "So, you think Dave is the type to try and rape someone?"

"Now, now," said Sister Jane. A hint of sternness had entered her tone: like Bambi's mother returning something to a shop. "Nobody's used the word rape, Jojo, don't you be the first. We'll see what Ellen has to say when she's had a rest, and some time to reflect."

Sunny was grateful to the gods, or whoever was in charge of stuff down here, that Aunty Jane had turned up and not an alternative female relative. If Sunny's or Ellen's mother had witnessed the hysterics, they'd have made twice as much noise themselves. As for Aunty Annie, she'd have run up Ku Klux Klan outfits from the bed sheets and hanged Dave on the spot.

"Betcha she won't talk for days." Jojo had no notion when to shut up. "She was like this once before, and she just stayed in her room then."

Sister Jane asked, with a frown, "This has happened before? What brought it on?"

"Something at work. She never explained. She did something wrong and she had to leave. She was just the same then — all droopy and silent. Drove me mam mad."

Knowing it didn't take much to drive Aunty Mo mad — not finishing your cabbage could make her bang her head off the kitchen cabinets — Sunny wondered what had happened. "I never heard about any of this," she said dubiously. "I thought she left her job to come to London."

"Obviously, we don't tell you everything," said Jojo smugly.

That was designed to sting, and it did. Sunny moved on, to ask the obvious question of the morning. "What are you doing here, Aunty Jane?" It sounded insolent, but Sunny had been rehearsing the question every which way and couldn't improve on this bald version. "I mean, out of the blue like this? And why us? Why not go to my mum, or their mum, or Aunty Annie?" She tagged on a hasty "I'm not saying you're not welcome. It's lovely to have you here." That wasn't quite true: Sunny was in the foothills of the sexiest relationship she'd ever experienced, and having a nun in full working order on the premises could be construed as a passion-killer.

"There's no mystery, girls. No big story." Sister Jane cut her sausage into neat, equal pieces. "I needed a break. A place to think. If I'd gone to one of your mams or to Annie, it would be gossip and cake all day, with no time to myself." She looked at both of them with a wholesome smile. "Besides, I haven't seen my beautiful nieces for ages, and I've never been to London. So here

179

I am." Her shining, candid face promised that there was no more to it than that.

"Well, we're really glad to have you. I'll move my stuff into Ellen's later on," said Sunny. "You can sleep in my bed." It was a bad word to even think around such a spiritual lady, but it tumbled around Sunny's brain just the same. *Bullshit.*

Leaving Sister Jane at the foot of Ellen's bed like Whistler's nun, Sunny and Jojo had sneaked out to spy on filming. Surprised to see the crew on a Sunday, they had big plans to snigger at Patrick from their vantage point behind a hedge, and possibly throw small items at him.

Little progress seemed to have been made with the redesign. No wonder residents were getting restless: neatly manicured lawns had been swapped for the Somme. A huge light, two cameras and a dozen faces all pointed at Patrick, who wore a look Sunny recognised. It was the same focussed, yet "Beam me up, Scotty" look he'd worn when out with Sunny and her girlfriends: she'd last seen it the night Penny had treated them to the director's cut of her latest break-up.

"This is boring." Jojo said what Sunny was thinking.

A clapperboard, with "StyleScaping" scrawled across it in chalk, slapped shut, and Patrick was off on take forty-four, explaining for the forty-fourth time why ponds are a good idea.

Sunny hadn't been interested in ponds forty-three takes ago and she still wasn't. "Let's go back."

Her gentle nudge toppled the crouching, spherical Jojo into a nettle patch like a Weeble. Choicest Irish swear words filled the warm afternoon air.

"Cut!" Serena's voice sounded furious, and her face looked that way, too, when it appeared round the side of their hedge. Sunny couldn't help noticing that Serena's hair looked fabulous, though. "May I escort you ladies back to your block?" she asked, tightly.

Marched to the steps like naughty toddlers, Sunny said "sorry" a lot to compensate for Jojo's Muttley-esque mutterings. "By the way," she asked, just as Serena shooed them in through the heavy doors, "what's 'StyleScaping'?"

"What is it?" The question seemed to irritate Serena. "It's the title of the programme."

"Oh." Serena was gone without a goodbye, leaving Sunny to muse that perhaps the producer and the presenter didn't *quite* share a vision, after all.

"Knickers!" Jojo was saying wonderingly.

"Knickers," said Sunny more flatly, for they were surrounded by the things. A thong hung from the lift handle. Camiknickers straddled the bottom stair. Some rubber pants reclined on the post pigeon-holes, and there were tummy-tamers slung over the light fitting. Looking up at them, Sunny put out her hand to the banister and encountered a pair of edible briefs. "Ewww!" She backed away, as if they'd bitten her. "What the hell is going on?"

Irritatingly, Jojo knew. "Mrs Wilde's placed knickers all over the common parts in the hope that the Cad won't be able to control himself in the face of such temptation. She's taking turns with Leonard to patrol." Nodding approvingly, Jojo said, "Could work."

"In that strange other universe where people like you and Mrs Wilde live, it just might," agreed Sunny, trying to open the lift without touching the thong.

Ellen was up, invalid-like in her dressing gown, when Sunny and Jojo got back to the flat.

"I scared you, didn't I?" Tears welled up in Ellen's eyes. "I'm sorry."

"Don't be sorry. Just get yourself together." Longing to probe, Sunny tied her metaphorical hands behind her metaphorical back. (With some metaphorical rope.)

"I never said a proper thank-you for throwing the party. It was such a nice idea." Ellen looked sheepish. "Even if I did ruin it."

"You didn't." Sunny paused, then had to laugh. "Well, you did, obviously."

Sister Jane put her head round the kitchen door, clapped her hands and said gaily, "If we set off now, we'll just make six o'clock Mass!"

The girls froze. None of them had been to Mass since they'd left home. They weren't even sure where the nearest church was, although they could find all the chip shops blindfolded. Sunny gulped. This was serious stuff for Catholic offspring: perhaps Sister Jane was empowered by the Pope to goad them to Mass with an electric prod.

Sneakily, Ellen got in first with a "I don't really feel up to it, Aunty Jane."

With a covert glare at her, Sunny thought, "Funnily enough, you haven't felt up to it since the day you stepped off the plane."

Next up was Jojo, who said aggressively, "I don't believe in all that crap."

Ellen groaned, but Sister Jane said, "Luckily, it believes in you, Jojo." She turned to Sunny. "Do you have an excuse ready, or do you just not want to go?"

Such frankness was novel in their family. Sunny was wrong-footed and burbled for a while, "Well . . . erm . . . now . . . yeeeeeees . . . hmmm."

"You don't want to go." Sister Jane didn't sound angry. She didn't sound disappointed. "How about a game of cards, then?" she said, producing a pack from her neat navy handbag.

CHAPTER
FOURTEEN

By Monday, Sunny had been transplanted into Ellen's room. She was forced to type hunched on the edge of her bed, but this wasn't the reason she was doing far more staring at the wallpaper than typing.

Fear was holding her fingers back. Fear that what she wrote would come true. Patently preposterous, this fear wasn't entirely overridden by Sunny's common sense: some small, pagan part of her couldn't be smothered. "Fabio is flesh and blood," she said out loud, feeling ridiculous.

It felt sacrilegious to waste such a perfect day for working. Sun streamed into the room, courtesy of the foolish summer which was still hanging around in early September, despite the fact that it was expected elsewhere in the world. More importantly, Jojo had been shoehorned out of the flat by Sister Jane, who had been shocked to hear that none of the girls had ever seen the Tower of London.

"Come with me, Jojo," she'd said briskly. "I need somebody to help me find the way on the tube."

This had seemed unlikely: Sister Jane would manage nicely if parachuted into the Arctic Circle with a knitting needle and a copy of *Woman's Own*, whereas

Jojo refused to use the tin-opener because it was "too complex". Sister Jane's determination had overpowered even Jojo's Olympian stubbornness and off the mismatched pair had gone.

Still in her dressing gown, Ellen had taken her first ever sick day. Quiet and wan, she took Jojo's place on the sofa and watched *Quincy*. Unlike her sister, she didn't shout advice at him.

Despite all this peace and quiet, despite the hundreds of ideas she had, Sunny couldn't write. She sighed, and strained her neck to see out of the window. She smiled. Patrick was being daubed with powder by a make-up girl.

Soon that face, so familiar to her, would be on thousands of television screens. "He'll be famous," murmured Sunny to herself. She wondered if he would still find time to get to the Volunteer every Thursday.

The phone rang. Grateful for the distraction from her shamefully blank laptop screen, Sunny yelled, "I'll get it!"

When Sunny heard her mother's voice on the other end of the line, she panicked. The elder Parkinsons regarded telephones as cunning, money-eating machines. Sunny's mum had dragged her English husband back to the land of saints and scholars and cheaper houses ten years ago, and ever since she had phoned Sunny on the dot of five-thirty on the last Sunday of every month.

"Mum? It's a Monday," Sunny realised in alarm. "Is it Granddad?" A horrible thought dawned. "Oh, God, don't tell me Snookums has snuffed it?"

"Snookums?" scoffed Mary Parkinson. "That auld cat'll bury us all. Well ..." she paused ". . . not literally." Mary wasn't a natural comic: she had a prosaic mind, tuned to anxiety. She excelled at roast dinners and worrying. "I'm, er, calling, on the off chance, to see if you've, em, heard from anybody. Out of the blue, like."

Sunny recognised that cagey tone from her childhood. It had been used for delicate subjects that the demure Mary wished would just go away. Where babies came from had been discussed in this tone of voice. When Father Frank had been in the *News of the World*, Mary had used it to tell Sunny that he had just been checking the boy for snake bites.

"Heard from *anybody*? Or somebody in particular?" Sunny enjoyed toying with her mother: she was spectacularly toyable-with.

"Oh. Just any old body." Mary sounded so laid-back she was in danger of toppling off her leatherette combined telephone table and seat.

"Somebody in blue, perhaps? With a crucifix round her neck?"

"She *is* there!" screeched Mary, her composure collapsing. "Put her on!"

"Aunty Jane turned up on Saturday, but she's out at the moment. Hang on." Sunny frowned. "Didn't you know she was coming to see us?" The aunts were in constant telephone communication with each other, sharing every banal aspect of their lives.

"How would I know?" gabbled Mary. "The convent called us to see if we knew where she was. I was

186

ashamed of me life. I've been up the wall. Mo and Annie have been up the wall. The convent's been up the wall."

So, Sunny concluded, Dublin was basically up the wall. "Didn't she tell the convent, er, guards that she was going away?"

"Isn't that what I'm telling you?" Like a mother who's located a missing toddler, Mary's relief was expressed as anger. "And they don't have guards in convents, you little heathen."

"Maybe they should. Then their nuns wouldn't escape."

"Tell me the truth. Is she all right?" Mary's voice quavered. She expected the worst at all times: Mr Parkinson used to say, as he came through the door from work, "Sorry to disappoint you, love, but I'm home."

"She's great."

"What is she saying? Is she going back?" Mary sounded frightened. "She's not thinking of giving up the cloth?"

"What cloth?" Sunny was a fine product of secular schooling. "Oh, you mean being a nun? As far as I know, she's having a break, then she resumes nunnage." Sunny played down her own surprise at the dramatic nature of Sister Jane's defection. Evidently, it wasn't the simple "break" her aunt had claimed: Sister Jane wouldn't worry her sisters without good reason.

"Oh, TG." Mary liked to use handy abbreviations. TG stood for "Thank God". Occasionally she used ITFW, or "In the Family Way", and she had recently begun to daringly suggest that the man in the post office, with the pastel leather blouson, might be TWI — "That Way Inclined". "Tell her to ring me. She can reverse the charges."

This reckless offer hammered home the gravity of the situation. Sister Jane's innocuous change of scene was looking like a jailbreak.

It wasn't a tough question. "Yes," Sunny told Sarah over the phone, later that afternoon. "I do think you've lost your marbles."

"Am I the only person bothered about what we feed our innocent children?" Sarah was attempting a kind of Mother Teresa vibe, which didn't sit well with her smoky, sexy voice that was designed for cigarillos, swearing and ordering men to assume the position.

"You're the only person who's bothered about Her. You seem to think that Liz is some kind of luncheon-meat Sharon Stone. She's ordinary. She's no threat to you." Sunny relented slightly. "All right. If I concede that you haven't lost your marbles, maybe we can agree that you've lost your sense of proportion? If the government allow Bilnius Red F, why should we worry about it?"

"It's concerned citizens like me who get the government to study these things." Sarah softened her tone. "All I've done is set up a little website for anybody who's concerned about Bilnius Red F. I don't know what you're making such a fuss about."

"A little website with the address www.porqypeecesisevil.com." Sunny didn't bother to add a sarcastic comment: that particular lily needed no gilding.

"It's just a warning shot across their bows."

"Listen to yourself, Napoleon. This isn't war. Alfie is your husband." Sunny enunciated clearly and carefully, as Sarah seemed to need reminding.

"I know I'm overstating," said Sarah, sadly, like a naughty child being made to apologise. "But if you heard the way Alfie sides with Her against me when we discuss Bilnius Red F . . ." She tailed off.

"Hey, hey," said Sunny gently. "Alfie loves you, Sarah, and only you. His relationship with Liz is all about work."

"No, I wish you were right, but it's more than that," squirmed Sarah, sounding reluctant to go on. "Remember you said me and Alfie needed to talk? Well, we did and guess what? He said he gets something from her that he can't get from me."

"I don't believe it."

"His very words." Sarah seemed to be doing her level best to sound angry. A connoisseur of her best friend's moods, Sunny knew she was longing to cry.

Without a typescript of the conversation, Sunny had no way of knowing if Sarah was reporting it accurately. Trying to simplify what was turning into a tangled mess of motive and suspicion, she insisted, "Look, the real issue here is your relationship. All this Porqy Peeces stuff is a smokescreen, but you'll only make things worse between you and Alfie if you let your jealousy of Liz blow a hole in the advertising campaign."

"I'm doing it for the kids," Sarah said, self-righteously. "I don't have a jealous bone in my body."

That would have been so easy to dispute: Sarah had once tried to have a temp deported for winking at Alfie in the lift. Sunny chose the diplomatic route. "Be careful. Think about this."

"Believe me," said Sarah miserably, "I don't think about anything else."

"I'll stay in with you, if you like. I don't mind," Sunny told Ellen. "Honest."

"I'm not a newborn. It's safe to leave me on my own." Ellen had washed her hair, relinquished the dressing gown and was putting a salad together. "Besides, Jojo and Aunty Jane will be back soon. It's almost seven."

Sunny theorised that they might have been imprisoned for treason. "I wouldn't put it past Jojo to shout out that the Queen is a man or something."

Doing something healthy with a bunch of basil, Ellen smiled wanly. Post-party, all her smiles were wan. She was a tepid version of her old self: Ellen Lite. At least, Sunny comforted herself, she was smiling.

"I'll only go if you're sure," she said, guilt tickling her about her desire to rush off to Chelsea Wharf and rugby-tackle Fabio, instead of staying at home with her cousin.

"Oh, Sunny, go! Go!" Ellen had a tower of too-clever-by-half law books piled on the kitchen table.

"I've work to do after I've eaten, and they'll be back any minute."

"All right then." Not normally so soggily protective, Sunny hated to leave Ellen tonight. "If you want to talk . . ."

A wry smile creased Ellen's lips. "You'll be there for me?" she mimicked the daytime chat shows Jojo worshipped. "Will you support me one hundred and ten per cent?"

"At the end of the day," deadpanned Sunny, "I love you to bits." She hesitated, going the same rosy colour as her new wrap-over cardigan. It needed to be said, but there was never a right time in their family. "I do, you know."

"Oh, get out and be there for your boyfriend." Ellen threw a spring onion at her. As Sunny pulled on a fitted jacket that Ellen was bound to recognise from her own wardrobe, Ellen said abruptly, "I'm much better. Really. What happened on Saturday wasn't just about Dave." Seemingly uncertain about how to express herself, Ellen looked down at the wilted basil. "I mean, he shouldn't have done what he did . . . but there's more to it than that."

Well, thought Sunny, that's as clear as mud. "You'll tell me when you're ready," she said, borrowing Sister Jane's attitude. It fitted rather well, unlike the jacket, which contorted her into a chic hunchback. "Oh. Forgot to tell you. My mum rang." She reported the conversation. "So Sister Jane is a nun on the run."

"That's a dramatic way of putting it. She's obviously going through something far more significant than she's

191

letting on, though. Maybe she's losing her faith." Ellen dropped her handful of herbs, her eyes wide. "Oh, dear God," she said, terror-stricken. "This doesn't mean they'll visit, does it?"

That "they" was the unholy trinity of Sunny's mum — Mary — Ellen's mum — Mo — and Annie, the spinster aunt who had "stayed at home with Mother". Occasionally, they booked an Aer Lingus flight to check up on the girls. Mary and Mo liked to ensure that they were eating properly, and Annie liked to check for signs of sexual activity.

"No." Sunny laughed indulgently, but the laugh died in her throat. "Would they?" she asked, desperately.

"Not if Aunty Jane talks to them, calms them down." Ellen sighed. "I couldn't take my mother at the moment."

There hadn't been a moment so far in Sunny's life when she *could* take her mother. All three girls were allergic to their mums, and, interestingly, the older trio had been allergic to *their* mother, whose "powers" Sunny worried she'd inherited. Sunny hoped that if she or Ellen (or, in some unlikely, science-fiction-style conception, Jojo) ever had daughters, this traditional distaste would stop, but there was no guarantee. Sometimes she suspected that all the women in their family were daubed with a secret mark on their foreheads that made their daughters want to avoid them.

"Does God mind if you suddenly start believing in Him and pray for something selfish?" Sunny ruminated.

"Probably. If He's got any sense. And if He does exist, He'll have a *lot* of sense," Ellen pointed out. "Nope. God's not going to help. If the mums and Annie want to visit, they'll visit. All we can do is strap on our bullet-proof vests and wait for it to end."

Tuesday was an even more fortuitous day for writing: *everybody* was out. Ellen dashed off to work, in her sharpest, severest suit. Jojo and Sister Jane headed for the London Eye, after a vehement, whispered argument between Jojo and Sunny while Sister Jane was out of the room.

Jojo had hissed, "I don't want to go on the fecking London Jayzus Eye."

"I hope you're using up all your nasty swear words before you step out with a nun," Sunny had whispered back.

"Feck off."

"I see you are." It wasn't often that Sunny got a chance to bait Jojo, and she'd made the most of it. "Bring a camera. Then we can all share the fun."

Jojo had pulled herself up to her full four feet eleven. "I warn you, I'm not on nun duty for the whole time she's here. It's not fair."

"Be good," Sunny had chirruped as she'd waved them off. "Why not take in a museum as well?"

So, the flat was empty. She could get down to some serious writing. She assembled her notes. She got out her thesaurus. She re-read the scant lines she'd already written.

A quick bath, first, she decided. To get in the mood.

Playing peek-a-boo with her toes in the surprising amount of bubbles you can bully from an own-brand product, Sunny gave herself a good talking-to: she'd spent last night with Fabio, and he'd been warm, loving, appreciative, passionate and playful, without once lapsing into Sergio-speak. As soon as she'd finished soaking, she'd attack her work with renewed vigour.

Ellen was battling cling film in an attempt to swaddle a left-over sausage. She stopped to note, "Your hands look like prunes, Sunny."

"Yeah. Had a longish bath earlier," said Sunny nonchalantly. "If I tell you something that's worrying me, do you promise not to laugh?" She felt in need of Ellen's intelligent logic.

"Of course. I'm not Jojo." Ellen winced at the sausage, now kinkily encased in clear plastic, and lobbed it into the fridge.

Sunny described how Fabio had admitted he loved her on the night of the party.

"I don't see your problem." Ellen peered into the fridge. She was on a throwing-out mission and no foodstuff was safe. "Aha!" She pounced on a jar of mayonnaise that could have been bought using groats. "It sounds really romantic to me. Like something out of a book."

"Exactly," whined Sunny. "*My* book."

"Ah. Jojo's witch theory." Ellen smiled ruefully, before unscrewing the mayonnaise and suppressing a scream.

"It sounds ridiculous, but what if she's right?"

"She's not right. These things don't happen. It's coincidence."

"It's a hell of a one."

"So it's a hell of a coincidence. It's still more likely than you being a witch." Ellen prodded a lump of Cheddar that was wearing a stylish fur stole. "You're always saying that love makes the world go round, so why not just go with it?"

Sunny wasn't used to declarations of devotion. "Patrick didn't say he loved me until our first-anniversary row."

"I remember. He got the date wrong, and you threw a cheese sandwich at him, and then you realised he was right."

"So I threw a cheese sandwich at myself to make up for it, and he told me I looked good with Cheddar in my fringe, and that he loved me."

"Thank God Fabio's more conventional. It could take years to engineer a situation where you have cheese in your hair."

"Oi, missus, my boyfriend's not conventional. He's romantic."

"Enjoy it, then!" Ellen sounded ever so slightly exasperated.

If you discounted rolling about on fur rugs with Italian nobility, this was Sunny's favourite way to end the day: a mug of hot milk and her cousins around the kitchen table.

The quiet circle of three conjured up her childhood. Ellen and Jojo were constants in a turbulent world, and she appreciated them, even though she had murderous impulses towards Jojo daily and could never fathom Ellen's cool approach to life, particularly men. Sitting here with them in the lamplight had a timeless tinge; instinctively, Sunny knew she would feel nostalgic for it some day when life drew them apart.

Jojo spoke. "You have an awful double chin from this angle, Sunny."

"And I love you, too." Sunny felt far too tranquil to point out that Jojo possessed a double everything.

"I've got an update on the Chudleigh Cad," Ellen told them. "According to Mrs Wilde, none of the decoys have gone yet, although she has suspicions that a thermal longjohn by the bins was tweaked." She disturbed the skin on her milk with her forefinger. "I have a suspect."

"Who? Who?" asked Sunny, expectantly.

"Guy!" Ellen was emphatic.

"No, no, no," scoffed Sunny, disappointed. "He's got too much to lose. If it got in the papers it could ruin his career."

"But he has the motive," said Ellen, galvanised. "He and Chloe are arguing about babies, so their sex life is probably fraught. Maybe he can only, you know . . ." she looked uncomfortable ". . . *find relief* by stealing knickers. *And*," she ploughed on, as the others geared up to disagree, "he hardly ever works, so he has plenty of time to skulk about and plan his deeds."

"You make him sound like Jack the Ripper. Are you like this in court?" asked Sunny.

Ellen reminded her that Guy was "at large" on the night of the stake-out. "You said he stopped by Mrs Wilde's pants."

"Yes. To stare in disbelief, as any sane man would."

Jojo was adamant. "It's so obvious. It's Boiled Egg."

"Poor old Ben?" laughed Sunny, who'd changed her tune about him. "He's far too timid to do anything so daring."

"Isn't it usually timid men who have these sort of compulsions?" mused Ellen.

"Hmm . . ." Sunny was tripped up by her own argument.

"And we know for a fact he's sexually frustrated because he can't even talk to a woman without going puce," said Jojo.

Ellen was coming round. "Maybe it *is* him. He fits the profile. Maybe it's not Guy but Ben."

An idea had been cooking for a while in Sunny's mind. "What about *Ernest*?" she asked, imbuing his name with malevolence.

Pooh-poohing energetically, Ellen defended the dapper little man. "He's too proper. He gets his clothes delivered straight from the 1940s."

"All right. Try this for size." Feeling that a showy theory, a kind of *Da Vinci Code* one, was called for, Sunny said confidently, "It's Mrs Wilde, looking for attention."

"The truth is," said Ellen, "we'll probably never know who the Cad is."

"You're right. I'm off to bed," said Sunny, on the tail-end of a virtuoso yawn.

Jojo asked, "Got any more pages for me?"

"Nope." Sunny avoided her eye.

"Ah. I see." Jojo had found a fleshy bit and she waggled her dagger, as usual. "Too scared to write in case it comes true?"

Sunny blew a raspberry, which startled Marmite so much she spat a hairball into the sink.

Archly, Jojo said, "There's an easy way to test your powers."

"Don't say 'powers'," snapped Sunny. She relented to say, "How?" in as offhand a way as she could muster.

"Well," said Jojo slowly, fully aware that she had all Sunny's attention, "I'd write something really specific, something like . . ." Jojo was no actress: Sunny could tell that there was nothing remotely off the cuff about her inspiration. "I know! Send Lucinda and Sergio off on an exotic holiday and see if Fabio suggests that you go away together."

"Sleep tight," cooed Sunny, making her way to the door. "Don't let the bedbugs maul you to death."

As Ellen slept that night, the tip-tap of typing sounded from under the covers of the bed opposite. Possibly the tip-tap of somebody typing the details of an exotic holiday.

CHAPTER
FIFTEEN

All this talk of knickers had highlighted an unpalatable truth: Sunny's pants weren't up to a love affair with an Italian count. In fact, she doubted if her tatty collection of once-white bikini briefs and their counterpart tired bras was worthy of a fling with Leonard. When she'd been dating Calum, her two "good" sets (one green, one pink) had sufficed for their infrequent trysts, but disrobing with Fabio was becoming a habit she was glad to encourage, and she needed more window dressing.

After an uncomfortable ten minutes in a Marks & Spencers changing room, while an amiable middle-aged woman ran a tape round her bosom and chatted easily of overspill and chafing, Sunny filled a basket with cheeky, sexy bras and pants. She could practically hear the school leaver on the till thinking, New boyfriend!

Meandering through Soho, near Waldhorn Truss Levy's offices, Sunny felt nostalgic for this lively, filthy corner of London where the hookers and the executives coexist peaceably. Turning a corner, she almost meandered into Alfie.

Very much in his natural habitat in his Paul Smith plumage, Alfie kissed her, as he always did. "I hear you're in love. That must be why you look so pretty."

Alfie always said the right thing. Sunny missed him, she realised. "You work too hard, Castro. I don't see enough of you these days."

A nervous voice chipped in, "Whoops! My fault, I'm afraid!" Liz caught up with Alfie.

"Hello again." Sunny jumped out of the way of a grown man on a weeny scooter. "What are you two up to?" She stopped short of asking if they were off for an afternoon of rumpy-pumpy in an expense-account hotel room: it seemed the wrong question for a woman wearing polyester culottes.

"Another bloody meeting," Alfie enlightened her. He looked tired, as if somebody had taken a wet cloth and blurred his edges.

Liz tugged at Alfie's sleeve, like a child might. "Just popping in here for mints," she said, and ducked into a newsagent's.

Instantly, Alfie leaned towards Sunny and spoke so intensely that the raucous street noises fell away. "Sun, do you know what's up with Sarah? She's behaving very strangely."

Oh dear. "Never get involved with a couple's fights" was one of Sunny's cardinal rules. She'd lost friends that way. "Is she?" This was sufficiently non-committal, she felt, without sounding rudely uninterested.

"After bugging me to get involved, she's now pulled out. She's ranting about this stupid bloody Bilnius bastard thing, which Porqy Peeces's advisers have told

200

me is harmless in such small amounts." Alfie grimaced, confused. "I'm starting to think she might have some kind of issue with Liz."

Poor Alfie, thought Sunny. Astute enough to clamber up advertising's greasy pole, he couldn't recognise his own wife's overwhelming jealousy. "It sounds like you need to talk," she advised, with repetitive banality.

"It always turns into a row," Alfie lamented. "And I'm so damned tired all the time." He looked it. His cheeky face was as white as his bleached linen shirt.

"It'll be all right." Sunny injected as much confidence as she could into the trite reassurance. "It's you and Sarah: it's always all right."

The smile that Alfie dredged up wasn't convincing. Liz emerged from the shop, waving her Tic Tacs in a buoyant manner, and Sunny said goodbye to them both.

Glancing back as she reached the corner, Sunny saw that Liz had taken Alfie's arm. The woman's comfortably built torso leaned towards Alfie's in a conspiratorial way.

The sun went in. Soho looked like the dingy slapper it is at heart, and Sunny vowed to knock the next forty-something she saw on a scooter into the gutter.

"Am I keeping you up?"

"No. No. God, no." Patrick corrected his slump, opened his eyes wide and assumed the expression of a Labrador who'd just got a tip-off about a job lot of Winalot. "I'm having a great time."

"Why were your eyes closed?" Sunny was sardonic.

"Can I get away with saying I was resting them, like my nan does?" asked Patrick, with what he evidently hoped was a lovable grin.

It wasn't. "Nope."

"Then, I suppose, the truth is, I'm knackered. Sorry, Sun. I was fascinated to hear all about your new knickers, honest, but Serena is a hard taskmaster."

"She looks it."

"I presumed that presenting was cushy. It's bloody hard." Patrick picked up his Guinness wearily. "I'm used to work, but this talking-to-camera lark is tough. I miss getting my hands dirty." Patrick held up pristine hands with a scowl.

Archly, Sunny said, "I see the title's changed." When she got no reply, she said, wonderingly, "*StyleScaping*. Hmmm. Not terribly you."

"No." Patrick was curt. "I was overruled."

"By the demanding Serena?"

"You don't like Serena, do you?"

Taken aback, Sunny answered, "Of course I do," far too quickly.

"You don't. I can tell." Patrick toyed with a beer mat. "You jealous?"

"Eh?" Sunny's eyes widened. "What exactly would I be jealous of?" The list in Sunny's mind was long (better hair, longer legs, snazzier job, a degree in something difficult), but she didn't intend to share it with Patrick.

Evenly, Patrick replied, "I thought you might be jealous because I get on so well with her."

202

"Whoah there, Mr Big Head," protested Sunny, noting Patrick's casual assertion that he "got on so well" with Serena: just why that should vex her Sunny wasn't sure, but it did. "If you want to cosy up to a tyrannical stick insect, that's your business. Why should I be jealous? After all, it's years since we . . ." Sunny's self-righteous head of steam gave out. "Since we, you know," she plumped for.

"Yes, yes, I realise that." Also embarrassed, Patrick harrumphed awkwardly. "I didn't mean . . . Just an ego trip. Sorry." He let his head droop back. "Ignore me. I'm too tired to think straight. Just talk and I'll contribute occasionally."

So Sunny told him about Jojo's sore feet, which were accustomed to padding from sofa to bed but which now tramped all over the capital; about Sarah's kamikaze attempts to get Alfie's attention; about the Stop Press news that every one of the decoy knickers had been filched. She ended with, "And, by the way, Ellen is much better." Sunny was quietly dismayed that Patrick hadn't already asked after her.

"I know. I popped in on Sunday. We had a good chat. She's going to be all right."

"A good chat? On Sunday?" Sunny was confused. "Are you sure? She was monosyllabic."

"Well, like I said, we chatted."

"Do you still think we were right not to call the police?" That evil little doubt was loath to leave.

"Yes." He was emphatic. "I don't think Dave is a danger to society."

"Would you say that if you were a girl?"

"Yes, but I'd say it like this." Adopting a shrill falsetto, Patrick squeaked, "I don't think Dave is a danger to society."

Determined not to laugh, Sunny scolded, "You know what I mean."

"Listen. You did the right thing." Patrick was serious now.

"You're getting very butch in your old age," murmured Sunny.

"How's the latest pastel-porn extravaganza coming along?"

"The book's going fine, thank you very much." Sunny was tart. This was a well-trodden conversational path.

"All this romance bollocks. Why would any independent, intelligent woman need doors held open for her? Does a confident woman need to be showered with OTT compliments?" One of Patrick's favourite tirades, it had barely changed over the years. "A woman wants a partner, not a protector."

"Sometimes even strong, independent women like to see a red rose on their pillow," said Sunny, passionately, with a suspicion that they weren't just discussing her frothy work: Fabio was being criticised, too. "What's the harm in telling a 'woman' " — she sketched quotation marks in the air with her fingers "— that she looks good?"

"It's demeaning," Patrick contended. "It implies that you paint your face like a good little girl and wait for a man to notice."

204

"You never did." Ouch. Sunny hated the spiteful side of herself that fired barbs like that.

"I always thought you looked . . ." Patrick caught her eye and grinned. "Change of subject, methinks. It's my round."

"Patrick." Sunny caught his sleeve as he passed her on the way to the bar. "Don't say 'methinks'."

Beastless, Sarah was at number thirteen's kitchen table when Sunny drifted in from the pub. "Hiya!" she sang happily, not sounding at all like a woman who was hanging her husband up by his reproductive parts and leaving him to dry. "Your aunty and I are just admiring your purchases."

The pile of new underwear lay between them, in all its silk and satin glory. Spluttering and stammering, Sunny scooped up the knickers and bras. Sunny was the product of a home where all the adults left the room, coughing, during the mating scenes in wildlife programmes: there was no way of coping with her nun aunt fingering her lingerie.

"I've stood down from helping Alfie," said Sarah, with artificial glee. "Now I can really show them!"

Sunny knew a brave face when she saw it. It pained her to see Sarah groping so blindly down the wrong path. "So you're convinced that Bilnius doodah is the big bad wolf and can cause real health problems?"

"Of course!" said Sarah, passionately. She added, perhaps more revealingly than she knew, "And even if it's harmless, it shouldn't be in what claims to be a natural product."

"I'm boring myself by now, but I have to say it again: can't you sort this out with Alfie and Porqy Peeces?"

"Whose side are you on?" demanded Sarah.

"I didn't know I had to take sides," said Sunny, sadly. This was moving way too fast.

Sister Jane interrupted. "Poker?" she suggested, flourishing the pack of cards she always seemed to carry in that capacious handbag, along with a rosary and a flask of tea.

It changed the subject but not the mood. Sarah and Sister Jane were evenly matched, and at about midnight Sunny bowed out and crept to her bed.

It was a phrase Sunny rarely heard. "You work too hard," Fabio had cooed down the phone on Saturday morning.

"We-ll . . ." Not liking to contradict him, Sunny had carried on excavating her Cadbury's Whirl with her tongue.

"Today will be dedicated to pleasure, *cara*."

A vivid snapshot of Fabio, naked on a futon with Jaffa Cakes placed strategically along his body flashed before Sunny's excitable eyes.

"Today you go to the spa."

It was churlish to be disappointed, so Sunny was looking carefully delighted when Fabio drew up in a silver Aston Martin.

"Flash," thought Sunny, wondering just how many cars her boyfriend owned. Sharp as ever, in impeccable tailoring, Fabio shone with wealth and well-being, as if he'd been styled for a starring role in an Italian movie.

But he wasn't a character in a film; he was here beside her, and he was in love with her. And he owned an Aston Martin. Truth, Sunny now knew, is stranger than fiction.

Roaring out of the drive, Fabio hooted the horn at Patrick, who had to jump into a hedge to get out of their way. Nosing across Putney Bridge, drawing envious looks from every male with eyesight, Fabio said abruptly, "You had a relationship with him?"

Sunny proceeded with caution. "Well, yes. About a zillion years ago."

Slapping the steering wheel with his palm, Fabio spat, "I knew it! I was so blind." He snorted like a racehorse after the Grand National.

Alarmed, Sunny said, Judas-like, "It was no big deal." She salved her conscience by adding silently, "Well, it wasn't to him."

Stationary at the lights, the car throbbing, Fabio was evidently trying to remain calm, which had the effect of making his girlfriend extremely nervous. "And yet you remain friends. This puzzles me."

"Why?" Uncomfortable, Sunny fiddled with the array of buttons on her door. The window slid up. "We get on well." The window slid down. "Not *that* well." The window slid up. "He makes me laugh." The window slid down. "A bit."

"He makes you laugh." Fabio seemed to be examining this idea. He didn't seem to be mad about it. "You were lovers. How can you forget this?" Fabio's face, designed to smile, bore a scowl. "And please, *cara*, stop playing with the window."

"Don't you like Patrick?" Sunny asked pathetically.

"Like him?" Suddenly, Fabio guffawed like an operatic villain. "I HATE HIM!" He revved the engine, and they sprang away from the lights. "I did not know of your history when first I met him. Now I know. NOW," he yelled unexpectedly, "now I know." He slammed the gears. "I hate him like I hate every man who has seen your beautiful white body. I wish he was dead, but no, he is OUTSIDE YOUR WINDOW!" When Italians shout, they *shout*. "He is . . ." and here Fabio sneered dramatically ". . . he is PLANTING FLOWERS!"

The air between Sunny and Fabio crackled with the ferocity of his emotions. Sitting stock still, Sunny was anxious, but perversely delighted. At last, a man with passion. Instinctively, she knew that Fabio wouldn't buy a camper van if she left him: he'd probably throw himself off the nearest mountain (possibly one that his family owned). "You don't have any reason to worry," said Sunny soothingly. "I never loved him." Something deep inside her wilted when she said that, but she had to think of Fabio.

"But you laugh, ha, ha, ha, and you make the chat and you smile like a Cheshire cheese Cat when you are with him." Fabio's command of English plummeted as his anger rose.

Finding this sexy, Sunny said again, "You mustn't worry yourself."

"I have told you, *cara*," he said angrily, "I AM THE JEALOUS MAN!"

And I am the aroused woman, thought Sunny.

208

The spa was part of a hotel that seemed to have been dipped in taupe paint. The floor of reception was taupe; the Hessian walls were taupe; the receptionist's lip gloss was taupe. It brought out his eyes.

"Di Sica Carelli." Fireworks over, Fabio was self-possessed and polite, as usual. "We have a booking for the spa."

That "we" puzzled Sunny as they were led down taupe corridors. She knew she'd bagged herself one of those rare males who could approach moisturiser without giggling, but the thought of a man spending a whole day at the spa was unthinkable.

"You're just having a massage, yeah?" she said to Fabio. Most men could manage a massage. Even her dad had had a massage, although it had happened ten years ago, and he still went red when he talked about it.

"Plus a facial peel. And manicure, pedicure. Some reiki, if there's time. Arun is an absolute master." He kissed her at the door to the changing rooms. "See you later, *cara*."

The dressing gown was ultra-soft, and the waffle slippers so white that Sunny felt sorry for them having to accept delivery of her grubby toes. Sunny's previous spa visits had all been the result of gift vouchers from boyfriends. She had tumbled excitedly in, holding the vouchers aloft as if they meant peace in our time. Then it would dawn on her that she was only entitled to two treatments, and pretty mealy-mouthed ones at that. "Choose from a mini facial or an express manicure," a receptionist would tell her sullenly. "The rest is extra." Usually, Sunny would stump up for one other treatment, bitterly regretting her choice as soon as she'd made it, wishing she'd plumped for a lava wrap, or for having a weird electronic machine rolled over her face.

Today, there were no choices to be made: she was booked in for the whole experience. Lotions were spread on her. She was wrapped in seaweed. Aromatic oils were applied to her pulse points. The soles of her feet were pressed. Careful and delicate attention was paid to every millimetre of her neglected surface area.

This was such a treat. It was such a wonderful gesture, the ultimate in luxurious pampering. And it was so fucking boring.

Magazine articles raved about the "feel-good factor" of spas: why didn't they ever mention the "feel-self-conscious factor"? It just wasn't right to have a stranger's nose hovering inches from your paper-knickered arse. When the technician asked her to turn over, Sunny performed an awkward heave and flop, terrified that she'd be the first client to roll off the narrow couch and slide, on a slick of aromatic oils, across the limestone floor, out through reception and under a bus.

Standing helpless against a white tiled wall as two beauticians hosed mud from her naked body, Sunny recalled similar scenes in Amnesty International literature. Didn't other women feel embarrassed during this sadism? Didn't they cringe when the pedicurist commented, in a caressing voice, "Rather a lot of hard skin here"? Didn't they itch to slap away the hand of the trichologist as she merrily "evacuated" pores with a gigantic magnifying glass? Perhaps they were too busy feeling good.

When her four hours of personal-space invasion was up, she took a deep breath and confronted the glass in her changing room.

Sunny wasn't expecting rosy, healthy skin and eyes as bright as a summer day: she'd had too many beauty treatments to be that naïve. But neither had she expected the apparition that met her eyes. Matted hair, scarlet cheeks, a face so oily it looked as if somebody had been diligently rubbing grease into it for hours. But then, Sunny reminded herself, somebody had.

Tugging her jeans on was tricky over her super-smooth, fragrant, hairless but horribly slippy legs Her camisole stuck to her clammy breasts, and there was seaweed up her nose.

It was predictable that Fabio should look like a star ready for his close-up. His hair was glossy, without the Rasta ringlets his girlfriend had acquired. By the look of his clothes, spa elves had pressed his suit and polished his shoes while he was in the floatation tank. Lounging against a taupe column in reception, he was completely motionless, like an artfully arranged portrait.

Fabio looked so celestial that Sunny's oiled, plucked, massaged and reiki-ed brain allowed one of those self-lacerating thoughts through her defences. *He's too good to be true*, squeaked her ying. *Shut up with that crap!* barked her yang. Or maybe it was the other way round.

CHAPTER
SIXTEEN

There were good answers to Fabio's question "Why haven't you ever cooked for me, my darling?", but Sunny didn't want to bang on about food poisoning, or cracked teeth, or the dumpling that had concussed Marmite. Instead, in her posts-pa daze, she went straight to the ready-meal section of one of the posher supermarkets, filled a basket with expensive ready meals and was back out in the sunshine in ten minutes flat.

From her left, over by the conga line of trolleys, she could hear a chant, a rhythmic repetition of something sung. Oh, Gawd, thought Sunny, a protest. She hated high-street protests, studiously avoided petitions and zigzagged into fast traffic to avoid charity salespeople.

Looking resolutely ahead, a navy-blue shape managed to catch her eye. I'm seeing imaginary nuns since Aunty Jane arrived, she thought, amused.

But this blue blur really was a nun. And it stopped chanting to shout, "Yoo hoo! Sunny, love!"

Every sinew in her oiled legs shrieked, "RUN," but Sunny knew she had to turn round. "Jesus, God on a bike," she blasphemed impressively, taking in the scene by the trolleys.

Huddled together stood Sister Jane and Sarah. A little to one side, on a crate, sat Jojo, murder in her eyes.

Walking stiffly towards them, Sunny read the homemade placards they were holding. Sister Jane's read, "PORQY PEECES — BIG SISTER IS WATCHING YOU." Sarah was brandishing "FASCIST SNACK". They were both shouting, "JUST SAY NO TO BILNIUS RED F!"

"Catchy," murmured Sunny.

"Just trying to get our message across." Sarah was defensive and rigid.

"Jojo's not chanting," Sunny pointed out, maliciously.

"Jojo's fecking starving," said Jojo. She didn't seem to share the others' fervour.

"Is this necessary?" Sunny asked, wearily.

"Somebody has to stand up for consumers' rights." Sarah's mask was back in place. "Don't they, Sister Jane?"

"Absolutely." Sister Jane, eyes now twinkling at warp speed, started the chant again and thrust a leaflet into Sunny's hand.

Scanning the prose, and ignoring the picture of a rabbit having something poured into its eye, Sunny said anxiously, "This could be libellous."

"Let them sue me. I'm performing a public service." Sarah poked the warm air with her placard, before exhorting Jojo, "Put a bit of life into it, woman."

After a Saturday being sadistically pampered, and a Sunday exploring Fabio's peaks and gullies like a

213

determined sherpa, Sunny vowed to spend Monday immersed in her writing.

She had to admit it: Lucinda and Sergio had started to bore her. They were in love, they had sex, they peeled fruit for one another. She slumped back in her chair, like a listless schoolgirl in an interminable maths class, and made the mistake of peering out of the window.

Things were more interesting out there. Some turf had been laid across the boggy garden, zigzagging from corner to corner. A team of young guys, like worker ants with fit bums, were busily patting it down, while more of their ilk manhandled large trees about.

Serena was talking urgently into a mobile phone, writing things on her clipboard and shouting at Patrick to put his mug down and get into position. Over by the catering van, Patrick gulped his tea and trotted over to where a taped X decreed he should stand.

He was barely recognisable in crisp chinos and groovily layered, obviously new T-shirts. His face looked different, and it wasn't just because of the teased and gelled hair. Patrick's eyes looked fatigued, she noticed with a pang. He needed an early night, with Ozzie and a *Seinfeld* boxed set.

Serena strode over to Patrick and tweaked a strand of his hair. Patrick didn't shy from Serena's presumptuous touch; he smiled at it.

Only a mean-hearted girl could be annoyed if the man she'd left years before was looking tired not because of work but because of a broomhandle named Serena.

Which made Sunny a mean-hearted girl.

"Be glad for him," she told herself. "All his dreams are coming true." Sunny reminded herself, comfortably, that all hers were, too.

"Oi, leave my aunty alone." Sunny had a big and particularly meaty bone to pick with Sarah when her friend rang her later that afternoon. "I don't want her getting involved with your nutty protests."

"Involved? She's the linchpin." Sarah was defiantly unapologetic. "If only there were more liberated free-thinkers like your aunt, I wouldn't have any trouble getting the message across." Sarah gushed, possibly to deflect more bone-picking. "What a role model. She must have had a massive influence on you when you were growing up."

"Er, yes. Massive," concurred Sunny untruthfully. Sister Jane had certainly influenced her never to wear top-to-toe navy, but her main role in Sunny's youth had been to inspire teenaged conversations with various cousins about whether Aunty Jane had ever "done it". "Are you sure that liberated and free-thinking describe her?" asked Sunny. "The Catholic Church isn't exactly a hotbed of liberal thought: they're still trying to convince gays it's something they ate."

"What's a nun if not the first feminist?" demanded Sarah. "Sister Jane opted out of patriarchal society to enter a female world. She chose not to marry and have baby after baby, like other Irish women of her generation. Nobody is the boss of Sister Jane. Unlike her cowed, dependent sisters, handcuffed to their husbands and pathetically reliant on their goodwill."

215

Unsure whether Sarah was using the term "sisters" literally or metaphorically, Sunny couldn't help thinking of her mother and her other aunts. Cowed? Hmm. Annie in full flight was anything but cowed: she'd been the victim of an attempted mugging once, and it was the only incident on police files where they'd been called by the assailant. Sunny's own mum didn't seem pathetically dependent on her husband. She ran the house like a boot camp, expecting and receiving total obedience from Sunny's dad, who had given up smoking, drinking, carbohydrates and fun under her watchful eye. "You'll live longer, thanks to me," she was fond of telling him, prompting him to mutter into his newspaper, "And thanks to you, it'll feel like it." No, Sunny didn't come from a line of forelock-tugging, please-don't-hit-me women: they were all independent types. And all barking mad, of course. Even Sister Jane was showing marked signs of O'Brien eccentricity.

"I'm glad you get on so well. And I agree that she is one in a million. But she's naïve and —"

"Hold on, that lady is not naïve," laughed Sarah.

Exasperated, Sunny finally said exactly what she was thinking. "Look, she's sincere. She doesn't have your mixed motives."

"I don't know what you mean," said Sarah, and from the other end of the line, Sunny could hear butter trying, but failing, to melt in her friend's mouth.

It was a good idea, a nice idea, a thoughtful idea. It was Ellen's idea: "I bet Aunty Jane would love to go to a musical," she said.

"Yeeuk. I hate musicals," Sunny protested, dishing up a confused dinner of pasta with curry sauce. "I mean, why keep bursting into song? And the plots are crap. And the blokes are gay. And they're so expensive. I always want to leave in the interval."

"Have you finished?" enquired Ellen, patiently. "Maybe I should start again. I bet our middle-aged, quiet-living, conservative, gentle-natured aunt who is a nun would like to go to a show and maybe we should treat her to one, because she's barely left the convent in the past twenty years, and she's obviously going through a bit of a crisis, and we love her."

"Which night shall we go?" asked Sunny weakly, arranging some stale poppadoms on a plate.

"Well, let's see. I'm free until, ooooh, approximately 2048," smiled Ellen.

The incident with Dave had unhappened. Ellen was laughing, she was enjoying her work, she was even making her habitual jokes about being hopelessly single. Sunny was relieved to see the old Ellen again, but there had been no gradual recovery and that worried her. One day Ellen had been morose and preoccupied; the next she was making her own muesli and wondering whether to dye her hair. The subject of Dave and the party was superglued shut. Sunny instinctively knew that this was an unhealthy attitude. There might come a day when the party, and the mysterious Dublin incident, and any other lurking horrors might clamour to get out into the daylight all at once.

"I'm not quite so available, because I have a handsome, wealthy, mad-about-me boyfriend." Sunny dodged the flung yoghurt pot. "I know I can do next Saturday, though. No need to check with Aunty Jane, she's bound to be free. Which tourist attraction is she at today?"

Wandering in, freshly showered and smelling like a plastic bouquet, Jojo had the answer. "She's round Sarah's."

Groaning, Sunny said, "They'd better not be planning any more silly supermarket protests."

"They're grown-ups," said Ellen, snapping a poppadom. "That's their business."

"No." Fabio shook his head, as if miserably conscious of his shortcomings. "I do not know Spam."

"Good. Well, don't bring it up," warned Sunny illogically as they entered the spiffy champagne bar. She spotted them immediately. Alfie and Sarah sat, like bookends, at either end of a large leather sofa in the middle of the flatteringly lit panelled room, enough space between them to park a Ford Focus. With a fixed grin, Sunny whispered to Fabio, "Fasten your seat belt, it's going to be a bumpy ride."

"Seat belt?" he whispered back, looking puzzled.

"Never mind." They had reached the frosty pair. "Hello, you two!" sang Sunny, as if she'd never been so pleased to see anybody in her life. She bent down and kissed Alfie, who seemed to be trying to smile, but his mouth wasn't in the mood. She did the same to Sarah, who received her kiss, and Fabio's, with the kind of demeanour Ann Widdecombe might display if bear-hugged by an Elvis impersonator. "Isn't this nice?" Sunny lied.

"Yes," said Sarah flatly. "Isn't it?"

"It's good to see you." Alfie was trying a bit harder.

"But you have no champagne!" Fabio waggled a finger at them. "This won't do!" He went straight to the bar. Sunny considered going with him; in fact, she considered going home, but she remembered her manners and sat between her friends. She judged it carefully and placed herself perfectly in the middle of the Sahara between them.

"So." She slapped her knees with her hands. "What's new?"

Alfie leaned his head back on to the sofa. "You really don't want to know."

Conversationally, Sarah said, "I've gone mad, apparently," obsessively pressing down the strict pleats of her Prada skirt like, well, someone who'd gone mad.

"Not here, please," groaned Alfie.

"Sunny knows everything," snapped Sarah. "She's as disgusted with your lady friend as I am."

"Ooh. Well." Sunny didn't relish being roped in. "Now then." She defended her neutral position as eloquently as she was able. "Ahhhh . . ."

"Lady friend? Give me strength," muttered Alfie, running his hand over his downy head.

Sarah, looking resolutely at Sunny and not at her husband, spoke in a clattering staccato. "I should stick to what I know. I'm the little lady at home. I should bake cakes, mop floors, keep quiet. According to my *husband*." Sarah pronounced the title like a baroque insult.

"Does that sound like me?" Now it was Alfie who was appealing to Sunny and ignoring his wife.

"Well. Hmmm." Sunny, splat in the middle, looked beseechingly over at the bar, but Fabio was chatting in his easy way to the pretty barmaid. Even in her present predicament, Sunny took a second to admire his beauty. The brown of his velvet jacket seemed to meld with the warm wood around him. His face glowed among the muted tones. He looked, she thought with a chill, like an elaborate piece of computer-generated imagery in a big-budget movie.

She was dragged back to the war zone as Alfie spat, "Mop floors! I don't want her to mop floors, Sunny, I want her to be happy. But it would be nice if she didn't flush my career down the toilet in the meantime. Is that asking too much?"

Sunny cottoned on: it didn't matter what she said. She could have recited the ten times table wearing her bra for earmuffs; they weren't listening to her, or to each other.

"He should try it sometime, vegetating at home with a couple of mini-hims." Sarah leaned over and poked Sunny's arm. "How would he like it if he spent his day with small people who consider Postman Pat the pinnacle of Western culture?"

"Has she forgotten the nannies?" Alfie asked Sunny, who was guiltily thinking the same thing. "The string of young women who not only do all the boring bits for her, like bringing up our children, but are handy for mindless bullying when the mood takes her."

"Actually, Sunny —" Sarah prodded Sunny sharply on her shoulder to regain her attention "— I haven't forgotten the nanny. As it's me who has to find them, interview them, train them and then sack them when they chat on a mobile while our sons play with knives, I'm not likely to, am I?"

"Do you know," laughed Alfie maliciously, "I feel sorry for her. Poor little thing, having to deal with staff as well as shopping, lunching, having her nails sharpened, while I fritter away every waking hour in an office, earning the vast sums of money it takes to run such a cold, selfish, deluded, spoilt bitch!"

There was an infuriated noise from Sarah's end of the sofa. Even Sunny was shocked at Alfie, who was usually so mild and so slow to anger. She frowned at him, disappointed, and he lowered his eyes.

Fabio put a tray of champagne and glasses on the table. "Are we all happy?" he smiled.

"I know the English phrase for this," said Fabio gently against her hair, as he held Sunny close in the Chudleigh Court lift. "It is the brush-off, no?"

"It is not the brush-off, *no*," said Sunny decisively. "Honestly, I can't think of anything I'd rather do than mess about naked with you, but having dinner with Sarah and Alfie has left me kind of sad."

"Why?"

"*Why?* echoed Sunny incredulously, pulling away to look at his face. "Couldn't you feel the killer vibes?"

"We spoke of films and what we like to eat. It was perfectly pleasant."

"But they wanted to kill each other with their soup spoons." Sunny leaned against his nice, broad, velvet chest again. "Never mind," she said, wondering disloyally at his lack of empathy. "It really got to me. I'm so fond of them both, and they're going through hell. So I'd kind of like to be on my own. Do you understand?" she asked.

"Of course, *cara*." Fabio kissed the top of her head. "But you must promise me that when you want to talk about these things, you come to me, darling?" There was a question in Fabio's dark eyes.

Sunny understood the code. "I'll come to you." Not Patrick, she added silently, and somewhat guiltily. It was time to start trusting Fabio with her innermost thoughts and feelings. It was time to unfold.

As if to underline what she would be missing by staying at Chudleigh Court, Fabio's goodnight kiss was a belter. "Ooooh," she breathed, as they stopped for air. "That's made me go all tingly. You give me shingles, Fabio," she teased.

"I hope not." Fabio drew back to look sternly down at her. "This is a painful, blistering rash. Do you feel unwell?"

"No, no, I . . . Never mind. Goodnight, Fabio."

"I love you, darling. I'll miss you."

As Fabio retreated reluctantly to the lift, Sunny felt a spasm, like sudden hunger. She wanted to tell him she loved him. "Fabio!" she shouted softly.

He turned, expectant.

"I'll miss you, too," was all she said.

CHAPTER
SEVENTEEN

"Marmite!" That cat was getting too cocky. Sunny yanked the curtains closed. "You are a fugitive. An outlaw. You are deep underground in the FBI witness-protection scheme. You do *not* sit in the window licking clumps of God knows what off your arse."

Now that Jojo was being frogmarched around London's historic sites, Marmite had taken to hanging around Sunny. Glad of the company, Sunny gave the cat an absentminded tickle every now and then as *Fatal Crescendo* took shape.

The sharp rat-a-tat-tat at the front door could only be Mrs Wilde. "She saw you!" Sunny locked Marmite in the bedroom and dragged her feet to the front door.

"That knocker could do with a dab of Brasso," Mrs Wilde greeted her.

"Hello," said Sunny, rummaging in the attic of her brain for a good excuse for having a cat-shaped item in her window. "I can explain." Sunny had plumped for *I was making a glove puppet for a young friend and was testing it at the window.* She swallowed hard but was interrupted before she could embark on this flimsy narrative.

"I'm canvassing residents to see if there are any fresh leads." Mrs Wilde stared imperiously down at Sunny.

"So, this isn't about the —" Catching herself just in time, Sunny didn't use the cat word.

"The what?" Mrs Wilde was querulous, her pencilled eyebrows raised high over tired brown eyes. It occurred to Sunny that if Mrs Wilde lost five stone, stopped buying kaftans, smiled occasionally and gave up drawing on her eyebrows, she might be presentable. Possibly, back in the neolithic age, when Leonard had somehow found the nerve to ask this slab of angry flesh to marry him, she had been attractive.

That must have been long ago, and maybe Leonard had been on medication, because the man lurking in her shadow looked incapable of such a feat. Without thinking, Sunny heard herself ask, "How long have you two been married?"

Her face crumpling in confusion, like a folded boxing glove, Mrs Wilde said, "What's that got to do with the price of fish?"

From behind her, a nervous voice said, "Fourteen years, three months, four days and . . ." He paused. "Two hours."

"How romantic." Sunny bent round Mrs Wilde's girth to smile at Leonard. "You know it exactly."

"Yes," murmured Leonard. He didn't look a romantic figure, with his balding head and drooping cardigan. His small mouth, almost hidden behind a grey moustache, smiled a tiny smile at Sunny. "It was a memorable day."

224

"Certainly was. Leonard's top hat was two sizes too small." Even Mrs Wilde was smiling now. "The photographs look like I married a peanut."

Acutely sorry for Leonard, Sunny shot him a sympathetic look, but those mild myopic eyes were back on his brogues.

"But I didn't marry him for his looks," said Mrs Wilde decisively. "Or his intellect. Or his personality." Behind her, Leonard shrank even more. Any more of this nostalgia and he'd be Marmite's height. "Or his —"

"We don't have any leads," interjected Sunny, eager to save Leonard any more of this casual humiliation.

Disappointed, Mrs Wilde left and Marmite was free to roam the wide open spaces of number thirteen once more.

An army marches on its stomach. And a writer writes on hers, Sunny thought, rubbing her eyes and heading for the kitchen. Dinner felt like years ago.

"You're playing Monopoly." Sunny was suspicious, frowning at her aunt and her flatmates. "And the television isn't even on."

"Pull up a chair," suggested Sister Jane.

"Run. Save yourself," said Jojo blankly.

Amused, Sunny leaned against the sink, arms folded. "Who's winning?"

Ellen pointed her small metal dog at Sister Jane. "She has God on her side."

"We all have him on our side," said Sister Jane. "Ellen, you owe me a hundred pounds in rent, love."

Marmite, who seemed to dislike this new regime as much as Jojo, jumped on to the board and batted the top hat across the room.

"That's it!" squealed Jojo. "We can't play on. I can't remember where I was!"

"You were on Baker Street," said Ellen calmly.

"And you're in the shit," warned Jojo, replacing the top hat with a thump.

"Ellen's in the what?" asked Sister Jane, turning to Jojo with a very particular look, part innocent child, part Stalin.

"She's in the poo," Jojo corrected herself.

"Aunty Jane," laughed Sunny, "as far as I'm concerned, you can stay for ever."

"Be careful," said Sister Jane, as she counted her wafer-thin money. "I might just do that."

Reading the card she'd picked, Jojo spread the news that she'd won second prize in a beauty contest. "Did you hear," she asked Sunny, "that the Cad got Sister Jane's pants?"

"Yes." Sister Jane beamed proudly. "He must be hard up to want my old navy bloomers, but he's got them. They disappeared on my way back from the launderette."

Unsure whether it was the correct etiquette to laugh at a nun's missing knickers, Sunny put a hand over her mouth. Ellen, her lips a wobbly line, concentrated on marshalling her little plastic houses and hotels.

"Who had access to the washbag?" asked Sunny intently.

"Listen to Inspector Wexford," mocked Jojo.

226

"Shuddup," said Sunny succinctly.

Sister Jane gave the question proper attention. "Well, I paused on the stairs to chat to one of those pretty girls next door. A pizza delivery man passed us. And Mrs Wilde, who was going up to the top floor to complain about some modern furniture she'd seen being delivered. Er, Guy, that nice-looking chap, stopped to say hello."

"It was him," Jojo chipped in. She looked to Sunny for corroboration and got a raise of the eyebrows.

"Ernest from the basement passed us as well. Said a very pleasant 'good evening'."

"What was Ernest doing on a floor *above* his flat?" Ellen wanted to know.

Sister Jane was stuck for an answer. "I couldn't tell you. But he had a very nice jacket on. And a lovely cravat."

"Do humans still wear cravats?" asked Sunny.

"Ernest does. Altogether a very well-turned-out man." Sister Jane threw the dice. "I think I heard he was widowed."

"Yes. His wife died last year," said Ellen. "An ambulance came in the middle of the night. It was terrible."

"It was brilliant," corrected Jojo, eyes gleaming. "We all got up, and had cocoa, and watched them take her body out."

Breaking the silence that Jojo had precipitated, Sunny asked tetchily, "Surely there's somewhere we could send her in for repair?"

★ ★ ★

Sister Jane minus her wimple was an unsettling sight.

"You have hair," said Sunny, in surprise, as they met over the kettle the next morning.

"Well, of course I have hair, you foolish chit." Sister Jane smoothed down her fringe. "I have the best hair in the family, Mother used to say."

Her modest boast was probably justified, but the bar wasn't set very high by Mary, Mo and Annie, who had experimented over the years with home perms, demiwaves, highlights, lowlights and rinses. Overtreated, tonged, rollered and pincurled, they'd all ended up with heads reminiscent of 1970s football-club managers.

"The grey suits you." Sister Jane's natural waves were simply cut. "Are you going to get rid of the rest of your costume?"

"No. Not yet, anyhow." She put her neat head on one side. "Would that bother you?"

"No," lied Sunny, imagining her middle-aged aunt suddenly going about in hotpants. "But does this mean you're not a real nun any more?"

"It's not as simple as that," laughed Sister Jane. "I'm a nun, all right. I'm just a nun on holiday. Now, get on with your work, and later on we'll all go for a lovely walk."

Alone again with her fictional lovers, Sunny decided it was time to add some more spice. Sergio and Lucinda's passionate and eye-popping encounter beside a waterfall was a pretty accurate recreation of the last night she'd spent with Fabio. Apart from the waterfall.

Sunny preferred things to be this way round: something happened and then she put it into a book. The days when she had been nervous to put pen to paper (or finger to keyboard) in case the ludicrous things she wrote came true seemed far away. Fabio was still larger than life, and utterly unlike anybody else she'd ever been in a lip-to-lip situation with, but he wasn't following her script. No luxurious trip had been mooted, no first-class air tickets had been tucked into her napkin. Fabio was his own man.

And, rather satisfyingly, *her* own man.

Sergio needed a schmaltzy line to throw at the ever-swooning Lucinda. "We are all we need," Sunny prompted him to say into his lover's perfect ear.

Without warning, a wave of longing trembled through her. She wasn't seeing him until Saturday. It would be a very long two days.

"Ready for that walk?" trilled Aunty Jane, from the hall.

Walking is good for you. Sunny knew that, she just never did it.

Not that Sunny had anything against walking: it was a necessary part of everyday life. Even Jojo walked to the fridge and back. But they both distrusted the whole philosophy of walking for its own sake. "Going up the towpath and back again," Jojo whinged. "What's the point?"

"Fresh air!" sang Sister Jane. "Exercise is food for the soul!" She strode ahead, her newly unfettered grey curls ruffled by the breeze tickling the riverbank.

"Has she told you anything about her plans?" asked Sunny discreetly.

"Not a dicky bird." Jojo wiped her perspiring face. "She still hasn't rung home, you know. Me mother called the other night in a right state."

"Look, girls!" shouted Sister Jane merrily, a hundred yards in front. "A heron!"

Under her breath, Jojo said, "If I want to see a heron I'll switch on the Animal Planet channel. But then," she qualified, "why would I want to see a fecking heron?"

"Don't you feel better for a good walk?" beamed Sister Jane at her nieces, slumped around the flat like abandoned mattresses.

"Oh, much, much better," wheezed Sunny, who was lying across the cooker.

A tinny rendition of a Beyoncé song suddenly rang out. "Ah. My phone." Sister Jane delved into the pocket of her Aline dress and fished out a mobile. "Hi," she said insouciantly into it.

"A mobile? Beyoncé?" Sunny perked up. "Do you think she texts her nun mates on that thing?" she asked Jojo, who seemed to be asleep up against the coatstand.

"Dunno. Shuddup. Feck off," drawled Jojo, dragging herself towards her bedroom and slamming the door behind her.

Into the phone, Sister Jane was saying, "Hold on a moment, I'll just go into another room." Passing Sunny, she asked, amused, "What are you looking at me like that for? Amn't I supposed to know how to use a mobile?"

230

"It just seems odd. Do you use them in the convent?"

"Oh, you'd be surprised. We have electrickery and horseless carriages as well," laughed her aunt. "Anyways, I'm not in the convent. I need it to keep abreast of things."

"What things?" Sunny was suspicious.

"Important things. Things that aren't any of your business," smiled Sister Jane. "Yet. I'll just finish this call and then I'll make us all a nice pot of tea." She reverted reassuringly to type as she pulled Sunny's bedroom door to.

The door didn't quite close.

Eavesdropping is a bad habit, just one of many that Sunny felt ashamed of. And enjoyed enormously.

"Yes, that's right," Sister Jane was saying. "I want to order thirty yards of it, please. Oh." The nun sounded disgruntled. "Metres? I'm no good at metres, dear. Can you work it out for me?" She listened for a moment, then said, relieved, "Grand. And I can pick it up in an hour? So that'll be twenty-seven metres of flesh-coloured PVC. Thank you."

Patrick, pint in hand, was in the middle of a long story about Ozzie's teeth. "The back ones seem to be rotting," he was saying worriedly.

A wry "Really?" was all that Sunny could muster up. Lovable though Ozzie was, she didn't relish updates on his decaying molars.

"That's what makes his breath stink. Some mornings he jumps on the bed to lick my face and it's as if somebody's thrown a tramp at me."

"You really know how to impress a girl with your suave talk."

"Oh, sorry," apologised Patrick indignantly. "Not romantic enough for you? Hang on a minute, I'll strew some petals on the lino and start speaking in rhyming couplets. Mine dog has breath like cheesy feet/But you smell twenty times as sweet."

Sunny held up her glass. "My liege, your rhyme's a pretty sound/But move your backside, it's your round."

It was quiet in the bar. A dissatisfied patron had beaten up the jukebox, so the only sound to disturb the dedicated drinking of the regulars was the whirr of the hand-dryer in the gents', which refused to switch itself off.

Returning with the drinks, Patrick asked Sunny why she kept looking at the door.

Sunny shrugged. "Didn't know I was."

His face sagged. "You didn't invite Fabio, did you?"

"God, no!" Sunny could just imagine Fabio transplanted to this grotty pub, enquiring about the vintage of the wine-box and sticking to the gummy carpet in his handmade loafers. She noticed Patrick's relief. "Would it be that bad? He's lovely when you get to know him."

"That won't happen," laughed Patrick, as if she'd just said something outrageous. "He hates me."

"No, no, no," fibbed Sunny transparently. "He knows that we used to go out together, and he's protective of me."

"A billion years ago," Patrick scoffed. "And what does 'protective' mean, exactly? Don't you mean 'possessive'?"

Sunny gave up. If Patrick was determined to believe the worst about Fabio she couldn't stop him. "Will we make Ozzie dance?" This was a useful standby for dull moments. Sunny leaned down and held the easygoing mongrel by his front paws, while he hopped about on his back legs.

Patrick reacted as he always did when Ozzie pranced: he started off giggling, then dissolved into, "Aw, don't, it's not fair, we're making him look stupid," and gave Ozzie extra pats, and hugs, and a little slop of Guinness.

The distraction gave Sunny another chance to look at the door. Her outlaw demeanour was a result of the only lie she had ever told Fabio (apart from the mandatory one about how many men she'd slept with). "I'm staying in tonight," she'd said, super-casual. "Got to get to the end of this chapter. Darling, don't call me, it's too distracting." And then she had slipped on another of Ellen's jackets and nipped off to the pub.

In her own defence, Sunny cited Fabio's jealousy of Patrick, but that reasoning was as full of holes as Jojo's CV, and Sunny knew it. Her boyfriend was undoubtedly jealous, but her own cowardice was the problem. She should have been able to tell Fabio where she was going and who with, but a shaky little voice argued against that sensible, mature plan. *What if you lose him?* this voice wheedled. *A little white lie is simpler.*

Sunny listened to that voice, even though it had guided her to romantic disaster since it had first piped up, round about her first period. Yes, it had advised, *go out with that boy with the cold sore who breaks in to parked cars: your mum will love him when she gets to know him.* When she'd met Calum, the very same voice had squeaked, *You might as well carry on seeing him, even though he's a thoughtless shit. Nobody else is interested in you. And you don't want to die alone, under your tower of back copies of* heat.

Sunny attended to that voice as if it was Confucius and not her stunted, terrified subconscious.

"What was that big shiny thing that was delivered to the gardens today?" asked Sunny, doing her best not to look furtively around her. It was highly unlikely that Fabio had bugged the pub, she told herself. "A big kind of steel ball, about ten feet high, with a hole in the middle."

"Just a sculpture."

"The times I've heard you go on about modern art in gardens," reminisced Sunny cruelly. "The names you've called poor Diarmuid Gavin for daring to put a girder in somebody's flowerbed. How times change . . ."

"It'll add some drama," said Patrick quietly.

"Urgh. That is Serena-talk. You don't say things like that!"

"It's sharp," persisted Patrick. "It gives focus, and bite, to the design."

"So you pull up our rosebeds, give us a shiny doughnut, and then, to add insult to injury, you tell us it gives bite to the design? Have you heard what the other residents are saying? They want their grass back." Sunny shook her head. "This is pure Serena."

"I like it," said Patrick doggedly.

Changing tack, Sunny's voice softened. "Are you sure you're comfortable with how things are going?" she asked gently.

"Yeah. Everything's on schedule and on budget. It's great." Patrick tickled Ozzie under his scruffy chin.

"But how do you feel about it?" asked Sunny, in best psychoanalyst mode. "How do you really feel about presenting something called *StyleScaping*?"

"I feel fine." Patrick's face was clear and unfurrowed. He smiled distantly at her.

Sunny realised that he wasn't going to tell her how he felt. A chill breeze, unexpected on this warm day, danced through the Volunteer and disturbed the discarded peanut packets on the lino.

CHAPTER
EIGHTEEN

Messages were being sent from Sunny's brain to Sunny's legs along the lines of "Hup! Hup! Off to the bathroom with you!" Sunny's legs were pretending not to hear, pleading that it was a Saturday and they needed a lie-in. Sunny was sorely tempted to stay in bed and dream vaguely saucy dreams of Fabio, but there was a novel to be finished.

As Sunny emerged, with bed hair and, even worse, bed face, into the hallway, the front door slammed. Sister Jane was out early. She yawned to herself. Probably heading off for some liberated free-thinking with Sarah. Perhaps they were going to burn down Sainsbury's.

After a quick shower, Sunny wandered into the kitchen and was confronted by Sister Jane's handbag on the middle of the table. Large enough to smuggle toddlers through customs, it nevertheless hung off her arm at all times. She'll be worried about it, thought Sunny, dialling the number of Sister Jane's mobile. Which immediately rang from inside the handbag. Sunny called Sarah.

"This is early for you." Sarah had caller ID, and knew her friend's schedule.

"Yeah. Work, you know," sighed Sunny the martyr. "Is Sister Jane there?"

"She should be here any minute. Don't try and talk her out of it."

"Out of what?"

Sarah's tone changed abruptly. "Nothing. She's, erm, having her legs waxed."

"What's going on?"

"That's her at the door. Got to run."

"Tell her I've got her handbag." Sunny made a snap decision. "I'll bring it over."

"Bye." Sarah ended the call without ceremony.

Sunny smelled a rat so big she could saddle it and ride to town.

Hot, bothered and sweating like an extra from *Gandhi*, Sunny finally turned in to Sarah's road. It was too hot to be rushing like this. The ribbon on her left espadrille had come off and she had concocted a funny walk to keep the shoe on her foot. The gargantuan handbag banged against her hip as she plodded down the wide avenue. She was not happy. At the far end of the street, a taxi purred at the kerb. She squinted: was it outside Sarah's gate?

There was a flurry of activity at Sarah's door. Sunny sped up. It wasn't easy to cover ground in a broken espadrille, but when she saw Sarah and Sister Jane bolt down the path, she broke into a flat-footed, lurching run. "Noooooo!" she yelled, thumping along like Frankenstein's younger monster.

Whether they heard her or not, they zoomed through the gate, and Sister Jane reached the taxi first. She had to be helped by Sarah. In fact, she had to be pushed and shoved and manhandled by Sarah, because Sister Jane was dressed as a gigantic slab of Porqy Peeces and was rather too wide for the door.

"STOP!" pleaded Sunny, waddling pigeon-toed along the pavement, waving the outsize handbag like a flag of surrender.

She could tell that they had seen her. Instead of politely waiting, the five-foot portion of luncheon meat redoubled its efforts to squeeze into the cab. Little nun legs frantically scrabbled, peeking out from beneath the pink costume, which apparently hung on some kind of clever framework around Sister Jane's body.

"Drive!" commanded Sarah, as she finally heaved her companion through and fell into the taxi behind her. The vehicle pulled smoothly away, leaving Sunny to come to a leaden, duck-like halt on the road behind it.

At least she knew what the PVC had been for.

How Sunny envied the passengers on the bus home. They all had nice normal problems. That black man reading the *Guardian* was probably concerned about whether or not he was going to get promoted at his IT company. That four-year-old swinging his legs and occasionally asking, "Do you have a vagina?" to embarrass his mother was worry-free, beyond the fear of getting his least favourite Petits Filous.

Sunny was positive she was the only person on the bus worried about a nun disguised as luncheon meat. It was a surreal problem, fathomless. Perhaps it was nothing to worry about: Sister Jane might be simply strolling round a park, feeding the ducks, in her nice Spam dress.

Ellen will know what to do, thought Sunny, as she plodded over Putney Bridge.

The espadrille had gone too far. Sunny took it off and hurled it over the bridge into the river. Instantly, she felt guilty for polluting the Thames, and instantly, she appreciated just how hot a bridge can be under a bare foot. Her walk morphed into an even funnier one, as she edged towards Chudleigh Court. Hopping and yet not hopping, Sunny crossed the road in morris-dancer style. On the other side, she stopped, one leg folded, flamingo-like.

Maybe it was a mirage. Sunny rubbed her eyes. No, the white Bentley really was there and Fabio was holding the door open. His outline danced in the sunshine. Out of place in the sweaty bustle of the street, Fabio was still. Looking directly at Sunny, in her damp camisole and one shoe, his smile was dazzling.

"Please step into the car, beautiful," said Fabio. "It is my surprise. A holiday. Just the two of us. We are all we need."

Sunny put her foot abruptly down. And swore as her sole sizzled.

The club-class lounge was cloistered and quiet, like an air-conditioned chapel furnished by John Lewis. Sunny, clammy and bewildered, was a blot on its luxe landscape. She wasn't wearing the expression of a young woman off on a jaunt with her lover; it was more the expression of a young woman who is scared she is a witch, whose aunt has run away dressed as Spam and whose foot hurts. She didn't avail herself of the freshly squeezed orange juice, and she didn't pluck a newspaper from the neat rails. She wasn't interested in the complimentary muffins, and she hadn't noticed the water feature.

The dark, riotously handsome man rubbing her foot was answering questions that evidently puzzled him. "But, *cara*, why are you interrogating me?" he asked. "What is my mother's name? Did I have a childhood pet? Do you suspect me of being a spy, of having a false identity?" Fabio's good humour was intact, somehow.

"No, no, obviously no," scoffed Sunny, aware that the true reason was even crazier: she was attempting to reassure herself that Fabio was real. It had struck her on the way to the airport, as she digested the latest spooky turn of events, that she knew very little about him. If he were to go missing, her description for the police would be sketchy: "Tall, beautiful, brown eyes, richer than little Richie Rich, likes veal." "I'm curious, that's all. You know so much, *too* much about me, but you're a mystery to me, Fabio."

"There's no mystery. I'm the man who's madly in love with you."

Suppressing a growl of frustration, Sunny finally conceded that you can have too much romance. She was after answers.

"There is something I must do." Fabio planted a kiss on her head and was gone.

240

Head drooping, Sunny was angry with herself for being so anxious. She was on her way to the di Sica Carelli villa on Capri. A week of unimaginable luxury (peppered with holiday sex) lay ahead. She was a lucky, lucky girl.

A television screen above the cappucino bar was tuned to BBC World. A snippet of breaking news filtered through Sunny's self-absorption. "Oh, noooooo," she wailed.

A sensible voice was saying, "In an apparent protest against controversial food additive Bilnius Red F, a demonstrator disguised as a slice of luncheon meat infiltrated Parliament just moments ago."

In wide screen, technicolour perfection, beamed live from the lobby of the House of Commons, Sister Jane was lobbing gobbets of Porqy Peeces at the Prime Minister of Great Britain.

"Stop that right now!" Sunny forgot where she was and jumped up, wagging her finger at the screen. "You're a very naughty nun!" Hot with shame, she peered around to see if anybody was staring at her. The businessmen, dotted around the room like pinstriped babies, all focussed on their broadsheets: it would take more than a tatty, shoeless woman with imaginary friends to make them look up from the FTSE Index.

On the screen, the small pink agitator was scampering nimbly across the tiles of the ornate Gothic chamber, dodging outstretched arms at every turn. She was relentless in her pursuit of the Prime Minister, his shoulders already splattered with pink goo, who was being hustled away by a cordon of stony-faced men.

241

"Shame on you, sir!" the little blob shouted, propelling an eggsized dollop in a graceful arc over the heads of his security.

"Ooooh, good shot!" murmured Sunny, despite herself. "Right in the eye."

"LIVE FROM PARLIAMENT," read a banner at the bottom of the screen. The commentator struggled to keep up with the action. "Extraordinary scenes here, in the cradle of our democracy, as a slice of luncheon meat terrorises the PM, despite the best efforts of Special Branch."

As a platoon of uniformed police cornered the plucky little serving of Porqy Peeces, Sunny didn't know whether to cry or cheer. She was glad that her aunt's short but colourful reign of terror was over, but she winced to see her middle-aged relative caught in a half nelson live on national television.

Looking very pleased with himself, Fabio returned, holding up an elegant pair of strappy sandals he had somehow sourced among the accessory franchises and newsagents of the airport.

"Sorry." Sunny pulled a contrite face. "We're not going to Capri, Fabio."

"Then where . . .?"

"Have you ever been to the House of Commons?"

There were hours of tension and tedium before the cousins and their renegade aunt were safely back in number thirteen. The three girls, exhausted from their vigil at the police station waiting for their aunt to be bailed, were pale.

"Thank God for Fabio," breathed Ellen.

Jojo added, "Thank God for his money, you mean." The cost of bail had straightened Sunny's hair. It was only due to some very fancy footwork on the part of Fabio's very fancy lawyer that Sister Jane's identity had been withheld from the media.

"Right." Sunny, along with Jojo and Ellen, followed Sister Jane into her bedroom and closed the door behind her. Arms folded and expressions grim, they looked like three disapproving mothers of a wayward teenager. Sunny waded in with, "Are you going to explain what you thought you were doing?"

"I was throwing Porqy Peeces at the Prime Minister," said Sister Jane, brightly. "Never liked the man. It was great gas."

Ellen frowned. "You have to promise us you won't do anything like this again."

"Hopefully I won't have to." Sister Jane's answer prompted a heartfelt group sigh.

Ellen went on. "You could be in very serious trouble, Aunty Jane."

"You have to help me, girls."

Softening, Sunny said eagerly, "You know we'll do everything we can."

"Could you show me how to put on lipstick?" Sister Jane held up a tube of Rimmel gloss.

"What?" Sunny was bemused.

"I have a date," Sister Jane told them, pouting to apply the lippy. "Oh, no, that looks awful."

Jojo sniggered, "You can't have a date!"

"Can I not?" asked her aunt, slyly.

"Who with?" spluttered Sunny, re-crossing her arms, awkwardly.

"Ernest."

"Ernest!" All three girls squeaked in amazed synchronicity.

"This is the best yet," laughed Jojo.

Sunny wasn't amused. "Do you mean a 'date' date?" She winced at the slapper's mouth her aunt had daubed on. "That colour is much too bright, Aunty Jane."

"That's why I need your help. I've never used this stuff in me life." She looked around at their faces and seemed to find them funny. "Would you look at you all! I'm not running away to join the circus. I asked Ernest if he'd accompany me to dinner and he said he'd love to."

"You asked him?" Ellen's voice was small.

"It's the twenty-first century, in case you girls didn't know. We can vote and everything."

"But you're a nun," said Jojo helpfully, as if their aunt might be unaware of it.

"And a good one, too. I'm going out for dinner with a man because I've never done it and I want to see what all the fuss is about. There won't be any hanky-panky."

Sunny turned her head as if her aunt had struck her. The image conjured up by her words was too much.

Jojo had a nice line in leers. "Shouldn't think old Ernest can hank or pank these days."

"You'd be surprised. He's taking me to a disco afterwards."

244

Now all three of them were lost for words.

"Out, out." Sister Jane waved her hands at them. "I have to get into me glad rags. Then you can come back and do me hair and face."

"But you're on bail!" Sunny protested, stumbling backwards out of the room.

"I believe I'm allowed to eat on bail."

"We were taking you out tonight," protested Ellen, as their aunt shooed them out like a flock of geese. "To an Andrew Lloyd Webber."

"Uuurgh." Sister Jane screwed up her face. "What would I want with a musical?"

There were at least a dozen good reasons to holler at Sarah, all so impressive that it was difficult for Sunny to prioritise as she dialled the Chiswick number. Was she more annoyed about missing her impromptu sex-fest in the Italian sun, or about being in debt to Fabio for many thousands of pounds, or about her aunty being exploited in a game of marital ping-pong, or . . .? As soon as the receiver was lifted at the other end, she knew she was calling to make sure that Sarah was all right.

"Oh, Alfie, it's you." Sunny had last seen him an hour ago, his face taut with worry. "How are you feeling?"

"Not great."

"And Sarah?"

"In the bath. Hopefully, I can trust her not to storm any ramparts while I'm at Liz's."

"Liz's?" Sunny didn't mean to sound so horrified. She wondered if Alfie knew just how inflammatory this would seem to his terrorist wife.

"Yes. So much shit is going to hit so many fans that if I stand on the roof I'll still be covered in the stuff," said Alfie, with weary fatalism. "I'd better do what I can to mend fences tonight."

That made practical business sense, even if it did just hammer a few more nails into the luncheon-meat coffin of his marriage. "I'm here if you want me."

"Why didn't I marry you, Sunny?"

"Because you love my best mate." It was time to remind him.

"Oh, yeah. Knew it was something."

"Aunty Jane isn't a bit sorry," marvelled Sunny, trudging through the drizzle with Ellen and Jojo. The argument about who should go and get the fish and chips they desperately needed had been so ferocious that the only answer was for them all to go and get wet.

Ellen was also marvelling. "Did you hear her say, 'oh, shush, it was only a bit of fun. Maybe now the government will do something'?" Ellen, her hair slick against her forehead, looked exasperated. "Fun! Attacking the Prime Minister!"

With backdated outrage, Sunny complained, "And fancy her not wanting to go to the musical! I mean, she's a middle-aged woman, she's contractually obliged to like Andrew Lloyd Webber."

"Do you reckon she'll get a snog off Ernest?"

"JOJO!" shouted Ellen and Sunny together, and Sunny batted her with the wrapped cod suppers.

"I'm only saying," said Jojo, smirking unattractively.

"She looked quite pretty with make-up on," said Sunny, a hint of warmth creeping into her disapproving tone. "Her eyes looked very young."

"And that new dress suited her." Ellen was thawing, too.

Not Jojo. "Did you see Ernest's cravat?" she whooped scornfully. "And the old fool had combed his moustache."

"He's a gentleman. There aren't many of them left," said Ellen, absently.

"No." Sunny added privately, I got one of the last ones. A warm glow crept over her, which may have been the packages she was clutching but probably owed something to Fabio, too.

"God, I'm looking forward to those chips." For once, Jojo spoke for them all. "Come on, hurry up. I'm going to make a massive butty with mine and share it with Marmite, in front of *Who Wants To Be A Millionaire?*" She quickened her pace as they turned the corner into the gardens.

The three of them stopped dead. For a brief moment, Sunny considered flinging the fish and chips over her shoulder and sprinting out into oncoming traffic, but common sense prevailed. This had to be faced up to.

She led her cousins to the three women peering like hens through the etched glass of their block's double doors. "Hello, Mum, Aunty Mo, Aunty Annie," she said.

And then the squawking began.

CHAPTER
NINETEEN

Maybe I'm a foundling, theorised Sunny hopefully. Maybe these three women are nothing to do with me. That's it, she decided. They discovered me on the steps of a church and took me home, little suspecting that I am, in fact, Norwegian royalty. "How are the chips?" she asked, dutifully.

"Gorgeous!" Mo, the perennially cheerful mum of Ellen and Jojo, responded as if she'd just dined on the finest foie gras. "There's nothing like a chip," she said emphatically, adding, "when you're hungry," for the sake of clarity.

Full of unwelcome relatives, the kitchen felt even more cramped than usual. "So," Ellen was saying, with a convincing simulacrum of a smile, "how long are you over for?"

"As long as it takes," said Annie darkly. She said everything darkly, partly due to her deep voice, stewed daily in Benson & Hedges, and partly due to her habit of looking suspiciously out from under eyebrows that had never encountered a tweezer. Her greying perm shook from side to side as she sighed (darkly), "I never thought it would come to this. My own sister on the news. Mother would turn in her grave if she was alive."

"Mother" was invoked often, usually performing an acrobatic manoeuvre: turning, spinning, twisting, leaping. She was getting more exercise in her coffin than she ever had in her little terraced house, where her main exertion had been throwing the newspaper at her husband.

Annie was angry with their absent sister. "Why isn't Jane here? Where does a nun go at night, for Jayzus's sake?" she demanded rhetorically. There was a zealous gleam in Annie's eye, and she was eating her chips as if they'd personally insulted her. Ellen and Sunny had one of their psychic conspiracies: they both knew they had to steer the conversation away from where Sister Jane might or might not be.

Ellen dived in with, "I rang a nice B&B just down the road and they've got room for you."

Mary and Mo smiled, but Annie asked, like a CID inspector, "Do they have kettles in the rooms?"

"Yes," busked Ellen, who had absolutely no idea, and would have sent her aunt there even if they had Rottweilers in the rooms.

Sunny's mother, Mary, asked, "Did Jane tell you girls where she was off to?"

"No," said Sunny quickly, popping more tea bags in the pot.

"Don't think so," hedged Ellen.

"She's on a date," said Jojo.

Although she only had a tea bag to hand, Sunny briefly considered devising a way to maim Jojo with it. "No, she's not. I'm sure she's not," she said placatingly.

Some situations you can't placate, and a kitchen full of shocked, squeaking Irish housewives is one of them. Annie threw her chip paper in the air, Mary put her hands to her head like a Munch print, and Mo started wailing, "No, ah no, ah no!" as if Sister Jane had sailed off on the *Titanic*'s maiden voyage.

"It's just dinner!" shouted Ellen. It took a lot to make her raise her voice, but ten minutes in to the aunts' visit and she was already bellowing like a market trader. "It's dinner! With a nice old man!"

"A MAN!" screamed Annie, as if this fresh detail was too much.

"Well, she's not a lesbian," muttered Jojo, adept at throwing oil on flames.

Mo spluttered, tears in her eyes, and a chip in her shampoo and set, "Who's a lesbian?" She turned to Mary. "Mary, our Jane isn't lesboid, is she?"

There was more of the same for quite some time. Hysterical misunderstanding, insane overreaction and ear-splitting laments; it took Sunny right back to the old days.

More tea and a Bronze age Battenberg helped. The howling tapered off. Annie said venomously, "Now we know why she ran away. She's man-mad!"

"She didn't exactly run away," said Mo diplomatically. She was traditionally the least confrontational, and least conservative, of the three. Sunny had run to Mo's for refuge when her mother had ranted about *Top of the Pops* being satanic propaganda. Sunny had envied her cousins having Mo for a mother, which, according to Ellen, was a bit like somebody who was covered in spiders envying somebody covered in cockroaches. "Jane just forgot to tell the convent she was leaving. It was right after they offered her the job."

"Which job?" asked Ellen, interested.

"Mother Superior," her mother told them.

"Blimey," said Sunny admiringly. "Isn't that a big deal in nun circles? Like being made managing director or something?"

"It's an honour," said Annie. Darkly. "We were so proud, and then she throws it all away. If Mother was alive, this would kill her."

"Mother was over the moon at having a nun in the family. After Declan, you know . . ." Mo's voice tailed off, and she looked down at the tablecloth, as her sisters glowered at her.

"Never mind Declan. That's history," said Annie, in the *very* deep voice she used for hushing up family secrets.

Exchanging a delighted glance with Ellen, Sunny looked forward to grilling Aunty Mo later on. Mo had always been an excellent source of O'Brien scandal: she lacked the iron discretion of the others. As far as Sunny knew, her uncle, Declan, had considered being a priest before he discovered that his true vocation was to service photocopiers, but evidently there was more to it than that.

Mo muttered, "It was his word against the bishop's," and resumed picking at her Battenberg.

"Thank God I recognised her legs sticking out from that cooked-meat get-up." Annie lit a cigarette. "If it

252

wasn't for Josie's distinctive knees we wouldn't know what she's been up to."

Sunny coughed theatrically. Nobody smoked in their flat, but she lacked the nerve to tell her aunt.

From where she perched on a kitchen unit, Jojo said flatly, "Put that out, Aunty Annie. There's no smoking here."

If a pin had had the courage to drop, you could have heard it. Annie looked confused and shocked, as if somebody had just flashed her. She turned slowly to stare at Jojo. "I beg your pardon?" she said, in her best faux-English accent.

"You can't have a fag in here," said Jojo, who seemed blithely unaware of the change in atmosphere. "Go on. Put it out."

"I'll put it out when I'm good and ready, miss," said Annie slowly, her expression still one of arch disbelief. Turning back to her sisters around the table, she said, as if to herself, "Some little chits should think about the way they treat their elders and betters." Taking a long drag on her cigarette, she asked Mo, "Is that the way you brought the child up? To cheek the poor aunt who sacrificed her youth to look after Mother?"

"No, no, oh no," said Mo, pink-faced and flustered. "Jojo, you shush, love," she said mildly.

"We'll all get cancer." Jojo was not a natural shusher.

"Ah, get away," sneered Mo. "Cigarettes don't give you cancer. Mother smoked eighty a day all her life."

"And died of lung cancer," Jojo reminded them.

"God rest her soul," the aunts muttered.

Annie was clear-eyed about the facts. "But that wasn't the cigarettes," she said. "That was next door's pigeons."

Over the seventeenth pot of tea, a debate was raging amongst the aunts. Annie was loudly declaring, "You can't hear a word these pop singers say these days."

"Which is a blessing." Mo was backing her up. "The only word they know is the F one."

Nodding sagely, Mary added, "And they're only half dressed."

Quietly, and sourly, Ellen said, "Coldplay are usually fully clothed."

"I mean, what do you make of that fella, the Prince?" scowled Mo. "The little black fella with the big hair."

"Is he a fella at all?" queried Annie.

"Well, he has a moustache," pointed out Mo, eruditely. "He throws himself around on big high heels, and it's all eff this, eff that and eff the effing other."

"I like him," said Jojo happily.

Sunny was certain that Jojo wouldn't know Prince from Prince Philip. Evidently, the argumentative O'Brien streak had crossed the generations. Sunny made her contribution, deciding quixotically to side with the aunts. "It all went downhill when the Beatles stopped washing," she said sadly, precipitating the perennial "Who's your favourite Beatle?" discussion. The aunts all took their traditional positions: Mo cited Paul for his "lovely eyes" and his long marriage to Linda; Mary plumped for George because he was no trouble and believed in God; Annie favoured Ringo because he had "a bit of the old personality". This only left John for Sunny. She had never liked him, partly because he reminded her of her maths teacher. For the purposes of this debate, however, he became a genius.

Punctuated by short bursts of "Love Me Do" and "I Wanna Hold Your Hand" in Irish falsettos, the discussion roared on. The kettle was put on again, even older cake was exhumed from the cupboard, and Sunny had to admit that her mother and aunts certainly livened a place up.

The doorbell sounded. All disagreement about whether Paul or George looked better in an aran stopped dead.

"Is that her?" hissed Annie.

"Only one way to find out." Ellen went to let Sister Jane in.

"Look at the time," hissed Annie, menacingly, as Sister Jane's footsteps drew nearer down the hall. "It's gone eleven. She's lost the run of herself."

"Now there's a surprise!" Sister Jane's voice was bright as she put her head round the door.

"Jesus, Mary and Joseph!" shrieked Mary, putting her hands to her cheeks. "Where's your wimple, Jane? Where's your habit?"

"In the wash." Sister Jane winked over at Sunny. "Youse all look very well, I must say."

"Is that lipstick?" Mo's voice was small.

Annie's wasn't. "You've painted your face, Jane!" she roared, standing up to glare down at her sister.

"If you don't mind me saying . . ." Sister Jane looked calmly up at Annie ". . . you could do with a touch of powder yourself."

Giving cheek to Annie, Mother's representative on earth, was unheard of in the family. A mushroom cloud of shocked silence threatened to take the roof off.

Sunny spoke. "Did you have a nice time?" she asked politely.

"Very nice, thank you," smiled Sister Jane. "We had a delicious steak and some gâteaux, and a little dance. Then Ernest took me for a walk along the riverside."

"A walk . . ." gasped Mary, clutching her neck, as if the word was code for sodomy.

Squinting malevolently, Annie asked, "Have you a drink taken, Jane?"

"We had a glass of Chianti."

"Ah Jayzus, Chianti," wailed Mary, shaking off Mo's placating hand. "The jig is up. She's going to hell in a handcart. Chianti, and her a Mother Superior."

"I'm not a Mother Superior." Sister Jane sounded sharp. "Yet."

Still standing, and obviously keen to regain control, Annie asked pompously, "Do you have an explanation for your behaviour, Jane? Can you tell us why you humiliated the family on national television and why you're gallivanting about with men in steakhouses and up and down riversides?"

"No." Sister Jane yawned. "I'm off to me bed. See you tomorrow." She smiled over at her nieces, standing in a dumbstruck row by the sink. "Don't keep these old ladies up too late, girls."

256

Her nose inky, and her arms full of Sunday papers, Sarah shook Sunny out of bed with delighted shouts of "Look at this! We're in every edition!"

Spread out on the kitchen table, the papers made depressing reading for Sunny, who could imagine the aunts' reaction. Flicking from the *Sun*'s headline "NICE TO MEAT YOU, P.M.!" to *The Times*'s "SECURITY QUESTIONS RAISED BY FOOD ADDITIVE STUNT", Sunny said nothing.

The mix of bravado and apprehension on Sarah's face was familiar. The squeals of glee and the hearty hugs for her nunnish partner in crime didn't convince. "You're regretting this already, aren't you?"

"Why would I?" Sarah laughed a little too heartily, like a Noël Coward heroine.

"You're scared it's gone too far."

"We've got the whole country talking about Porqy Peeces," enthused Sarah, her face lit with brittle energy. "They'll have to listen to me now."

"What if Bilnius Red F isn't that bad?"

"It is." Sarah suddenly thumped the table. "It is," she said in a smaller voice. "Please, Sunny," she sounded pained. "I've already had my telling-off from Alfie."

When did she get so thick-skinned? wondered Sunny. "Alfie and I are hurt and annoyed and . . . and . . . we're worried that you're going to prison." She added, "You twat," feeling that the situation merited it.

"They wouldn't dare put a mother and a nun behind bars for using their right to free speech," said Sarah coolly. "And why are *you* hurt, for God's sake?"

Spluttering, Sunny embarked on a list. "You've been doing this behind my back. And implicating my aunty."

The victim of sudden deafness, Sarah leaned over a paper, seemingly engrossed in the newsprint.

"When did you cross the line?" Sunny couldn't let her off the hook, particularly as she was certain that Sarah was writhing with regret. "When did you become so obsessed with one dodgy little ingredient in a tin of pressed meat that you decided to ride roughshod over your family and mates?"

"When my husband decided to bonk his client." It would have made sense if Sarah was shouting, but she was quiet, conversational even. "I've found out that he's been seeing her when he's been claiming to be at meetings. Quiet little dinners. A show. Even a trip to the zoo." Sarah managed a smile. "Like a couple of schoolkids dating."

"Are you sure?" Sunny was horrified. Alfie had never been a liar.

"I confronted him last night, in the middle of his spiel about how I was endangering his career, our marriage and, oh, just about everything, from the Northern Ireland peace treaty to the future of the white rhino. He confessed. Said he does see her outside the office. She's *sympathetic*, apparently." Sarah returned to studying the papers. "And I'm not. I'm a cow."

Sagging like a bag of dirty laundry, Sunny mewed, "You're not a cow." She reconsidered. "Well, actually, you are, but you're my favourite cow in all the world."

258

"Thank you," laughed Sarah. With a teary gleam in her eye, she asked, in a choked voice, "What have I done, Sun?"

"Come here." Sunny folded Sarah up in a firm hug as sad as it was fond.

"Have I lost him?" gulped Sarah, fear mangling her words.

Without a crystal ball, Sunny couldn't answer. She tightened her embrace. "It'll be all right," she whispered, fingers tightly crossed.

CHAPTER
TWENTY

Sunny's family were like hand grenades. She couldn't take her eyes off them for five minutes or they went off and debris filled the air. She had only nipped out for milk and sugar, but when she got back to the flat, all the air left her lungs: Fabio was sitting among them, a teacup in his hands and a look of abject terror on his face. "Fabio!" she said, abruptly.

"Oh, Sunny!" said Fabio gratefully, as if she was a heavenly apparition. His eyes pleaded eloquently for rescue.

"I was just telling Fabio about the time your knickers fell down during the school nativity play." Mary's face was contorted with laughter. "We have a video of it, and we play it every Christmas."

"I need you in the hall, Fabio. Urgently," Sunny babbled.

"Thank God!" Fabio stood up, and sprinted to her side. "Excuse me, ladies," he said, graciously, if a little belatedly.

"Leave the door open," commanded Annie, a woman who had burst in on many pubescent snogs.

Gritting her teeth, Sunny dragged Fabio into the room she shared with Ellen, taking care to leave the door ajar. "I'm sorry!" she hissed into his gorgeous face. "Don't chuck me!"

Laughing, Fabio kissed her nose. "It would take more than that."

"I'm not going to grow older like them, honest!" stammered Sunny. "I won't wear elasticated trousers, I won't cite Richard Madeley as the epitome of male sex appeal, I won't fry everything and then wonder why I've got hips the size of Malta. Honest."

"I believe you." Fabio nodded, exaggeratedly, like a mime.

"Was it terrible?" she asked, sympathetically.

"It was terrible," confirmed Fabio with a shudder. "They talk at the same time, and so quickly. They keep touching me." He plucked at his shirt as if he could still feel their hands on him. "They ask me if I know the Pope. They ask me if I am serious about you." He threw her a sly look. "What do you think I said?"

"I think you said we're madly in love," whispered Sunny.

"I told your mother that I want to protect you for ever," said Fabio solemnly. Then his eyes widened, like a beautiful cat awakening. "Sunny, you said 'we' . . ."

"I did, didn't I?" teased Sunny. Something about Fabio's demeanour among the O'Brien battalion had touched her heart, shooing away her final reserve. Of course she was in love with this man. Not just because he was "perfect" but because of the tenderness he inspired in her. "I love you, Fabio."

Silent, they gazed at one another: a kiss would be too brusque.

The spell was broken by a loud howl from Annie. "There'd better be no monkey business out there!"

Urgently, Fabio begged, "Please don't make me go back."

"No, no. You go. Run and don't look back."

Fabio's exit didn't go down well at the kitchen table, but he got excellent reviews from the older generation.

"Lovely hair, hadn't he, Annie?" This was towering praise from Mary, who was the official family critic for all television and film stars' hair.

"Lovely shoes." Annie, usually so critical, went further.

"Lovely manners," Mo added.

"Lovely speaking voice." Mary had gone dreamy.

"Lovely —"

Jojo interrupted her mother. "Yeah, he's lovely. Can we move on?" She held up the cat, awkwardly. "Nobody's even noticed Marmite's runny eye."

Perversely, Sunny was grateful for Jojo's begrudging shift of focus. She was in love with Fabio, and the feeling was too precious to share. I love him, she told herself, and it felt as if central heating had been switched on in her tummy.

With Sister Jane AWOL since morning, the aunts refused to leave the premises all Sunday in case she returned. Sunny and Ellen, smiles clamped firmly in place, listened to their unending stream of consciousness, covering an impressively wide range of subjects: single mothers, Cliff Richard, exactly how much weight

Sunny needed to lose. Sunny noticed Ellen's fists slowly clenching and unclenching, almost continually.

By the window, Mary broke off from a long treatise on why fried food is good for you to squawk, "Isn't that Patrick down there?" His fate was sealed. Within moments he was in the kitchen being subjected to a fond interrogation and having every aspect of his appearance discussed loudly to his face, as if he wasn't there.

With a sympathetic smirk at Patrick, as Mo asked excitedly about the "fillum" he was making, Sunny slipped out to answer her mobile. "Fabio," she purred. "I love you, you know."

Sunny sensed him melt. "I can never hear that enough, *cara*."

From within the kitchen, a gale of laughter sounded. "Who is there?" asked Fabio. He was no actor, and the throwaway air of his "Is that Patrick?" didn't ring true.

"The aunts are hooting. I don't know how but they get drunk on tea," fudged Sunny. "Of course Patrick isn't here. Why would he be? I told you, we're not that close any more." Turning, she saw Patrick emerge quietly from the kitchen.

Sunny didn't take in Fabio's reply. She was gazing at Patrick. He had heard: his downturned smile was proof of that. Putting a finger up to make him hang on as he strode past her, she finished her call with a gabbled, "Got to go; I'll ring you back. Love you."

Sunny grabbed Patrick's arm, a gesture he didn't welcome, judging by the look on his face. "Hey! Hold on. That was just —"

"No need to explain," said Patrick lightly. "Now I know why you were so furtive in the pub. I'm a big secret, am I?" He smiled wryly, prising her fingers from his shirt. "I don't want to get in the way of the big romance you've been waiting for, Sun, especially not if it's love at last."

"You're not in the way." Sunny shook her head, as if this was nonsense.

"I've been thinking for a while that maybe we should knock our Thursday nights on the head, now that you've got a serious bloke." He jiggled his keys, self-consciously. "And I really don't need the glares any more."

"Glares?"

"Fabio gives me evils whenever he passes me." He paused, remembering. "We're talking vicious evils here."

"So, we'll just pack in Thursdays, then?" said Sunny.

"May as well. You've got better things to do these days."

"Well, sort of . . ." It was hard to dispute it without betraying Fabio. Perhaps Patrick was right and there wasn't room for two men in her life. "The end of an era," she said wistfully.

"Hardly," laughed Patrick. "It was just an old pub."

"I'd better get back to the aunts," said Sunny, all wistfulness banished. "See you."

"See you." With a final jiggle of his keys, Patrick was gone.

Sunny leaned against the closed front door, anger bubbling in her chest. Why was Patrick such a wimp when it came to her? An overheard phone call, a few dirty looks and he cancels their weekly date. He couldn't even let her say, sentimentally, that it was the end of an era; he had to laugh and diminish the way she was feeling. Where was the depth of emotion that she expected from an ex-lover? She kicked the door with a yelp of fury.

This was outdated outrage, she knew. It wasn't just about today. It was about musty old events that should have been tidied away years ago. She punched the door again. Bloody Patrick. Bloody, bloody, bloody Patrick.

It was a family summit. They'd never had one before, but Mary had found the idea in a magazine at the hairdresser's and was keen to try it out. "We all sit down together and discuss the problem, frankly and calmly."

Somehow they all wedged in around the table. Chairs were in short supply, so Sunny volunteered to sit on the bin. Sister Jane was very erect, with a closed expression.

"Would you like to start us off, Annie?" asked Mary, with the requisite respect for her older sister.

Unafraid, Annie kicked off with, "Have you a fancy man or what, Jane?"

Sister Jane raised her eyes eloquently to the cracked ceiling, but didn't answer.

Before Annie could sling another claw-hammer of a question, Ellen said, in a measured, carefully non-confrontational way, "Aunty Jane, your sisters are worried about you. They think you might be unhappy

265

or confused. Can you share your feelings with them and let them know what your plans are?"

An admiring silence blanketed the family summit. Mary nodded approvingly: presumably, this was exactly the type of civilised thing the magazine article had promised. All eyes turned to Sister Jane, who said, with her customary self-possession, "There's no need to worry about me. I'm happier than I've ever been."

There was a pause, which Sister Jane chose not to fill.

Straying from the family-summit template, Mary's patience snapped. "Is that it?" she asked, with a hint of anger. "Don't you owe us a little more than that? We've been tearing our hair out. And according to the girls, you don't even go to daily Mass any more!"

Without looking at Mary, Sister Jane said firmly, "I'm very sorry that you've been upset. I know what your nerves are like," she said, almost in an undertone. "As for Mass . . ." she regarded her nieces with narrowed eyes ". . . I go to 6a.m. round the corner at St Teresa's before they're up." She glanced at Ellen, devilishly. "Even you, Ellen."

"Am I allowed to say something?" Mo asked Ellen timidly. "I'm not au fait with these family-summit doobreys." She coughed, then said nervously, "Jane, is this fella Ernest the reason you left the convent?" She sounded terrified of hearing the answer.

"Ernest would be very flattered to be cast as the dashing hero. No," said Sister Jane firmly. "He isn't the reason. Sure, didn't I only meet him when I got here? We've had dinner. He's a very interesting man, been all over the world with the navy. He's lonely now, and he says he likes having a lady to put a clean cravat on for." She raised an arch eyebrow at her audience. "It's all quite chaste and innocent, I assure you."

"Of course, of course," spluttered Mary and Mo, as if nothing had been further from their minds.

Annie asked the question that hung in the air. "What are you going to do next?"

"I've given this a great deal of thought," said Sister Jane gravely, as her sisters and nieces all leaned in. "I'm going to retrain to be a lap-dancer."

Sighs were exhaled loudly all round. Mary slapped the table. "I don't understand you, Jane," she snapped, irritably.

"And I don't understand you," said Sister Jane, bluntly. "I never have. I couldn't fathom why anybody would choose another life instead of becoming a nun. It was the only thing in the world I wanted to do. But you would never have swapped places with me, would you, Mary? Of course not. Each to their own. We don't have to understand each other." She softened, looking as if she regretted her harsh tone. "But we should love each other."

Mary tutted, as if this was useless information. Sunny could tell that her mother was overwhelmed, but the impatient tilt of Mary's head had a galvanising effect on Sister Jane.

"I've had a long day and I'm off to bed," she told them, rising slowly and with a stiffness that was unusual. "If you're really here to reassure yourselves that I'm all right, then you may as well get yourselves off home."

"That's really all you've got to say for yourself?" Mary's voice sounded strangled. "After we came all this way?"

Harrumphing eloquently, Annie hung back from contributing her usual scorching remarks.

Mo fearfully asked, "Are you going to accept the position of Mother Superior or not?"

"Goodnight," said Sister Jane, as she left the room.

Jojo stood up. "I declare the family summit finished," she declared. "Stick the telly on, will you, Ellen? There's a George Clooney film just starting."

Trailing through the airport on Monday evening, Sunny said sadly, "Life's very complicated, isn't it? I mean, I expected to be euphoric when they finally left us in peace, but I feel all deflated."

"They looked so sad," said Ellen. "Like a little huddle of refugees."

"Did you see Annie?" gloated Jojo. "She was like a burst balloon."

Ignoring her, Sunny asked Ellen tentatively, "Do you think Aunty Jane is being a tiny bit, well, mean? She could have given them a bit more than she did."

"Not at all," said Ellen firmly. "It's her life, and she's entitled to live it without a Greek chorus of closed minds. She'll tell them what her plans are when she's good and ready."

It was becoming clear to Sunny just how alike Ellen and Sister Jane were.

Summer seemed to have fallen in love with London and was still reluctant to leave. The mellow warmth was refusing to ripen into the sunny chill of early autumn. Typing furiously on the end of her bed, Sunny squinted in the low sun, aware of the nagging feeling that they were all on borrowed time: this Indian summer couldn't last much longer.

Day after day, the sun proved her wrong. Every single one of those days, Sunny heard Fabio say that he loved her, and now she could say it back. The feeling it gave her was at least as warming as the unscheduled weather.

The Chudleigh Cad's career carried on, haphazardly, despite Mrs Wilde's eccentric investigation. The thinnest Thin Girl had been the latest victim, losing a brand-new pair of Lycra seam-free pants in an audacious snatch from their balcony.

Suspicion bloomed. Each resident had their own pet theory. Ernest was keeping a close eye on Boiled Egg. Ben himself had taken to leaning out of his window to take Polaroids of Guy's movements. Guy, being Guy, loved the attention and made sure to offer his best side. Sister Jane refused to be drawn into what she called "character assasinations", and carried on with her exploration of London. Jojo changed her mind and alighted on a different suspect every day. Sunny was utterly confused: she suspected everybody and nobody.

All the residents agreed on one subject: the emerging new garden was *awful*. Modern, stark and *über*-chic, it didn't suit the sober tastes of Chudleigh Court. The knotted tubular statue baffled Ernest: "What's it meant to *be*?" he whined. Everybody, even the trendy Thin Girls, bemoaned the loss of their pretty little goldfish pond, which had made way for a pebble-edged Japanese-style water feature.

Aware of these rumblings, Patrick carried on filming to a very punishing schedule. As Sunny watched from the window, mug of tea in hand, she saw his confidence grow and his style develop. He's good, she admitted to herself. The two of them chatted whenever their paths crossed, and they shared daft jokes, but the closeness fostered by their Thursday nights was evaporating.

So far, there were no daisies, not one, in the emerging garden. It really didn't matter, Sunny told herself, often, that Patrick had forgotten.

CHAPTER
TWENTY-ONE

"Aren't you missing something mindless on the telly?" enquired Sunny, politely.

Jojo had been sitting on a chest of drawers for half an hour, in a scarlet polyester robe edged with feathers, picking at her feet. For most people, picking at their feet wouldn't rank as a hobby, but Jojo wasn't most people. "Am I outstaying my welcome?" she asked, with what sounded like satisfaction.

"I'm trying to work. You're very distracting."

"I'm just sitting here, quiet as a mouse."

"In red polyester. Lobbing bits of toenail about. You're hard to ignore."

"You're writing very fast. When can I have the new chapters of *Fatal Crescendo*?"

"I'm just getting to the end."

"What predictions have come true lately?"

"None. I am officially not a witch. It was all coincidence."

"Yeah." Jojo scoffed.

"It was," said Sunny placidly, determined not to let her cousin rile her. Since realising the depth of her feelings for Fabio, her absurd fears had shrunk. In the words of the poet Michael Ball, love changes everything. "It was coincidence. Projection. Whatever."

"You think?" insinuated Jojo.

"I know."

"That's all right then." Jojo meant just the opposite.

"Yes. It is." Sunny felt secure. Soon she'd be lying beside Fabio, showing him her book. Jojo couldn't unsettle her.

But she could throw toenails at her.

Sitting up in bed, his honey-coloured shoulders co-ordinating divinely with the ivory linen pillows, Fabio was in tears. "You are genius." His grammar foundered on the lump in his throat. "You are best writer in world." He shook his head in disbelief at his girlfriend's talent. "Best lover, best writer. Where did you come from?"

Praise was always welcome, but Fabio was sounding unhinged. "It's good, I hope, but . . ." Sunny knew that her book was good *of its kind*. "I'm no Jane Austen."

"No, you're better," insisted Fabio with spirit. "She is dull old bag. You write sexy and modern."

Partial to a bit of Austen, Sunny fidgeted at the comparison. "Let's wait and see what Camilla says." She would know what Camilla thought of this masterpiece in a couple of hours.

"She will love it. Or I will kill her." He sounded serious.

The small office reeked of the pot-pourri on Camilla's desk. Probably marketed as something like "Forest

Sensation", the smell made Sunny feel as if she'd been buried in a shallow grave by a houseproud serial killer. "So," she asked nervously, "did you like *Fatal Crescendo?*"

"No." Camilla shook her dated, expensively coiffed head. "I LOVED it, darling."

"Phew."

"Apart from the ending. What am I to make of it? They declare their love to each other and wander off into the sunset?"

"Isn't that the classic romantic ending?"

"Haven't you heard? Marriage is back in fashion," declared Camilla. She tossed the manuscript across the desk. "Go home and write me a fantastic proposal scene. Quickly as possible. Now, off you pop. I have to make some calls to the Coast."

Fabio wasn't helping. "That is *very* distracting," murmured Sunny, as he nuzzled her neck like a big, friendly lion.

"Come back to bed, *cara*," he begged, sulkily.

"I have a deadline, darling." Sunny, sitting on the end of the futon with her laptop on her knees, arched her neck where he was kissing it.

"It is always work, work, work with you. It is a shame, because you are so good at play." Fabio slipped his hands under the towelling robe Sunny had borrowed from him.

Gulping and giggling, Sunny flailed half heartedly at this onslaught. "Oh, I give in," she declared, theatrically, turning round and throwing herself full length on him.

Trying manfully not to look winded, Fabio pushed the Sunday papers out from under them on the bed and wrapped his arms round Sunny.

"Hang on." She disentangled herself from a dismayed Fabio.

"No, no, no reading," he admonished, sulkily but sexily, pulling her face to his.

Sunny wouldn't be distracted. "Oh, God." She straightened out the *Sunday Times*. "This is terrible, Fabio. It says here that Porqy Peeces have recalled all their tins from supermarket shelves because of the doubts over Bilnius Red F."

"Who is he, this Bilnius Red fellow?"

"Never mind."

Gathered round the dinner table, the flatmates and their cuckoo in the nest, Sister Jane, were dissecting another of Jojo's baked potatoes.

"Mine's burnt," lamented Ellen.

"Mine's raw," sighed Sister Jane.

"Mine's lovely." Jojo was imperturbable.

Cutting off a wedge of her own potato to donate to her aunty's plate, Sunny asked, "Any plans yet?"

"Trying to get rid of me?" Sister Jane asked, with a wink.

"Of course not." Sunny was surprised by her own sincerity. Until the past few weeks, Sister Jane had been a vague, navy figure from her childhood. Now she felt as if she knew her aunt in a way that she didn't know her own mother. Sister Jane could be frustrating, with her sphinx-like refusal to explain herself, but she was also fascinating and funny and things had a habit of happening around her. "I'd like you to stay for ever."

"That's nice." Sister Jane accepted compliments the way she accepted insults: placidly. "You'll see the back of me soon enough."

"Running off with Ernest?" tittered Jojo.

Sunny tapped Jojo on the head with Sister Jane's raw potato. It was strangely enjoyable.

"Ow," complained Jojo, rubbing the spot.

"Girls," said Sister Jane, gently.

"Where's me new ending for *Fatal Crescendo?*" demanded Jojo, in the surly tone you might expect from somebody who's just been assaulted with a tuber. "The proposal scene?"

"Still working on it," hedged Sunny. She had started, and rewritten, it countless times.

"Scared, are you?" Jojo was smug. "Scared it'll come true?"

"Yeah," nodded Sunny, sarcastically. "I'm absolutely terrified that the gorgeous, intelligent, romantic, wealthy man I'm head over heels in love with will ask me to marry him."

"Yeah," concluded Jojo, stealing Sunny's last forkful of edible dinner. "You are."

Sarah only smoked at times of stress. On the way to Chiswick, Sunny stopped at an off-licence to buy forty cigarettes for her, along with three bottles of rosé. If the shop had stocked horse tranquillisers, she might have considered getting those, too. Poor Sarah, Sunny kept thinking. Poor, poor Sarah.

As the Castros' wide front door opened, Sarah, crumpled and tear-stained, wailed, "Please don't say you told me so."

"Come here." Sunny took her friend in her arms and let her cry it out. It was only the first instalment of many sobbing sessions that long evening. Sarah didn't usually cry, but then Alfie didn't usually walk out on her.

Gulping the wine as if it was keeping her alive, Sarah spilled the sorry story. Alfie had come home early that afternoon with the contents of his desk in a cardboard box.

"They sacked him?" Sunny was incredulous. "He's the top dog at Waldhorn Truss Levy."

Apparently, political wranglings had been going on within the company for some time. "Alfie didn't tell me about them. Didn't want to worry me, he said. The Porqy Peeces crisis handed them his head on a plate," said Sarah, eyes downcast with what looked curiously like shame. "We had what you could call words," she said, wryly, sinking another half-glass. "Then off he went, shouting 'divorce' over his shoulder."

"He'll be back." Sunny sounded certain. The Castro marriage was her touchstone. They *had* to be all right. "And until he is, you've got my shoulder to cry on." She tapped her left shoulder. "This one," she clarified, "right here."

★ ★ ★

Real life was too diverting for Sunny to apply herself to the proposal chapter. She'd spent a morning receiving panic-stricken updates from Sarah ("He's got a solicitor!", "He's rented a bedsit in Hammersmith!"), and now Jojo was demanding her attention.

"I told Guy you'd come," she said.

"Why? I'm busy," snapped Sunny, her nerves stretched. "If you want to accept Guy's invitation to tea, off you toddle. Include me out."

Jojo could be very persuasive, particularly when she threatened to tell Ellen that the jacket that had mysteriously disappeared from her room was hidden in the bottom of Sunny's wardrobe, with a red-wine splash across it.

Pressing Guy's doorbell, a realisation hit Sunny. "You'll tell Ellen anyway, won't you?"

"Probably."

The door opened and, surprised, both girls jumped back to allow Mrs Gibbs to shuffle out past them. "Mind aht," she gurgled, swaying on those infamous bad legs.

"Greetings, ladies." Guy ushered them into his flat. "Mrs Gibbs 'does' for me," he explained.

"Really?" Sunny found it hard to believe that Mrs Gibbs could leave anywhere cleaner than she found it. If the old lady ever went missing, they could simply follow the trail of cigarette ash and phlegm.

"Sit, sit." Guy ushered them into his overcrowded sitting room. "Make the place look attractive." Curious items from all over the world jostled on shelves. A stuffed owl squinted at Sunny as she sat gingerly on a chaise longue.

"You have a very eclectic collection here," said Sunny, dusting off a word she rarely dared to use.

"I've been lucky enough to go round the world with my work," smiled Guy, with that smile that was always the same. He gazed about at the kilims and the aboriginal paintings. "I usually bring something back." He slapped the nose of a large, unnerving tribal mask that hung on a nail. "UHURU!" he grunted suddenly. "NOKWANGA ZUM!" He nodded, as if accepting imaginary applause, and explained, "That's a voodoo chant I learned in Africa. Amazing guys, those witch doctors."

"Fascinating," said Sunny, politely.

Jojo turned a Papuan nasal flute over in her hands. "Wasn't Uhuru the woman in *Star Trek*?" she asked, with knife-sharp casualness.

"Careful with that," warned Guy. "It's a thousand years old." He left them alone while he went off to make tea.

"This is a fecking museum," muttered Jojo.

"I think it's interesting," lied Sunny. The room, with its dead animals and anthropological oddments, gave her the creeps.

"Where's Chloe?" Jojo raised her voice to ask. She saw boundaries only as funny little lines put there for her to waddle across.

From the kitchen, Guy shouted, "Oh, she needed some space," over the sound effects of jangling spoons

278

and boiling kettles. "Whatever that means." There was a synthetic jocularity about him. "She'll be back."

Jojo pointed silently to a large framed photo of Guy on the mantelpiece, centre stage and commanding the room. Presumably Guy's publicity shot, his handsome face was attempting to look gentle yet firm, sensitive yet sadistic. *Cast me!* it begged. *I can be anybody, from mentally deficient to action hero!*

Pointing to a much smaller, two-inch by two-inch, photobooth snap of Chloe that was tucked awkwardly behind a carving of a wombat, Sunny whispered, "No wonder she needs space." In a flat this size there was barely room for Guy and his ego, never mind a woman.

Shaking her head, Jojo said knowingly, "No, I reckon *this* is why she left." From beneath a cushion on the armchair, she extracted a very purple, very glittery thong.

"No!" yelped Sunny.

"No what?" grinned Guy, returning with a full tray.

Freewheeling wildly, Sunny improvised with her customary skill. "I was just saying, no, that wasn't you playing the corpse in *Midsomer Murders* the other night."

Like any actor, Guy preferred to dwell on what he *had* been in. "I did pull off a cracking dead window cleaner in *The Bill* seven years ago. Really had to dig deep for that. Even washed a few windows to get inside the character's head."

"Gosh. Amazing." Sunny gushed, holding his gaze desperately, aware that Jojo was cack-handedly stuffing the thong back under the cushion. "Any other appearances coming up?" she asked absently.

"Nothing concrete. A few callbacks."

"Fab. Great." Sunny had no idea what he meant.

"Sugar?" asked Guy.

"I don't know." The innocuous question panicked Sunny. Was he holding the sugar bowl in a pervy manner? Could she detect sexual deviancy in the way he poured the milk?

Jojo plunged in with a fearless question. "Who do you think is the Chudleigh Cad, Guy?"

His reply was airy. "Don't know, love. Don't care. Some nutter with no girlfriend and too much time on his hands. Oops." Guy looked archly from one visitor to the other. "Have I just described myself, ladies?"

A natural pooh-pooher, Ellen was pooh-poohing vehemently. "The glittery thong is purely circumstantial," she told Sunny and Jojo. "We all know that Chloe wouldn't wear something like that, but it's not enough on its own. If you had found a whole stash of underwear, and somebody claimed them as missing, that would be different. You need more evidence."

"Easy." Jojo was nibbling all the chocolate off a Kit Kat.

"Easy?" queried Sunny, dubiously.

"As pie."

CHAPTER
TWENTY-TWO

Camilla's answerphone message had left Sunny in no doubt. "I'm tired of waiting for the proposal scene, darling," she'd threatened. "Hurry up or I'll be angry. And you wouldn't like me when I'm angry."

I've got news for you, Camilla, thought Sunny wearily, as she knuckled down to work. I don't like you when you're not.

The bedroom door swung dramatically open, interrupting Sunny's first trickle of inspiration in days.

"We're in!" Jojo was smiling, devilishly.

"In where?"

"Guy's flat." Jojo was so pleased with herself she performed a short jig. "I bunged Mrs Gibbs a tenner, and she's letting us in while she 'does'. Well, come on," she chided impatiently. "What are you waiting for?"

Sunny was waiting for her common sense and her personal decency to catch up with her. She took off, before they could spoil things.

Predictably, Mrs Gibbs was in a foul mood. "Gettamoveon," she ordered, slapping Sunny with a damp duster. Sounding as if she was gargling wet nails, she launched into a recital of her ills as Jojo set about rifling Guy's flat. "You should see me veins, like knotted rope. And don't talk to me about piles."

Sunny had no intention of ever doing this. Overwhelmed with guilt at what they were doing, her overwrought imagination transformed every squeak of the floorboards into Guy's return. "This is *wrong*," she flung at Jojo, elbow deep in a desk drawer. "Let's forget it."

"Wimp," spat Jojo, striding into the bedroom. She looked around, with the eye of an expert, and said, "Aha!" before flinging open one of the bedside cabinets. An avalanche of ladies' underwear tumbled out on to the shag pile with a soft thud. "Gotcha, you perv!" Jojo shrieked, falling to her chubby knees and throwing the scanty lingerie into the air.

"Oh, my God." Sunny was rooted to the spot. She hadn't seriously expected to find anything. This was a little too real for her liking. "It's Guy. He really is the Chudleigh Cad."

"You bet your sweet bippy he is!" whooped Jojo. "Get a load of this!" She twirled a scarlet brief round her forefinger.

"Stop it!" begged Sunny, disturbed by Jojo's delight and by the suspicion that they were in over their heads. "This is serious, Jojo. He's stolen these knickers and terrorised all the women in the block. You shouldn't be laughing."

A nice pair of peach camiknickers on her head, Jojo disagreed. "It's funny," she said gaily. "And nobody's really been terrorised." Jojo was not impressed by modern theories of stress-related trauma: her considered

282

advice to manic depressives would be, "Get over it". "I can't wait to see Mrs Wilde's gob when she sees this little lot."

"But what do we do now?" agonised Sunny, aware of Mrs Gibbs's eyes on them.

"We'll unmask him at the Residents' Association meeting tomorrow." Jojo was definite, with no room for doubts.

"Ewwww," shuddered Sunny, contemplating the little Everest of underwear. She couldn't fathom why a handsome, self-assured man like Guy would stoop to nicking knickers. "Should we, you know, take one?" she suggested timidly. "Just to show Mrs Wilde as proof?"

"Great idea." Jojo scooped up a flimsy black pair. "These'll do."

Mrs Gibbs's litany of personal woe had tailed off. "Got another tenner?" she asked, in her OAP From Hell voice. The girls looked over to see a small piece of paper in her nicotine-stained grasp. There was handwriting on it. "It in't half interesting," she leered.

Jojo looked to Sunny, who tutted impotently and handed over a ten-pound note. Gingerly, Sunny accepted the creased paper, only to have it snatched by Jojo.

Greedily reading, Jojo hooted. "Holy shit!" she exclaimed. "This nails him!"

Sunny read over her shoulder. The first few lines made her acutely uncomfortable: Chloe was telling him how much she loved him, and how it broke her heart to leave. The last two sentences, however, were worth her ten pounds and her damaged conscience. "I can't live with your seedy other life any longer. I can't sleep beside you knowing the trophies you collect to feed your addiction are right beside the bed."

"Wow," gasped Sunny.

Jojo went further. "Double wow with extra nuts," she said.

Either side of Fabio on a white leather banquette, Sunny and Sarah leaned over him, laughing like, well, like drunks.

"Did you see . . ." Sunny was lost for words.

"Yes, he . . ." gasped Sarah.

"And then he . . ." Sunny managed to squeal.

"And I . . ." squawked Sarah.

"HA HA HA HA HA HA HA!" bellowed Sunny, whose careful up-do had tumbled out of its clips.

"Your hair!" screamed Sarah, as if they had reached comedy nirvana.

"I know!" hollered Sunny.

This struck Sarah as possibly the wittiest thing she'd ever heard.

When Sunny had suggested that they take Sarah out to cheer her up, Fabio had said of course. No, he'd reassured her, of course he didn't mind. Between the two women, he sat very straight and sipped his cappuccino, looking rather like a man who minded.

The laughter had turned to raucous sobs on Sarah's end of the banquette. The taxi ride to her house involved a lot of hairstroking, a lot of soothing and a lot of "He'll come back, of course he will".

284

Unconvinced, untidy and wobbling like a tightrope walker, Sarah's erratic progress up her path prompted an attack of drunken guilt from Sunny, as she watched from the purring taxi. "Should I go in with her, make sure she's OK?"

"*Cara*," said Fabio, placing a restraining hand on his girlfriend, "you can't live Sarah's life for her. Alfie has gone: she must face it."

"He'll come back," asserted Sunny for the umpteenth time, as the taxi drew away.

"Perhaps. We must hope," said Fabio, sweetly, but with distance, like a kindly priest. "Now, do you mind if we change the subject, my darling?"

He sounded so wistful that Sunny laughed sympathetically. "Oh, I'm sorry, Fabio." She quelled a burp. "It's no fun watching two birds get drunk."

The taxi sped up, and Sunny felt a lurch, as if a thread that connected her to Sarah had just been tugged. She turned to Fabio and quelled the pinprick of guilt by kissing his beautiful mouth. It almost worked.

Sunny let herself in stealthily, tiptoeing to the light switch. She let out a strangled "Eek!" as she saw Sister Jane and Ellen, sentinels in dressing gowns, at the kitchen end of the hall.

Sunny sobered up in a nanosecond. "Who's dead?" she asked baldly.

"Lots of people," said Sister Jane, with a glance up and down her dishevelled niece. "But nobody we know." She turned to Ellen. "Coffee, I think?"

"By the bucket," agreed Ellen.

"Have I done something?" Sunny obediently slurped the coffee they gave her.

"There speaks a guilty conscience," said Sister Jane, batting Marmite off the table. "Actually, it's not about you. It's about this young lady."

"You?" asked Sunny, surprised, turning to Ellen. "But you're never the problem."

"One day," mused Sister Jane, looking at the ceiling, "my darling niece may develop the talent to keep her mouth shut. But this, Lord," she lamented, "is obviously not the day." Frowning at Sunny, Sister Jane said, "Perhaps, sometimes, we take it for granted that Ellen is fine, just because she doesn't complain," she paused, "like the rest of us do." Leaving a moment for Sunny to digest this, Sister Jane went on. "Ellen has shared something with me tonight that I think you should know, too. Then we can understand her a little better, and maybe —" she stroked Ellen's hair tenderly "— love her a little more." Sister Jane laid her mug in the sink. "I'll leave you to it, girls," she said, and closed the kitchen door behind her.

A silence fell that Ellen, staring at the table, didn't seem about to fill.

"OK, I'm scared. You can start any time you like," said Sunny, who had gone cold during Sister Jane's intro. "What's happened?" she asked. Then, when Ellen still said nothing, "Can I help?"

Clipping Sunny's last word, Ellen suddenly looked up, past her cousin, and began to speak, mechanically, as if reading a transcript. "Do you remember when I left my job in Dublin?"

Sunny nodded.

"I didn't leave. I was sacked."

"No, you can't have been!" The words, dumb and impetuous, sprang from Sunny's mouth.

"I was sacked," repeated Ellen, still staring at a point somewhere over Sunny's shoulder. "The senior partner, Donal Courtney, told the other partners that I mishandled an important case."

"You would never do that!" protested Sunny with certainty.

Ignoring her, Ellen trundled robotically on. "Donal was lying. He . . ." Ellen faltered for the first time. ". . . had some sort of *crush* on me." Her voice was that of an automaton again, devoid of emotional emphasis. "He took me to meetings, involved me in strategy making. He told me things I didn't need, or want, to know about his problems with his wife. One evening, he insisted I stay late and help him prepare for court. I was reaching for a file when he reached inside my blouse."

It was as if Ellen didn't hear Sunny's shocked bleat.

"He tore it open," continued Ellen, dryly, with no emotion. "I struggled to push him away. He threw me, hard, against the bookcase. I banged my head. I was crying. He pulled my bra down, and he was kissing me. Even though my head was bleeding. I screamed and kicked, and I got away from him. I fell over a swivel chair. But I got away. I couldn't face work the next day, or the next. When I went back, Donal summoned me to a disciplinary meeting, where he sacked me with the full backing of the board."

"NO!" Sunny couldn't help herself. This was a horror story.

"He said he'd given me every chance, but I kept messing up. He said he couldn't cover for me any more." Ellen's eyes were intent on the middle distance. "I had to clear my desk." She startled Sunny by turning to look at her. "I know what you're thinking."

"Do you?" asked Sunny, mildly. More than anything, she longed to wrap her arms around Ellen, but her cousin was emitting very efficient signals repelling any sort of physical contact.

"You think I'm a coward. I think I am, too. I should have told the truth. Stopped him doing it to somebody else. But I couldn't face it." She flexed her fingers. "Being interviewed, *photographed*, asked if I'd led him on. I would have had to defend myself, and I didn't have the strength. I let him win. I've let him win over and over again since that night because I can't forget it, or get over it." Choked, Ellen's self-possession was begininning to unravel.

This was hard to listen to. Sunny felt agitated with anger and defeated by sadness. She imagined her dignified, modest cousin exposed and bleeding, somehow getting herself home; it was a vile picture. "If you really want to know what I'm thinking, it's that you have absolutely nothing to explain or feel guilty about, Ellen. You're the victim here."

"I *hate* that word!" snorted Ellen, with a vehemence that made Sunny flinch. "I don't want to be a victim.

It's not . . . not *me*. But every time I see *that* look in a man's eye, I freeze. Suddenly, I hate him. Do you get it?" she asked wildly. "I hate any man that fancies me!"

"I get it." Sunny needed to cry, but she wasn't about to burden Ellen with her own emotions. "This brings us neatly to Dave, doesn't it?"

"Mmmm," agreed Ellen, wrapping her own arms around herself in the hug that Sunny didn't feel permitted to give. "He just made a very gentle move on me, that's all. And I freaked." She crumpled at the memory. "Christ, I terrified him. He put his arms around me, kissed me on the lips . . ." Sorrowfully, Ellen admitted, "Nobody's kissed me since *him*."

"Oh, Ellen, you poor thing," soothed Sunny.

"Oh, Ellen, you mad thing," corrected Ellen tartly. "I went berserk. I knew Dave was only trying to show me how he felt. I tried, I really tried, to relax, but suddenly he was another Donal, a pig who only wanted one thing and didn't care whether I was willing or whether he had to take it from me." She closed her eyes. "He thought I was joking at first, and just grabbed me tighter . . ."

"Oh dear," empathised Sunny.

"Exactly. That's when I went ballistic."

"Poor old Dave," Sunny said sadly. "He was almost lynched."

"For nothing. For expecting me to be normal."

"You are normal. Don't start," ordered Sunny. "You were learning to trust Dave, and one day you would have felt secure enough to kiss him. And," she suggested timidly, "to tell him."

"I couldn't even tell you," said Ellen miserably.

289

"You have now," Sunny reminded her comfortably. A suspicion tapped her on the shoulder. "I've just twigged: Patrick knows, doesn't he?"

"Yeah." Ellen nodded. "Somehow, one evening, when we were waiting around for you, it all came out. He's a good listener, I suppose," she ended sheepishly.

Now, Sunny understood how Patrick was able to take control with such assurance at the party: he knew the back-story. "Will you scream if I hold your hand?"

"No," smiled Ellen, and held out her slender white hand. "Actually," she said after a moment, "that's rather nice."

"One of my strengths," Sunny boasted. "Hand-holding."

Over cornflakes the next morning, both Sister Jane and Sunny were adamant.

"I can't face it," said Ellen briskly, snapping on her bracelet watch.

"You owe him," Sunny reminded her, tossing sugar over her flakes.

"It would mean he can stop blaming himself," said Sister Jane.

A promise to tell Dave was extracted sometime between a row over the last yoghurt and Ellen's departure for the office.

This outing to Hammersmith would eat into precious writing time, but Sunny had to do it.

290

"Welcome to my world." Alfie pulled open the door and swept an arm extravagantly over his surroundings. "Quite the palace, I'm sure you'll agree."

"It's . . . nice." Sunny took in the room, which was boudoir, kitchen and living area all in one economical, tatty package. "Such a bonus," she said, "when one can switch on the kettle without getting out of one's bed."

They both laughed, a conspiratorial snigger with years of history in it. Sunny threw her arms around him. "What are you doing in a bedsit, you idiot? You're far too old, and far too bald, to live in one room."

"But it's so handy for the mini-mart," argued Alfie, taking two glasses out of a depressed Formica cupboard. "Down one flight of stairs and I'm in a twenty-four-hour paradise of Pringles and long-life milk."

The bedsit had been decorated by a pattern fanatic. The sofa bed's jazzy tartan argued vociferously with the floral curtain at the window. "This is the best you can do?" said Sunny, dubiously. "You've got pots of money, Alfie Castro. Is this self-flagellation, like those old martyrs who wore hair shirts and ate nettles?"

"I do have a hair shirt, but it's by Dior," smiled Alfie. "No, Sunny, this is the best I dare do. Rich old Alfie Castro won't be rich for much longer if his life carries on collapsing." He paused, corkscrew in hand, to muse, "Sid James never filmed that one, did he? *Carry On Collapsing*." He handed Sunny a glass of cold wine. "Babs Windsor would play Sarah, the sexy Spam avenger. Hattie Jacques would do her comedy-nun routine. And Sid could play me, reduced to one room by the flyover, rediscovering the launderette."

"You'll get another job . . ." Sunny clicked her fingers, not very well ". . . just like that."

"You never could click your fingers properly," smiled Alfie, leading her to the lumpy sofa. He drank the wine in two gulps. "Have you seen her?"

"I'm seeing a lot of her," Sunny nodded. "She doesn't know I'm here. She's in bits, Alfie."

Alfie seemed to shrink. "Yeah."

"Why don't you go home?"

"Is that what she wants?" he asked, without looking up.

"Yes! Yes!" Sunny beefed up the exclamation points. "She needs you. She misses you. She's sorry."

"Aha," said Alfie, mildly. "Did she say that?"

"Well . . ."

"Not big on sorries, my wife." Alfie shook his head. "It's all gone wrong. It doesn't feel the same." His laugh was short and rasping. "I sound like one of your heroines."

"You can mend things, Alfie. You have to talk. You were meant for each other."

"I would have agreed, once upon a time. Sarah doesn't want to talk, she wants to make speeches. She stopped thinking about my feelings months ago." He looked almost shy as he said, "It hasn't been nice in our house for ages, Sun."

"She's still the same Sarah. Underneath."

"Maybe the same Sarah is not a nice woman. And maybe the best thing for me is not to be too near her."

292

Alfie was choosing his words carefully. "That came out extremely badly, but I can't think of any other way to put it. She's not good for me." He shook his head, as if he could hardly believe what he was saying. "I don't want to go back."

This was difficult to listen to. Sunny crossed the maze of mismatched carpet tiles and grabbed the bottle to refill their glasses. "How's the job hunting?" she asked, brightly. "Where have you been for interviews? Partridge Haldane Associates were always sniffing round you." The world of advertising is an incestuous one, with creatives shuffling from company to company, lured by bonuses, and perks, and the relative merits of the executive loos.

"If they had a bargepole," said Alfie comfortably, "Partridge Haldane wouldn't touch me with it. Nor would any of the big-hitters. I am the opposite of Viagra as far as the advertising business is concerned."

"But you're famous in West One," argued Sunny. "You're the man who got the nation buying recycled toilet roll. You coined the phrase 'Bobby's in the shed'. It was you who convinced four out of seven teenagers that they couldn't live without a fun-fur cover for their mobile."

"Yes," concurred Alfie. "That was me. But more importantly, I'm the man who put Porqy Peeces out of business."

"Hmm." There was no getting away from that. "You deserve a second chance. Somebody will recognise what an asset you are."

"So I can carry on making teenagers buy stuff they don't need?"

"Hang on there, matey. That's sacrilege. Advertising agencies exist to make people buy stuff they don't need." She scrabbled for an analogy. "That's like Aunty Jane saying Jesus was a bit of a chancer."

"The most surprising thing about all this —" Alfie looked sideways at Sunny, as if he didn't expect her to believe him "— is the relief. After spending all day, every day, stressing out about my job, and my marriage, and making enough money to keep the Castro show on the road, suddenly I have ordinary, small problems again, like trying to make sure I don't run out of clean pants and what to have for dinner. Advertising has chewed me up and spat me out and, Sunny, *I don't care*." He smiled and slapped his knees. "How are the twins?"

"You shouldn't be asking me." Sunny saw an opportunity to press her point home. "You should be with them. You're their daddy." She paused, before saying, "They're great, as usual. Charlie picked his nose and was gallant enough to offer me the bogey. Sam threw a tea party for every battered teddy in the house. They're fine, but they need their daddy."

"Not half as much as their daddy needs them," Alfie said.

"Then go home, you stubborn little advertising genius, you." Sunny poked him.

"We'll work out access. I'll never let the twins down."

"Access?" The cold word rattled Sunny.

"I've decided to let Sarah keep the house."

294

"Christ, you've been thinking about this." Sunny was alarmed.

"What else have I got to do? Man cannot live by daytime TV alone." Alfie polished off his wine. "I'll get some kind of job. Maybe I can retrain. I'll have to pay maintenance."

"I don't want to hear this." Sunny was adamant. "I think you should go home. Where they love you."

"That's just the point," said Alfie. "They don't."

CHAPTER
TWENTY-THREE

"Why do you think God gave you feet?" was Sister Jane's waspish response to what Sunny thought was a very sensible question — "Why are we walking back from the supermarket when a bus goes past the door?"

"To make Nine West rich." Skipping to keep up with those muscly little nun legs, Sunny said, "Sarah sounded very down on the phone."

"I'm very proud of the campaign, but I didn't foresee the personal toll it would take on the poor girl." Sister Jane strode across the road, holding back the traffic with one small, magisterial hand. "Husbands don't seem to stick around these days."

"My dad's not going anywhere," Sunny consoled her, adding distantly, "He wouldn't dare."

"My husband's pretty reliable," said Sister Jane unexpectedly.

Sunny pulled a face she'd never made before: part mule, all amazement. "Your what?" she asked, in a giggly, hysterical whisper. "Aunty Jane, I know you're full of surprises but —"

Raising her eyes to heaven, Sister Jane said, "Sometimes I forget what a pagan you are. I'm married to the Lord, Sunny. In a metaphysical way."

"Which means you don't have to do his ironing. Or have his dinner on the table." Sunny found another advantage her own mother would welcome: "And you don't have to listen to him droning on about golf."

"That's one way of looking at it."

"He's a model husband, in many ways." Sunny warmed to her subject. "Doesn't make a mess around the house. Never leaves wet towels on the bed. You can trust him around your girlfriends."

"Well, he's married to most of them as well, remember."

"Oh, yeah. Poor old henpecked God." She looked accusingly at her aunt. "I hope you don't all nag him at once. He's got a lot on his plate, you know. War, famine, disease, etc., etc."

"Like any good partner, we do our best to help."

Craftily, Sunny suggested, "So, technically, you were being unfaithful with old Ernest at the Angus Steakhouse? Was God jealous?"

"If he ever decided to assume that very human emotion, I'm sure he wouldn't waste it on Ernest. And less of the old, if you don't mind. He's only ten years ahead of me."

"You'll never get old." That cheeky face was perennially young. "It must be something they put in the Communion wine."

"Stop it now." Sister Jane couldn't help tittering. "Some respect, if you don't mind, for my vocation."

"How did you know you had one? A vocation, I mean?" Sunny was intrigued.

"I've always known," said Sister Jane matter-of-factly. "Besides . . ." She paused, looking both ways as they crossed a side street.

"Yeah?" prompted Sunny, when her aunt hesitated. "Besides?"

"I knew I didn't want to see the same old face over a boiled egg every morning." Sister Jane put a hand to her mouth. "That sounds terrible."

"No, it doesn't," smiled Sunny, revelling in these cosily shocking revelations.

"Don't get me wrong, I know Mary loves your dad, and Mo loves Uncle Brendan, but seeing some man get older, and fatter, in the opposite armchair, watching the telly every night, arguing about whether to have a conservatory or a carport . . ." Sister Jane shuddered. "It's not for me."

"But surely life in the convent is kind of samey?" Sunny had a mental image of a very big, very quiet house full of mousy women praying and averting their eyes.

"Not at all!" Sister Jane assured her, as they passed the brash, confusing window of a bookie's. "We teach, and we take in exchange students, and we look after the local homeless, and we have a football team."

A nun's football team was almost too comical to resist, but Sunny managed.

"I've always been a bit of a rebel," said Sister Jane contentedly.

Becoming a nun wasn't Sunny's idea of rebellion: her teenage wildness had involved eyeliner, getting sick on sweet martini and staying out till, oooh, well past ten.

She looked at her aunt's sturdy figure. Perhaps it *was* rebellious to go and live in what amounted to a feminist commune, instead of toeing the party line by finding a suitable boy and settling down to produce little people just like you. "I never thought of it like that before," said Sunny.

"No. There's no space in your day to think." It wasn't unkind, the way Sister Jane said it, but the comment made Sunny uneasy. "Every minute of your time is taken up. Music blaring, your computer screen flickering, chattering on your mobile, rushing off to restaurants and discotheques."

"Aunty Jane, nobody goes to discotheques these days. It's clubs."

"Clubs, then. And the television is never off." Sister Jane slowed and looked at Sunny with interest. "Is it ever peaceful enough for you to hear the little voice within you? Do you have a quiet place?"

"That's a strange question!" Sunny rebuffed it with a laugh.

"Obviously not," said Sister Jane enigmatically, stepping up the pace again.

"Love the halter-neck," murmured Guy into Sunny's ear. "Shows off your shoulders." His insinuatory voice felt as if it was inside her head. She leaned away from him: she knew too much about Guy to welcome his compliments.

She spotted Patrick in the scrum of residents at the meeting and shoved her way through to get to him.

"How come you're here?" she asked. "You don't live in the flats."

"Mrs Wilde asked if she could hold the meeting in our production tent. Said we should attend. There's some big announcement, apparently."

"I know, I know." Sunny rocked excitedly on her heels and whispered, "They're going to unmask the Chudleigh Cad."

Patrick tensed. "They're what?" he asked, seemingly incredulous.

"Me and Jojo found out who it was." Sunny was bursting with excitement.

"You mustn't do this," said Patrick vehemently. He was staring deeply into her eyes, like a stage hypnotist. "Please, Sunny, don't let this happen."

"What's the matter with you?" Sunny backed away from him, treading on a Thin Girl, who apologised for leaving her foot in the way.

"Please," pressed Patrick, laying a hand on her bare arm, as Mrs Wilde began her spiel, standing on a crate at the end of the tent.

"Welcome, one and all," she said grandly. "This is an auspicious day for the Residents' Association." It was impossible to ignore Ernest's hand stabbing the air. "What is it?" asked Mrs Wilde, irritably, palpably keen to get to the exciting bit.

"As the *StyleScaping* chaps are present," began Ernest, his moustache rippling with emotion, "I would like to protest in the strongest terms about the changes to our gardens." To a chorus of "Hear, hear", he continued. "In particular, I would like to condemn the modern art they have inflicted upon us."

Serena looked resolutely at the floor, while Patrick bit his lip.

"Personally," began Mrs Wilde, "I *like* the statue. It's very . . ." She seemed at a loss to describe it, and abandoned that line of reasoning. "Perhaps we all need reminding that the fees from Curiosity Films will enhance our Residents' Association events for quite some time." She rattled on, ignoring interruptions from the floor. "For instance, our Christmas party can at last enjoy a professional Santa. Remember last year? When our Santa let us down at the last minute?" Mrs Wilde glared at Ernest.

Clearing his throat, Ernest said, "My dear wife passed away the night before."

"That," said Mrs Wilde absently, addressing her clipboard, "is the kind of thing I'm up against." She clapped her hands, quelling the hubbub of dissent. "We're here today to discuss something far more important. Tireless detective work has resulted in an important discovery. Ladies and gentlemen, the Chudleigh Cad has been caught!"

A bubble of surprise broke over the crowd. Ernest raised his eyebrows at Sister Jane, who raised hers back, and settled his cravat. Ben looked nervously about him, and the Thin Girls let out a collective "Oooh!" of anticipation. Mrs Gibbs asked, "What did the old bladderbag say?" loudly enough for the old bladderbag to hear.

Sunny sneaked a look at Guy, who seemed blithe about what was about to happen: that actorly ego had convinced him he was untouchable. Even though he was a "creepy, crazy madster" (Jojo's memorable phrase), Sunny felt a pang of sympathy. Was a public unmasking really necessary?

Up on her orange-box podium, Mrs Wilde didn't look as if the finer points of ethics bothered her much. She handed over to Jojo, who was confident and self-possessed, gazing around at the assembled residents like a presidential nominee addressing a rally. "This," she declared, holding aloft a Woolworths carrier bag, "belongs to one of you." She upended the bag and the black knickers with a distinctive red ribbon on them fluttered to the floor.

Gasps and exclamations filled the air. "Is there any grub at this do?" spluttered Mrs Gibbs.

Sunny felt a sharp dig to her ribs. "Stop her!" Patrick was hissing, looking pained. "Please!"

"I can't," mouthed Sunny, disturbed by his passion. He was so disappointingly lukewarm when it came to her, how come Guy's plight moved him so much? Besides, she reminded herself with a healthy pinch of self-righteousness, Guy had to face up to his problem.

The middlingly Thin Girl stepped forward. "They're mine!" She rescued her tiny pants, and stroked them as if they were a little chiffon hamster. "Where did you get them?"

"Yes," shouted Guy. "Come on! Who's the Chudleigh Cad?"

Sunny had to admire his nerve. She kept her eyes fixed on his face as Jojo unfurled the incriminating note.

"*This*," she said, bright-eyed and evangelical, "was written by the Cad's girlfriend." She cleared her throat and began to read. " 'I can't live with your seedy other life any longer.' "

As Sunny watched, a subtle change crept over Guy's face, like a storm cloud building in the distance.

" 'I can't sleep beside you knowing the trophies you collect to feed your addiction are right beside the bed.' " Jojo folded the note, with slow precision, back into its original folds. She swept a long, tantalising glance around the assembled residents.

Guy swallowed hard. He had gone very still.

Sunny's head felt hot as she heard Jojo say, very distinctly in the hush, "That note was written to GUY STALBRIDGE!"

All faces swivelled towards Guy. Everybody took a small but definite step away from him. He stood, like a statue in the middle of a flattened cornfield, with a stupefied look.

Sunny felt a surge of pity. She glanced at Patrick, who looked as baffled as Guy. He was frowning and seemed about to say something, but Guy beat him to it.

"It wasn't me," he said weakly, before utilising his actor's projection. "This is a mistake," he boomed, defiantly.

Up on her stage, Jojo waggled the note. "It's signed by Chloe," she said, condescendingly. "And how else do you account for the knicker mountain in your bedside cabinet?"

"There's a simple explanation," said Guy, his demeanour reminding Sunny of his walk-on part in a Battle of Britain TV film. He continued, more limply, "But I don't want to go into it."

Nervous laughter sounded from the residents. "Yeah, right," shouted Ben, whose boiled-egg appearance could evidently be misleading. "Perv!"

"How could you?" The thinnest girl looked close to tears.

"In my day —" began Ernest.

Ernest's potentially fascinating reminiscence was doomed to go unheard: Mrs Wilde yanked Jojo off the crate and reinstated herself on it. "Let him speak," she demanded, imperiously.

Guy, looking surprised to have her as an ally, said, "I can explain. But it's difficult. You see . . ." He paused, and looked at his feet, his lips a slender line. After a deep breath, he raised his head and admitted, "I do have an addiction. But it's not what you think. It's a sex addiction." He laughed, unconvincingly. "Yup. I can't get enough. It's never off my mind. I proposition all and sundry."

Goggling at him, Sunny felt vaguely affronted: he'd never propositioned *her*. She caught Patrick's eye. He looked bemused, as did everybody else.

"The underwear by my bed . . . Well, yes, they are trophies, for want of a better word." Guy had gone red. A classy claret, as befitted his socio-economic status. "I always manage to keep a pair of undies from the birds — *ladies* — I sleep with."

Two of the Thin Girls cast wondering looks at their middlingly thin friend, who avoided their eyes to stuff the panties into her chic little handbag.

"But," Guy's voice wobbled with emotion, "I have NEVER stolen knickers from a stranger in my life. It's all part of the sexual encounter for me. Sorry to disappoint you, folks, but I'm not your Cad."

A buzz of confused chatter erupted. Mrs Wilde agreed with Guy from her prominent position. "No, Guy, you aren't the Cad." She had the crowd's attention. Obviously enjoying herself, her floral crimplene bodice shook as she roared, "But I know who is!"

This was turning out to be the most action-packed Residents' Association meeting ever. Sunny remembered long evenings spent debating the merits of compost heaps: tonight would go down in RA lore. It was the Kennedy assassination of Residents' Association meetings. She shrugged dramatically at Jojo, who was looking highly disgruntled, but she studiously avoided Guy. At a guess, his expression wouldn't be benign. As for the newly sensitive Patrick, his head was in his hands.

"The callous brute has been using a position of trust to carry out his disgraceful deeds," thundered Mrs Wilde. "No woman has been safe from his grubby attentions. We have all trembled beneath him, but today his reign of terror ends."

The audience was rapt, waiting for the second, and hopefully more reliable, revelation of the evening. Sunny's mind raced. She was still adjusting to the fact that Guy was just an innocent sex maniac. Who on earth, she wondered, was Mrs Wilde about to name?

"The Chudleigh Cad," howled Mrs Wilde, "is Patrick Smith." A scarlet fingernail pointed in his direction.

Slowly lifting his head out of his hands, Patrick met her gaze.

"Deny it if you can!" shouted Mrs Wilde triumphantly.

"Obviously, I'll deny it," said Patrick equably.

"Eh?" Sunny pushed her way back to Patrick's side. The residents muttered around her, like a mob of villagers in a Frankenstein movie. "Patrick, tell her she's wrong!" she urged.

Mrs Wilde stepped from her box, like a sprightly hippo, and walked with self-conscious pride to a parade of lockers where *StyleScaping* personnel stashed their personal belongings. "Please note the name on this locker," said Mrs Wilde, like a conjuror about to perform a trick.

" 'Patrick Smith,' " read her audience obediently.

"*Voilà!*" With a flourish, Mrs Wilde tugged the door open. A job lot of knickers tumbled out on to the floor. "Need I say more, ladies and gentlemen?" simpered Mrs Wilde, her wider-fit sandals obscured by scanties.

Aghast, Sunny yanked at Patrick as if he was a one-armed bandit. "Tell them!" She was wild-eyed. "Tell them they've been planted there, Patrick!" The surly mood of her neighbours was scary. "Tell them you've never seen these knickers before."

Patrick squeezed his eyes shut, then laid his palms over his face. In a resigned voice he said, "She didn't plant them. I knew they were there."

With relish, Mrs Wilde sneered, "You put them there, didn't you, you sick, twisted goat of a man?"

"I did." Patrick held out his hands as if to be cuffed. "It's a fair cop."

"He thinks it's funny!" Mrs Wilde appealed to the crowd, which was already on her side.

"It's not funny," scowled a small redhead in ill-advised shorts. "Them's my best briefs." She stooped down and snatched back her property.

The Greek woman from the second floor who always had spinach in her teeth said, "I feel violated," in a heavy accent and retrieved a very large pair of faded bikini bottoms. "In my country . . ." She tailed off menacingly, leaving details of a Greek fate unclear.

Ben, who was coming out of his shell considerably, shouted, "Let's get him!"

Sunny stepped in front of Patrick. "You're wrong. You're making a mistake," she squeaked, in a voice with all the gravitas of candyfloss.

Mrs Wilde shook her head. "You heard it from the horse's mouth," she reminded Sunny. "I propose a vote. Please write your suggestion for Mr Smith's punishment on the slips of paper that Leonard is handing out and give them to me on your way out. I'll assess the results and inform you anon."

Patrick turned his face to the wall, as the residents scribbled angrily and left the tent. Sunny, a ferocious guard dog in a halter-neck, stood by him, glowering at everybody.

The thinnest girl said, with a sad shake of her head, as she passed, "He hasn't even said sorry."

A sigh shook Patrick's frame.

"Why should he be sorry for something he didn't do?" asked Sunny passionately and rhetorically.

Serena, who had been silent up until now, took Patrick by the shoulders as the last vote was cast. "Did you do it?" she asked him, her voice shaking.

Patrick nodded.

Sunny gasped.

Serena unleashed a long string of unladylike words, then added, "Thank you, Patrick, thank you so much. They say there's no such thing as bad publicity, but you've proved them wrong. If this gets out . . ." Serena twirled her beads and eyed Mrs Wilde. "We need to talk," she said.

"We do, don't we?" said Mrs Wilde contentedly, and allowed Serena to lead her off into a corner.

Demoralised, Patrick was slumped against the locker that had incriminated him. Sunny shook her head. "I don't buy this," she said. "I know you wouldn't do this."

"In that case," said Patrick, without looking at her, "you obviously don't know me as well you think you do." He turned to her. "Sun, tomorrow, Thursday, could we meet up again, just this once?"

"Of course." Sunny nodded, her eyes crinkling warmly at him.

"I really need to talk."

CHAPTER
TWENTY-FOUR

Even without Abba apparently performing live for the Gonks in Jojo's bedroom, Sunny would have found it hard to concentrate on *Fatal Crescendo*. The spectre of Camilla, teeth bared and horsewhip in hand, was a compelling incentive, but Sunny's fingers slumped on her keyboard like so many sausages.

A cartoonish image of Patrick tiptoed through her mind. He was sniggering unpleasantly and holding a tiny pair of knickers to his nose, like a wine connoisseur. It didn't ring true.

And yet . . . during a long night spent on the edge of Fabio's futon staring out at the posh Chelsea moon, Sunny had been forced to admit that Patrick had been around at vital moments in the Cad's career. He had the opportunity to snatch the giant pink knickers while she snored in the tent. He'd been around the day her own pants had been kidnapped. He'd visited the flat on the very day Sister Jane's underwear had walked. Since filming had started, he'd been at Chudleigh Court almost every day.

It would all be circumstantial without the confession. But even with the confession, Sunny couldn't absorb it: Patrick was almost *too* sane. He didn't fit the template of the Chudleigh Cad, and she was yearning to hear the archetypal simple explanation in the Volunteer. Quite what form that explanation would take was beyond her.

Jojo opened the bedroom door and aimed a pair of pants at Sunny's head. "Yours," she explained. "Mrs Wilde is returning Patrick's pervy pile."

"Don't say that," muttered Sunny.

Behind Jojo, Sister Jane looked in to say, "Mine are the only knickers that haven't come home to roost." She looked mildly proud.

"Odd," said Sunny, shuddering at the thought of Patrick touching her aunty's underwear.

Obviously glad to be first with the news, Jojo told Sunny, "Patrick's punishment has been decided. He has to have counselling, but he's being allowed to film the rest of the series as long as he doesn't step inside the buildings."

"Like a dog with the mange," murmured Sunny.

"No, like a loony who can't keep his mitts off ladies' knicks." Jojo preferred to call a spade a spade.

It had to be done. Mid-morning, Sunny dragged Jojo to Guy's flat and a large dollop of humble pie, with some grovel on the side, was consumed on his doormat.

Guy was surprisingly forgiving. He seemed to find Mrs Gibbs's sideline in snooping amusing, rather than disturbing, and he exhorted them both not to worry about it. "Friends again," he smiled benevolently.

Evidently, any spotlight was welcome, even an unflattering one.

There was no time for lunch. Sunny was too busy not writing a proposal scene, but Fabio wouldn't take no for an answer. With premature guilt about the lie she would have to concoct in order to meet Patrick later, Sunny gave in and joined him in the back of a large chauffeur-driven Bentley. "Nice," she understated. "Where are we going?"

"Paris!"

"No, really, where are we going?" Her heart sank. Fabio meant it. "Oh, how wonderful," she said in a monotone, gluing a wide smile on to the end of it.

"It is a surprise. To make up for the last time we tried to do this." Fabio was grinning and delighted with himself.

"Lovely. A surprise." Sunny wished he'd notice that she didn't like them much. "What time do we get back?"

"In three wonderful days."

"But I haven't even got a suitcase!" panicked Sunny.

Proudly, Fabio told her, "It is taken care of. Jojo packed for you."

"Oh, that's all right then." Sunny wanted to scream, but instead she kissed her thoughtful, romantic, generous, down-right irritating boyfriend.

According to Fabio, the Hôtel Georges V was the Parisian choice of royalty and Madonna, and Sunny had to admit that the Material Girl knew her stuff when it came to luxury. Their suite was splendid, in the true meaning of the word. The soaring ceilings were painted with eighteenth-century frescoes. The lamps shed discreet pools of light on the antique damasks. Sunny assumed she'd need a travel card to cross the bed. It was absolutely magnificent.

Her suitcase, open on a special rack, was everything Sunny had feared: it was classic Jojo. She'd tucked a Gonk in but had neglected to include underwear. Thoughtfully, she had provided a furry hat, and she had also been diligent enough to pack one slipper. There were all Sunny's oldest T-shirts and two pairs of trousers, one of which had dog poo on the turnups. There was cleanser, and moisturiser, and mildew remover. There was a hairdryer without a plug and the winceyette nightie Sunny huddled in when she had period pains. All in all, not noticeably Madonna-like.

Peering over her shoulder, Fabio murmured, "We must go shopping, *cara*," and snapped the case shut. "After."

It was impossible to remain churlish when a man whose sexiness was way off the Richter scale was sliding your shoulder straps down and kissing your freckles. Sunny turned to Fabio and soon they were on that bed the size of Sunny's first flat.

Sex with Fabio always left Sunny feeling as if tiny elves had been expertly massaging her body. Languorously, she stretched her limbs on the bed, shouting, "Darling," loud enough for him to hear over the roar of the power shower. "Where's my laptop?" It was verging on sacrilege to think about work in this opulent room, but Sunny had no choice.

Back came a shout. "I do not bring your laptop."

Sunny took a deep breath. A low surge of panic swelled in her chest. Three days before she could get back to *Fatal Crescendo* . . . Camilla would be filing her teeth into points.

Another shout came from the bathroom. "This trip is for pleasure. We do not think about work."

"Correction," thought Sunny acidly. "*You* don't." In fact, she realised, Fabio never thought about work. He seemed to own one of those money trees her father was always on about. Trying to keep calm, and trying to locate the pocket she kept her gratitude in, she reminded herself that a man as privileged as Fabio couldn't possibly grasp what it meant to earn your own living. How would he guess that writing books not only paid the bills but shored up Sunny's shaky self-esteem? Sunny took a deep breath and prodded herself to be grateful and appreciative. Fabio couldn't be expected to understand her work.

As he emerged, lithe and absurdly wantable, from the shower, Fabio's outline shimmered in the steam. Outside on the Avenue Georges V, the sun nipped behind a cloud and the room darkened. Fabio disappeared for a moment, making Sunny blink. It was only an illusion. He was back again.

Maybe it was her fate, Sunny mused. Perhaps a wicked fairy had stood over her bassinet and, with a wave of her sticky wand, decreed that Sandra Parkinson would always have niggling problems to spoil her fun. Surrounded by Parisian comfort and glamour, with the

314

benefit of hot and cold running sex, Sunny was fretting about Patrick.

This anxiety had to be hidden from Fabio, who would feel betrayed if he guessed what was going on in her head. Sunny kept recalling the meaningful way Patrick had said he needed to talk to her, and she keenly remembered how wonderful it had felt for her life to be balanced for once: she had the love of her boyfriend, plus she was the trusted confidante of her ex.

Now everything was out of kilter again, as Sunny silently willed the devoted Fabio to leave her side long enough to let her call Patrick before he got to the pub. It seemed like hours before Fabio asked if he could slip away for a brief chat with the manager, who was an old family friend.

"Yes! Yes! No problem!" Sunny had to sit on her hands to stop herself from ushering him out of the door. One lingering kiss later, he was gone, and Sunny scrambled over to the telephone.

Hands shaking, and feeling like a spy, she confronted the international dialling system. Her fingers were fat and disobedient, and she had to keep stopping to take deep breaths before starting again.

Something was wrong. Instead of the familiar beep-beep of a mobile ringing, she heard a pre-recorded French message. She tried again. No joy. "What's wrong with it?" hissed Sunny, redundantly, shaking the phone and tapping it on the side of the desk: this was the extent of her expertise with hardware. She dialled again, only to hear the Gallic bint repeating herself.

Ellen can get hold of him for me, thought Sunny, willing herself to stay calm, confident that her diligent cousin would still be in her office. This time the capricious French phone system co-operated. "Ellen!" she said, her voice wet with relief as the phone was picked up at the other end.

"Sorry. Ellen's on a training course. She'll be back tomorrow."

That bad fairy was on a roll: Ellen's mobile was off and remained that way. Even Sister Jane was permanently engaged: some kind of prayerthon, perhaps.

Sunny tried Patrick's mobile again. Once more that recorded mademoiselle explained something, clearly and calmy, and once more Sunny regretted sneaking her Walkman into French classes back at school.

"Aha!" An idea struck Sunny, a good one. She could ring Jojo and ask her to pass on her message.

It was peculiarly infuriating listening to the phone ringing gaily in Chudleigh Court when she couldn't get through to Patrick, but Sunny was accustomed to her ruinous technological karma. She composed herself. Jojo was not the ideal person to rely on in a crisis. If her cousin detected any sign of desperation, she would flick into Aunty Annie mode and sadistically hold back any help. Jojo had to be handled with care.

"Hi! How are you?" sang Sunny gaily, as if Jojo's happiness was the one thing in the world she cared about.

"How'd you think I am?" growled Jojo. "What do you want? *My Name Is Earl* is on." Jojo didn't play by the rules of chat. She didn't offer any details she wasn't specifically asked about, and she didn't ask how other people were: this might imply she cared.

"Listen," said Sunny, casually. "Could you wave out of the window to Patrick for me? Put him on?"

"S'not here."

"But he must be."

"It's pissing down. There's nobody here. They all went home early."

"Nooooooo," wailed Sunny, forgetting herself.

"Is something the matter?" Jojo was more interested now. "What's wrong? Has Fabio dumped you?"

"Of course he hasn't," snapped Sunny. "Listen, if Patrick rings to ask where I am, will you say I'm very sorry but I was whisked away on a trip? Tell him that I'm really, really sorry. Will you?"

"I don't always answer the phone." Jojo could smell blood. "There's the first episode of a Robson Green two-parter tonight. If he rings during that, I'm not answering."

"No," hissed Sunny. "You couldn't leave your mate Robson on his own to do a favour for me."

"He's me favourite," stated Jojo simply, as if that explained everything. "I have to go. Marmite wants another choc ice."

"Don't let me keep you," said Sunny to the dial tone.

Anticipating Patrick's puzzlement, annoyance and eventual disappointment was making it even harder to think straight. He needed her, and Sunny was going to let him down. He would conclude that she didn't give a damn.

For some time after that she stared at the tapestry on the wall and tried to remember Patrick's home number. These days she never used it: they always talked on their mobiles. It was in the memory of her mobile which sat by her bed in London, diligently unpacked by Jojo. She knew the first three numbers, but after that it all went fuzzy. "8925," she muttered, like a witch making an incantation. "8952." She screwed up her eyes. "9825." She cursed. "I think there might be a four in it." Suddenly she hated fours.

Regarding Fabio across the immaculately laid table, Sunny felt proud. This was the perfect setting to showcase his beauty. He had calmly steered her through a menu that reminded her of the French GCSE she had failed, he had known what a "sommelier" was and had dealt with him, he had passed Sunny a linen handkerchief to stop her blowing her nose in a napkin. "You are *perfect*," she whispered at him, her ungracious gripes forgotten and her Patrick-flavoured fretting quelled by the vintage wine.

"I do not like that word," smiled Fabio. "It is dangerous."

"Maybe," agreed Sunny, but it was the only one that covered him. "If we skip dessert . . ." she leaned closer in the candlelight ". . . can we go upstairs and make love like maniacs on the rug?"

"WAITER!" called Fabio, a little raucously for such an establishment.

★　★　★

Perhaps, thought Sunny, as she scribbled wildly, I should *always* write my novels perched on a gold-leafed loo in the small hours. She had crept away from the sleeping Fabio to make the most of sudden inspiration, and the missing chapter was pouring out of her Biro on to Georges V notepaper.

The bathroom was so *über*-luxurious that it had a telephone hanging there on the marble wall, presumably for those vital calls that just *had* to be made whilst weeing. It was tempting, but Sunny resisted. Even if she managed to beat the bad fairy and get through to Patrick, she couldn't speak to him in case she roused Fabio. Explaining why she was phoning her ex-boyfriend secretly in the middle of the night would take some doing.

Instead, she applied herself to *Fatal Crescendo*'s proposal scene. She was happy with it so far: it was romantic enough to satisfy Camilla and unlikely enough to satisfy herself. The leaky pen halted as Sunny examined the word she'd just used: unlikely. Jojo was right, she thought bitterly, I *have* been scared to write a proposal in case it came true. Jojo didn't quite understand, though: Sunny wasn't frightened of being proposed to; she just didn't want Fabio to echo what she wrote. When, *if* he asked her to marry him, there must be no mystic overtones: she had to believe he was doing it for love alone.

So, the more unlikely the better. Lucinda and Sergio had been swiftly relocated to Japan. No sooner had they arrived than the local volcano started to grumble, as they do, and now the terrified but well-groomed couple were fleeing a river of molten lava. The lava was gaining on them, but Sergio managed to snatch Lucinda out of the way of their "fiery foe" (Sunny was on form) for long enough to ask her to marry him.

Yawning, Sunny crawled back to snuggle alongside Fabio. However rich and resourceful he was, even Fabio wouldn't be able to conjure up an erupting volcano in Paris.

CHAPTER
TWENTY-FIVE

The subdued couple boarding the flight to London couldn't possibly be the same playful pair who had been tugging each other's underwear off with their teeth just hours earlier, could they?

They could.

All had been nuzzles, kisses and tickles until Fabio had glanced at the bill when they were checking out. "No, no, we did not use the phone," he told the receptionist. A clammy sweat broke on Sunny's brow as he turned, good-naturedly, to her. "We didn't need anybody else, did we, *cara*?"

Her carefully casual "Hmm?" spoke volumes.

"Ah." The penny, or possibly the euro, dropped with Fabio. With a disappointed sigh, like a headmaster who'd discovered Sunny, yet again, forging a note to get out of games, he asked, "If I dial the numbers on our bill, will Patrick answer?"

Sunny nodded and started to explain. "But, Fabio, Patrick was expecting to see me, it was important, he had something to tell me, and I couldn't just let him down, so I was trying . . ." She limped to a standstill, conscious that she wasn't improving matters. "When I say 'important', I don't mean *important*," she continued, confusingly. "And obviously I *could* let him down. Of course I could. But . . ."

Fabio had paid the bill, silently. With a sad smile, he'd gallantly picked up Sunny's luggage, heavy with the new clothes his black card had bought for her.

In the facile luxury of the first-class lounge, she sat next to him, studying his dejected profile, wondering what she could say to repair the rent in their intimacy. A plea for leniency along the lines of "Your jealousy made me lie to you" was wisely shelved.

On the plane, Fabio stared out of the window, his tigerish eyes distant. Sunny watched her fellow passengers get on, her fingers drumming on the armrest. Fabio had perked up a little, but she still felt uncertain, as if her (rather snazzy and ostentatiously new) shoes had been transported to shifting sand. Then she noticed something that took her mind off the injured young god next to her.

One, two, then three, four Japanese people entered the first-class cabin. Graceful and smiling, with sleek black heads, they were just the vanguard of a whole Japanese platoon. They filed past her and took their seats, returning her stupefied stare with polite nods.

Chattering mutedly, they kept coming, until every other passenger in this section of the plane was Japanese. It was like — she paused to try and swallow — being in Japan.

"Stay calm," she told herself. To fulfil the prophecy, a river of molten lava would have to flow down the aisle.

Take-off went smoothly, with no volcanic activity, and soon lunch was being served. Japanese conversation flowed in tuneful staccato around her as everybody unfurled their napkins. Mmm, lasagne, thought Sunny, with Homer Simpson inflection, as she hungrily eyed the tray in an approaching stewardess's hands.

The plane lurched suddenly, as if the giant toddler playing with it had dropped his toy. Sunny's tummy fell like a lift in a skyscraper, and the stewardess stumbled, tipping the tray.

Fabio had, of course, the reflexes of a panther. The lasagne took off independently, but he managed to sprawl across Sunny and take the bullet for her.

Shocked Japanese gasps segued into a flutter of applause. The stewardess, mortified, fussed at Fabio with a damp cloth; the unimpeachable white of his cotton shirt was splattered with blobs of lasagne, like a tomatoey map of the world.

Waving her away, Fabio was looking deep into Sunny's eyes. He peeled off his soiled shirt, causing the stewardess's cloth to pause, mid-flourish. "*Cara* . . ." The eyes fixed on Sunny's own were wholly tender now. The pasta-based drama had chased away the vestiges of Fabio's grand Italian sulk. "Will you . . .?"

His lips this close always made her head swim, but Sunny wasn't too giddy to note that if she squinted, the lasagne dripping from his glossy hair looked just a little like lava.

Despite this, a voice that sounded just like her own, but was rather loud, shouted, "Yes, Fabio, I will!"

★ ★ ★

The pop of champagne corks brought neighbours out of their front doors like meerkats.

"Congratulations!" said Ernest, accepting a glass on the landing, which was filling up with Chudleigh Court denizens.

"Congratulations!" said Boiled Egg, accepting a glass.

"Gimmethat, you snotty little know-nothing," grunted Mrs Gibbs, swiping the bottle.

"Is that the ring?" The Thin Girls gazed, goggle-eyed, at the pyramid of diamonds weighing down Sunny's left hand. Glam enough to make the Beckhams' Christmas list, it had apparently been passed down through seven generations of Fabio's celebrated family. Dazed, Sunny stared at it. The ring threw back the dying light of the dusky landing as dazzling strobes.

"I've never seen anything like it," she admitted.

"You're so lucky," said all or some of the Thin Girls.

"They'll probably get divorced." Jojo had her own angle on the celebrations. "Most people do."

Bouncing about like an Italian spaniel that had just been let out of a car boot, Fabio pressed fizz on to anybody who passed by, and kissed Sunny at least twice a minute.

One of these kisses almost knocked her over. Sunny giggled and righted herself. "I feel so strange," she whispered.

Ellen, at her side, looked concerned. "Good strange or fainty strange?"

"Oh, good strange," Sunny assured her. "Excellent strange." She laughed and a tear dribbled out. "Never-been-happier strange." Her head felt exceedingly hot and quite empty. "Perhaps I should sit down." She laid a hand on Ellen's arm.

Propped up in an armchair, Sunny felt mildly ashamed. She was a robust girl and usually left the Victorian histrionics to her mother, who liked nothing better than to zigzag across family gatherings squawking, "Who put the lights out?"

"Sorry. I don't know what came over me. My legs went all funny," Sunny said sheepishly.

"It's the excitement," said Ernest.

"It's that ring," said the thinnest Thin Girl. "I'd faint if somebody gave it to me."

"She's probably pregnant," drawled Jojo from across the room.

"Shut up, you!" said Sunny, with unexpected vehemence from an invalid.

Fabio knelt in front of his fiancée and asked tenderly, "You don't regret saying yes, do you?" It wasn't a serious question, and everybody round him smiled benevolently.

"God, no," whispered Sunny, and she threw her arms round him, as all the surrounding females teared up. "No, never," she whispered into his hair.

Mrs Wilde turned up, telling Sunny, with insulting incredulity, that she'd done very well to nab Fabio. "Reminds me of my Leonard in his younger days." Leonard had coughed uneasily at this and plucked at his safari shorts. Mrs Wilde had been particularly impressed to hear that Fabio had surreptitiously flown over to Dublin to ask Mr Parkinson for his daughter's hand. "Very traditional," she commended.

Sister Jane said, with some glee, "I can picture your da's face when Fabio turned up on the doorstep."

"Yeah," laughed Sunny, tinnily. She'd been grimacing at the thought of that meeting. What, she wondered, could Fabio have made of the psychedelic hall carpet her parents were so proud of? She suspected that none of the Carelli di Sica houses could boast a collection of eggcups depicting seaside towns of Ireland or a doorbell that chimed "Wake Me Up Before You Go-Go". The ring on her finger proved that Fabio didn't hold the avocado bathroom suite against her, and that he was man enough to cope with tumbletwist loo-seat covers. "They got on just fine, according to Fabio."

"Mr Parkinson is a gentleman," said Fabio. "He had many tales of hardware shopkeeping to tell."

Hoping that her dad hadn't partaken of too much Baileys during these many tales, Sunny asked, "Did he tell you about the time Terry Wogan came into the shop?"

"He did."

"Ah." Too much Baileys. Over the years, Mr Parkinson's encounter with Mr Wogan had grown longer and longer: the current version culminated in Terry Wogan exclaiming that Sunny's dad should really have a television show of his own, as "It would be better than that rubbish you see nowadays." "Sorry," she said.

"I enjoyed his talk."

326

"Of course you did." Ellen patted Fabio on the back. "He's so polite. A few family Christmases will soon knock that out of him."

While Fabio was re-enacting the pasta-splattered proposal to an admiring audience of tipsy neighbours, Ellen nudged Sunny to ask, "Why didn't you cancel Patrick? He stopped me in the gardens the next morning, wondering what happened to you."

"Oh God. Did he wait long at the pub?"

"Closing time."

"Why didn't he ring the flat?" squeaked Sunny.

"He did."

They let that hang in the air, imagining Jojo cosied up to Robson Green and ignoring the phone.

Ellen said uncomfortably, "I suppose you don't want to hear this, but he seemed, well, hurt." She dropped her voice even further, making Sunny incline her head to hear. "Are you sure?"

"About what?" Sunny caught on. "About Fabio? Of course I am!" She studied Ellen, wondering where such a question had come from.

"It's just so quick . . ."

"For you, maybe, Miss Cautious. Not for me." She laughed at her cousin's grave face. "Honest!"

A finger tapped her on the arm and Sunny turned to face Sarah, who had obeyed a texted summons. She was speechless when she heard the reason. "Good luck," she said, holding Sunny rather too tightly. "I'm thrilled." She didn't look thrilled. She looked shrunken, as if her sundress belonged to somebody else.

"This can't be easy," said Sunny, in an undertone.

327

"Oh, it's easy. It's easy because I love you, Sun," Sarah assured her, her face obviously holding back a waterfall of tears. "I'll just, you know, slip away, and . . ."

"I understand." Sunny watched her go, wishing she could guarantee one of her trademark happy endings for her friend.

Head buzzing with the excitement, Sunny slipped into the bathroom for a moment on her own. Through the high, open window, she saw the film crew, gathered around Patrick, who was doing something horticultural with a hoe.

"Five minutes, everybody!" A shout dispersed the little crowd.

"Oi! Patrick!" Sunny knelt on the cistern and leaned out. "Come up and have a glass of champagne!"

Finding her face at the tiny window, Patrick shaded his eyes and called up, "I'm blacklisted. Remember?"

"Ooops, of course," she shouted. "Listen, about the other night . . ." It was a strange position to apologise from, but she did her best. "There was nothing I could do. I'm so —"

"Don't worry about it," he interrupted her, from down on the lawn. "It didn't matter."

"But —," Sunny was determined to push an explanation out.

"Forget it, Sunny," yelled Patrick. "You're a busy girl. It's cool. What's the champagne in aid of?"

Struggling to keep her balance, Sunny bawled, "I'm getting married!" Her knee slipped and she fell, pressing her face into an empty bottle of Toilet Duck.

She bobbed up again to hear Patrick shout, "I'm very happy for you."

"When will we have that drink? And that chat?"

"At your wedding!" Patrick grinned cheekily, just as a make-up girl jerked his chin down and came at him with a powder brush.

Sunny stared at him for a long moment before she clambered down from the cistern. Ellen's reportage was flawed: Patrick didn't look even slightly "hurt". Ironically, this had the knock-on effect of making Sunny feel slightly hurt. Impatient with her own childishness, Sunny reached up to pull the window shut. There was a definite chill in the dusk: the long summer was fading at last.

Visitors had dribbled away, trailing good wishes in their wake. Fabio had gone on ahead to his place to "get it ready", whatever that might entail.

"I forgot that Patrick's not allowed indoors." Ellen was elbow deep in suds, washing glasses. "Doesn't feel right. Like he's some scuzzball. We all know he isn't."

"Well, he is, actually," said Jojo, teasing Marmite with an Iced Gem. "He stole knickers for wanky fun. He's massive scuzzball."

"I still don't believe it," said Sunny defiantly.

Sister Jane said decisively, "It's not a nice topic for today. Today is a special day. Let's not talk about scuzzballs."

"He is, though."

Sister Jane persisted. "Let's talk about Fabio. About the future. There are going to be a lot of changes around here."

Sunny started, and glanced at Ellen, who had done exactly the same.

"Oh, yeah," said Ellen, as if it had just struck her. "You'll move out."

"Well, not right away," quibbled Sunny, who had been so dazed by the proposal and by her own acceptance that she hadn't thought past it.

"So . . ." Ellen turned to her sister. "We'll be here together, Jojo. Alone."

"We'll need a new rota." Jojo seemed quite pleased. "I want to do less hoovering."

"Such a sentimentalist," laughed Sunny. "I know you'll miss me really."

"Yeah, I will," said Jojo. "It'll mean more rent."

"Will you live in Italy?" asked Ellen, with a sulky look.

Sister Jane chipped in. "Fabio was telling me he has plans to buy a place in the States. He might want to move there."

"Hang on, hang on, ladies." Sunny held up her tea towel. "We've only just got engaged. Let me get used to that idea first."

Tickling Marmite's chin, Jojo told the cat, insinuatingly, "She's got cold feet already."

"I'll ignore that, if that's all right with everybody," sighed Sunny.

"By the way, I did as I was told," said Ellen briskly, dunking a glass. "I spoke to Dave."

"And?"

"And he walked away." Ellen rubbed the glass ferociously, as if trying to whittle it into an amusing shape. "Can't cope. Wished me well and all that, but he's not in my life any more."

"God. Bloody hell." Sunny felt impotent: launching into a list of Dave's shortcomings was tempting, but that wouldn't help Ellen. "I'm sorry. I wish he'd reacted differently," she found herself saying woodenly.

"Me too." Ellen held the glass up to the light. "This one needs another rinse."

One of the James Bond touches that Sunny particularly liked about Fabio's apartment was the panel of switches near the front door that controlled the lighting. Various "moods" could be evoked with a flick of the finger. Sunny had sanguinely expected "seduction", but she walked into "workplace".

"Something smells good," she said, brushing Fabio's neck with her lips as she slipped off her jacket. "Oh, it's *you*."

"We have quite a night ahead of us," he promised her.

"You betcha," she responded, with more than a hint of Benny Hill. She let him take her by the hand and lead her into the sitting room. "What are they?" She'd anticipated hundreds of tiny candles and was taken aback by the array of files and folders on the low glass table in front of the fireplace. They reminded her of homework and didn't fit in with her racy plans for the evening.

"Sit, sit." Fabio lowered her to the goat-skin rug and knelt down beside her. "*This* —" he opened the nearest folder "— is wedding venues." He patted the file and said, with a boyish raise of one eyebrow, "My favourite is the family chapel in Tuscany, but we can talk about that." He dragged a pile of brochures towards them. "Honeymoon ideas." Pointing to an A4 envelope stuffed with papers, he said, "Those are catering companies, mainly British ones, but I have some Italian suggestions as well, depending on where we hold the ceremony. Of course," he said, looking cheeky, "we could always have two weddings. So many decisions." He sprang up, like Marmite would if she didn't eat chocolate twenty-three hours a day, and went to the kitchen. "You make a start. I'll check on dinner."

Immobile, Sunny stared at the coffee table. It looked like her parents' coffee table had looked during her GCSEs. It wasn't a look she liked. "Er, Fab-ee-yo," she wheedled, raising her voice to be heard over the noise of pasta bubbling. "Isn't this a bit premature? Can't we enjoy the moment and let the details take care of themselves?"

The chef came to the door of the kitchen and leaned gracefully against the jamb. He pointed a wooden spoon at her. "For you, it might be premature. I've been thinking about this since I saw you leaning on that washing machine."

"Oh, Fabio." Sunny's bones turned to jelly. "You're so sweet." She picked up the nearest leaflet. "Ooooh!" she said, with an exaggerated gurn of delight. "Bridesmaids' shoes!"

CHAPTER
TWENTY-SIX

It was the first time that Sarah had seen Fabio's apartment. She was impressed. "Taste. Style. Elegance." She pointed to the marble floor in the en suite. "And Mickey Mouse slippers. I can tell you're a frequent visitor."

"Oh, Fabio has enough class for both of us," tutted Sunny, sending the slippers under the loo with a swift kick.

Spotting the stack of bridal magazines in the sitting room, Sarah picked one up. "You're keen. Going to grab him while he's hot?" She flicked through page after page of white dresses and dreamy smiles. "Am I a bridesmaid?" she asked, apparently amused by the idea.

"I haven't got that far," protested Sunny, trying in vain to switch on the coal-effect fire. The weather had changed with a vengeance. "We can't agree on where or when."

"You've done the who, that's the important bit." Sarah squatted by the cold grate. "Ple-ase let me be your bridesmaid," she wheedled, mischievously. "You were mine, after all."

"What a day that was." Sarah's wedding had been a riotous blur of confetti, and laughing, and very bad dancing.

"Remember Alfie telling me that I couldn't invite anybody I'd slept with?"

"Yeah," laughed Sunny, "and you stood up and tipped all the invites in the bin."

They both laughed, comfortably, and stopped dead at exactly the same moment. Sarah said softly, "How did he seem to you?"

"Terrible. He's —" Sunny stopped, frowning. "How did you know I went to see Alfie?"

"More to the point, why didn't you tell me?"

"I was going to," said Sunny, uneasily. "I wanted to try and help. I needed to see how he was for myself."

"Don't panic. I'm not annoyed." Sarah sucked her teeth. "He'll barely speak to me."

"He can't get a job."

"Yeah. He managed to tell me that."

"If you apologised . . ."

"For what?" Sarah flared up. "For caring about people's health? For doing the right thing?"

"For screwing up his job." Sunny held Sarah's gaze.

"I *am* sorry about that," said Sarah, huffily. "But he won't listen to me. He only listens to *Her*."

"Not Liz again." It felt like ancient history to Sunny: Liz's name hadn't come up during her visit with Alfie.

"He's been with her." Sarah pouted. "Twice."

This baffled Sunny. Once again she was hurled into a boiling cauldron of doubts about Alfie. Something else

334

occurred to her. "Hang on. How do you know? And you haven't told me how you knew I was at his flat?"

"I'm psychic." Sarah pulled a mystical face.

"You're about as psychic as Marmite's behind." It dawned on Sunny. "You're watching him."

Sarah nodded. "We all need a hobby."

"You're crazy," said Sunny with feeling. "Instead of sitting down face to face and communicating with him, you'd rather sit in a car wearing dark glasses."

"I need to know." It was almost a whine. "He's still seeing her, even now when there's no excuse. They don't work together any more."

"Well, maybe they . . ." Sunny worked feverishly to cobble up a feasible reason for them to meet.

"Maybe they're at it!" snapped Sarah. She yanked a small notepad out of her handbag. "Look," she said earnestly, flicking over the pages. "Monday. 3.18p.m. He went to her house and stayed there for one hour and twelve minutes." Flushed, she appealed to Sunny. "What else could they have been doing?"

"That's a long list, starting with Scrabble and ending with contacting the dead. You have no proof that they're having an affair." Sunny snatched the pad. "This is scaring me, Sarah." She read out a few entries at random. "8.09p.m. Kentucky Fried Chicken. 11.47p.m. Lights out." Sunny stared at her friend. "You're sitting there till all hours? Who looks after the twins?"

"The nanny, of course. Although they had to sleep on the back seat on her night off." Sarah grabbed the notebook and stowed it away. "It's better than sitting in that big house, worrying. Missing him." Sarah threw Sunny a pleading look.

"You can be bridesmaid," she relented. "But you have to wear a dropped-waist peach dress with matching bag."

Sarah laughed, as Sunny hoped she would.

"I'm very impressed. Very." Years of exile in Dublin had softened Trevor Parkinson's accent, but Sunny's dad was still recognisably a Londoner. "Presentable. Polite. Charming. He had your mother fluttering like a teenager."

"I can't deny any of it," agreed Sunny happily, gazing across the room to where Fabio was immersed in compiling a guest list. "He's a dream."

"And not short of a few bob," said Trevor Parkinson in an undertone, as if speaking of gynaecological matters. "Did we get this wrong, or is the young fella a count?"

Fear of fainting fits and palpitations had ensured that Fabio's title had been kept from the aunts during their trip. "No, you heard right."

There was an intake of breath at the other end of the phone, and Trevor turned his head away to shout excitedly, "Mary! He *is* a count! He's a count!" An outbreak of squeals greeted this, as if somebody had thrown hot fat over a hen. "Your mother says, will that make you a countess?"

"Ummm." Sunny didn't know the answer, and had to ask her intended. "Apparently, I'll be a contessa. I'll be Contessa Sandra Carelli di Sica." She said it slowly.

It sounded like somebody else, not the girl curled up with her knees under her chin in the Venetian mirror opposite. "Flipping hell," she added.

"She'll be a contessa," shouted Trevor dutifully over his shoulder at the other end of the phone. There were more noises, which could have been her mother giving birth to farmyard animals but were in fact a simple question. "Your mother says, what will that make her?"

Resisting the exquisite temptation to say, "The same neurotic old bag she's always been," Sunny broke the news that her mother wouldn't get a title. "She'll still be the same old Mary Parkinson, I'm afraid."

"Ah." Trevor spoke to his wife again. "You'll be a duchess, love," he told her.

"Dad!" gasped Sunny, as the noise of a casserole dish hitting lino flew across the Irish Sea.

It was tricky, having a foot in both camps. Not quite living with Fabio but not quite part of Chudleigh Court any more, Sunny never seemed to have the right clothes. Her favourite mascara was always where she wasn't. She surprised herself by missing her old life at the flat. Even Jojo had her good points when she was a taxi ride away.

Now that Camilla had accepted *Fatal Crescendo*, Sunny should have been embarking on her next little epic. Entwined Hearts's fees weren't juicy enough to allow much leisure between novels. However, the apartment was designed for relaxation, not labour, and Sunny was finding inspiration hard to come by.

Life with Fabio centred on quality. They watched art-house foreign films, ate simply prepared organic meals and listened to Satie. Oh, for a quick blast of *Corrie*, thought Sunny, as she nestled against Fabio and watched a compelling African drama about the disputed ownership of a goat.

One Wednesday night, she arranged to eat with her cousins, despite Fabio's unexpected grumpiness at the suggestion. His idea of togetherness exceeded even Sunny's needy definition. To keep him happy, she texted him half-hourly as she and her cousins sat chatting aimlessly and amiably in the kitchen.

Just as Sunny was asking, "Where's Aunty Jane?" they heard a key in the front door and a familiar Irish voice shouted, "Yoo hoo! It's meeee!" which was Sister Jane's customary entrance.

"Yoo hoo!" shouted Sunny and Ellen together. For some reason known only to themselves, this made them laugh every time. They were still giggling when Sister Jane reached the kitchen. She wasn't alone.

"Dave," gasped Sunny.

"Jayzus, Dave," gasped Jojo.

Ellen brushed past her aunt and their visitor with a speed that rendered her brusque. Her bedroom door slammed behind her.

"It's all right," said Sister Jane quietly to Dave, who looked ready to flee. "We'll get the kettle on."

In silence, they listened to it boil. Sunny asked in a dull voice, "I can't remember, Dave, do you take sugar or not?"

338

Dave took two, he informed her, his general demeanour that of a man on trial for his life.

Sunny did her best to hand him a mug of tea in what she hoped was a non-judgemental manner, but inwardly she was seething with unasked questions. How could he show his face after letting Ellen down so badly? She didn't share Ellen's philosophical acceptance of his decision: if he had real feelings for a woman, then he should take the rough with the smooth. "Penguin?" she offered, dully.

"We've only two left," whined Jojo, who had none of Ellen's graciousness, particularly where chocolate-covered biscuits were concerned.

Sister Jane, with a reproving look at Jojo, took both the Penguins and handed one to Dave. "There's something you should all know," she said, stirring her tea. "Ellen didn't get in touch with Dave."

Suddenly, Dave looked different to Sunny. He seemed taller, and the jacket she had condemned as an anorak blossomed into a windcheater. "Oh, my God. You know now, though, about . . ." She left the end of her sentence dangling, uncertain how to allude to Ellen's ordeal and its aftermath.

"Yes. Sister tracked me down and told me everything," said Dave, casting about for somewhere to park his Penguin. "I feel terrible." He looked wiped out. "I had no idea."

"How could you have?" sympathised Sunny, who had flipped deftly from Dave's hanging judge to his staunchest supporter. "Nobody knew. We were so pleased when you came along and made Ellen so happy." She smiled at the confused modesty that overwhelmed Dave's mundane features. "You must have felt awful after the party."

"You all thought I was a rapist or something." Dave wasn't an eloquent boy. "I'm not. I'd never hurt her."

Jojo asked, "Are you finishing that Penguin?"

The noise of a door opening down the hall interrupted them. "Dave?" Ellen used a small, anxious voice.

"Right. We're off out." Sister Jane was matter of fact. "You too, miss," she said, before Jojo could argue.

Turfed out on to the streets of Putney, the three evacuees debated where to go. For want of any better suggestions, they decided to head for the new tapas bar on the High Street.

"The joint is jumping," said Sister Jane, as she pushed her way in.

Looking around, they recognised many of the faces throwing back tequila. "There's the bloke who does the clapperboard," Sunny pointed out. "And isn't that one of the cameramen?" The crew of *StyleScaping* had invaded the place, getting merry and eating their own weight in *patatas bravas*.

"Sunny!" yelled Patrick from the bar. "Have a tequila!"

"You're drunk." Sunny was amazed. Patrick occasionally got giggly after his tenth Guinness, but she had never seen him so red of face, or wobbly of leg.

"I am! But I'm going to get much drunker!" he promised her. "Have a tequila!"

340

"No thanks. I've got some nail-varnish remover in my bag that tastes better." She turned to her companions. "What'll you have, Aunty Jane?"

Before Sister Jane could answer, Patrick yelped, "Have a tequila!" in what was becoming quite a monotonous way.

"Do they do sherry?" Sister Jane asked.

"Have a tequila!" advised Patrick, loudly.

Eventually, and against their judgement, they had a tequila. And another one. After that Patrick didn't seem drunk at all.

"What are we celebrating?" asked Sister Jane, pouring her third tequila into a pot plant.

"Our slot!" shouted a make-up girl. "Oooh! Whoops!" She cackled and put a hand over her mouth. "That sounds a bit rude, dunnit? And you a nun." She squinted at Sister Jane. "You are a nun, aren't you?"

"Yes, dear," said Sister Jane.

Serena appeared. She had the enviable knack of getting drunk without looking as if she'd rolled down a hillside. "Let me explain, Sister," she said smoothly, swaying only slightly on her delicate high heels. "A slot is the day and time our programme will be aired. We were originally scheduled for 6p.m. on Fridays, which is pretty good." She reached up and tousled Patrick's hair, which was un-Serena-ish enough to be the result of strong drink. The tequila also seemed to have magically erased her anger about cad-related publicity. "But when the suits saw our rushes, they moved us to eight-thirty on Thursdays."

"And that's a better slot?" Sister Jane asked.

"It's BRILLIANT!" shouted Patrick. "Have a tequila!"

Sunny looked sceptical. "How would you know about slots? You'd never even stood in front of a camera until a few weeks ago. And I have a tequila, thanks," she added, hurriedly.

"I know because Serena told me so," said Patrick, in a happy, dopey voice. "And Serena is the cleverest woman in the universe."

Serena looked modest, but didn't dispute the accolade. "It really is a massive boost for us. It means more viewers, more media interest and of course more fame and fortune for this man!" she ended, with a raucous giggle, presumably borrowed from a page-three girl.

"I'm really, really pleased," said Sunny. And she was. It was true. But she was also marvelling at the Frankenstein monster she'd created when she'd egged Patrick on to take the job. All that attention from make-up girls and lighting experts seemed to have rendered him more handsome than he used to be. His jaw was cleaner, and he had pecs now. She narrowed her eyes. "Patrick Smith, you've been going to the gym," she accused.

"Have a tequila," he suggested, but quite quietly.

Serena said smoothly, "Of course he has. He has to be buff on the screen. He has wonderful raw material. It's a shame to waste it."

If Sunny had ever dared to call Patrick "wonderful raw material" he'd have laughed her out of the tapas bar and into the river.

"Come on, Aunty Jane, let's move to a cooler spot," Sunny said, knowing that Patrick wouldn't even notice they'd gone. Leaving Jojo at the bar to get a bottle of sparkling water, she and her aunt colonised a table by the door.

Sunny brought up something that had been puzzling her. "Aunty Jane, the phone bill was in the flat and —"

Cutting her off with a look of embarrassment, Sister Jane said, "Oh, goodness, yes. I'm so sorry, dear. I'll pay for all the overseas calls, of course. I meant to mention it earlier."

"That's not important. I was just wondering what's going on." Sunny saw her aunt's expression close off. "Whoops. I'm being too nosy."

"No, no," said Sister Jane, uncertainly. "I'll tell you when there's something to tell."

"Fine." Sunny smiled at her aunt. The woman had gone through nearly six decades being mysterious, and she wasn't about to give it up now.

Jojo set down their overpriced fizzy water. "I told the barmaid to give us free olives, but she wouldn't, the cow."

"Imagine that," said Sunny. "Somebody immune to your charm."

Sister Jane said slyly, "I can see somebody who isn't immune. A chap at the bar is staring at you, Jojo."

In disbelief, presumably, thought Sunny, swivelling her head.

A burly, suede-headed bloke averted his gaze as all three women turned and caught him.

"Bloody hell, he *was* staring," conceded Sunny, with blatant and quite rude astonishment.

"It's a free country," said Jojo, nonchalantly.

Sister Jane pushed. "He's smitten, unless I'm mistaken."

Sunny could have questioned the wisdom of listening to a professional celibate's view of the cattle market of modern dating, but she held her tongue. Covertly, she kept her eye on the guy. Built like a rugby player, short and squat, he wasn't her cup of tequila, but he was attractive enough in his way. She recognised him as one of the television gang. And he was definitely stealing glances at Jojo.

For her part, Jojo refused to play the coquette. "Have you got a problem, mate?" she shouted across the throng.

Cringing, Sunny buried her head in the menu. She heard the staring man answer, "What's your name?"

"None of your business, slaphead."

There is Hard to Get and there is Castrating Harpy: Jojo was effortlessly the latter. Surprisingly, her acidic retort was met with gales of laughter from her victim. "What a woman!" he said, admiringly.

Sunny peeped over the top of her menu. She had half expected Jojo to be having a secret preen, to see her looking smug about attracting attention in a crowded bar. But no. Jojo was utterly unconcerned. This girl didn't play hard to get: she *was* hard to get. The man at the bar evidently relished a challenge, because he kept up the staring.

"Ooh, Jojo's clicking!" said Sister Jane excitedly, using the slang of her Dublin youth. "He's mesmerised."

And presumably on the run from an institution, mused Sunny. She wondered what was going on back home between Dave and Ellen. She wondered how her fiancé was coping, on his own, with his vast reference library of wedding suppliers. She wondered why the crop-headed bloke had sent them over another bottle of mineral water instead of chatting up a normal woman instead. All this wondering was hard work, and she was relieved when one of the defiantly un-Spanish barmen shouted, "Let's be 'aving ya!" at eleven o'clock. Soon she'd be hurtling Fabio-wards in a taxi, away from complicated emotional showdowns and besotted rugby players.

"Come on," she chided her aunt and cousin. "Let's get a move on."

It was difficult to negotiate a route out of the bar, as the *StyleScaping* posse were on the move, too. Like a herd of drunken cattle, they lowed and lurched, blocking the exits with their exuberant leave-takings.

A loud "Get off me!" sounded behind her and Sunny turned to see Jojo enveloped by her admirer.

"Call me!" he begged, slipping a card into her back pocket.

"In your dreams, fat boy," spat Jojo.

"You kill me!" He laughed, backing away with a puppy-dog look on his face.

"Christ, if ever a man needed therapy," muttered Sunny, grabbing Jojo and propelling her towards the door. "Can we get going, please?"

"Listen to her!" Jojo snatched her arm away. "Annoyed we're not the centre of attention, are we?"

"No," blustered Sunny, "not at all. I just want to get back to my husband to be, if you don't mind."

"'Husband to be!'" aped Jojo gleefully. "Excuuuuuuuuse me."

"Girls, girls," reprimanded Sister Jane.

"'Girls! Girls!'" echoed Patrick, but louder and with more spit. "Not going home already? We're all going back to Serena's place."

Wild-eyed, Serena shushed Patrick. "All?" she hissed. "*Us*, not all, Patrick." She turned her green gaze on Sunny. "Sorry. I've only got a tiny place."

"No need to apologise," said Sunny sincerely. There were many spots on earth she wished never to visit and Serena's tiny place was one of them. "Be gentle with him," she couldn't stop herself adding. "It's a school day tomorrow."

"Oh, it's not like that," Serena assured her. "Just a coffee and a chat."

LEAVE HIM ALONE, YOU CONNIVING BITCH! Sunny wanted to bellow into that beautiful face. LEAVE HIM ALONE! HE'S GOT TO DIE OF MISERY, WANTING ME FOR EVER AND MOURNING THE CHANCE HE MISSED! Surprised by the vehemence of her inner voice, Sunny cleared her throat and said, "Well, it was nice to see you," like a polite child after a birthday party.

"Likewise." Serena was already disengaged, scanning the crowd for Patrick, who had been swallowed up.

"Are we all set?" Sister Jane was standing a little way down the pavement. "Come on, love. You were keen to get home."

"Yeah. Yeah. Hang on a minute." Sunny was scanning the crowd, too. She spotted Patrick just before Serena did. That three-year-old child had broken into her brain again and had just come up with an excellent plan. There was one thing that Patrick could never resist after a few drinks. Sunny knew that it would interest him far more than the offer of heavy petting in Serena's tiny place. "PIGGYBACK RACE!" she yelled.

"YEAAAAAH!" bellowed Patrick, just like she knew he would.

Serena scowled. Sunny smiled smugly. Sister Jane yelped as a cameraman scooped her up and shouted, "Hang on, Sister!"

Hopping on to Patrick's back was like jumping into a time machine. Sunny's whole body remembered the old days. She leaned into him the same way. Her knees hugged him like they used to. The rasp of his hair against her cheek was the same. It took the air out of her for a moment.

Then Sunny spotted Serena's face. It was pale and pinched. Nobody had dared to swing her on to their back, and the sight of her made Sunny feel like the class bully. "Hold on," she said urgently. "Patrick, why don't you —"

He didn't hear her sudden change of heart and didn't swap her for a lighter jockey. They were off, galloping towards the finishing line, which had been specified as the other end of the bridge. Drunken men have a marvellous capacity to make snap group decisions: Sunny had often posited that it might just solve the world's problems if the UN and all the dictators and warlords got mullered together one Saturday night.

"Giddy up!" squealed Sister Jane, her skinny steed scampering into the lead.

Jojo's swain had of course refused to take no for an answer and had dragged her up on to his back. Even with such a burden, he had the stamina to threaten Sister Jane's lead. To an encouraging "Put me down, you bullet-headed thick!" from his passenger, he raced down the pavement, scattering innocent passers-by.

"Go! Go! We're losing them!" panicked Sunny, all regrets about Serena dissolved by her competitiveness. "Faster, Patrick! The make-up girl has overtaken us!"

"She's lighter than you," puffed Patrick, ungallantly. "You never used to be this heavy."

"That's my healthy, fashionable curves," Sunny pointed out, insulted. "FASTER!" If only, she thought, she had a whip.

Jojo and Sister Jane were neck and neck at the lights. Sister Jane was deeply into the spirit of the race, leaning over to nobble her niece with a merciless tickle. Jojo was immune to tickling, and she was immune to the charms of her mount. "Put me down or I'll rip your ears off!" she was warning him, as Sunny and Patrick drew level with them.

The make-up girl's good start had evaporated: the lighting guy beneath her had a stitch. The assistant director and the production PA had bucked tradition:

she was carrying him. She looked as fresh as a daisy. "You're history!" she goaded Patrick, good-naturedly, as they waited for the lights to turn.

"You're cheese," said Patrick, who was no good at insults even when he was sober. "You are so fucking cheese."

"Stop calling her cheese," whispered Sunny. "GO!" The green man was up.

The untidy race staggered over the crossing. Sunny and Sister Jane vied for second place, after the Herculean PA. Behind them, Jojo was scuppering her own chances by coming good on her threat about her partner's ears.

Across the bridge they thundered, clattering into each other, red-faced and hooting, tailed by a baying audience. Sunny was laughing so much she thought her chest would crack, and she was having the same thought she always had when a piggyback race erupted: why don't I do this every day?

Good-natured honks and shouts sounded from passing cars. Suddenly, one car screeched to a halt, almost mounting the pavement.

"Watch it, mate!" laughed the PA, who swerved, but hung on to her lead.

The driver's door flew open. Fabio, his handsome face transfigured by blackest anger, jumped out.

"Fabioooo!" cried Sunny, delighted to see him, not taking the murderous look seriously.

"Can't stop!" Patrick panted, galumphing past.

"Put her down!" Fabio ran alongside, that murderous look still in place. Wearing only cashmere

PJs bottoms, his bare midriff was as defined as a xylophone.

"It's all right," gasped Sunny from her rocky seat. "I'm fine," she gabbled, as she was bounced towards the finishing line. It was clear that Fabio wasn't play-acting: she quailed at the thought of what might be about to happen.

"I SAID, PUT MY WOMAN DOWN!" bellowed Fabio, with the kind of projection that can stop even a piggyback race.

But only for a moment. All the competitors gave Fabio a puzzled glance, then resumed their rush to the far side of the bridge.

"I AM WARNING YOU!" Fabio ran easily alongside Patrick, who was now a clear second after the PA.

"Can this wait?" panted Patrick.

"Fabio, please," begged Sunny, glowing scarlet with embarrassment. Not being a Neanderthal miss, she was unaccustomed to being called anybody's "woman". "It's all right."

"IT IS NOT ALL RIGHT!" bellowed Fabio. His eyes really were flashing, like Sunny's make-believe heroes. He was pumped full of anger, a Duracell bunny of rage. This would not, could not, end well, thought Sunny, suddenly a very reluctant passenger as Patrick thundered on.

A loud, tattered hurray went up from the hangers-on as Patrick and Sunny pipped the PA at the post. Sister Jane jogged in a triumphant third, and last of all, behind the make-up girl, were Jojo and her long-suffering partner, whose ears were bright red. His expression, however, was blissful. "Aren't you the feisty one?" He smiled down at Jojo, after depositing her carefully on the ground.

"And aren't you the twat?" she replied, brushing down her rumpled market-stall velour as if it were Dolce & Gabbana. "Look at me! You've ruined me outfit!"

The winners were slapped on the back and praised with the kind of fulsome emotion tequila induces. "You were brilliant, mate!", "Amazing!", "Awesome!"

Only Fabio struck a sour note, with his slightly less admiring, "You have gone too far, little man."

Twittering at Fabio's elbow, all Sunny's pleas were ignored. She bit her lip. Fabio stood as solid as a block of granite, ready for a confrontation. She hoped that Patrick, even with all that alcohol rushing around his blood, would cool things down.

"It's late," said Patrick, not quite concealing the amusement he felt. "Why don't we all say goodnight and you can take Sunny home?"

"Do not presume to tell me what I can do with my own fiancée." Fabio's voice was steely. Sunny noted that she had been upgraded from "woman" to "fiancée".

"I'm not, I'm not, mate." Patrick laughed and held up his hands.

The crowd gathered nearer, sensing a fight in the offing. The perfect end to the perfect night, thought Sunny, unless you had the awful feeling it was all your own stupid fault.

"Everywhere I go, there you are, Mr Cad. Why is this?" The archly puzzled face Fabio pulled was so exaggerrated that Sunny struggled not to giggle along with some of the others. "Perhaps you want to steal something that is mine?"

Aware that she was that something, Sunny cringed. She could feel Serena thinking, "They're actually fighting over that girl with the big bum and the messy hair?"

"She's not 'something', she's a person," said Patrick with a new seriousness that made the crowd step back. Slowly, he said, "And she's not yours either."

Like a rocket, up went Fabio. "Explain yourself!" he hissed, his fists curling at the end of his taut arms. "She is mine. She will never be yours again, Smith."

"I meant, she doesn't belong to anybody." Patrick looked at Sunny for the first time since the confrontation had ignited. "Sunny's very much her own person."

"Yeah," thought Sunny, glad to be backed up. Fabio's eighteenth-century outrage was as insulting to her as it was to Patrick. She laid a restraining hand on Fabio's arm and was astonished when he shook it off bad-temperedly. He had never been brusque with her before.

"I have had enough." Fabio was shaking his head, and his dark hair swung like a shampoo commercial. "Always, you are *there*. You are watching, waiting, for our relationship to stumble."

352

"I don't know what you're on about, Fabio, but I'll tell you this." Patrick folded his arms. "I don't want a fight."

A disappointed ripple ran through the onlookers. "Yes, you do," encouraged Jojo, shaking off the arm that the heavy-set man was attempting to snake around her shoulders.

"A fight?" Fabio laughed. "You think I would fight you in the street like a dog?" He lowered his head, keeping his burning eyes on Patrick's wry ones. "But we will meet again, Mr Cad, and we will settle this."

Willing Patrick with all her fibre not to trill, "Ooooh, I'm scared," Sunny stepped in front of her panting fiancé. "It's time to go home," she told him, steadily.

His glittering eyes turned to Sunny. "Yes," he said, gently. His breath was still ragged, but he was reassuringly her old Fabio once more. "Let's go home, cara."

CHAPTER
TWENTY-SEVEN

London was Sarah's private road. She drove as though speed limits were meaningless numbers daubed whimsically on sign-posts by elves. Double yellow lines, though decorative, meant little to her. The fact that she talked non-stop while careering across roundabouts on their way to the leisure centre did little to improve Sunny's already grim mood beside her.

"Yes, seriously, it almost came to blows. WATCH OUT!" bawled Sunny, grabbing the dashboard.

Sarah was accustomed to screams from the passenger seat, and she blithely carried on cutting up fellow motorists, presumably interpreting their two-fingered salutes as some sort of accolade. "Kind of sexy."

"In books, maybe. Not in real life," fibbed Sunny.

"Did Fabio take his —"

"Shirt off? Obviously."

Overtaking a bendy bus takes balls, but Sarah had those in abundance. "None of this is about some piddling piggy-back race." Sarah sounded thoughtful, as the bus driver's fruity insults faded behind them. "It's about Fabio's insecurities."

That wasn't a word Sunny associated with her proud, self-possessed man. "Fabio is as secure as . . ." Despite being a writer, Sunny was crap at anologies. "As a very secure thing," she ended, quietly.

"I admit," said Sarah, "he has looks, wealth, power." She paused. "*You.* But just imagine for a moment how you'd feel if there was a female equivalent of Patrick in his life. A kind of Patrick with boobs who Fabio was completely relaxed with, had private jokes with, teased relentlessly."

"Why'd you have to come over all sensitive and insightful?" grumbled Sunny. "I rely on you to be callous and flip." This wasn't true. The sardonic face that Sarah presented to the public was at odds with the attention she gave her friend's problems. Sarah's wisdom had pulled Sunny back from the brink of many a romantic precipice. It was one of the reasons Sunny loved her and one of the reasons why the recent Liz-related lunacy had been so troubling. "I just want to get on with being annoyed with Fabio, thank you very much. I'm not in the mood to *understand* him yet."

"If a person didn't know better," Sarah said airily, belting the wrong way down a one-way street, "a person might think you were still in love with Patrick."

"I expect that kind of Disney-talk from Ellen." Sunny attempted the repressive look copyrighted by her aunty Annie. "Not you. You know the whole story."

"Sorry." A novel word for Sarah, it sounded sincere.

Sunny rubbed her eyes: red and rabbity, they testified to her long night wrangling with Fabio.

It hadn't been the sort of wrangling she liked. It hadn't been sweaty, or exciting, or *sans* clothes. This had been a wrangle about whether or not it was acceptable for twenty-first-century men to stride about with their shirt off calling their women "woman". The opposing viewpoints were simple enough: Sunny thought it wasn't acceptable, and Fabio thought it was. A weary deadlock had ended with Fabio's gentle touch on his fiancée's arm, and a sleepy kiss, before they'd fallen into a drugged sleep. Nothing had been resolved, but a plaster had been applied to the wound.

"One good thing came out of last night," Sunny remembered, with a wide smile. "Ellen and Dave are back together!"

"Aww!" said Sarah expressively, evidently big-hearted enough to enjoy other people's joy while her own love life lay in ruins.

"This is Ellen, remember, so it's all very tentative, but Aunty Jane reports that she let him hold her hand in front of her."

"Whoopee doo." Sarah seemed unimpressed.

"And they're going away for the weekend."

"Now that's more like it," said Sarah approvingly. "Somewhere divinely romantic, I hope."

"They're going to a conference called 'Valuing Ancillary Relief Claims In Family-law Cases'." Sunny tried not to look at Sarah, but in the end she had to and they both burst into satisfying peals of laughter. "As long as they're happy," she said, wiping her eyes, as Sarah parked with her usual élan. Sunny peered out at the quiet suburban street. "This isn't the leisure centre." She buckled up again, asking suspiciously, "What are you up to?"

"You wouldn't have come if I told you the truth," said Sarah matter-of-factly. "It's showdown time. High noon. The day of reckoning." She dabbed on lip gloss in the rear-view mirror. "Armageddon."

"Speak English."

"I'm going to confront Liz over her relationship with Alfie." Sarah pointed at a tidy semi. "That's her house. Have you ever seen anything neater?" she sneered. "Looks as if she Dettols it every night."

"This is a bad idea." Sunny felt cornered. "Please turn the engine on and let's go swimming."

"I'm going in."

A veteran student of Sarah's moods, Sunny knew when to give in. "I'll be right here when you come out," she said, comfortingly.

"No you bloody won't," Sarah corrected her. "You're coming in with me."

A lopsided battle ensued. Predictably, it ended with Sunny stamping up the short path behind her avenging angel of a friend.

"Go easy on her," she whispered as Sarah rang the doorbell.

"But of course," said Sarah ironically. "Listen to that!" she scoffed as the chimes of the bell faded. " 'Edel sodding weiss.' "

"Shhh, she'll hear."

A foggy form sharpened up in the frosted glass of the front door. Liz, her hair dishevelled, opened the door a crack. "Oh, my goodness!" she exclaimed.

"We need to talk."

"I don't think —" began Liz, meekly.

"No, you don't think." Sarah pushed at the door. "May we come in?" she said, Manolos firmly planted on the welcome mat.

"Thanks for seeing us, Liz," said Sunny politely, as if the poor woman had any choice.

"Tea?" asked Liz, obviously nonplussed. She seemed to be operating on default hospitality mode. "I've just taken a cake out of the oven."

"But of course you have," said Sarah, looking Liz up and down.

Aware of the critical appraisal, Liz fussed with her fringe and put a self-conscious hand to the tie neck of her blouse. An apron dotted with cartoon cats protected a lumpy skirt from the ravages of cake-making. She looked every inch the frump, but Sunny also took in the gentleness of Liz's gaze.

"A slice of cake would be lovely. Thanks." Sunny nodded and beamed, positioning herself firmly as the Good Cop.

Off Liz sped to the back of the house, leaving Sarah to mimic, " 'A slice of cake would be lovely,' " at Sunny. "This isn't a fucking social call."

"Don't swear in here," begged Sunny. She had an odd feeling that the little china shepherdesses lined up on the mantelpiece might commit hari-kari by plummeting into the grate at the sound of the F word. "Liz likes her beige," she whispered, looking about at the bland sofa and bland walls.

"How chic." Sarah picked up a cushion hand-embroidered with cats, between two talons. "Alfie must have a secret desire for co-ordinating Dralon that I knew nothing about."

"It's cosy," said Sunny, approvingly. The room was dated, but it had the comforting charm of a favourite aunty's home. "No design statement. No fashion-victim styling." She looked at Sarah and hastily added, "Not that your house is like that."

"No, not that my house is like that." Sarah narrowed her eyes at Sunny and threw a cushion smothered in needlepoint roses at her.

"Oh." Liz was at the threshold with a big tray. She seemed puzzled by the sight of adults throwing cushions, but evidently decided to let it pass. She surprised her visitors by taking the lead. "Would you mind telling me why you're here?"

"We need to talk about Alfie." Sarah waved away the proffered china cup.

"Really?" Liz looked guarded.

"I know what's going on."

A blush can look cute, but the deep crimson that flooded Liz's jowls did not improve her. She looked like a strawberry in a bad wig. "Ah," she said, delicately.

"Yeah. *Ah*." Sarah was not in a delicate mood.

"How did you find out about us?" Liz gazed deep into her PG Tips.

Sunny put her cup down. She was shocked. She had fully expected Liz to explain away the time she spent with Alfie. She glanced at Sarah, who was carefully maintaining her Bad Cop demeanour. Dismay underpinned the scowl: Sarah had wanted the simple explanation, too.

"I followed him," said Sarah defiantly. "Nothing to be proud of, but I fight fire with fire," she warned the mumsy little pudding on the opposite armchair.

"I see. I suppose you're angry?" Liz looked up with a little grimace on her face, like a Beast caught finger-painting the dado rail.

"Just a touch," said Sarah icily.

There was a long pause, during which a carriage clock on a shelf ticked off each self-conscious second. "He said he didn't feel able to suggest that kind of . . . *activity* to you," said Liz uneasily, eyes darting over her knick-knacks. "He said you'd be shocked."

Chin wobbling, Sarah managed a half-laugh. "Me? I'm the most open-minded, liberal person you could meet." She turned to Sunny for corroboration. "Aren't I? Aren't I broad-minded?"

Assuming the question was a sanitised version of the more direct "Am I not a goer?", Sunny answered with an assertive nod. In her single days Sarah had shagged and snogged her way through Waldhorn Truss Levy, leaving panting, exhausted men flapping in her wake like goldfish out of their tanks. It did seem odd that Alfie turned to this mousy woman for . . . for what? Even Sunny's imagination didn't stretch to an activity that would shock Sarah.

She glanced speculatively at Liz over her teacup. Were there nipple clamps under that pinny? Did Liz have a way with a whip? Perhaps she forced Alfie to lick her shoes and do the housework dressed as Doris Day?

Sunny reached for a slice of sponge. More cake might stem the disturbing images in her head.

"I've always been interested in that kind of thing." Liz dared to smile modestly. "I showed him a few tricks. He was very grateful." She found the courage to look Sarah in the eye. "Although he can get overexcited."

Cake, cake, thought Sunny, desperately. More cake.

Without the solace of home-baked Victoria sponge, Sarah's nostrils were flaring as she said in a sepulchral voice, "How can you sit there and talk to me like that about my own husband?"

"I'm sorry." Liz immediately reverted to mouse mode. "I know you've been having problems." She looked at her plump hands folded neatly in her aproned lap. "Perhaps you should join us for one of our sessions?"

There wasn't enough cake in the world to cover that suggestion. "Liz!" gasped Sunny. This conversation was proof that books can't be judged by their frumpy covers. Give Liz ten more minutes, thought Sunny fearfully, and she'll be roping me in to take pictures.

"You have some nerve!" hissed Sarah. She looked ready to fly off the sofa.

"Well, so do you," squeaked Liz, obviously at some cost to her nerves. "You barge into my home, after ruining my life, to cross-question me about Alfie. I shouldn't have let you in." She stood up abruptly. "I'd like you to go please." Issuing orders wasn't one of her skills, and Sarah stayed put, although Sunny half stood, then bounced back down again.

"I'm not going until you promise you'll never see Alfie again," demanded Sarah.

"Why are you hounding me?" Liz looked ready to burst into tears and stood wringing her hands, chapped from cake-making and ornament-polishing. "What have I ever done to you?"

"He is my husband," enunciated Sarah, coldly.

"And Porqy Peeces was my life," shrieked Liz, making Sarah blink rapidly at the sudden change in volume. "My grandfather worked himself into his grave building up that company. My father left it to me on his deathbed. I didn't know where to start. God knows, the world of cooked meats is a fast-moving one. But I did my best. I put my heart and soul into it." Liz stepped towards Sarah, who sank back into the very cushions she'd been ridiculing. "I modernised the factory, and I tightened up production, and I got us into the black. We were expanding, taking on more staff, and the advertising campaign would have put us in a different league. Then you turn up." She jabbed a bitten nail in Sarah's general direction. "With your slogans and your soundbites and your stunts."

Interrupting, Sarah showed she could shout, too. "But you were peddling poison!" she yelled. "To children!"

Liz held out her hands hopelessly. "It was as safe, no, safer actually than most of the processed food on offer. If you'd worked *with* me, I would have reassessed the research, I would have put our people on to it."

"And baffled us all with science so you could go on peddling the same rubbish," accused Sarah.

"No," said Liz, passionate at last. "That is not the Porqy Peeces way of doing things. I would have taken professional advice, and if you were right I would have done whatever it took. But we'll never know if you were right, because it was trial by television and Porqy Peeces was found guilty."

"Of course I was right," Sarah snapped.

"It doesn't matter now. The factory's empty. My staff are laid off." Liz sank down into the beige embrace of an armchair. "I let them all down."

"Well," harrumphed Sarah, seemingly at a loss for a clever remark. She was looking uncomfortable.

"When I think of poor Betty," wailed Liz suddenly, causing Sunny and Sarah to exchange puzzled looks. "Sixty-two. Been our dinner lady since 1973. Where's poor Betty going to get a job now?"

Poor Betty. Sunny visualised an old lady in an egg-spattered overall wandering around a job centre, crying, with a ladle in her hand.

By the look of Sarah, she was thinking of poor Betty, too. "You can't hold me responsible," she said sullenly. "If Porqy Peeces was wholesome, none of this would have happened." She looked to Sunny, possibly for support, but the look on Sunny's features was a pained one. Sunny knew that vengeance, jealousy and suspicion had been every bit as instrumental in Sarah's vendetta as public health.

"It didn't have to come to this." Liz's self-control was hard won, judging by the stormy look in her eyes.

"If you'd been able to keep your hands off my husband," spat Sarah bitterly, getting to the point at last, "perhaps poor Betty would still be frying eggs. Blame the pervy shenanigans you and Alfie get up to. Don't blame me." She stood up, as if to go. She looked even nearer to tears than Liz.

"Pervy?" Liz tried the word for size and didn't seem to like it. "What's pervy about DIY?"

Leaning down to pick up her bag, Sarah pulled a face. "DIY?" she spat angrily. "Is that some kinky term you people use?"

Theories about what depraved behaviour the letters might stand for cavorted through Sunny's mind. None of them were nice, some of them were physically impossible. Then it came to her. "You actually mean Do It Yourself, don't you, Liz?"

"What else would I mean?" queried Liz, innocently. "He put up those shelves a couple of days ago." She pointed to some wonky MDF planks supporting the carriage clock and a DVD collection that betrayed a *tendresse* for Pierce Brosnan. "At the moment we're putting together a little three-legged table." Liz simpered slightly as she said, "He'd noticed that I had nowhere to display my Victorian-reproduction dolly. He's thoughtful like that, isn't he?"

Sarah was still speechless, indeed she was frozen in time and space, so Liz rambled on, "He's turned the legs beautifully. He couldn't even knock a nail in at first and now he's dovetailing his joints like billy-o." She glowed with teacherly pride. "He said you wouldn't understand, but I felt he should give you more credit. You do understand, don't you?" said Liz, with cautious kindness, like a child approaching a pit bull terrier.

364

"No," confessed Sarah. "I don't."

Neither did Sunny. Over the next half-hour, Liz was happy to fill them in. Apparently, very soon after they'd been introduced at the Waldhorn Truss Levy offices, Alfie had told Liz that she reminded him very strongly of his grandmother.

At this point, Sarah had turned a laugh into a believable cough. Sunny glared at her: they both knew that Alfie's late nan had been reminiscent of Frankie Howerd, only not so feminine. They also knew that Alfie missed her very much.

Carrying on with her tale, Liz recounted how she and Alfie fell into the habit of carrying on their chats after their meetings ended. She stressed that these conversations were always entirely innocent, but that she began to discover how deeply unhappy he was.

Sunny laid a hand on Sarah's arm to stop her shouting, "Objection, Judge!" or something similar and nodded at Liz to carry on.

"Alfie was so disillusioned with his job. He felt like a hamster on a treadmill, he said."

"Oh," tutted Sarah, "he's been saying that for years."

"Really?" Liz seemed shocked. "Yet you never suggested he might give it up?"

"How could he give up his job?" exclaimed Sarah. "He earned a fortune. He was at the top of his game. Nannies don't grow on trees, Liz."

"No." Those myopic eyes could be quite searching. "Anyway, when your, er, the protests started, and I began to fall apart, Alfie was very supportive. And there was *no* funny stuff," she said firmly, looking like a woman whose stuff had never raised even a titter. "When he got the sack, and he felt that you wouldn't want him any more, he —"

"Hold on, lady!" Sarah butted in. "I never said that."

"I don't know the rights and wrongs of it." Liz brushed the interruption away. "But since then, he's been coming here to relax. And to talk about his children. And about how much he loves you." She smiled at Sarah. "Yes, that's mainly what we talk about. If you don't mind me saying this —" Liz risked a touch of feeble defiance "— we talk about what went wrong."

Sarah seemed to swallow this, although Sunny knew she would loathe the thought of such a prim miss knowing her private business.

"And we get on with our DIY!" finished Liz, with a flourish. "Alfie likes to use his hands, and he gets such pleasure out of seeing the finished article get some use. He feels that you might not welcome his handiwork in your beautiful house."

"We-ll ..." Sarah surveyed the lopsided shelf doubtfully.

"You should see the look on his face when he's making something. It's as if he's meditating," said Liz.

"I can imagine," said Sarah softly. Looking chastened, she put her head in her hands and said shakily, "Liz, I owe you a massive apology."

Sunny sighed with happy relief. Sarah was repaying her faith in her at last.

Then Sarah was lifting her head, and Sunny saw that her eyes were glittering demonically. "I've had an idea," she said.

CHAPTER
TWENTY-EIGHT

Yawning in an extravagant, tonsil-baring manner that she would never expose Fabio to, Sunny accepted a mug of tea from Ellen.

"How come you're here so early?" Ellen seemed puzzled. "Even when you lived here, you rarely saw the kitchen at this hour."

"Technically, I still live here." Sunny regretted the tetchy note in her remark and continued more equably. "Me and Fabio are on Aunty Jane duty. Even Jojo deserves a bit of a break, so we're taking the holy one off to Buckingham Palace. He's just parking the car."

A good, old-fashioned Irish republican, Ellen turned up her dainty nose. "Rather you than me."

"I thought it would be nice for Fabio," smiled Sunny, wryly. "Might remind him of some of his more spartan properties." She sipped her good, strong, number-thirteen tea meditatively. "I probably won't be able to concentrate on HM's décor. My mind is buzzing with Sarah's plans."

Ellen cocked her head, inquisitively, and Sunny told her about the "showdown" with Liz.

"So, after all that fuss, there was no affair, and there was possibly no need to shame Porqy Peeces in public. Sarah was left with various kinds of egg all over her face," Sunny explained. "Then she had a brainwave. She asked me and Liz who we thought would be the best person, no, the *only* person to rehabilitate Porqy Peeces. We just looked blank, and Sarah stood up and shouted, 'ME!'" Sunny shrugged her shoulders, still finding the turnaround hard to accept. "So, get this — Sarah and Liz are going to work together. Sarah's overseeing the new recipe, so she can endorse the launch of the new product, getting loads of press and publicity all over again."

"Simple but brilliant," said Ellen, admiringly. "If Sarah says it's good for you, everybody will believe her because she was the one who exposed them in the first place." She shook her head. "Genius. They'll be in every newspaper and magazine."

"They'd better be. Sarah's already promised a big wodge of Alfie's money to refinance the company." Sunny opened the fridge and shut it again, confounded by its emptiness. "She's off to see him this morning to try and mend all the bridges she's been busily burning."

"Sometimes life gives you a second chance," said Ellen, quietly, as if to herself.

Beetling into the kitchen, in a startling peacock-blue polyester satin creation, Jojo grunted a command at them. "Telly!" she belched, caveman-like.

With a long white finger, Ellen flicked on the television. "Hey, that's Chudleigh Court!" she gasped.

"This is weird," laughed Sunny. They were watching a live outside broadcast on breakfast TV of an interview with Patrick, but they could also see the real thing through the kitchen window. The crew were bunched behind the cameras over in the Zen corner (or the "bloody silly" corner, according to Ernest) as Patrick fielded questions, through an earpiece, from the presenters in the studio about his "ground-breaking" new programme.

"He's there!" Sunny pointed delightedly at the television. "And he's there!" She pointed out of the window, happy as an ape who's just discovered fire. "And he's there!" She skipped back to the television again.

"Yes, we grasp the concept." Ellen was not so easily impressed.

"It's a headfuck!" laughed Sunny, just as Sister Jane appeared.

"Is it, indeed?" said the nun, with the gentlest disapproval.

They all gathered round the TV, laughing as Patrick fielded the inane probings ("So you're the Jamie Oliver of gardening?") and cooing about how pretty their block looked in the background.

"He's so professional," said Sister Jane.

"Something's distracting him." Sunny frowned. Patrick missed a beat and stumbled over his embarrassed rebuttal that *StyleScaping* would make him a green-fingered sex symbol. "What's all that commotion?"

Ellen, who had crossed to look out of the window, gasped, "You're so not going to believe this."

Unnerved, Sunny dithered by the screen. Suddenly, Fabio was on the television. Squealing, "But you're parking the car!" she rubbed her eyes, viciously, like a squirrel on speed.

It made no difference. That really was her fiancé live on national TV, legs apart, hands on hips, bellowing, "We have unfinished business, Smith!" in faultless romantic fiction style.

Eyes wide, Sunny had to forego the luxury of breathing for a moment or two. The presenters back at the studio also struggled to make sense of the glamorous interloper. Evidently, they decided to run with this new development, because they transmitted Patrick's bemused "Here? Now?"

Circling him, Fabio shouted, "I have had enough! I must defend the honour of my loved one!" in his thrilling baritone. He tore off his shirt with the ease of much practice, and slapped Patrick's cheek with a handy pruning glove.

Glued to the TV, Fabio's loved one was reeling. "Defend my honour . . .?" As far as Sunny knew, her honour was in no danger whatsoever: it was perfectly happy, sitting up in bed and taking solids.

"You wrote this!" accused Jojo.

"Even I couldn't come up with this tosh," winced Sunny.

Fabio reached down to a pile of gardening implements. Selecting a rake for himself, he tossed Patrick a hoe.

Deftly, Patrick caught it.

"*En garde!*" snarled Fabio, adding, with aristocratic condescension, "You understand the terminology?"

"I understand all right, mate." Patrick lobbed the geranium he'd been cradling over one shoulder. Abruptly, his entire body language changed. Up jerked his chin, and he stood erect and tense as a ballet dancer.

"Please, no," whispered Sunny, looking through her fingers. It had never come up in conversation with Fabio that Patrick had been shortlisted for the British Olympic fencing team at university.

"Maybe one of them will get killed!" Jojo licked her lips.

Without another word, Sunny took off. The others hard on her heels, she raced down the stairs and out into the cool morning. Most of the other residents had the same idea and were gathering around the two men.

Mrs Wilde, in a towelling dressing gown that flapped disconcertingly in the breeze, was shouting, "Teach the Cad a lesson for us, Fabio!" Behind her raced the Thin Girls, in darling little PJs, and the Greek woman was bringing up the rear in a nylon nightie. Chloe was an unexpected addition to the mob.

"STOP!" Sunny howled as she raced towards the cameras. "STOP THIS!"

In the midst of the gathered camera crew and gawpers, Fabio and Patrick were entirely intent on each other. As if, thought Sunny, puffing to a halt, they were in love. Slowly and gracefully, they brought their unlikely weapons up in front of their faces, before swooping them round in a full circle. Then they leaned in and shook each other's left hand.

"Aw, is that it?" A Thin Girl at Sunny's shoulder sounded disappointed.

"This is dangerous," Sunny reminded her. "One of them could get hurt."

"I know!" The Thin Girl's face glistened with excitement.

"*Allez!*" shouted Fabio, and leaped towards Patrick, legs apart, one knee bent, in a classic lunge. The rake clashed woodenly with the hoe, then clashed again. It was a harsh noise, and Sunny grimaced, pulling her hands back into her sleeves and bringing them up to her face, like a child watching a slasher film.

The two men darted round each other, their gardening implements meeting rapidly in the air. Springing about the polished pebbles of the Zen garden, they neatly combined gardening and violence in a way rarely seen on early-morning telly.

Eyes narrowed, Serena was following this development. Sunny tried to analyse her expression as Serena listened to unheard commands through a headset. She hoped the slender woman might step in and stop this parody, but she was disappointed. The cameraman hoisted his camera on his shoulder, and, on a word from Serena, took off with the rest of the onlookers, as Fabio and Patrick charged across the newly laid zigzags of grass.

"Oooh!" gasped the *StyleScaping* crew, as Patrick staggered back, prey to a sly parry from Fabio's tool.

"Yessss!" they wheezed, as Patrick recovered. He pursued Fabio towards the mini pagoda, forcing the count to speed backwards with impressive agility.

The female Chudleigh Court contingent had huddled together and were chanting, "GO! GO! FA-BEE-YO! BEAT THE PERVY SO AND SO!" Sunny marvelled at this partisan mob's ability to organise themselves so speedily. She wasn't half as creative, squeaking, "Oh, please be careful!" as the opponents clattered past her.

Things moved fast in a duel. One moment Fabio and Patrick were prancing daintily round each other, the next Fabio had managed, with a thrillingly animal grunt, to lock his arm round Patrick's, pulling the pair of them close together at chest level. Their contorted faces were an inch apart, the hoe and the rake waggling. With a massive effort, Patrick pulled away and dragged the combat over to another corner of the garden.

The clamour of the weapons had to compete with the excited feminine chants and the blokey shouts of support for Patrick. Negotiating damp grass in slippers seemed to be a doddle for Fabio's acolytes. They thundered after the action, turning and reversing with the ease of figure skaters.

Just as agitated, but far less co-ordinated, Sunny stumbled over her own feet and tumbled headlong. The sensation of damp earth on her scraped palms took her right back to primary school.

A brawny hand helped her up. Mrs Wilde, an unlikely still point in the chaos, said admiringly, "Your fiancé is very brave to face such an ogre."

"Please, Mrs Wilde." Sunny dusted down her jeans. "That ogre is a friend of mine."

Peering down at Sunny, Mrs Wilde asked, "Whose side are you on, Miss Parkinson?"

"Surely that's obvious?" replied Sunny.

"Highly diplomatic." With a tight smile, Mrs Wilde rejoined the scrum, a wildebeest in terry towelling.

After a moment, Sunny galloped after her, cursing the woman for being so unexpectedly perceptive. There was a dingy truth that Sunny was avoiding as she scrambled over the landscaping: she didn't know whose side she was on.

Of course, *of course* she wanted Fabio to win: she just didn't want Patrick to lose.

The mob changed direction as suddenly as a shoal of angel fish. Sunny was wrong-footed as they swarmed past her in pursuit of Fabio and Patrick, who were goading each other through themed flowerbeds.

Close to hysteria, the middlingly Thin Girl breathed, "Oh, Fabio's just like a hero out of a book!"

"Well, he's not," snapped Sunny, negotiating a dwarf conifer with bad grace. "He's an ordinary person, like you or me, and this is barbaric."

Speeding backwards, Fabio was fighting to stay upright. Patrick clearly had him on the run as he pressed him towards the catering van with his trusty hoe.

At Sunny's shoulder, Ellen shouted, "COME ON, PATRICK!" Shrugging her shoulders apologetically at her cousin, she hollered, "AND COME ON, FABIO, IN THE INTERESTS OF NEUTRALITY!"

It was easier to stand still, to let the cameraman and the *StyleScaping* personnel and her hormonally imbalanced neighbours pass her by. Sunny, panting, hands on knees, watched them with the same detached interest she brought to David Attenborough nature programmes. Beyond them, the two men who meant most to her were trying to kill each other with garden items.

That sly question of Mrs Wilde's had triggered something. The extent of Sunny's feelings for Patrick hit her with a clarity that was as exhilarating, and as unwelcome, as a bucket of icy water.

Their connection was deep, far beyond the pallid limits of pub-based friendship. Patrick was embedded in Sunny's past and she couldn't just winkle him out and discard him.

With a migrainous twinge, she recalled how readily Patrick had stepped aside when Fabio materialised. It was as if the two men were *conspiring* to part her from Patrick; Fabio with his jealousy, and Patrick with his passive acceptance of its consequences.

Even if Patrick can do without me, I don't intend to do without him, Sunny decided. She was committed to, and madly and dizzily in love with Fabio, and her decision could only complicate their relationship: somehow, she would have to reconcile the two men.

The same two men currently trading blows with B&Q hand tools.

The action was intensifying. Sunny rejoined it just as Patrick pressed Fabio up the steps of the catering van, causing the lady in it to drop her spatula and back up against the canned drinks.

Fabio caught his heel and stumbled awkwardly up the steps, inducing a loud whoop of female horror.

"Finish him off, Pat!" yelled an electrician, earning him the combined wrath of the Thin Girls, who beat him with tiny, lovely fists.

The hoe and the rake danced above the spitting fat of eggs frying. Patrick had the upper hand, but suddenly Fabio reached up and grabbed the frame of the cramped van's skylight.

With dazzling strength and energy, which almost provoked a mass stroke amongst the ladies, Fabio heaved himself up. Having swung his body back, he pulled his knees up to his chest and swung forwards, both feet landing squarely on Patrick's chest. "AHA!" he snarled, triumphantly.

"Oooch!" Sunny empathised with the pain of the blow.

Stumbling and out of control, Patrick careered down the steps. He was only halfway to his feet when Fabio bounded down to join him. Scuttling backwards, Patrick stepped into a wheelbarrow. A rake in his chest pushed him out of it.

Eyes slits, hair flying, Fabio looked like a pirate, and he fought like one. He was merciless. On and on he lunged at Patrick, every move transparently personal.

Through the Japanese-style water feature they splashed. Around the topiary pyramid and across the crunchy new lilac gravel on the path.

"Don't hurt each other!" squeaked Sunny, her plea drowned by a prosaic, and spitty "MU-U-RDER 'IM!" from Mrs Gibbs, all nine of her hairs still in rollers.

Just then, Sunny would have swapped places with *anybody*, even somebody taking their driving test, kissing Andrew Lloyd Webber or in labour with quads. And yet . . . she wasn't immune to the tug of the pheromones pulsing through the air like fog.

Fabio sweated as he did everything else: tastefully. As he pirouetted around Patrick, a droplet fell from his fringe down his finely wrought nose to make an enviable journey down the smooth contours of his chest. Sunny was flummoxed by how ardently she desired him, as he jigged about, jabbing at one of her oldest friends with a piece of gardening equipment. *I suppose that's why I'm marrying him*, she concluded.

"AHA!" snorted Patrick, utilising the fencer's rather limited vocabulary. He was forcing Fabio towards the hated sculpture.

The speedy rhythm of their unlikely weapons meeting was in time with Fabio's feet, as he desperately tried to force Patrick away. He couldn't quite manage it, and Fabio's back inched nearer and nearer to the swooping metal abstract.

Everybody was wincing in anticipation of his pain. Sister Jane turned away. Sunny was paralysed.

The men fenced frantically now, clambering to a climax. In the stillness, the hoe and the rake blurred.

Almost upon the steel doughnut, Patrick brought his hoe round in a pitiless swoop that knocked the rake right out of Fabio's grasp. It landed near Ernest, who immediately assumed the look of a man composing a pithy letter of complaint.

The little oestrogen army froze, terrified for their champion. Sunny knew her man: he wasn't beaten.

Before Patrick had a chance to finish him off, Fabio pounced on a discarded trowel and brandished it like a dagger.

"Oh, come off it!" scoffed Patrick, obviously tired of the whole thing. He thrust forward and the crowd groaned in anticipation.

They had underestimated the Italian. Cornered, Fabio growled like a wolf and managed to wrap his trowel arm round Patrick's at chest level. His speedy, unexpected move knocked the hoe out of Patrick's grip. In a second, or two at the most, Fabio had manoeuvred his adversary against the statue.

"AAAARGH!" Patrick's howl, as his back slapped against unforgiving metal, quietened the crowd.

Sunny's throat shrank.

Patrick was bent backwards at a ludicrous angle. Fabio pressed his advantage home by leaping, Errol Flynn-like, on to the steel structure and pressing his trowel to Patrick's throat.

Every gesture was perfect. Fabio looked like an antique etching. Apart from the trowel. "Do you surrender?" He was breathing hard.

"Yes," gargled Patrick, the tiny shovel constricting his Adam's apple.

Triumphant, Fabio raised both arms high in the air, basking in the rapturous ovation from his gaggle of devoted fans. Launching himself athletically into the air, he landed, catlike, with both feet on the ground.

Sunny's own feet had turned to lead. Beside her, the least thin Thin Girl was wiping her forehead and saying, "Whoo! Fencing rocks!" but Sunny couldn't celebrate. Somebody had to lose, she knew that, but it was ugly to see Patrick flat on his back. Particularly when she'd admitted to herself just how much he meant to her. However, deep down, in her pagan subconscious, which had no truck with etiquette, she was aware of a burning pride in her victorious man. This emotion shocked her. And slightly disgusted her.

"We're back to the studio!" called Serena, hoarsely. She bent double, and hung there, looking every bit as exhausted as the duellers.

Holding his trowel to one side with ostentatious regard for safety, Fabio reached down to Patrick. Hesitating for a second, Patrick took his hand and allowed Fabio to help him up. To swelling cheers, the two men embraced, holding the pose for a moment as the crowd went bananas.

Something swelled inside Sunny, too. There was hope. Perhaps they'd fought out their resentments and dark, male antipathies.

Then they untangled themselves. Fabio looked for Sunny's face in the milieu. He smiled gorgeously at her, just as Patrick's fist met his chin. Flying back, Fabio hit the grass with a damp "thwack". He lay there, winded, with Patrick standing over him.

The spectators stood silenced, and transfixed. "Was that meant to happen?" puzzled Jojo.

Unexpectedly, Patrick held out his hand to the man he'd just caught with a sideways uppercut. Fabio, a snarl corrupting his handsome features, sprang up without Patrick's help. Spitting vehemently on the ground, he turned and stalked away, in the direction of Sunny's block.

Watching him go, Sunny ran towards Patrick, whose closed expression gave no clues to his motivation. "What was that for?" she yelled. She might love the guy (within the strict, sisterly limits she'd sketched out), but she wasn't blind to his faults. "He beat you fair and square!" She was panting with anger.

"Yeah," Fabio's fans started up again, emboldened by Sunny. They hadn't had time to think up another rhyme so they threw random remarks. "Knave!" thundered Mrs Wilde. "Big bully!" jeered Chloe. Ben chose to shout, "Chonker!" which baffled everybody.

Anger from Patrick was a surprise. "What the hell has happened to you?" he yelled at Sunny, deftly turning the tables on his attacker. "You enjoyed that farce, didn't you?" He gasped as he moved his neck.

"Oh, God, you're hurt," whined Sunny, deflated like a balloon by his look of pain.

"Like you care," spat Patrick, with more emotion than Sunny had ever seen him expend. She barely recognised his face, transfigured by fury. "You used to be so down-to-earth. Now look at you — creaming your pants over your poncey boyfriend challenging me to a ridiculous duel. God, Sun, you make me sick." He strode away, pursued by Serena and her staff.

Staring after him, Sunny willed herself not to cry. Never before had Patrick shouted at her like that, not even when she'd given his favourite overcoat to Oxfam and he'd had to buy it back. Her girly dream of nestling in between him and Fabio, holding both their hands, dissolved, soggily.

Murmurs ran through the crowd. They lurked, eager for more action.

They got some tepid fodder when Fabio paused on the steps to turn and yell at Sunny, "Are you with me, woman?"

Sunny turned. She regarded him for a long minute. "Yes, Fabio, I am," she said, and went to his side.

CHAPTER
TWENTY-NINE

There is a moment in *The Wizard of Oz* that everyone who sees the film remembers. It made Sunny shudder with delight whenever she thought of it: Dorothy steps out of the ruins of her farmhouse into a bold, new, technicolour world. Oz is a magical place, fizzing with life, in exciting contrast to the black-and-white world she's left behind. Her sepia existence has been flooded with colour.

Sunny's relationship with Fabio aped this trick, with one subtle difference: it managed to do it the other way round.

Following Fabio off the grass at Chudleigh Court had been a momentous step for Sunny. Oddly, it felt more meaningful than accepting his proposal. Despite that preremptory "woman", and despite her newly minted honesty regarding Patrick, Sunny had still gone to Fabio's side.

An important page had been turned, and Sunny spent almost all her time at Chelsea Wharf now. After such drama, there was a need to consolidate. Her greedy daydream of a future that included both her current love and her ex was exposed as a shallow fancy. Even if there was a way to muzzle Fabio, Patrick had stated unequivocably and in front of witnesses that she made him sick. It wasn't the sort of review she'd relish on the cover of her books — "Makes me sick" Patrick Smith, *Gardener's Weekly* — and it had pricked her bubble with a pop they could hear in Oslo.

It was a time for snuggling up to Fabio, and talking. As a couple, they weren't big on talking (their areas of expertise were Gazing Into Each Other's Eyes and Advanced Snogging), but now there was a lot to talk about.

Fabio's chivalry, for a start. To Sunny's untutored eye, it looked suspiciously like good, old-fashioned chauvinism, marketed under a new name: his Bilnius Red F.

Then there was the matter of Sunny's honour. Surely, she reasoned disloyally, it had been Fabio's own honour that he had defended so prettily and so publicly (the tabloids had loved it).

Uncomfortably aware that there must be issues that Fabio itched to discuss, most of them Smith-related, Sunny was prepared to be as honest and as open as possible. He deserved that, and their love was elastic enough to cope.

Given all this juicy debating material, a casual observer at Chelsea Wharf might confidently expect the air to be full of expletives and flying inherited china. But no. There were no rows. There was no discussion of the duel or the illicit punch after it. Sunny and Fabio were polite to each other. Sooooooo polite. With their "Thank you"s and their "Sorry"s and their "Would you mind?"s, the only politer people Sunny had ever come across were her mother's bridge club. And she couldn't remember there being anything remotely sexy about her mother's bridge club.

Ditto, there was, suddenly, nothing sexy about Sunny and Fabio. They made love as often as before, and nothing had really changed, except that everything had changed. It was impressive but mechanical. Sunny found it hard to get comfortable afterwards: she blamed the futon.

Sunny lit some candles. The darkness was creeping across the walls of the apartment, and she wanted to keep the shadows at bay. Next door in the kitchen, she could hear Fabio preparing supper. It might be scallops, or spaghetti: it wouldn't be out of a tin, and it wouldn't need a blanket of tomato ketchup to render it edible. "I'm a lucky girl," she cooed, tweaking the waxen lilies on the dining table.

"Ten minutes, *cara*." Fabio emerged to fuss with the cutlery. "I said, ten minutes . . ." He looked her up and down.

"Oh. Sorry. Ten minutes." Sunny dashed off to the dressing room. She kept forgetting that Fabio liked her to dress for dinner. She tugged on one of the many new dresses Fabio had bought her. These days, gifts came at her like mosquitoes. Every time Fabio left the apartment, he returned with a pretty little something done up in tissue. This latest dress was silk, the colour that dead roses can be. It was exquisite, and it demanded full make-up and a head of tamed hair, so the scallops got to the table before Sunny did.

384

"You look beautiful," said Fabio, admiringly, waving away her apology. "I'd wait for ever for you."

"That's so nice." Polite, again, Sunny wondered how he would have reacted if she'd emerged in a cardie, buttoned-up wrong.

"I was going to ask for the lady of the house, but you seem to be her."

"God, you're funny." Alfie swung the front door wider. "Never seen a man in an apron before?"

"Yes, but not *you*." She leaned over to kiss him. "Glad to see you back at home." She squeezed him for good measure. "Where you belong."

In a blur of gold hair and dirty knees, the Beasts rushed over and wrapped themselves around Alfie's legs like koalas. Charlie shouted, "Sunny!" and Sam shouted, "Shunny!" They were both giggling like a *Friends* audience.

"Boys, who's looking after Tigger and Pooh?" asked Alfie, urgently. "You know what they're like. Quick! Quick! Make sure they haven't eaten all your fishfingers!"

Off roared the twins, leaving the grown-ups smiling indulgently after them. "They're *so* easy to manipulate," confided Alfie. "It reminds me of the graduate trainees back at the agency."

"The graduate trainees didn't keep stopping to kiss you, and put jam on your face, though."

"Not all of them, no. Were you hoping for an audience with Superwoman?"

"Yeah. I need some fortifying girlie chit-chat."

"You'll have to make do with me." Alfie covered his stubble with his hand. "Does that help to sustain the illusion?"

"Yes. In fact, you're quite beautiful. For a bald girl." Sunny hoisted herself on to one of the chrome stools dotting the kitchen. A piece of fishfinger flew at her, but, rather impressively, she managed to catch it in mid-air and throw it back.

"Guys . . ." warned Alfie.

"Where's Sarah, then?" asked Sunny, fidgeting on her stool. She'd been trying to find that elusive comfortable position ever since Sarah had bought the chairs for an astronomical sum three years ago, and she wasn't about to give up.

"In the study with Liz." Alfie threw up his hands in resigned confusion. "One minute she wants to boil Liz's head, the next they're bosom buddies, huddled over spreadsheets all day long. I don't pretend to understand my wife."

"But you do love her again?" checked Sunny.

"I always loved her," admitted Alfie. "But she was getting hard to like, you know?"

"I do know. That's our Sarah," agreed Sunny. "So . . ." She looked around her theatrically. "I see no tear-streaked nanny. Does that mean . . .?"

"Yup. I'm it." Alfie leaned, relaxed, against the worktop. "I get the boys up, feed and water them, play with them, take them to the park, separate them when they beat each other with Sticklebricks, pull the marbles down from their nostrils, watch *Bob the Builder* with them, tickle them, bath them, somehow

386

herd them back to bed." He wiped a hand over his face. "It is at least eighteen times more tiring than being the big cheese at Waldhorn Truss Levy, but a million times more satisfying. I mean, look at them."

Obediently, Sunny looked at them. Much 'as she loved the twins, they looked just like every other two-year-old she'd ever met: covered in food debris and making loud, crap conversation. "Just like me and their mother after one vodkatini too many."

"Only rather more coherent," offered Alfie.

"So this is permanent, this set-up?" Sunny had missed an episode or two in the soap opera of Sarah's life.

"Absolutely. The advertising business had wrung all it could out of me. I'm a house-husband from now on, and I'll leave breadwinning to my energetic, dynamic and, frankly, irritating-if-she's-not-working wife." Almost bashfully, he said, "The answer was staring us in the face the whole time. I had grown to hate being in the office, and Sarah had grown to hate being at home. Duh!" He slapped his head. "It doesn't take Poirot to work it out. I had to take a step back from business, and Sarah had to plunge in. Now, we're both challenged and inspired and fulfilled, and all those other ten-dollar words that women's magazines bandy about."

"It's obvious, when you put it like that," agreed Sunny. "Perhaps *too* obvious. Humans can be dense, can't they? Even the smart ones, like you."

Ignoring the compliment, Alfie confided, "This Porqy Peeces jape is inspired, you know. We've put a lot of money into the company. I think it'll make us a fortune."

387

"Good," said Sunny. "Then we'll all be rich as . . . What was that bloke's name?"

"Croesus," said Alfie, who'd listened at school. "I don't think we'll ever attain the dizzy heights of your titled fiancé. You'll be lighting candles with fifty-pound notes after you marry him."

"Oh, I'm sure I'll have somebody to light my candles for me."

"But of course," agreed Alfie. "The important thing, Sun, is that after all our trials and tribulations, everybody's getting their happy endings, aren't they?"

"They are." A gobbet of fishfinger hit Sunny in the fringe.

Sunny had only popped in to collect her Wallace and Gromit DVD. She hadn't expected to have to defend herself against Jojo's taunts. "I'm just waiting for a good storyline to strike me!" she told her diminuitive cousin.

"You're scared to write, you witch!" Jojo told her. "Scared. Scared. Scared."

"I don't need this," Sunny muttered. Her lack of inspiration was worrying enough without Jojo poking her short-arsed oar in. Sunny suspected that the real problem was her sudden propulsion into the world of the superrich: she simply didn't *need* to write another book.

A loud crash from outside silenced Jojo, mid-retort. They both dashed over to the window. "Jayzus!" shrieked Jojo. "Leonard's dead!"

Leonard certainly didn't look well. His chicken-thin legs stuck out from beneath a tree that had apparently toppled from a *StyleScaping* lorry.

Speeding down the hall, Sister Jane shouted, "Tell them I'm on me way. Tell them I've been trained in first aid. Tell them not to move him."

"DON'T . . . Oh." The instructions died on Sunny's lips as Leonard was manhandled, like a rag doll, across the grass and down the basement steps by assorted crew members.

Sunny caught up with her aunt, and they found Leonard laid out in Ernest's bedroom. Ernest was closing the wardrobe door carefully, with a strangely furtive movement. "Right, I'll leave you ladies to do the nursing," he said, when Sunny appeared.

"Call an ambulance, Ernest, would you!" Sister Jane called after him.

"How is he?" whispered Sunny, going to the other side of the bed.

"Unconscious. Possibly mild concussion." Sister Jane felt Leonard's waxy face. "He'll live."

"What should we do with him?" Sunny always admired people who knew what to do, and her aunt was one of those people. Left to her own devices, all Sunny would prescribe for Leonard would be sweets.

"First thing is to turn his head to one side, so he won't swallow his tongue. And if he vomits, it won't choke him." Never handsome, Leonard wasn't looking his best, but Sister Jane turned his sallow head with a tender touch.

The door banged open, and Mrs Wilde trundled in, almost filling the small room. "Leonard!" she roared, her face contorting. "What have they done to you?"

"They dropped a tree on him," said Sunny, realising how comical it sounded and doing her best not to laugh. This earned her a look of deep disapproval from Sister Jane, who was gathering up a pile of books from Ernest's bedside table.

Mrs Wilde goggled at the nun. "He hardly wants to read now!"

Ignoring her, Sister Jane tucked the books under Leonard's slippers. "His feet should be higher than his head," she elucidated.

Bending over her husband, Mrs Wilde bellowed into his face, "CAN YOU HEAR ME?" She raised her hand to slap him, but Sister Jane caught her fleshy arm just in time.

"That won't help," said Sister Jane, shocked. "Perhaps you should wait outside."

"But that's my husband lying there," wailed Mrs Wilde, tragically. "Cut down in his prime."

If this was Leonard's prime, Sunny thought, his decline wasn't going to be pretty.

Another unwanted visitor joined them. Serena looked anxious. "Is he . . . ?" she asked.

Sister Jane started to undo Leonard's tie. "He's going to be just fine." She added, with emphasis, "As long as he gets some peace." Her disapproval didn't seem to register with Mrs Wilde and Serena.

"Not content," began Mrs Wilde, relishing the easy prey that Serena suddenly represented, "with importing deviants, you proceed to drop a tree on my spouse. Where will it all end?" Various chins wobbled with distaste.

"I deeply regret this terrible accident." Serena spoke like an official letter: conciliatory, but not about to accept responsibility. "I can understand how you're feeling."

"I doubt it," snorted Mrs Wilde. "Unless somebody has thrown a tree at one of your close relatives?"

"Nobody threw a tree at Mr Wilde." Serena held up a forefinger to emphasise this important fact. Ignoring Sister Jane's appeal for quiet, she went on, "The lorry in question has functioning reverse lights, and even has a loud warning beep. My PA personally advised Mr Wilde to get back, that he was in the lorry's path, but he replied . . ." Serena referred to a small notepad. "He replied, 'I'm going to get my hands on that little bugger at last.' He was chasing a small tortoiseshell cat."

Stiffening as she tussled with Leonard's shirt collar, Sister Jane looked up at Sunny.

Never good at dissembling, Sunny's expression plainly said, *That little bugger was mine.* Abruptly, she turned away, and toyed with a candlestick on Ernest's mantelpiece.

"Doing his duty, to the last." Mrs Wilde dabbed her dry eyes with a proper hanky.

"According to various witnesses, the cat then raced behind the lorry, which had to brake sharply, sending the tree flying off the back," Serena continued.

Sunny gripped the candlestick harder. Ernest's wardrobe door was slowly swinging open, with a ghostly squeak.

"So, it was the cat's fault." Serena concluded. "The owners of the cat are responsible."

Amber diamonds glowed inside the wardrobe, among Ernest's tweed trouser bottoms. Marmite, a sock clamped in her mouth, was preparing to jump out.

Sunny kicked the wardrobe door shut, turning all heads towards her.

Luckily, Serena and Mrs Wilde had bigger fish to fry, but Sister Jane shushed her, motioning at Leonard.

"Sorry!" mouthed Sunny, keeping an eye on the wardrobe.

"Poppycock," Mrs Wilde decreed. "I hold you fully responsible. I intend to sue, but for now you can pack up your cameras, and your trees, and your degenerate presenters and go home." Mrs Wilde had drawn herself up to her full height, and her bosom seemed to have expanded: perhaps she had a special valve in her bra for use during confrontations.

"Read your contract," spat Serena. "I have one more day and I'm using it."

"I have read my contract," boomed Mrs Wilde, her face alive with spite. "You are not meeting required levels of site safety. I can terminate our agreement just like that." She clicked her fingers. She was noticeably better at it than Sunny.

"If I can't have another day . . ." Serena's voice trembled, her hauteur dissolving ". . . I can't complete the series."

If Mrs Wilde had known the phrase "Tell it to the hand 'cos the face ain't listening", she may have used it here. Not an obvious Jerry Springer afficionado, she simply said, "That is not my problem," and quit the room, like a bad-tempered carnival float.

Serena, seething, hesitated a moment before following her.

Uninterested in the dramas around her, Sister Jane was continuing to loosen Leonard's clothing. She'd had to battle to undo the button of his tight shirt collar, and now she was reaching for his waistband.

"Aunty Jane, you minx!" gasped Sunny.

"His clothing must be loosened." Sister Jane had no time for her niece's saucy asides.

"Marmite's in the wardrobe," Sunny whispered to her aunt.

Her aunt wasn't listening. Mouth hanging open, she was far more absorbed in Leonard's exposed underwear than one would expect a nun to be.

"What?" Sunny was nonplussed. "What's the matter?"

Sister Jane pointed at the navy-blue pants revealed by Leonard's open zip. "They're mine," she whispered.

Later, Sunny couldn't remember just how long she'd stared at Leonard's groin. "Oh. My. God."

"This means . . ."

"I know."

They regarded the comatose weakling in the bed with new eyes. Leonard was the Chudleigh Cad.

"The fiend!" Sunny relished the word. "What cunning. Pretending to search for clues and it was him all along! Leonard is a brilliant mastermind of crime!"

"Hardly." Sister Jane supplied some balance. "But he's definitely not a man at peace with himself." She patted his limp hand.

"Can you blame him? Married to *that*?" If she factored in Mrs Wilde, Sunny could only feel sympathy for Leonard. "What do we do?"

"We talk to a certain young man." Sister Jane stepped over to the window, which looked out on to the lawn, and knocked frantically on the glass. Patrick's feet came into view, and he bent down to peer in at the basement. "In! In!" mouthed Sister Jane. The feet disappeared.

"I'll, erm, like, go." Sunny started to edge around the bed.

"You will not."

"I'm not exactly his favourite person just now."

"Stay where you are." Sister Jane was using her special look.

"OK."

Sister Jane let Patrick in and closed the door carefully behind him.

"I can't stay. I'm an illegal immigrant." Patrick looked at Leonard, but he studiously avoided the Sunny-shaped figure on the far side of the bed.

It was odd to be so strained around Patrick. This was the man who'd taken a splinter out of her bottom after an ill-advised banister slide, but Sunny didn't feel able to look at him. The twin realities of how much he meant to her and how impossible it would be to keep him in her life gave the little tableau around the bed a horrible poignancy. She doubted if Patrick was affected the same way. After all, she made him sick.

"How is he?" asked Patrick.

"Depends." Sister Jane snapped the elastic on Leonard's underwear with one finger. "You see, I recognise these. They're mine."

Patrick groaned and rocked back on his heels. "Leonard," he whispered. "You promised."

"Now I know why they weren't returned with the others. The real culprit had hung on to them."

"Where do we go from here?" asked Patrick, intently.

"Let's give the poor wretch some space." Sister Jane shepherded Patrick over to the window, and beckoned the reluctant Sunny sharply over. "Right, young fella." She folded her arms. "Tell us all."

With deep reluctance, Patrick began his tale. "One morning, a few weeks ago, I was the first into the production tent, and I found Leonard hunched over one of our spare lockers. He was furiously stuffing knickers into it. I knew I'd found the Cad. He was moving his hoard because his wife's investigations were making things hot for him." Patrick shook his head at the memory. "What a state he was in. Shaking, sobbing, hysterical. I sat him down and asked if he wanted to talk about it."

Patting his arm, Sister Jane smiled proudly. "Good lad," she said.

"Well, I'd always thought he was a quiet little man, but he talked non-stop for what seemed like hours. It all poured out. He's had a shit life, poor sod. Overbearing mother, bullied at school, ignored at work, lost his virginity at the age of forty-seven to Mrs Wilde in Lyme Regis, after a wedding dinner of rissoles. It hasn't been a barrel of laughs for Leonard. Apparently, he's always had this desire to steal underwear, but he'd controlled it until recently. He can't explain it, swears it's not sexual. He likes ladies' knickers because they're soft and feminine and, well, nice. There's very little niceness in Leonard's life. I asked him why he couldn't just buy the underwear, but he said he'd die of embarrassment. This is a very repressed man."

"Didn't it bother him that his female neighbours were living in fear?" Sister Jane asked.

"According to Leonard, he blanked that out. But who knows? I didn't try to psychoanalyse him, I wanted to calm him down. He seemed relieved to be getting it out. Then I told him I'd help him to tell his wife. And he went berserk. Lost it, gibbering about suicide, strangling himself with a thong." Patrick cast his eyes to heaven. "So I was stuck. Something told me that Leonard wasn't serious about killing himself, but he was definitely going off the rails. I regret it now, obviously, but I made a deal with him. I promised that I would get rid of the evidence if he promised to stop. I warned him that he had to pack it in right there and then and get some counselling."

Sister Jane leaped ahead of the story. "So you hid the underwear in your locker, but it was searched before you could dispose of it."

"Exactly. I reckoned it was safe there; I had a key. I've never had to smuggle contraband knickers before, and I can tell you that it's surprisingly tricky. Every time I was poised to shove them into a bag, somebody wandered by. I never seemed to be alone. Now, I realise that Mrs Wilde got her hands on a set of keys and searched all the lockers." Patrick shook his head at the memory. "And then she ambushed me."

"And you shouldered the blame," said Sister Jane.

"What else could I do?"

"You could have exposed Leonard. Nobody would have blamed you if you had." Sister Jane took his hand and squeezed it. "You're an old softie, Patrick."

Sunny would have put it stronger than that. You're a hero, she thought, amazed. Patrick had absorbed all the disgust of the residents, just to protect a man he hardly knew. Along with admiration, Sunny felt an irrational irritation. How come Patrick would martyr himself for Leonard but leave her stranded all those years ago? Then she remembered the punch he'd dealt Fabio. She couldn't forgive Patrick that. He looked less of a hero, suddenly.

Patrick shook his head. "Serena and the guys knew I wasn't the Cad. In private, I told them that much, but I wouldn't give them Leonard's name. If that tree hadn't fallen on him, nobody would ever have found out."

"I'm glad we know the truth," said Sister Jane. "But it's having wider repercussions. Mrs Wilde is kicking you all out. She won't let you finish filming."

"She can't —"

"They've been through that. She can."

Sunny addressed Patrick directly for the first time. It felt odd, like talking to somebody she'd lost touch with. "If," she began slowly, "you expose Leonard to his wife, she'll owe you an apology, and probably let you finish filming."

"No." Patrick didn't meet her eye. "No way."

"You wouldn't have to do it in public. Just tell Mrs W." Sunny couldn't let him waste all his hard work on the programme.

"I promised." Patrick looked up at the ceiling.

"You're ruining your big chance," said Sunny, exasperated. She gestured towards Leonard. "In the long run, it's better for him, anyway."

They all three looked over at Leonard's pathetic figure. And they all jumped, startled. The bed was empty.

Through the window, Sunny glimpsed two shaky legs ascending the steps to the lawn. "He's awake!"

Dashing out to the garden, they tailed the concussed Leonard, who was approaching his wife. Mrs Wilde and Serena were still arguing vociferously. Various crew lounged around, waiting for the outcome. They perked up at the sight of tiny Leonard, dishevelled and unzipped, tapping his wife on the shoulder.

"You're not dead," nodded Mrs Wilde. "Good. Help these oiks pack up, Leonard. They're —"

"SHUT UP!" bellowed Leonard, his spindly limbs shaking like café cutlery.

Mrs Wilde leaned away from him, puzzled. "I beg your —"

But it wasn't her day for finishing sentences. "LEAVE THESE PEOPLE ALONE, YOU RANCID SOW!" Leonard ordered his wife, at a volume that loosened her hairgrips.

"Leonard, have you gone quite —"

Sunny, Sister Jane and Patrick gaped in shock as Leonard — David to Mrs Wilde's menopausal Goliath — raved on.

"BACK TO THE FLAT!" He advanced on her. "BACK! BACK, I SAY!" he roared, as if training a dim circus lion.

"Do you think it was the knock on the head?" Sunny asked Sister Jane.

Sister Jane pulled a mystified face. "He must have heard us talking."

"But . . ." Mrs Wilde was stammering. Leonard had her on the ropes, and he pressed home his advantage.

"DIDN'T YOU HEAR ME, LITTLE WOMAN? STOP MEDDLING AND GET HOME. THIS MINUTE!"

The crew raised expressive eyebrows at one another. Leonard had called Mrs Wilde a little woman, which was both highly inaccurate and very dangerous.

And yet he lived. Mrs Wilde could have felled him with one swipe of a paw, but instead she was studying him, her eyes flickering over him as if she was trying to confirm that this really was her husband. "Leonard," she said, and the voice was coquettish. "Oh, Leonard." It had melted to a girlish tinkle. She turned and wafted (much as a trawler might waft) towards the entrance to their block.

Leonard looked about him at the open mouths and wide eyes. "Carry on," he said jovially. "As you were. You can film tomorrow, no worries there." And off he skipped after his wife.

Nobody spoke for a moment or two. They had witnessed something extraordinary. A worm had turned. A dictator had fallen. Leonard had got out of his pram.

If Sister Jane hadn't been there, and if Patrick had been the old Patrick, not this new one who didn't want to talk to her, Sunny would have voiced her theory that there just might be some bedroom action on the cards for old Leonard. Mrs Wilde had looked quite moved by his new-found butchness. Maybe, Sunny conjectured, with all the certainty of one who knew nothing about psychology beyond reading *Take a Break*'s problem page, Leonard would have no further need to wear ladies' panties.

"I'd better get back to work." Patrick looked uncomfortable. "You won't tell anyone? About my secret?"

"No," sighed Sister Jane. "We'll make sure everybody still regards you as a monster of depravity, Patrick, if that's what you want." She tutted, but gently and approvingly.

"See you then." Patrick aimed this farewell squarely into the empty space between Sunny and her aunt, before walking over to a gobsmacked Serena.

Ernest caught up with Sunny and Sister Jane. "For you," he said furtively, handing Sunny a large overnight bag.

"Thank you," said Sunny uncertainly. Then, "Oh, *thank you*," she gushed, but discreetly, as a faint mew escaped from the bag.

"She often visits," Ernest confided, in a low voice. "I didn't know she was yours."

"Yes, she's our Marmite."

"Oh." Ernest looked put out. "I call her Judith. After the lovely Miss Chalmers."

Two floors up, Sunny saw Mrs Wilde pull her bedroom curtains smartly across with an excited swish.

CHAPTER
THIRTY

A bottomless font of un-asked-for advice to her friends, Sunny was clumsy at counselling herself. She could ponder plots for days at a time, but examining her own emotions was hard labour, the mental equivalent of breaking rocks in the hot sun. Conjuring up a two-day seminar (with pie charts) on just where Jojo was going wrong would be a doddle, and if you gave her an hour's notice she could knock up a pamphlet on what Sarah should do with her life, but she was clueless about Sunny Parkinson. Or the Contessa Carelli di Sica to be.

Fabio's proposal had been accepted with very little contemplation. It was probably the single most important decision of her life, and now she wondered whether her loins had made it for her. These were unreliable at the best of times: in the 1990s, she'd thrown a bun at Ellen for disparaging Marti Pellow. She should examine, seriously and calmly, like the jury in an Old Bailey murder trial, whether she was doing the right thing.

Sunny gulped. This was grown-up stuff and had no place in the romantic, frothy story of her love for Fabio. Straying into the unmapped territory of her motives for saying "yes" was something, she now realised, she had carefully avoided.

Peeping round the sitting-room door at Fabio, she used the phrase she'd recommended to the Castros so many times. "Darling," she forced herself to say, "we need to talk."

"We certainly do." Fabio was erecting a flip chart. "We haven't even made a proper list of possible wedding venues." He picked up a marker pen and scribbled "Westminster Cathedral" in his flowery European hand.

Peeved that Fabio had commandeered the moment, Sunny regarded the flip chart and said, wryly, "I'm surprised you haven't brought in an overhead projector." How would she manage to shift the conversation from wedding venues to whether they should be getting married at all? Maybe, she thought, with sneaky relief, it would be impossible.

"No. I'm saving that for the list of honeymoon destinations." Fabio took in her baffled face. "I am making a joke!" He laughed. "Is that so unusual?"

"Well, yes," confessed Sunny. "You don't do jokes."

"You make me sound boring," said Fabio absentmind-edly, scribbling some more.

"Never," said Sunny decisively. "Nobody who owns a bum like yours could ever bore me."

The pen stopped in mid-air. "It is only my bum that interests you?" It was an absurd question, but it sounded as if Fabio needed a proper answer.

"No, of course not. All your other bits as well," Sunny assured him. This stuff was true and didn't need

Old Bailey contemplation. "I mean, you're more than the sum of your sexy parts. You're, oh, you're fascinating and mysterious and charismatic and . . . Why are you looking at me like that?"

"I'm waiting for the bit where you say you like me, *cara*."

Sunny was bewildered by his tone. "But of course I like you, Fabio!" She felt cold. They were creeping near that uncharted territory she was so wary of. "I love you, don't I?"

"Don't you?" he said.

His beautiful face was so sad that Sunny hesitated to speak. The conversation had taken the serious turn she'd planned. And dreaded. The air between them was gluey with unspoken fears.

The phone rang. With a monumental tut, Sunny snatched it up. "What?" she said, roughly. "OK," she said after a moment. "I'll be there right away." Sunny put the phone down. "I have to get back to the flat," she told Fabio. "Aunty Jane is leaving."

All was activity in the gardens at Chudleigh Court. Sunny, head down to avoid Patrick, dodged through the orderly disorder of a location shoot being dismantled.

There was similar upheaval inside number thirteen. Jojo was scuttling down the hall, carrying Sister Jane's spartan toiletries. Ellen was folding navy-blue items of clothing and handing them to her aunt, who was tucking them neatly into a case. Sensible flat shoes and heavy-gauge tights littered the floor.

"Aunty Jane," said Sunny. "Explain!"

Her second-best wimple in her hand, Sister Jane did just that. "I'm off to Guatemala," she said.

Sunny reeled. "And? You can't just say, 'I'm off to Guatemala,' as if you're nipping out for a pint of milk."

"Give me a chance and I'll tell you," laughed Sister Jane. "I've come to a decision about my future. I'm not going back to Dublin. I wasn't cut out to be a mother superior. I've been looking into a convent in Guatemala City. The sisters there run a charity doing wonderful work with homeless children. They change lives, Sunny."

"But why so sudden?" Sunny felt like a toddler about to be abandoned in her room without a nightlight.

"One of their key people has had to return to this country, and they have a place for me." Sister Jane put her head on one side. "Be pleased for me, love. It's a troubled place, and I'll be useful."

"You'll be brilliant. They're very lucky little homeless children." It struck Sunny that this woman, previously just a distant figure from her schooldays, had quietly woven herself into the warp and weft of Sunny's present day. "But what will we do without you?"

"Oh, shush," chided Sister Jane, fondly. "The same as you did before I arrived, you silly girl!" She stretched to fold her into a warm hug that smelled of Camay.

Ellen was brisk. "Come on, Aunty Jane. Pack that wimple, and I think we're done."

"Now . . ." Sister Jane looked around the room. "Have I everything?" She stood surveying Sunny, Ellen and Jojo. "I wish I could roll you girls up and pop you in my case!" she said. "Oh, go on, smile. I never saw such long faces. I'm only going to Guatemala." She realised what she'd said and laughed so infectiously that the others managed to join in.

Maintaining a lifelong habit of fuss-avoidance, Sister Jane was being driven to the airport by Ernest. "No tearful good-byes in the departure lounge," she said, hugging each of her hostesses in turn. "Thank you for taking me in and being so generous to a poor old stray. You've given me the time of my life," she said, the edges of her voice just cracking. "Promise me you'll look after one another. Promise, now?"

There was a chorus of yeses, Jojo's prompted by the merest of kicks.

"And promise me that you'll follow your hearts. It's what I'm doing, and I feel ten years younger. Look for that quiet place." Sister Jane seemed to find Sunny's eye, but it was only for a moment. Sunny might have imagined it. "Go to your quiet place and just listen."

There was a silence, broken by Ernest's cheery "All aboard!" from the gardens outside.

"That's me." Sister Jane gathered up her baggage. "Goodbye, goodbye, goodbye!" A navy-blue blur, she shot off down the hall and was out of the front door and gone.

"I can have her room." Jojo was either skilled at finding silver linings or breathtakingly callous.

Ellen said, "It's strange without her."

Sunny smiled. "She's only been gone ten seconds. If you look out of the window, you'll see her."

"No. I don't think I want to." Ellen stayed put.

"Me neither," said Sunny.

Ellen was regarding her closely. "Is there trouble at t'mill?" she asked.

"You could say that."

Jojo asked excitedly, "Did you catch him with a girl? Did you catch him with a boy? Does he take heroin?"

"Yeah," agreed Sunny. "All of those, plus he fancies Ernest. Now, despite your eagerness to claim it, this is still technically my room, so would you kindly sod off?"

Dragged out by Ellen, Jojo managed to squeeze in a couple more theories. "Is he violent? Have you gone lezzer?"

Perhaps, thought Sunny, as she closed the door and leaned against it, this is my quiet place.

She'd been wrong earlier: she and Fabio didn't need to talk. The truth, in its entirety, had swum into perfect focus just before they were interrupted by the phone call.

Sunny wasn't in love with Fabio. She was in love with being in love with him. Giddy on the romance of it all, Sunny hadn't noticed that she and Fabio essentially had nothing to say to each other. Sweet nothings were as deep as they would ever go.

A fat tear rolled down Sunny's face and dropped off her chin. She crumpled on to the bed. A little dream, long cherished, was perishing. Perhaps Sunny wasn't losing the love of her life today, but she was losing *a* love.

Fabio, with all his beauty, and charm, the way he smelled and the way he moved, was a stranger to her from now on. He wasn't hers to kiss or hold. This was a one-way road she'd just stumbled down.

Abba burst into noisy life in Jojo's room. Sunny groaned and put her hands over her ears. The last time she'd felt this bereft was when she'd finished with Patrick. Like now, she had felt compelled to end it, even though nobody had understood. Nobody except Patrick, that is. He knew they were flogging the deadest of dead horses.

Four, no, more, years had passed, but the pain was as citrus fresh as if she'd just ripped an Elastoplast off the memory. In those days, Sunny and Patrick had been best buddies in and out of bed. It had been so natural to be with him, like nudging your toes into slippers after staggering home in your party shoes, that Sunny had never stopped to think of what future they might, or might not, have. They didn't talk about love, or make grand declarations; they just spent all their time together and knew exactly when the other one needed a neck rub.

They were an uncomplicated couple, everybody said so. Only Sarah heard the low-level sniping from Sunny: "Why won't he talk about his feelings?", "He never says he loves me", "God, if only he'd be jealous once in a while". None of these little cracks had looked like fault lines, even when she'd said, enviously, one drunken night, "Alfie's passionate about you, isn't he? How does that *feel*?"

Not the first girl to mistake morning sickness for a dodgy curry, Sunny may well have been the first to take her pregnancy test in the loos at BHS. She'd been so certain the test would be negative that she was only doing it to placate the more worldly Sarah. The waiting queue must have exchanged raised eyebrows at her strangulated shriek, and a nice Scottish woman, in elasticated slacks, knocked on the door to ask if she was all right.

This development was so unexpected, such a hundred-and-eighty-degree turn, that Sunny loitered, dazed, by the onyx lamps crowding the lighting department for half an hour before she dialled Sarah's number on her mobile.

Despite the shock in her voice, Sarah had refused to be downbeat. "It's a whole new chapter," she'd counselled. "The next step is to tell Patrick." Aware of Sunny's cowardly leanings, she'd added, "NOW!"

There didn't seem to be a right time to share this amazing, devastating, wonderful news with the only other person it truly affected. Sunny prayed that he would react, that he wouldn't adopt the bland mask he dug out for crises. Eventually, Sunny had blurted it out while Patrick was flossing his teeth.

"What do you want to do?" he'd asked, as if she'd just told him they were out of bread.

Sunny, who'd seen all those chick flicks where the prospective dad, no matter how dire the circumstances, leaps around like an ecstatic chimp, burst into noisy tears. "I want to know what *you* want!" she'd wailed.

And so it had gone on. Patrick was passive and calm, with no real opinion. Sunny willed him to be decisive, to proclaim whether this extraordinary revelation in a chain-store loo was the best thing that had ever happened to her or a calamity. She was too close to its complex threads to come up with an answer. For every thought along the lines of *It'll kill Aunty Annie*, she would think, *perhaps it will have Patrick's eyes*. She was scurrying around in tearful circles.

"I'll support you whatever you want to do," Patrick had repeated, endlessly. And Sunny could only interpret this one way: he didn't really want a baby but he didn't want to force her into a termination either. No, she'd thought bitterly, he'd rather let me feel alone and helpless, shouldering all the worry and guilt myself.

No baby had arrived. Sunny had spent an afternoon in a very comfortable private clinic, reminiscent of a mid-standard B&B. Sarah had turned up, her face soft with unshed tears, to take her home. It had been Sarah's hand on hers in the middle of the night, and Sarah's soft voice comforting her through the cramps and temperatures. Like two World War I tommies sitting out a mortar attack in a trench, that night had sealed their friendship. When other people lost patience with Sarah, and despaired of her selfishness and her wildness, Sunny would remember how much she had needed from Sarah that night and how much Sarah had been happy to give.

It had been the next morning before she told Patrick.
"Oh."

"Is that a shocked 'oh'? You wanted me to do this, didn't you?"

"I . . . don't know."

Sunny and Patrick, as a thing, as a couple, had never recovered. They limped on for six more months, but the little baby who never was grew and grew in their minds, until they couldn't see each other over its head.

"He left me in the dark when I needed him" was Sunny's mantra whenever she thought of that time. If it hadn't been for Sarah's interference, the weekly Volunteer sessions would have atrophied in the first couple of months.

"I'm not going to let you two be blown apart completely. Just do what your fairy godmother says, will you?" Sarah had ordered, while administering medicinal house white.

So, Sunny repressed the worst of the memories, and somehow she and Patrick had reclaimed a quirky friendship from the gory carnage of their love affair.

Usually, Sunny was strict with herself and refused to revisit the pain of those days. Today, though, was so extraordinarily emotional that she felt a compulsion to scrutinise how she felt about the roped-off sections of her past. It unsettled her that Patrick was so much in her thoughts on the day that her love for Fabio sputtered out, but she felt strong enough to examine why that should be. At last.

But nobody can examine anything with "Dancing Queen" shaking the walls. Sunny heard Jojo leave her room and thunder down to the bathroom like a heifer.

"What is going on?" Sunny put her exasperated head out of her room as Ellen passed by with a stack of law books.

"She's going out to dinner. With that man."

"A date?" Sunny was taken aback.

"It's not a fecking date," disputed Jojo, rushing back to her room with a bottle of nail varnish.

411

Sunny couldn't engage with this latest twist. "Do you have to have Abba on so loud? And can't you shut the bathroom door while the bath's running?"

"Ah, go shag yourself," Jojo suggested. "I'm having fun. I'm allowed." She disappeared into the bathroom and turned the radio on.

Number thirteen wasn't her quiet place. As Sunny shrugged a linen jacket on, Ellen came up to her.

"Do you need me?" she asked, simply.

"I might, later," Sunny admitted. "I've got to get away just now."

"I understand."

And Ellen did, which was part of the beauty of the girl.

There was no tranquillity out in the transformed gardens, with its Zen corner, Japanese water feature, ornamental cabbages where the roses used to live, zinc summer house and, of course, the infamous statue. There were no daisies.

Lorries inched, braking and growling, out of the gates. The catering van was locked up and ticking over. Shouts echoed across the grass, as the various tents were collapsed. Electricians crouched on the path, coiling up long snakes of lead, and the reliably perky make-up girl sat glumly on a trailer, waiting to hitch a ride. Only the production tent was still up in the corner it had made its own. A few residents had come down to wave off the production and generally get in the way. Sunny jogged over to them, huddled around the door-shaped flap.

412

"Is anyone in there?" she asked the Thin Girls and Chloe, who were lighting up cigarettes.

"Nope. It's empty," said the middlingly Thin Girl, with a mock sad look. "Show's over."

Sunny dived into the cool interior. Emptied metal shelves loitered in the darkness like chrome skeletons. A large TV screen, blank and dead, squatted in one corner, flanked by DVD players and other paraphernalia.

Sunny sank into a director's chair on the other side of the tent, grateful for the muffling qualities of canvas. The raucous, good-tempered disarray outside seemed far away. She took a deep breath and tried to calm herself, so she could arrange her thoughts.

The TV screen flared. She squinted, dismayed. Somebody was in here. She peered over and made out Serena's profile in the dark, the fine nose outlined by the cold, blue glare of the television.

Fast-forwarding at a dizzying pace, Serena seemed to be searching for a point in the tape. She kept stopping the film, scribbling on her clipboard and setting it off again.

Sunny had never seen raw footage before. A timer took up one corner of the screen, and the picture had an unfinished, fuzzy look around its edges. She admired Serena's skill in sewing together a coherent programme from this patchwork of jumbled segments. None of it made sense to Sunny.

Unexpectedly, Patrick's face filled the screen and Sunny stiffened. "The most important skill for a gardener," he was saying, ear-gratingly loud in her precious silence, "is patience." Serena paused the action to write notes in her lap.

Sunny stared at Patrick, as still as if she'd been paused, too. He was exactly what she didn't want to see at this moment. He scrambled her thoughts more than ever, but she kept her eyes on that familiar face, two feet across and shining in the darkness. The lines around his mouth described his smile like contour markings on a map.

"Good boy," Serena said approvingly to her muted star.

Perhaps he smiled at Serena like that when they were alone. Jealousy, corrosive as acid, dripped on to Sunny's heart.

The PA looked in to warn, "Packing this up in ten minutes, boss."

"Fine." The video whizzed at breakneck speed, until Serena slowed it down to watch the duel. Completely unrelated to the rest of the footage, it was as if the crew had suddenly decided to make a cut-price swashbuckling movie. The camera dashed to keep up with Fabio and Patrick, often losing them altogether and then finding them again as they jumped on to the path or flashed past at close quarters.

This wasn't the version breakfast television viewers had been treated to: that had been vision only, with a commentary supplied by the bemused presenters. The real soundtrack was disconcerting. Patrick's mike, clipped to his T-shirt, had stubbornly stayed put through all his exertions, picking up his every grunt and strain and groan. It sounded as if he was giving birth to twins. "Aaaaargh!" he yelled and Sunny put her hands over her ears.

Serena had picked up her mobile. "Hello?" she said. Then, "Hang on, I'll have to read the figures to you." She picked up a sheaf of papers and strutted, oblivious, past Sunny out into the daylight.

The denouement of the duel was coming up. Sunny turned away. She didn't want to witness, yet again, one man she cared about defeat the other man she cared about. And she certainly didn't want to see Patrick swing that shameful punch.

"Gnuuuurgh!" Patrick's groan as he tried to fend Fabio off echoed around the dark tent. Sunny's eyes were clenched shut. "Uhhhh." That sounded like the wind being knocked out of Patrick as his back slapped against the sculpture. Sure enough, Fabio's voice, slightly distant but still picked up by Patrick's mike, asked, "Do you surrender?"

Scuffling, coughing noises followed, presumably as Fabio helped Patrick up. Then, oddly, Fabio's voice was picked up, every bit as clear as Patrick's. Sunny opened one eye and saw why: it was the post-duel embrace and their heads were close together.

"This is the end of it," Fabio was hissing into Patrick's ear, every word booming loud and crisp in the darkness. "She's all mine. Go find your own piece of ass."

And then the punch.

Mouth open, Sunny stared at the footage, which had moved on to a treatise on topsoil. She couldn't believe her ears. The Fabio she'd loved wouldn't use language like that about her.

Patrick, she now knew, had hit Fabio for *her*, and only for her. It hadn't been spite, it really had been about her honour. This set off a dizzying relay race of thoughts in her head, thoughts she couldn't process with Patrick up on the screen talking loudly about compost.

Sunny stood up and stumbled over chair legs, racing for the door in the darkness. She stopped short, and blinked, one hand shading her eyes. Somebody was standing by the open flap. It was hard to make out who it was. The light from outside shimmered around the figure's outline, breaking it up.

"*Cara*." Fabio had been watching the video, too. He took a step nearer, but he was still indistinct in the tricksy lighting. "Don't," he said, as Sunny opened her mouth to speak. "I'm sorry, Sunny. For calling you a . . . for being so disrespectful."

"Fabio," began Sunny, slowly, hoping inspiration would shape her jumbled feelings into words that would wound as little as possible. "I don't . . ." Inspiration, not for the first time, huffily turned its back. The only words available were arrow-sharp. She couldn't hurl them at him.

"I know." Fabio's rich voice was mournful and flat. He spoke as if he had been expecting this moment. "I know you don't, and I don't think you ever did."

"Oh, I did!" Sunny corrected him, with a large, tearful smile. "I have loved you, Fabio, I swear." Just because she was flat on her bum on the grass didn't mean that she'd forgotten the sensation of swooping through the air on a swing. "Things have changed. We should never have got so serious. It wasn't us," she said, lamely, realising how many layers of meaning there was under this prosaic, practically meaningless phrase. "Come closer, will you? I can't see you properly."

"Go to him." Fabio didn't move. His shape still shifted, fuzzily. "I've fulfilled my role. I must leave, and you must go to him."

Behind her, the title music of *StyleScaping* exploded tinnily on the soundtrack, making Sunny look round with a jump. Turning back to Fabio, she let out a startled, "What?" He was gone.

Sunny dashed towards the light of the open flap.

CHAPTER
THIRTY-ONE

Sunny found her quarry out on the street, loading tools into his car. "Patrick," she said, breathlessly (Sunny wasn't built for speed), "you love me."

Patrick looked up for a moment from his efforts to jam a rake into the boot. "Go indoors, take a tablet," he advised, with trademark composure.

"You do. You love me," laughed Sunny, bobbing up and down. After the turgid mental wranglings of the last couple of hours, she suddenly felt bubble-light. "I don't make you sick. Fabio said so."

The composure showed signs of crumbling. Slamming the boot, Patrick snapped, "Not funny, Sunny. I've no idea what this latest little game is about, but I'm not playing." He brushed past her, trailing a loamy smell of earth, and stalked towards the main gates.

"It's not a game." Sunny hopped to keep up with his long strides. "I'm being honest at last, after years of pretending. You do love me." She nipped in front of Patrick, getting in his way most efficiently, and stood on tiptoes to say, "And, Patrick, I love you, too."

"Oh, you," he sneered, sidestepping neatly. "You love everybody." He strode away from her, back into the gardens.

Sunny stared after his retreating back in some confusion. Extensive research in the romance section of the local library had taught her that declarations of undying love aren't met with such a surly response; the very least a girl can expect is flattered surprise. "Oi!" she yelled. "Hang on! You do love me, and I know you do, because that punch was all about me. I heard what Fabio said. You hit him for me."

Patrick walked even faster as his persecutor gained on him. "Don't flatter yourself," he grunted over his shoulder. "I hit him for my own reasons. That bloke gets on my wick."

A few heads were turning in their direction. Chloe and a Thin Girl exchanged amused glances. An electrician sat back on his heels to watch the show. Work slowed.

"All right then," conceded Sunny, "but why does he get on your wick? Because I got engaged to him!" There was no answer from Patrick, who was scowling round at their audience, daring them to comment. "Aha! Nothing to say. You did. You hit Fabio because YOU LOVE ME!"

Patrick's abrupt halt precipitated an awkward little backwards trundle from Sunny. Bending down, he kept his voice low, as if pacifying a cuddly, but dumb, pet. "Men don't fight over women outside the books you churn out. It turned you on, didn't it?" he accused. "Two grown men fighting over you like schoolkids?"

"Well, yes. Kind of." A comic shrug accompanied Sunny's admission.

"Thought so." Patrick took off again.

"Oh, for God's sake, Patrick," cajoled Sunny, trailing after him again and starting to feel stupid. She'd clocked the onlookers, too, and she was attempting a strange run, of her own creation, that looked like a casual walk but was very, very fast, in order to throw them off the scent of an impending "scene": this wasn't working, as the hybrid walk/run was quite a scene in itself. "I didn't mean that it turned me on as in *turning me on*, I meant that it was a thrill to know that you care that much."

Patrick kept walking, breathing heavily and avoiding Sunny's eye. Around him, delighted personnel pretended to pack lorries and disassemble camera accessories, while keeping careful watch on the action.

"You see!" Sunny was triumphant. "You can't argue with me. I think we really love each other." Finding a volume loud enough to get through to Patrick but subdued enough to foil the waggling ears around them was tricky. "I think we always have." Sunny was holding out her heart on the end of a stick for Patrick to take.

He batted it away as if it were a bluebottle. "Sunny, sometimes you really do take the sodding biscuit."

Dismayed, Sunny kept up her tortured lope as Patrick found his voice. "We tried being in love, remember? It ended badly. What's wrong with being friends? Before Fabbypants came along we were doing fine. Suddenly you, *you*, decide we're in love, it's a love story, no, hang on, it's the greatest love story ever, so you skip out from behind a bush, like some demented fairy, and land all this on me." He was heading for the sculpture at a rate of knots. "What do you expect me to say?" he ranted, suddenly unconcerned that he was providing a sideshow for the crew. "We're not all characters in your books, Sunny. At least, *I'm* not."

The fight gone out of her, Sunny stopped and leaned on the statue for the support that life wasn't offering. It was cold to her touch. Patrick kept walking, and he didn't look back.

A figure popped up through the hole in the heart of the steel monstrosity, startling Sunny. "You, sir!" Leonard pointed at Patrick's disappearing back. "Stop there!"

With a venomous "See what you've done now" look at Sunny, Patrick turned and folded his arms. "What is it, Leonard?" he asked, as cordially as somebody gritting not just their teeth but their entire skeletal frame is able.

"I've watched you youngsters together. It's perfectly obvious what's going on here," said Leonard, who had assumed the air of an elder statesman since the showdown with his missus. "You may dismiss me as an old fuddy-duddy, but I, too, know of the inextinguishable flame of romantic love. It won't be denied. You've felt it, Patrick. Can you deny that you fought for this maiden?"

A grunt of impatience escaped Patrick, who couldn't have looked more uncomfortable if his jeans were full of mice.

Slumped against the sculpture, Sunny kept her eyes on the floor. Patrick was unlikely to take lessons in love from the Chudleigh Cad.

"There was a moment such as this in the wooing of my wife when I could have lost her. I saw sense, as must you, sir." Leonard had a style all his own: Sunny was glad he was on her side, but she wished he'd get on with it. "This lady has declared her feelings, and the least you can do is listen."

Patrick's hands were on his hips now. He was tapping one foot, his discomfort and eagerness to get away so strong Sunny could almost smell it.

"You clearly have pride, sir," Leonard carried on in his ringing, pompous way. "Let me tell you, pride will wound a man more savagely than any bullet." He drew an enormous breath, settling into his theme. "How well I remember the sage words spoken to me by my father, a man who laboured for the East Anglia railways, in a responsible if humble capacity, for over three decades. He said to me —"

"ALL RIGHT!" Patrick raised his hands in abject surrender. "PLEASE STOP, LEONARD." He turned to Sunny, who had raised her eyes fearfully to his. "FOR CRYING OUT LOUD, I LOVE YOU, SUNNY! I DO, I LOVE YOU. I LOVE YOU MADLY." He paused, then yelled, "GOT THAT?" bad-temperedly, eyebrows raised, at the shocked object of his affections.

"Er, yeah, OK," replied Sunny, in a daze. None of this had gone quite how she'd expected.

Then something happened that always happened if she and Patrick looked at each other for long enough. They started to laugh. Patrick took two long strides towards her, stepped through the hole in the middle of the sculpture and threw his long arms around his

422

demented fairy. Around them, their audience were laughing, too, and there was even a smattering of applause.

"About bloody time," shouted an electrician.

Patrick was squeezing Sunny so hard she wanted to burp. Into her hair, he whispered, "Who was that daft count who didn't know shingles is funny, anyway?" he demanded.

"Stop making the jokes and kiss me," ordered Sunny, suddenly parched. She closed her eyes and Patrick's warm lips met hers, slow, assured and so right.

She'd found her quiet place.

Suddenly, everything was easy. Realistic enough to know that this golden light would dim, that she and Patrick wouldn't always talk so readily about their deepest feelings, that they wouldn't always sit as close as Siamese twins, Sunny was pragmatic enough to enjoy it while it lasted.

Through her new, high-velocity, rose-tinted specs, the Volunteer seemed the perfect venue for their reunion. The landlord's dandruff was fairy dust, and the whirr of the suicidal handdryer was tinkling background music.

"Here's to us," Sunny said, stealing some of the froth from Patrick's Guinness.

"So," asked Patrick, comfortably, with the air of a man who has been kissed, and kissed good, "have you got all that romance rubbish out of your system now?"

"You're saying that to annoy me, aren't you?" checked Sunny. On a nod from Patrick, she said, "In a way I have. I don't yearn for all the OTT trappings any more. But," she defended herself, "I never really did. I think I was just missing love in my life," she ended, in a small voice.

Patrick tightened his arm around her. "I wish I could make it better, about . . . His eyes clouded over. "About what happened back then."

"Why did you withdraw like that when I told you I was pregnant?" asked Sunny. She'd been longing to ask that simple question for years.

Taking a moment before he spoke, Patrick answered her gravely. "I honestly didn't want to pressurise you," he said. "I felt that any macho intervention would be unfair, that you needed space. It was your body, that was the way I looked at it. You had the casting vote, but I would support you, whatever your decision."

"Do you sometimes think about how things would be if we hadn't . . ."

Patrick got the gist of it without Sunny having to find the words. "I always think about him, her, on its birthday." He took a sip of his pint. "On what would have been the birthday, you know . . ."

Sunny knew. She always had a bad day on that date, no matter what she was doing or who she was with. "I didn't dare let myself believe that you even thought about what happened."

"Are you kidding?" Patrick's kind face was shocked. "Sun, it'll always be with me. It was the most painful situation I've ever been in. There were so many layers to it."

424

"That's exactly why I needed to talk it through," Sunny pointed out, agitated. "I took your silence to mean that you didn't want the responsibility of the decision. Or even worse, that you didn't really care."

"Sweetheart, I cared," said Patrick, pained. "I just wanted to wrap you up in my arms and look after you. Now, I see, I should have done more hugging and less analysing."

"That's a good rule to live by," smiled Sunny. She could feel deep, old scars beginning to knit together. Misplaced respect for her independence was far easier to absorb than indifference.

"I was trying to do the best thing for you. I got it wrong. Really wrong. We should have talked." Patrick smiled, and his breath this close was sweet. "Like we are now."

"Yes," she agreed. "And I shouldn't have gone ahead without telling you."

"There are a lot of 'shouldn't have's in our past." He absolved her with a kiss on the nose. "I wasn't prepared for the devastation it triggered off. I was in pieces. But, of course, I didn't talk about it." He sighed, as if impatient with the younger Patrick. "Didn't want to burden you."

"We were twits, weren't we?" Sunny found she could smile about it.

"Really large, impressive twits," concurred Patrick. "If anything like that happens again . . ."

"We'll talk," she ended his thought for him.

"Big time. Till we're blue in the face."

"We'll talk as if we're in a talking competition."

425

"As if we're being paid by the syllable."

"Seriously," pressed Sunny, "we won't lose each other like that again, will we?"

"No." He seemed sure. "Never. Never ever."

At their feet, Ozzie gave a muffled yelp in his sleep.

Basking in the certainty that she'd like the answer, Sunny asked dreamily, "When did you realise you still loved me? Because now it's bloody obvious to me that I never stopped loving you. I just bent it into friendship."

"I suppose I always knew. I pressed down hard on the feelings because there was nowhere to put them. When you started getting serious with Fabio, all sorts of emotions started popping up. Like moles on a lawn."

Patrick looked disturbed by the memory, and Sunny felt a rush of indulgent affection for him. "You're too good at hiding your feelings, Mr Smith," she told him, playfully.

"I was so *jealous* of the guy." Patrick shook his head, smiling in a disbelieving way. "Christ, it felt so good to punch him. Mind you, I hated myself for it." He gave Sunny a searching look. "Will you miss him?" Patrick's new emotional bravery knew no bounds.

"No," was Sunny's immediate, instinctive answer. She dared to expand on it a little, while they were still in their golden phase. "There'll be moments, though, when I will. I did love him, in a way." It gave her an odd ache to use the past tense about Fabio. "I know," she said, surprised by her own certainty, "that I'm never, ever going to see him again." She remembered how shadowy and blurred he'd looked in the obfuscating dusk of the tent.

426

Obviously needing some reassurance, Patrick tried to tease out some gentle criticism of his rival. "Did you ever have a really good laugh with Fabio? Honestly?"

"Oh, yes," fibbed Sunny. She pursed her lips, to admit, "Though I did say 'never mind' quite a lot when he didn't get my gags. But then —" a worrying thought struck her "— maybe I'm not funny."

"Oh, you are," said Patrick, darkly, and not entirely to her taste.

"He could be a little . . ." Sunny hesitated to damn Fabio so soon after their break-up.

With no such scruples, Patrick proffered some possibles. "A little poncey? A little arrogant? A little misogynistic?" He tried not to smile. "A little imaginary?"

Sunny shook her head. "You're horrible," she told the man she loved. She'd been about to say that Fabio had lacked empathy, but Patrick's joke nudged a bruise. Sunny had a lurking suspicion that she was the only woman in history to have sex with a fictional character. "What if *you* start doing the things I write?"

"That," said Patrick, "is not going to happen. Feel me, Sunny." He held out his strong, square hand. "That's flesh and blood."

Taking his hand, Sunny went further. "It's very nice flesh and blood." She kissed his fingertips. "As you've been so honest with me, I should confess that I was jealous, too. Of Serena." Or the Red Herring, as Sunny preferred to think of her, now.

"You don't say." Patrick raised his eyebrows. "Who would have guessed?"

"At one point I thought that you and her, you know . . ." She laughed at how silly that must sound to him.

"Oh, we did sleep together," said Patrick, matter-of-factly.

Sunny's eyebrows ended up on the smoke-stained ceiling. "I'm sorry, I could have sworn you just said you slept with Serena."

"I did." Patrick held her gaze. "Once. Drunk. Awful. Never again." Wistfully, he said, "Not you."

"She won't be very pleased that we're back together."

"Believe me, it won't bother her."

Even in a golden phase, it's not advisable to dwell on slim, beautiful, powerful women that your boyfriend has recently slept with. "Sarah will be glad we're back together. And Ellen. The 'I told you so's will deafen me." Sunny remembered something. "Ellen told me that she told you, about the thing, the you-know-what."

"Amazingly, I can decipher all that." Patrick stroked Sunny's cheek. "It must be love."

"You're a nice man, Patrick Smith. A good man." Sunny held his chin so that he had to look at her and take the compliments. "I mean it. Ellen couldn't even bring herself to tell me what happened in Dublin. She doesn't trust easily, but she knew instinctively that you were a safe haven."

Dumb with modesty, Patrick stared at his pint.

It was time to go. "Drink up, Patrick. I want to take you home and reacquaint myself with your rude bits." Sunny upended her crisp packet into her mouth and said through the crumbs, "I never thought I'd say this, but thank goodness for Leonard."

Leaning into each other, giggling at everything and nothing, their progress home was slow.

As they passed the towpath, Sunny noticed the outline of a couple kissing in the dark under the trees. Aww, she thought, benevolently, feeling a kinship with all lovers tonight. It dawned on her that the smaller figure was familiar. Horribly familiar. "That's Jojo," she whispered, nudging her new (and old) boyfriend.

"Kissing a man," goggled Patrick, rubbing his eyes.

"Presumably, she will now kill him and eat him," hypothesised Sunny. She gave Patrick a gentle punch that knocked the wind out of him. "See! Everybody wants love, deep down. Ellen and Dave are riding off into the sunset to an ancillary-claims seminar, and even Jojo's having a damn good snog by the river."

Hand in hand, they sauntered through the gates. The chic new garden was empty, all traces of the *StyleScaping* circus eradicated.

"Yuk," said Patrick, with heartfelt intensity, looking around him.

"Whaddyamean yuk?" Sunny was shocked. "It's your design."

"It's a travesty," said Patrick, bitingly. "It's nothing like my original plans."

"How come?"

"Compromises all the way. Budget. Time. *Serena*." Patrick raised an eloquent eyebrow. "Making *StyleScaping* was murder. Hanging about for hours, then talking

429

rubbish to c?ved,   ?ky in love." He set off back
done all the g, With   ?ernourished figure was soon
at the old p...
Apocalypse N?cks. C?   ?g her face with her hand,
"And your ?he hole ?   ? information'."
"Oh, God, I?d shook h?   ?er down on to the damp
"Tomorrow ?ed them al   ?led statue. "Have you
adamant. "And?ed Leonard?
sort out the old ?ed   ? the carpet of tiny,
"— ring Serena?s torch on the   ?om. "They're feisty
second series." ? But you erect?   ?d. "Pop up all over
"But you want? size. Admit it   ? not." She picked
"I want you t? him, too."   ?ext book is going
doing what you l?rd, unhesitatingly.   ?und him, like a
"That," said Pa?r, between you and   ? this girl who's
you, Ms Parkinson? young lovers."   ?n she thought
They'd ambled ?ght, turned back, a
against it, invitingl?ace. "Want to see   ?red Patrick.
Oblivious to he? pull his dressing   ?monds, near
scowling up at the? his groin.   ?'m qualified
plainly. "It's wrong. t Leonard had drawn
belong in this pretty ?e said, like a doctor
He pushed at it, sulk?us. "You promised.'
"Oooer." Sunny da?ard was as skittish
moved. Not much, ? yellow beneath
looked at each o?alettes belong to
understanding in that   my special tastes
For an answer, Patri? with her cast-offs.'
sculpture. Sunny brace?o his audience's ?
and gasping, they felt
Patrick.

said through the crumbs, "I never thought I'd say this, but thank goodness for Leonard."

Leaning into each other, giggling at everything and nothing, their progress home was slow.

As they passed the towpath, Sunny noticed the outline of a couple kissing in the dark under the trees. Aww, she thought, benevolently, feeling a kinship with all lovers tonight. It dawned on her that the smaller figure was familiar. Horribly familiar. "That's Jojo," she whispered, nudging her new (and old) boyfriend.

"Kissing a man," goggled Patrick, rubbing his eyes.

"Presumably, she will now kill him and eat him," hypothesised Sunny. She gave Patrick a gentle punch that knocked the wind out of him. "See! Everybody wants love, deep down. Ellen and Dave are riding off into the sunset to an ancillary-claims seminar, and even Jojo's having a damn good snog by the river."

Hand in hand, they sauntered through the gates. The chic new garden was empty, all traces of the *StyleScaping* circus eradicated.

"Yuk," said Patrick, with heartfelt intensity, looking around him.

"Whaddyamean yuk?" Sunny was shocked. "It's your design."

"It's a travesty," said Patrick, bitingly. "It's nothing like my original plans."

"How come?"

"Compromises all the way. Budget. Time. *Serena*." Patrick raised an eloquent eyebrow. "Making *StyleScaping* was murder. Hanging about for hours, then talking rubbish to camera, knowing that somebody else had done all the graft. You should see the state of the garden at the old people's home!" he moaned. "It's like *Apocalypse Now*. I need to get back to basics."

"And your old jeans?" suggested Sunny, knowingly.

"Oh, God, I miss those jeans," wailed Patrick.

"Tomorrow morning, put them on." Sunny was adamant. "And go straight round to Vine House and sort out the old folks' garden. And then —" she grinned "— ring Serena and tell her you don't want to do a second series."

"But you want me to be famous."

"I want you to be happy. You've got to get back to doing what you love."

"That," said Patrick, with a wicked leer, "would be *you*, Ms Parkinson."

They'd ambled as far as the statue. Sunny lounged against it, invitingly, in the hope she might get kissed.

Oblivious to her come-hither look, Patrick was scowling up at the steel shape. "I hate this," he said plainly. "It's wrong. It's bad. It's pretentious. It doesn't belong in this pretty garden around these nice people." He pushed at it, sulkily.

"Oooer." Sunny darted away from it. The statue had moved. Not much, but perceptibly. She and Patrick looked at each other, and there was perfect understanding in that look. "Dare we?" she whispered.

For an answer, Patrick leaned against one side of the sculpture. Sunny braced herself against it, too. Heaving and gasping, they felt it shift. "Harder!" encouraged Patrick.

430

Sunny pushed harder. The colossus moved, teetered for a second, then fell away from them. With a loud "whump", it collapsed on its side.

Lights came on all over the mansion blocks. Curtains parted. Sunny and Patrick stepped into the hole in the middle of the now horizontal artwork, and shook hands over their victim.

A figure in a dressing gown approached them along the dark path. "Who's there?" demanded Leonard, in his new strident manner. He flashed his torch on them. "Oh." He was surprised. "You, Patrick? But you erected this chap."

"And now I've cut him down to size. Admit it, Leonard," cajoled Patrick. "You hated him, too."

"Dreadful eyesore," admitted Leonard, unhesitatingly. "Ah, well. None of my business. It's between you and the lovely Serena, I suppose. Goodnight, young lovers." He turned to leave them, then turned back, a conspiratorial look on his thin face. "Want to see something?" he asked, starting to pull his dressing gown aside and aiming the torch at his groin.

Before Sunny could howl "NO!" Leonard had drawn his garment open. "Oh dear," she said, like a doctor examining a nasty ganglion.

"Leonard." Patrick looked furious. "You promised."

"And I've kept my word!" Leonard was as skittish as a kitten, his teeth glittering yellow beneath his moustache. "These chiffon pantalettes belong to my dear wife, who now understands my special tastes and has vowed to keep me supplied with her cast-offs." He clicked off the torch, much to his audience's relief.

431

"May you both be as lucky in love." He set off back along the path, and his undernourished figure was soon swallowed by the darkness.

"That," said Sunny, fanning her face with her hand, "defines the phrase 'too much information'."

"So," said Patrick, pulling her down on to the damp grass in the centre of the toppled statue. "Have you noticed what we're lying on?"

Contorting herself, Sunny saw the carpet of tiny, white, new daisies under her bottom. "They're feisty little buggers, aren't they?" She smiled. "Pop up all over the place, whether they're invited or not." She picked one. "It's just come to me what my next book is going to be about." Sunny wound herself around him, like a friendly boa constrictor. "It's about this girl who's madly, wildly, crazily in love with the man she thought she'd lost years ago."

"Will it have a happy ending?" murmured Patrick.

The stars above their heads were diamonds, near enough to pluck. "They're the only ones I'm qualified to write."

432